MW01470439

PRAISE FOR AN EMPYRIAN ODYSSEY

THE DARK SOLSTICE

"A compelling and addictive read, with mythology, romance, and betrayal. A must-read for fantasy lovers!"
-*Liz Konkel, Readers' Favorite*

"This is a wonderfully composed piece of work! The reader is brought into the story on every level with the detail that arouses all of your senses…the characters are so enticing, enriching, and unforgettable…I could not put this book down."
-*Jean Recha, Amazon review*

"An exceptional introduction to a series because it lays out the world so well. In the books that follow it will be easy for the reader to just dive in and enjoy."
-*Ray Simmons, Readers' Favorite*

THE HOUR OF EMBERS

"Truly masterful…the characters leap off the page with lush visual descriptions and lively dialogue, and the various gorgeous settings of the land set a high bar for atmosphere akin to Laini Taylor or Neil Gaiman."
-*K. C. Finn, Readers' Favorite*

"Reading this novel was like meeting old friends that I love and cherish. I enjoyed it so much that I read it once again immediately!"
-*Rabia Tanveer, Readers' Favorite*

"There is so much depth to this plot—politics, control, exploitation, subterfuge—that you fear to blink in case you miss something important."
-*K. J. Simmill, Readers' Favorite*

PRAISE FOR
AN EMPYRIAN ODYSSEY

THE CROWN OF THE DESERT

"Fans of epic fantasy rejoice! The Crown of the Desert is set to take you on a journey featuring grand sweeping landscapes, epic battles, and magical creatures from your wildest nightmares… I absolutely loved the book and can't recommend it highly enough."
-*Pikasho Deka, Readers' Favorite*

"I would not hesitate to recommend The Crown of the Desert to fans of the existing series, and the series in general to fantasy fans looking for heartfelt, well-developed characters, exciting worldbuilding, and a superb magical world filled with tension and high-stakes adventure."
-*K. C. Finn, Readers' Favorite*

"I was expecting tension, drama, action, and perfection, and I got them all. The tension was so thick I could feel it and loved it till the end. The cliffhanger, the struggles, and the subplots all worked toward giving readers a complete theatrical experience."
-*Rabia Tanveer, Readers' Favorite*

"The Crown of the Desert by N.L. Willcome is an evenly-rounded young adult fantasy that ticks all of the important boxes…Very highly recommended."
-*Asher Syed, Readers' Favorite*

"N. L. Willcome has crafted a fine fantasy adventure with multiple point-of-view characters and some excellent tension in The Crown of the Desert. The novel starts strongly and the momentum is consistent throughout the story. There are some very real surprises with Haven's fate being among one of the biggest…Overall, this is a solid read and a wonderful bit of autumn escapism."
-*Jaimie Michele, Readers' Favorite*

The Crown of the Desert is a work of fiction. Names, characters, places, and incidents either are the product of the author's imagination or are used fictitiously. Any resemblance to actual persons, living or dead, events or locales, is entirely coincidental.

Copyright © 2022 Nikki Leigh Willcome
First Edition
Printed by Amazon Direct Publishing
Cover photographs obtained through Shutterstock.com
Cover design by Nikki Leigh Willcome

All rights reserved.

ISBN-13: 979-8839374690

The Crown of the Desert

An Empyrian Odyssey: Book 3

N. L. Willcome

6

For Kypling

Epic tales are filled with extraordinary people who don't know they're in one.

And you are extraordinary.

Dramatis Personae:

Marsh lands:
Tamsin Urbane – leader of the Ma'diin
Haven – Watcher
Mr. Monstran – Haven's captor, servant to the Master
Enrik – Tamsin's friend, member of the Empyrian army
Numha – kazsiin to Tamsin
R'en – kazsiin to Tamsin
Kellan – Watcher, friend of Haven
Oman – eldest Watcher
Poma – former kazsiin to Hazees
Ardak - leader of the Exiles
Enok - Exile
Hronar – Exile
Treygan - Exile
Ko'ran - friend of Haven, Lu'sa's father
Commander Ruskla - Commander of the dam outpost
Lieutenant Farrows - soldier at the dam outpost
Mr. Brennan - healer, former horse master at the dam outpost
Calos – newest Kazsera of the marsh lands, tribal color is gold
Mowlgra – former kazsiin to Hazees
Saashiim – member of the islanders
K'al – Kazsera of the marsh lands, tribal color is purple
Benuuk – member of the Tamsin'diin, brother of K'tar
Samih – Watcher, deceased
Mora – seer, formerly from Alamorgro
Ysallah – Kazsera in the marsh lands, tribal color is red, deceased
Hazees – Kazsera in the marsh lands, tribal color is green, deceased

Dramatis Personae continued:

Empyria:
Georgiana Graysan – Empyrian rebel, former servant
Cornelius Saveen – Lord of Empyria and the Empyrian army
Tomas – former servant to L. Regoran, rebel leader
Reynold - Empyrian guard
Aden - rebel leader
Mr. Graysan – father of Georgiana, scribe to L. Regoran and rebel spy, deceased
Lord Regoran – former Lord of Empyria, Emilia's father, deceased
Lady Regoran – wife of L. Regoran, mother of Emilia
Captain Pak – captain of Empyrian guard

Cities:
Emilia Regoran – daughter of L. and L. Regoran, real father is L.Urbane
Sherene – former day maid to Tamsin
Lady Lavinia Urbane – wife of L. Urbane
Lord Urbane – former Lord of Jalsai and Empyria
Lady Allard – wife of L. Allard, escaped to the Cities
Brunos – manservant to Mr. Monstran
Lord Halbany – a lord of the Cities
Lady Halbany – wife of L. Halbany
Lord Findor – a lord of the Cities
Lady Findor – wife of L. Findor
Madame Corinthia – widow to Commander Corinthia
Mr. Brandstone – butler of Urbane manor
Commander Garz – high-ranking officer of the Cities armies
Lord Taul – a lord of the Cities

map design by Elizabeth Recha

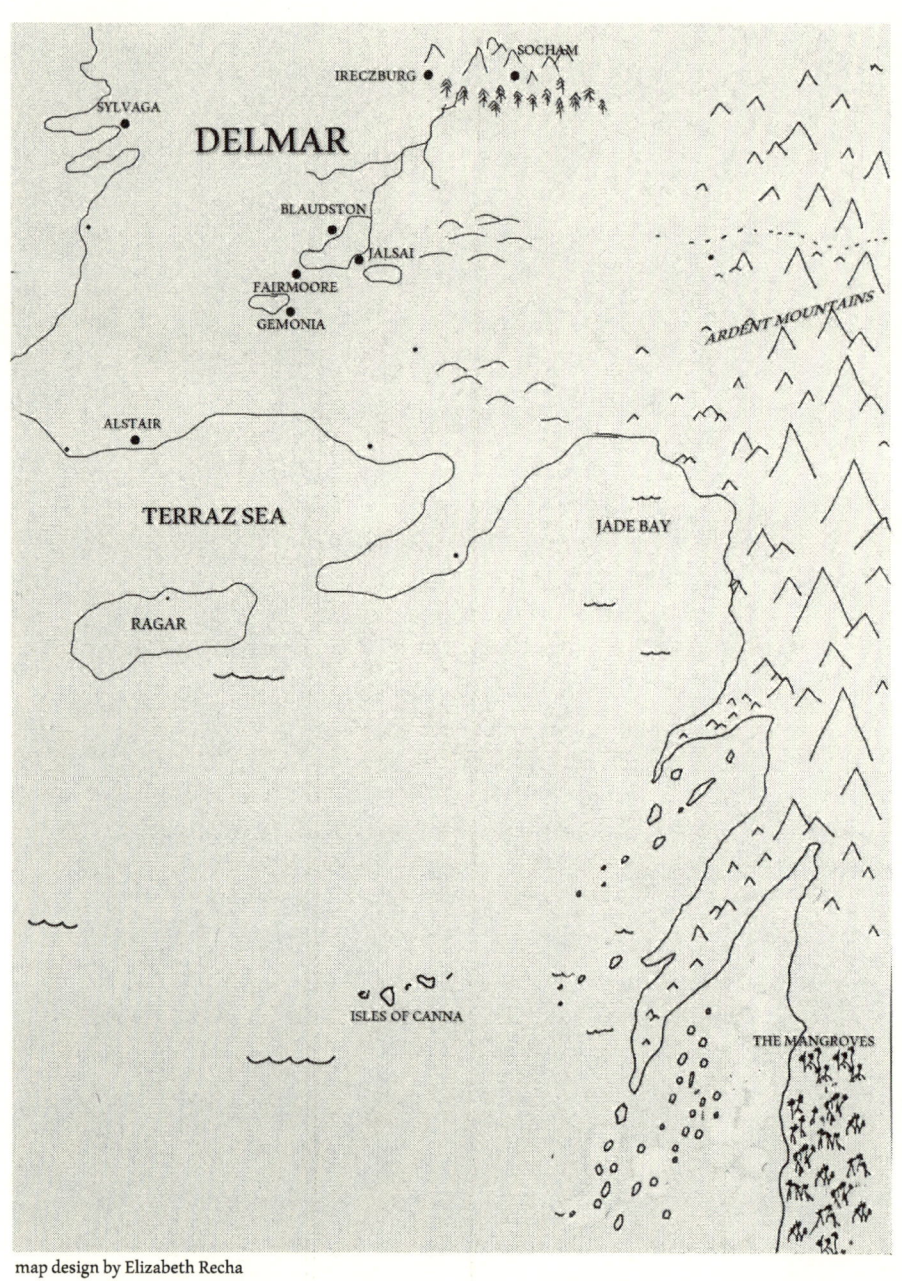

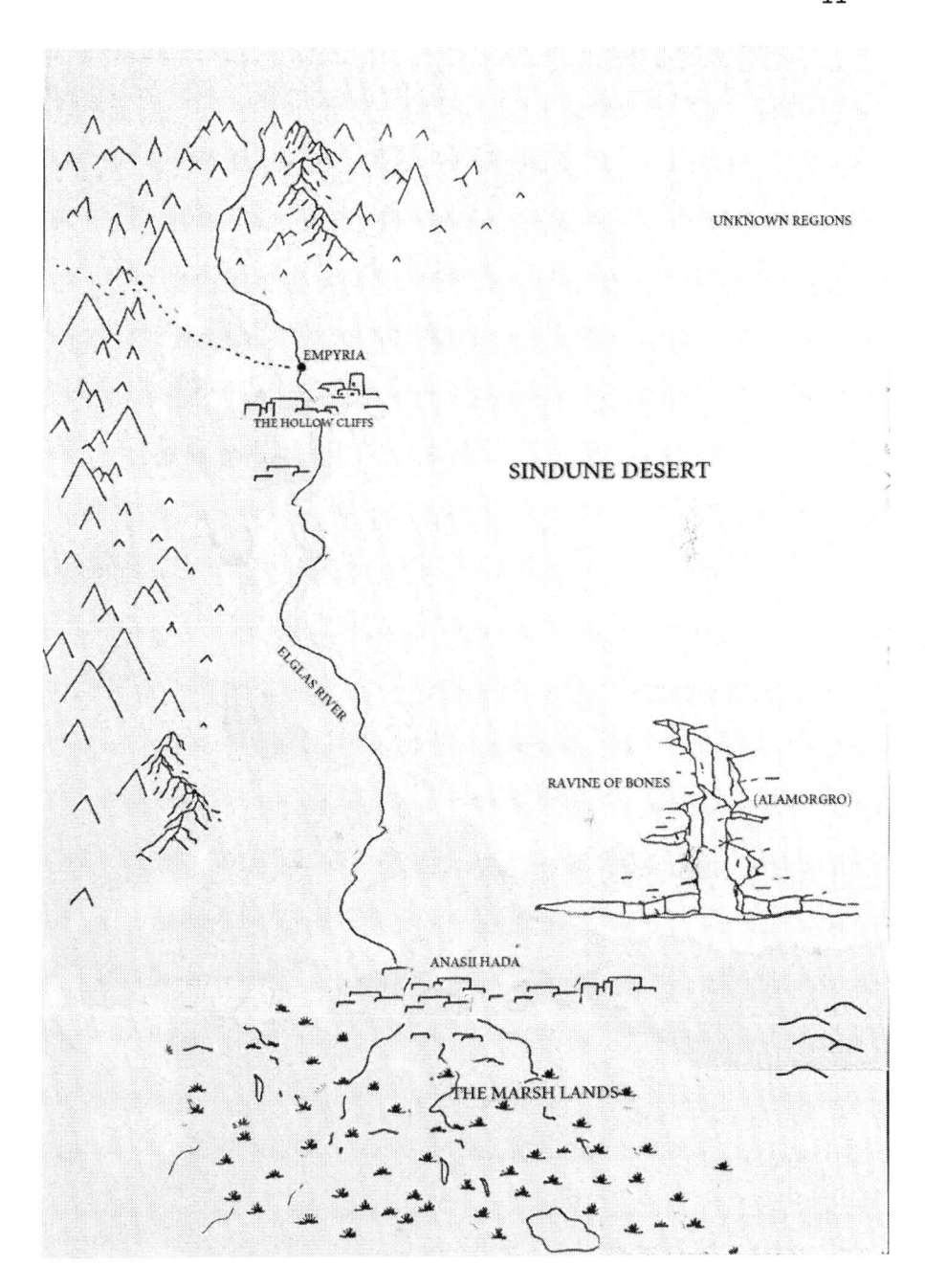

12

Mahirii's Prophecy

Her light will be born under the watchful eyes of the stars.
Her heart will break against the rocks.
Her tears will replenish the dry earth.
Her iron will ring through the darkness so all will know
That the sun has risen again.

Hers will be the fury.

Her blood will bind the roots of all that grows.
Her song will rally the weary.
Her people will fall to their knees.
Her strength will embrace them and send them to the water
Where all began and all will end.

Hers will be the judgment.

Her sword will carve the truth.
Her voice will travel the world.
Her allies and enemies will succumb to the fire.
Her ashes will soar higher than the heavens to the place
Where darkness and light collide.

Hers will be the fury.
Hers will be the judgment.
Hers will be the choice.
Hers will be the tide that changes the forces of earth and moves
Gods and queens.

Prologue

She flattened her palm against the rock, soaking in its strength and listening to its ancient story. For thousands of years, it had stood witness to the rising sun and moon, to the rain-soaked fields and trees that stretched out their roots into the soil. It had given way to the river, to allow life to reach the lands far to the south beyond its sight. It had even survived the Great Battle that turned those fertile fields and forests into a wasteland of ash and dust until nothing else remained. Then the hills turned into dunes and it became a monument in the desert, standing that way until the others came. It had known storms of water and thunder and storms of wind and sand and had endured them all. Then the others came with their axes and shovels and carved it to pieces, building temples and walls out of the ruins. But they gave it a name. They called it The Hollow Cliffs.

She brushed her slender fingers over the rough stone, making wavy strokes in the sand that had collected there. Wavy, blue, strokes.

She stood up and looked out over the desert waste. The storm was moving in, though it would be some time before it reached the figures below. They were still oblivious to its impending arrival, though she had seen it a handful of times before.

This was the moment that needed to happen. The girl had to leave the camp. If she stayed with them, then the events that needed to unfold would never have a chance. She needed to run, and he needed to go after her. If he didn't, then everything the Blue Lady had so carefully cultivated would come to an abrupt end. Yes, it was a risk. Bonding these two together forced the Watcher down a path he may not come back from and by doing so she might be giving the enemy the exact weapon he needed to win this. But she had underestimated the Watcher's significance. It was a sacrifice that needed to be made. Without this moment, the girl would not make the choice needed to fulfill her destiny.

That was the funny thing with destiny...it was not set in stone.

The wind rustled her indigo hood, not quite a warning, but rather a reminder.

She had not broken any rules. She was merely making the most of the storm. She had appeared to the girl in the desert, for she needed to draw her out to a vulnerable state. And she had appeared to her once before, when she was an impressionable little girl, appealing to her adventurous nature, for she would need it for what was coming.

The wind picked up and she crossed her arms. The Watcher's sacrifice was more than ample payment for her involvement. Of course, she had already seen these events take place; they were farther along in their journey, but the Blue Lady had wanted to come back to this moment. They were nearing the end and she was beginning to doubt if she had done enough. If she had done everything she could. She might be able to help, one final time, before their fates were beyond her reach.

"Then run, little she-hunter. Run."

Those were the last words Tamsin heard before the fear took over and she ran. She could still hear them behind her as she turned down another passageway. They seemed to echo in the rocky halls after her, chasing her like a shadow, snatching at her heels until she finally stumbled and crashed into the floor. But what was truly chasing her was more than shadows.

At first, she had fled blindly through the dark tunnels, the sound of the amon'jii's claws scraping against the stone driving her forward. But as her endurance waned, she knew she would have to run smarter, not faster. So she began choosing the narrower passages, forcing the large creatures to pursue her in an ever-thinning line. But they were relentless, voracious, and...hungry.

They clawed over each other and at the walls, snapping and snarling at each other just long enough to give her an extra moment here and a precious second there to gain an inch.

They could not burn her, for despite the reckless speed at which she ran she kept control of the fire raging in their hearts. But their voices lashed out after her, taunting her, cursing her. They promised a ruthless death. She wanted to cover her ears and scream.

'Get up!' her mind shrieked and her hands raked across the ground in answer, grasping at anything that would help her along. But her arms felt numb, and her legs were like wooden logs as she heaved herself back to her feet. The shock of what she had seen was setting in, slowing her down as it fought against her instincts to flee.

She gripped the tunnel wall for support and her hands flexed around an edge. She quickly felt along it and though she could barely see a foot in front of her she deemed it wide enough and slipped around it. There was just enough room for her to squeeze into the crevice and she forced herself to keep moving through it, even as the walls scraped her back, her arms, and her knees. She kept going, even when she felt like the walls choked all the air from the passage, even as they pushed what was left from her lungs. The tearing and snarling and shrieking from the main passageway grew louder and she grew more desperate to escape them until she was tearing at the wall herself, pulling her body through by her fingernails.

At last she felt an edge, and gripped it tight, thrusting herself out of the narrow crevice and into the cold night. She gasped as she was released and the bitter bite of the canyon air seized her. She stumbled forward and collapsed onto her hands and knees. She hugged herself around her knees, hoping the pressure would still her heaving chest and quiet her breathing. Surely they would hear her? She forced her lips shut, even though her lungs begged for more air, but she only allowed it through her nose. In and out. In and out as her chin quivered and the fear inside threatened to rip her open. It whispered insidious things to her, telling her to give up, that there was no way she was getting out of here alive. That everything that had happened had been for nothing. It fed off the heartbreak of her past and the horror that she had just witnessed.

18

Chapter One

12 days ago...

Something prickled under his skin as Kellan made his way back to the Watchers' muudhiif. He was on his way back from Tamsin's muudhiif for the second time and both times he had been turned away by one of her sha'diin, saying she did not wish to be disturbed.

Some Ma'diin steered clear of him as he walked by, while others met his gaze, but only briefly before looking away again. The air around the Ma'diin army's camp was equally quiet as it was charged. Tamsin had given the order yesterday that no one was to lift a finger nor weapon until she had decided what to do. The Ma'diin would obey the new Kaz'ma'sha, but unless she decided quickly, the other Kazserii might move to act without her and Tamsin's newfound reign would be over.

He paused and looked back over his shoulder in the direction of Tamsin's muudhiif. His instincts told him something wasn't right, but he didn't know what.

"Kellan?" He turned back and saw Numha and R'en walking towards him. He nodded in greeting to the two kazsiin.

"Did you talk to her?" Numha asked.

"No, she still doesn't wish to see anyone."

Numha bowed her head. "She's under a lot of pressure. I just wish she would let us help."

R'en gave an exasperated sigh. "I say we just go in there."

"We have to respect her wishes," Numha said. "If we don't, then no one will. The other Kazserii are getting impatient and some of them will use any excuse to stir up discord."

"I would love to see them try," R'en said, a little too eagerly.

Kellan looked back towards the muudhiif, that prickling sensation crawling under his skin again. "Then I'll go. The Watchers listen to no Kazsera. What I do won't affect the others. R'en, make sure the sha'diin stay outside."

R'en grinned widely and followed Kellan as he marched back to the muudhiif. Numha looked disapproving but did nothing to stop them.

A couple sha'diin gathered nervously in front of the muudhiif's entrance as Kellan returned.

"We told you, Watcher, Tamsinkazsera—."

With a swift swipe of his hand Kellan had his sword pointed at the sha'diin. "Step aside. You don't want me to say it twice."

A couple of them looked like they might reach for their own weapons, but intimidation got the better of them standing so near the cloaked killer and one by one they let him pass. Kellan still had his sword pointed at them as he walked through, but once he was inside he slid it back in its sheath, trusting R'en to keep them in line. He did a quick glance around the inside, turning to check the corners behind him, but the muudhiif was empty. His brow knitted together as that crawling feeling made its way into his stomach. The fire ring in the center was cold; not even an echo of smoke drifted up from it. He walked through and over to the annex.

"Tamsin?" he called out, lifting the flap that separated the private chamber from the rest, but that room was deserted as well. He cursed under his breath and returned to the main chamber. "R'en!" he shouted, scanning the room again for any clues as to where she had gone or what had happened.

R'en burst through the entrance flap a moment later, her sword at the ready.

"She's gone," Kellan said.

"What?" R'en's happiness at finally taking action vanished.

"She's not here!" he snapped.

"Where could she have gone? The sha'diin would have told us if she had left."

Kellan resisted the urge to slash the sides of the muudhiif open with his sword, angry at himself for letting her be alone for so long, especially after the recent intrusion that had resulted in Samih's death. Then he noticed something and went over to the wall, examining a section of reeds. "These binds have been cut," he said. He brushed away the frayed edges of rope and pushed slightly, sending the section tumbling over. It was just large enough for someone to fit through.

"Do you think he came back?" R'en asked. "The boy that killed Samih. Do you think he took her?"

A cold chill settled on him, freezing the quiet panic that threatened his rationale. He took a few deep breaths. "Find Numha," he said.

An hour later, they met outside the Watchers' muudhiif and Numha joined them as well as the other Watchers. They had made their way through the Ma'diin camp, keeping their eyes and ears open for any sign of Tamsin, but there wasn't even a whisper of knowledge of her whereabouts.

"What should we do?" Numha asked. "If the other Kazserii find out she's missing they're going to take matters into their own hands."

"We need to buy some more time so we can search for her," Oman said. As the eldest living Watcher, Oman was their unspoken authority, but even without that his calm demeanor was a steadying focus for the group, making him a natural leader. "Numha's right though. We should do this quietly."

"We'll split into teams so we can send word back when we find her," Kellan suggested. "Take only the Tamsin'diin with us."

Oman nodded.

"But the Kazserii won't wait much longer," R'en said. "They're getting restless."

"Then we won't keep them waiting," Numha said. "If Tamsin does not return—*if*," she reiterated at the looks she received from some of them, "then we will still have to deal with the northerners and the dam. We'll spread word to the other kazsiin to tell their Kazserii that Tamsin's ordered the army to the anasii hada immediately. Everyone will be too busy to notice she's missing and then that will give you a few days to find her."

They each looked around at each other, but no one could come up with a better plan, so they all agreed.

"Good," Numha said. "Get ready to leave within the hour. We will meet you—."

She stopped as a strange chuckling sound was heard coming from inside the muudhiif.

R'en made a growling sound from the back of her throat as she drew her sword and walked into the muudhiif, intent on cutting off the tongues of any wicked eavesdroppers. Oman, Kellan, and Numha followed her inside. There, still strapped to the main support pole was the witch woman, Mora.

It was she who was chuckling, and she smiled at the sight of the four. "You're missing your little Kazsera, aren't you?" she sneered.

They all looked at each other, equally surprised to hear the woman speaking Ma'diinese.

"I thought Tamsin told you to kill this one?" R'en said, pointing the tip of her sword at the seer. "If you don't want to, then I will."

"Tamsin told us to choose what to do with her," Kellan said, "but I am inclined to indulge you, R'en."

R'en took an eager step forward.

Mora stiffened and her chuckling ceased. "I can tell you exactly where your Kazsera is," she said.

R'en stopped but didn't lower her sword.

Numha stepped closer. "You know where Tamsin is?"

"I will tell you, but it will come at a price."

"You will say what you know, or I will free you of your tongue," R'en warned.

"Then you will never know what happened," Mora countered.

But Oman held up his hand. "Tell us and I will personally see you to the edge of the marsh lands."

"Not good enough," Mora scowled. "I will need something more real. Something more precious to you."

"What do we have that you could possibly want?" R'en asked, her irritation blinding her to Mora's request.

But Numha was not blinded. "She's a blood stealer," she said quietly.

No one spoke for a moment as they all realized what Mora was talking about.

Then Oman spoke up. "I will pay your price, witch."

The others looked unhappily at each other, but nobody spoke against him.

Mora started laughing, however. "It's not your blood I seek, Watcher."

"Then whose?" Kellan asked, his own patience starting to thin.

But Mora only smiled.

The answer dawned on Oman first and he stepped forward. "You have a deal."

Tamsin felt numb despite the adrenaline racing through her, despite the cool rock underneath her, and despite the heat from the amon'jii's mouth only inches from her face. She could see the confusion in the creature's own eyes, as if paralyzed from the clash of rage and curiosity created by the young woman in front of it. The young woman who could understand it and speak to it. A revelation born from the battle only moments ago, one that now gripped each of them like a fist of stone. But whose fist would crack first and crumble to sand? Would the revelation give way to mercy, or would it end here with an absolution for blood?

Her broken sword trembled in her hand, betraying how afraid she actually was. She knew every moment she hesitated was increasingly likely to be her last, but she felt just as paralyzed as the creature looked. How would it feel, she wondered, to be ripped apart by this animal? Would it be quick, or would she feel each tear from beginning to end? Would it be less painful than knowing she had failed and that everything she had worked toward was to end right here?

A crackle of thunder resounded like a hammer overhead, warning of an impending storm just as the jagged edge of a lightning beam reflected in the amon'jii's dark eyes. The creature lifted its giant head for a moment, sniffing the air. The skin rippled along its neck and Tamsin imagined if it had any hair then it would be standing on end by now. It turned its eyes back towards her and Tamsin knew if any rain was coming it would not be in time to save her.

But she didn't need rain. She had another weapon.

"*Why haven't you killed me yet?*" she asked it in its own snarling language. She still didn't know how she could, or even if she wanted to know how, but her understanding of the creature's language felt startling familiar. Like the first time she had created fire. It was there, it just hadn't been unlocked yet. And now that she did, it was…instinctual almost.

The amon'jii's eyes narrowed into slits. "*Becaussse He lied.*"

This was not the reply she had expected. "*Who lied? About what?*"

The amon'jii's skin rippled along its neck again, clearly agitated. Its lips pulled up over its teeth. "*He did. He said He wasss the only one.*"

Tamsin didn't know who the amon'jii was talking about, but an idea was starting to form. "*Can you take me to Him?*"

The amon'jii's nostrils flared. "*You can hear usss. You can stop the fire too.*"

Perhaps the person the amon'jii was referring to was like her. "*I can. Will you take me to Him?*" Though she didn't know who He was, this might be her chance to get into the Ravine.

The amon'jii's ribs expanded in and out several times as it seemed to think about what it was going to do. At the same time, Tamsin wondered again if these moments were her last. A minute ago, she had thought the amon'jii as animals, controlled by their basic needs to hunt, to eat, to kill. But they were becoming more complex by the moment. And with the information the Watchers had gathered about the amon'jii coordinating an attack against them, they were becoming more dangerous as well.

"*Come,*" the amon'jii said at last and it turned away from her to head back in the tunnels.

Tamsin took a quick breath, barely able to believe that she was still alive.

The amon'jii stopped at the mouth of the cavern and looked back at her. "*Come!*" it hissed. "*I will not attack you again.*"

Tamsin scrambled to her feet and did as the amon'jii commanded, following it into the Ravine of Bones. She reached the entrance to the tunnels and watched the amon'jii's large, dark body merge into the shadows. She looked back out over the rough terrain where she had just been, surrounded by the open air and the guarantee of morning light after the darkness despite the impending storm. It was very different than where she was about to go. To a place—

She looked back to the tunnel and her thoughts and breath caught suddenly, as if they had been snagged by a thorny bush.

The amon'jii had vanished.

She reached out with her senses, trying to feel for its heart again, but it was gone. She was alone.

And the amon'jii knew she was coming.

She struggled with her childlike fear of the dark and the knowledge that she was deep in the amon'jii's territory only heightened that fear as she made her way through the winding tunnels. The sweat on her palms and the rapid beat of her heart as she felt her way along the cold stone tried to undermine her reasons for doing this. With every little sound, every whistle of air, she imagined one of the animals right behind her, its fanged maw waiting to snap her neck and rip her to shreds. She thought she heard breathing right next to her once, but as she fumbled for her sword, she realized it was only her own, echoing against the rock.

Maybe she was crazy. Maybe she had finally lost whatever sanity she had left after the red sight had left her walking on unsteady ground. But no, it wasn't the red sight that had skewed her reality; that had happened a long time ago, back when she thought Haven had died in Empyria. That had been an empty, senseless form of insanity. Born from that had been a frame of fearlessness where the dangers in front of her held no power over her and for a time it had worked, but she wondered now if that nonchalant bravado had given her false confidence and she was now walking into a spider's web where she would be trapped and eaten alive.

But the more she thought about the amon'jii's words, the more she thought it might have been referring to Haven. As far as she knew Haven and the Watchers couldn't talk to the amon'jii, but he could manipulate fire and if there was even a chance that the amon'jii would lead her to him, she had to try.

She emerged into a large cavern with a dozen or so stalactites hanging precariously from the ceiling. The uneven floor was littered with boulders and shards from where some had fallen and exploded into hundreds of pieces. On the opposite side of the cavern were four more tunnels, each leading somewhere she couldn't see. She frowned, trying to figure out which way to go, when she saw movement out of the corner of her eye. She knew what it was even before she turned to face the rightmost tunnel, the opening easily twice her height, and saw a dark shape there, darker than the blackness that surrounded her. It took two steps into the cavern, its glowing eyes locked onto hers and it took every drop of her willpower not to turn around and flee.

Be calm, she told herself. Clear your mind. Don't let the fear rule you.

She did her best to stand up straight and appear confident as the amon'jii watched her, though she could not help her knees from shaking.

The amon'jii's nostrils flared in and out as if it were smelling her and its mouth hung slightly open. It looked like any other she had seen, but it was missing one of its front fangs.

And then it spoke. *"You are alone,"* it said.

She shivered. She did not relish her newfound ability to communicate with them at all. She nodded.

It bared its teeth in what she could only imagine was a smile. *"I am not,"* it said.

More dark shapes started to emerge from the other tunnels, their claws clicking on the rough stone.

Tamsin's mouth went dry. She counted: one, two, three, four, five…Five of them sauntered into the cavern, surrounding her, making the large space suffocatingly small. If there was ever a moment to be brave, this was it. If they sensed her fear they would see her as easy prey. And she refused to be that.

She reached out with her senses and was reassured when she could feel the pulse of energy from each of their hearts. She made sure she had complete control over them, which only took the blink of an eye, and then focused on the one who had spoken to her. *"You asked me to come here and I have come. Why?"*

There was a rustle as the amon'jii stirred, caution and intrigue flashing through their eyes and One-fang bared its teeth again. *"We were curiousss about the she-hunter who speaksss in flamesss,"* it said. *"Never hasss a Night Hunter been able to do thisss."*

"I'm not a Night Hunter," she said, assuming it was referring to the Watchers. *"I've never taken one of your lives before."*

One-fang flicked its tongue out like a snake. Before she could blink, one of the others lunged towards her. Her fingertips were already on the hilt of her broken sword and she whipped it out in front of her, ready to defend herself against the attack, but it never came. The amon'jii stopped just inches from the tip of her blade. Its lips twitched, but other than that it didn't move any closer.

"What is this?" Tamsin asked. Her back was damp underneath her shirt.

"You have the silver teeth," One-fang said.

"That makesss you a Night Hunter," the one in front of her said. It snorted in disdain and backed away. *"You are but a babe. Of courssse you haven't killed any of usss."*

"You said you wouldn't attack me again," Tamsin said, glancing at One-fang, but keeping her sword pointed at the other.

"And I won't, but they made no such promissse."

She felt the cold breath of panic brushing against her neck. *"Then why did they come?"*

"As I said, we are curiousss."

Tamsin knew she had to tread carefully. The danger she was in was very real and she knew their curiosity would only last so long. If she couldn't talk her way out of this one, then there was a very good chance that she wasn't getting out at all. Maybe against one or even two she may have had a fighting chance, but against all five...

"Do you let your children hunt the Wat—the Night Hunters?" she asked.

"No, but they are killed by the Night Huntersss nonethelesss."

"And you have killed Ma'diin children."

"Blood for blood. What isss your point she-hunter?"

"My point is that by your definition I am a child and I have killed no one. So, if any of you come near me again, I will have my blood for blood." Threatening their children had not been part of her original plan, but having to defend herself against so many had not been a part of the plan either.

A low growl erupted from a few of them and she raised her sword several inches so the blade was eye level.

"I will burn you until even your ashesss are no more," one said, turning its lips back into a gruesome snarl.

"Try," Tamsin said even though a voice was screaming at her not to goad them any further.

"Not yet," One-fang said. "I have questionsss for the she-hunter."

Tamsin took even breaths, feeling strangely calm in the face of her looming demise. "What do you want to know?"

"How do you know our language?"

"Did the Great One teach you?" one of the others asked. It was the smallest of the bunch, perhaps just old enough to be there with them, though Tamsin realized she knew nothing about their social system. Its question earned it a snarl from One-fang and it shrank back.

"Who is the Great One?" Tamsin asked.

"Tell her," the one that had threatened to burn her said. "She will not live long enough to tell anyone elssse."

"Is he your leader?" Tamsin asked.

"Yesss," One-fang said reluctantly. "But he isss not one of usss. Now answer my question."

Tamsin stared at him, hoping he would see the honesty in her eyes. "If I knew the answer to your question I would tell you, but I am just as surprised by it as you."

One-fang's eyes squinted suspiciously. "You are different than the other Night Huntersss."

She nodded. "My mother was a Night Hunter, but my father is from the north. I've lived there my whole life. I knew nothing of you or the Ma'diin until only recently."

"But now you are here. Why isss thisss?"

"Some of the northerners betrayed me and took someone I care about away from me. I came to my mother's people for help."

"Why would they help you?"

"Because the man I care about is one of them."

The one on the left arched its back and lifted its head as if to make himself appear bigger. *"Isss Horn Breaker your mate? Isss that why you are here?"*

They had to be talking about Haven, but she didn't know why. He was the only one to ever come to the Ravine and make it back alive. She answered slowly, *"He is the one the northerners stole, yes."*

Snarls and growls erupted from the amon'jii and some raked their claws against the stone ground.

Tamsin's heart pounded against her chest. She should have lied. *"What does Horn Breaker have to do with you?"*

"He isss a murderer!"

"He hasss slaughtered hundredsss of usss!"

The cavern filled with their cries of anger and outrage. Tamsin took an involuntary step backwards and all eyes turned to her again.

One-fang stretched its thin neck and let out a steamy hiss. *"The northernersss are like gnatsss on our hidesss compared to Horn Breaker and the Night Huntersss. Once we rid the world of them, we will defeat the northernersss too."*

"Why do you want to kill them? If you just left them alone, they would do the same."

"The Great One hasss promised usss. When the Night Huntersss have perished, we won't have to live under the rocksss anymore. We will take the land and our race will thrive."

"The Night Huntersss will not stop even if we do," the one who threatened her said. *"They thirst for our blood and live to break our bonesss."*

"And you do the same," Tamsin said. *"It has to end."*

"It will end when their eyesss are cold and every last body hasss turned to dust."

The one on the left was closer. Tamsin cursed herself for not noticing; she had been too preoccupied arguing with the others. She shifted her stance ever so slightly. The young one next to One-fang started pacing behind the others. She knew her time was running out. *"I am a leader among the Ma'diin. Like your Great One,"* she said. *"If you promise me now that you will stop killing the Ma'diin, then I swear to you that the Night Hunters will do the same."*

"Only the Great One can make such a promissse, she-hunter," One-fang said, *"and He hasss no interest in changing hisss plansss."*

The one on her left was inching closer. She could almost feel its craving for her death. *"Would you take me to see the Great One?"*

It paused and the others did as well, their eyes darting towards One-fang, the idea making them uncertain.

She held her breath. If this worked, then perhaps she had found a way to survive this after all. Or she was handing herself over willingly to the spider whose web she was caught in.

One-fang tilted its head, as if it were listening to something. *"If we took you, what would you say to Him, she-hunter?"*

In truth, she would try to kill him, knowing what he planned to do, but she did not say this out loud. *"That would be between us, don't you think?"*

"If you would try to sway Him from Hisss caussse, then you would be wasting your breath and only delaying your death."

"Why? Why does he hate the Ma'diin so much that he would wipe out their entire race?"

"You would not understand, she-hunter. He was betrayed and the makersss of the light onesss tried to kill Him."

"Who is he?" Tamsin asked, but even if they would've answered her they did not get the chance because a dark shape flew at her then. She crouched instinctively and raised her sword, but the shape was already past her. She had only a moment to realize it wasn't a bat when several more shapes darted past her, whirring through the air straight at their intended targets. One-fang and the other amon'jii shrieked in rage as the shapes pelted them, one after the other. Their mouths opened and Tamsin felt the pressure surge as they tried to release their deadly streams of fire, but her control over them was absolute and their jaws clapped shut in astonishment.

"Tamsin! Grab my hand!"

Tamsin couldn't believe the voice she heard and whipped around to see Enrik perched on a narrow ledge about six feet up the wall behind her. He held up something in front of him and sent another object shooting towards the amon'jii. He had some kind of crossbow and was hurling rocks at the creatures as fast as he could.

For a moment all eyes were on him and the amon'jii's shrieks were silenced as they zeroed in on their new prey.

"Tamsin!" Enrik shouted again.

Tamsin didn't waste another moment and rushed over to the ledge just as she heard the amon'jii's claws scraping into ground behind her in pursuit. Enrik reached down and Tamsin jumped to grab his hand. He clasped onto her arm and pulled while she scrambled up the rock face, using her feet and sword hand to find any kind of leverage she could. Enrik dragged her up to the top just as one of the amon'jii's claws struck the place she had been.

There was a dark opening at the back of the ledge just wide enough for the pair of them to rush through. The adjoining tunnel was too small for the amon'jii to follow, but they didn't slow down. Tamsin followed Enrik's lead, quickly but carefully shuffling through the craggy tunnel, using their hands to feel their way along the walls so as not to scrape their heads on any jutting rocks. The amon'jii's snarls grew fainter the farther they went until the walls finally gave way to a larger, bulbous room and the only sounds they heard were their own anxious breaths.

There were several more dark tunnels leading off from the room and Enrik pointed to one. "This way," he said.

But Tamsin stopped him. "Wait. Enrik—."

"Tamsin, we can't stop yet. They can get to us here."

"But—."

She was cut off again, this time by another burst of snarls, not far away.

Enrik's eyes widened and he glanced around quickly. He pointed to a ledge that sloped up from the ground and led to another tunnel about midway up the wall. "Go," he said hastily. "It'll take you to the canyon. I'll draw them away and meet you there. Go!" he repeated as she opened her mouth to protest.

Tamsin didn't like splitting up or the idea of Enrik being chased by those beasts alone, but she was moved by the urgency in his voice and ran up the rocky ramp into the next tunnel. The echoing sounds of the amon'jii advancing spurred her on and she kept going until she saw a softening in the darkness ahead. A grayish hue penetrated the black, giving angles and shapes to the rocky walls around her. The tunnel abruptly stopped and expanded into an enormous cavern, easily twenty times bigger than the one she had just left. The ceiling was checkered with gaping holes, exposing the clouded sky above and illuminating the misshapen stalagmites that littered the floor.

Tamsin saw an archway on the other end of the cavern with an even lighter illumination emanating from it. That must've been the way to the canyon. She rushed forward, weaving through the stalagmites that easily rivaled the size of any draft horse, though she was about halfway to the other side when she slowed, noticing how unusual the rocky formations were. None of them actually resembled a cone-like obelisk, wider at the bottom and tapering off at the top. These were wider, with smaller branches extending out to the sides and back to the ground. Some had flatter, fan-shaped off-shoots extended to its neighbors. Some even had—

Tamsin gasped and froze, for some even had…heads.

These weren't stalagmites. These were statues. Statues of the very creatures she had just encountered.

Tamsin took a steadying breath and took the moment to study one in front of her more carefully. It had been carved to resemble an amon'jii, exquisite to the point where she could make out the expression on its face. But there was more; these statues were different. The fan-shaped off-shoots protruded from their backs and some were extended and others curled around the bodies. They resembled the statues at the gates of Empyria.

Tamsin had a mind to wonder how these statues had found their way so far north to the desert city, but she also had the instinct to keep moving, knowing if she dwelt on this too long she might never leave this place because, even without wings, the real amon'jii were still out there looking for her. Though she remembered the way Haven had looked at the ones in Empyria, with suspicion almost. He had been suspicious of most things then and she hadn't known him long enough to know when he was truly wary. And she hadn't seen an amon'jii yet either. Coming from the life he had, it was no wonder why Haven had been so on edge in Empyria. She felt her own skin prickling as she tip-toed through the statues, making her way through them with an added level of caution. Even though they were only made of stone.

Chapter Two

The rebels were becoming more of a nuisance with each passing day—nay, with each passing hour. Cornelius Saveen stood on the veranda of his compound, looking out to the glass dome of the Armillary as it reflected the evening's rising moon. It wouldn't be long before he was summoned back; his office seemed to have a revolving door of officers with reports of supply raids or weapons gone missing or unexplained fires on the west side. But for a minute he just wanted to be left in silence to contemplate his next move, for the city should have been his. But it wasn't. Monstran was gone. His bestial manservant, Brunos, was gone. The other Lords: Urbane, Regoran, and Wohlrick had all been removed. Lord Allard was the only one left, but he was as malleable as hot wax and never left his compound so Cornelius, feeling generous, allowed him to stay. He also allowed Lady Wohlrick and Lady Regoran to remain at the Wohlrick compound together, but under close watch. The disappearance of Lady Allard and the late Commander's wife, Madame Corinthia, was troubling, but if they had set off for the Cities and tried to make contact with Lord Allard, they could still be useful. Empyria should have been his. The only ones still opposing him were the rebels, who were behaving more like thieves than a band of fighters, sneaking about and causing unease, even in his own ranks of soldiers.

The fires were just a distraction; he had figured that out immediately, meant to draw attention and soldiers away from the real targets. But even so, each one had been victorious for the rebels, for they had gotten what they came for and disappeared again without a trace. And that was the infuriating part: not one arrest had been made from one of the rebels' raids, because by the time his men discovered what had happened or been taken, the rebels were gone.

Cornelius and his top officers in the Empyrian High Guard had convened numerous times to theorize possible plans to counteract their terrorism and to guess their next targets, but so far everything that had been put in place had only served to stretch his men too thin, which of course Cornelius had thought could be one of the rebels' strategies. He had closed the bridge to the Armillary, posted extra guards on the wall and to the riverbank, increased his own security, and all of this on top of the two contingents he had sent to the dam and with Mr. Monstran.

Not only did he need more men, but he needed more men that were loyal to him. One of his captains had suggested conscripting men from the east side to join the army, offering more rations and supplies in exchange for their service. Cornelius had nearly demoted him right there for such an idiotic plan. Having open military enrollments would be like inviting the rebels over for cigars whilst the Empyrian soldiers spilled all their secrets.

He had closed the gates and Empyrian borders, under Monstran's advice, to deflect the Cities from sending troops to seize his newfound power from him. But now that Monstran had gone back to whatever rock he lived under, Cornelius found himself able to think clearly again, as if he had been living in a thick fog since he arrived. He was once again living in the harsh radiance of the Sindune sun, able to see a bright future for himself. For he knew now that cutting the Cities off from Empyria had been a strategic move on Monstran's part against Cornelius. The slithery, silver-haired man had wanted Cornelius to fear the Cities involvement if they found out what was happening. He wanted Cornelius to feel isolated, promising power, but feeling powerless as dissension grew around him. He had a feeling it was the same tactics he had used against his late uncle. Ones that had sent him to an early grave. But Cornelius wasn't going to be caught in the same mess that his late uncle had found himself in. He had his own plans.

Opening the borders back up wouldn't be simple, but it could be managed if the letter Cornelius had written to his ally in Jalsai was believed by the Lords Council. He had written to an old friend, Commander Garz, about how the rebels had taken over the city, imprisoned and murdered several lords, and had closed the borders themselves. He could easily manipulate the Council into sending several contingents, if not a solitary army, to "restore power" to the lords.

Cornelius smiled. Then all he had to do was clear away the last of the rebels as one of his servants would brush away the sand and all his problems would be over.

"Is that the last of them, Tomas?"

Tomas nodded, though the darkness around him shadowed his expression. "That's the last."

Georgiana Graysan nodded back, as she looked up the steps into the pantry of the kitchens at the Allard compound. "Stay safe."

"Always," Tomas replied, then he disappeared as he closed the hidden hatch from the pantry room floor.

The secret tunnel they had been using for a week now beneath the Allard compound was once again plunged into darkness, save for the small light from Georgiana's torch. She turned away from the steps and surveyed the new faces that Tomas had brought them. Four more men and one woman.

"Alright then, follow me," she said, pushing past them and down the tunnel, before they could ask her any questions. She would let Aden answer their questions once they reached the caves in the Hollow Cliffs. Not that she wouldn't know the answers; she just wanted to be alone with her thoughts for a little bit. She worried every time Tomas brought them more people. Worried that Tomas would get caught, worried that they would run out of supplies, worried that the soldiers would find them. It seemed worry was her closest companion these days. Ever since Lord Regoran's death, there was a constant shroud suspended over the rebels, as if anything more than a whisper would bring a net down upon their heads and ensnare them all. Their raids had all been successful so far, but that was all. The new leaders of the group seemed hesitant to do anything bigger than the supply raids. And that was another thing: with Lord Regoran gone, there was no clear leader. Tomas led from above, bringing new recruits and organizing supply drops to the caves,

Aden kept people organized below, and a handful of others coordinated the raids, but there was no one person in charge. Georgiana helped Aden in the caves, as they thought it was too dangerous for her to be above ground since her father had been branded a traitor.

That also did not help her worry. Since the last time she saw her father, she had not heard any word about his whereabouts. He had told her he had been sentenced to the malachite mines of Ragar across the Terraz sea, but there hadn't been any reports of caravans leaving the city, with prisoners or otherwise. And the last time she had been in the catacombs below the Armillary, he hadn't been there. She had tried to do as he asked: to leave him in the past, but it was an impossible request.

She had been wrestling with an idea, since there was only one person that could possibly know where her father was, but she knew Tomas and the others would not like it.

They came to the boulders that marked the end of the long march down the tunnel, climbed up them and into the caves of the Hollow Cliffs. There was a crude window that let in the moonlight from the canyon side where the Elglas cut its way through, but Georgiana led them away from it and through a small archway into another cave. There were two more archways and she pointed them out.

"That way will lead you down and out to the western edge towards the mountains and this one—" she led them over, "is where you'll now be staying."

Through the archway was the rebels' hideout. They walked past crates and barrels of supplies and chests of weapons that they'd taken from the soldiers, through the largest of the caves they occupied. Attached to this main cave were several smaller ones, which they used for sleeping quarters and storing other supplies like clothing and blankets. It may have seemed disorganized to the newcomers, but Georgiana was quite impressed with how quickly they had set up their temporary base.

She nodded to Barden, one of the rebels standing watch by the archway and he nodded back, used to seeing her running in and out of the tunnel that led back to the city. Then she spotted Aden, hunched over a table examining some papers. She led the newcomers over and introduced them.

"Welcome," Aden said, always pleased to meet new people.

"Can you show them around?" Georgiana asked him.

"Sure. Everything okay?"

"Yeah, I'm just a little tired. Thanks," she said and ducked away quickly before he could ask any more questions. She followed the crude tunnels marked with red paint, though she didn't need their guidance anymore to know where she was going. She found her bunk in just a few steps. It was roughly the shape of a hollowed-out egg and about as big as a wheelhouse, though there was nothing remarkable about it. The walls hadn't been smoothed down and she had to duck her head to get through the doorway. She put the torch she had been carrying into the hole in one of the walls and sunk down onto her rug. She had managed to bring a few items from her home, but most of it had gone straight to their makeshift kitchen. She and her father hadn't had much to start with, and that had never bothered her, but at least at home the memories of him had been imbued in the walls, in the rooms, in the candles on the table where they supped together every night. Here, she was just reminded of her loneliness. And that reminded her of her reason to fight.

It was perhaps why she had chosen this room in particular as her own. Not because the others were too superstitious or it had been the only one available, but Georgiana was the only one who didn't seem to mind the life-size statue standing next to the far wall. It was a beautiful statue, simple and cracked with age, but still in its entirety. It depicted a woman, standing with her face bent down and her arms bent in front of her as if to cradle something. The stone wasn't the same as the cliffs that surrounded it, more gray than beige. Georgiana thought it might have been brought down here in the days of the old Ottarkins, after Delmar had occupied it. A relic of the old religion they used to believe in. Georgiana's mother's religion.

Georgiana was young when her mother died and she learned little about it from her father, so she could only speculate as to who or what god the statue depicted. Tomas and a few other rebels still followed the old ways secretly, she had found out, descendants of the original dwellers of the city, but even they only had crumbs of the old religion to follow. Nobody knew who the statue was. So Georgiana didn't mind sharing her sleeping bunk with her. In fact, she found it rather comforting, as if someone was watching over her, like her father used to.

Georgiana leaned her head back against the cave wall and exhaled slowly through pursed lips. "I have to do something," she whispered into the silence. Though she wasn't talking about taking inventory of supplies or cooking meals for everyone in the caves. Those tasks needed to be done, but not by her. She looked at the statue, how the woman's face had melted into an expression of understanding by the carver. "I'm capable of more than they think I am," she said, as if the statue had tried to placate her. She wanted to do something useful, something important. Anyone could chauffeur people from one end of the tunnels to another. But she couldn't stay down here forever.

"I know you are," a voice chimed in from outside, then Aden stepped around the corner, almost doubling over to get inside. Georgiana was tall amongst her peers, but Aden was a good head taller than even she was. "Which is why you're here. If I let you go back, how many heads would roll?"

"Only one," Georgiana muttered grimly, remembering the vow she had made. There was only one man on her list that truly mattered: Cornelius Saveen.

Aden sighed. "Revenge won't help the cause. It'll only get you killed."

"Let me try and I'll prove you wrong."

"You wouldn't get within ten yards of him," Aden said. "And what would you even do? Have you ever even held a sword before?"

"Did you come here just to piss me off?" She crossed her arms in front of her.

"No, actually, the opposite." His steely grey eyes narrowed with a slight twinkle. "We're planning a weapons raid."

Georgiana's arms fell to her sides. "Weapons? That must mean..."

Aden nodded. "The others think it's time. Our numbers are growing and the other raids have all been successful so far."

"You're going to take on the Armillary."

"Not yet. We have the numbers, but most of them aren't fighters. We'll get the weapons we need to train them, then we can plan something bigger."

"Who's going to train them?" she asked. Aden was right about that at least. Cornelius' men were soldiers. The rebels were made up of fishermen, merchants, servants, and others who had worked their whole lives without ever touching something more than a knife.

"Barden."

Georgiana bit back her comment. Barden was a fisherman, like Aden, who had a preference for spears over nets, but other than that she couldn't see what qualified him to train them.

Aden heard her through the silence anyway. "I know, I know," he said, holding up a hand. "But he's the best we got."

This sparked an idea. "If I can get us someone better, will you let me train with the men?"

Aden narrowed his eyes. "Who do you have in mind?"

Georgiana shook her head. "Answer my question first."

Aden scratched the back of his neck with a frown. "Gia..."

"Aden, I have to do something," she said softly, tempering the restlessness that made her skin sizzle.

Her melted tone had the desired effect and Aden sighed. "Alright, but if Tomas overrules me—."

"I can handle Tomas," she said, hiding the grin that wanted to spread across her whole face.

"And I'm not promising you a spot on the raid. Just training."

"Understood."

"Alright then," he said. "Who did you have in mind?"

"A guard I know. His name is Reynold. He—."

"A guard? It's too risky Gia."

"We're friends," Georgiana lied. She and Reynold weren't exactly friends, but she had known him for years and he had been the one to warn her that her name had been on a list. The same list she had gotten when he helped her sneak into the Armillary. That same night Lord Regoran had been killed by Cornelius and Georgiana had helped Lady Allard and Madame Corinthia escape. "And he's helped us before. We can trust him. I just need to talk to him."

"I'll speak to Tomas the next time he comes below," Aden conceded. "But I should get back. Gotta find a cozy hole for the newcomers." Then he rapped his knuckles on the wall as he ducked back out.

Georgiana rested her head back against the wall again. Whether Tomas and Aden approved or not, she knew she had to talk to Reynold. And whether Reynold agreed to help them or not she had questions that needed answering. So one way or another, she was going back to the city.

Chapter Three

"Emilia, will you please stop that."

"Stop what?"

"Fidgeting. You're worse than Tamsin," Lavinia said.

Emilia glowered at her from across the parlor, but stopped tapping her foot all the same. She wanted to bark a dozen remarks back to her, but she held her tongue and crossed her ankles in front of her instead. Though it only lasted a moment and she couldn't contain her impatience anymore. She stood up and started pacing in front of the cold fireplace.

"Oh, for lords' sake," Lavinia muttered.

"They'll be here any minute," Lady Allard said and patted Lavinia's hand next to her on the sofa.

Emilia stopped a moment to look at the two ladies sitting as calm and serene as two swans in a pond and wondered how they weren't as nervous as she was. Maybe it was their age, or that Emilia had stopped drinking anything stronger than tea, or the inescapable reality that the father she had known for the last fifteen years was dead, or a combination of the three that made Emilia unable to sit still as they waited for the other lording families to arrive. Though Lavinia's serenity was starting to fade every time Emilia moved.

Despite the danger they had faced only recently, Lavinia and Emilia had decided to stay at the Urbane manor in Jalsai due to Lady Allard and Madame Corinthia's arrival. Madame Corinthia, after their arduous journey to the Cities, was to remain in bed until her child was born, so she remained upstairs in one of the guest rooms while the others waited in the parlor room. Lady Allard had stayed too, under Lavinia's insistence. Between the attack from the man looking for Tamsin and the stories Lady Allard and Madame

Corinthia had told them of Empyria's current situation, Lavinia had thought it best that they all stay together for the time being.

Lord Urbane had not been happy about their decision to stay at first, thinking only of their safety, but he was in no position to argue with his wife at the moment, and Emilia suspected he was secretly glad that they had stayed. Not only did it give him the chance to mend things with Lavinia, but they had found a way to help.

The sound of gravel crunching under wheels gradually grew louder as a carriage pulled up the long drive and stopped in front of the doors. Emilia flew to the window and pressed her nose uncomfortably against the glass pane to see outside. That was one thing she did miss about Empyria: nearly every room was open and exposed to the air. There were no such things as glass windows there, not even at the compounds. She watched as two ladies stepped out of the carriage, escorted by their husbands.

"Emilia, I must insist now that you sit down," Lavinia said.

Emilia peeled her nose off the window and sat down across from the two of them, crossing her ankles to keep her feet still.

The door opened and Mr. Brandstone, the Urbane's butler, entered. "Presenting Lord and Lady Findor and Lord and Lady Halbany," he said. His demeanor was perfectly calm and sculpted and even his dark, bushy eyebrows gave away no sign that he was anxious about the day's proceedings.

Emilia then got her first real look at the people Lavinia had invited for tea. They were the only people Lord Urbane trusted enough to let into his house, for the luncheon was just a cover so he could reveal himself officially back from the dead. Lord and Lady Findor looked like they could have been twins, both tall and slender with light brown hair and long, bent noses. Lady Findor wore a purple satin dress that bustled over the thighs to reveal a white and beige striped skirt beneath and an intricate collar made of white lace while Lord Findor wore a black suit with a purple kerchief tucked in his breast pocket. Lord and Lady Halbany were dressed just as nicely; Lady Halbany in a high-collared dress as well, with yellow flowers dotting the hem of her green-colored skirt, and Lord Halbany in a suit and neat top-hat. Lord Halbany was taller than his wife and had a curled mustache while Lady Halbany let her bright copper hair twirl out from her bun in little ringlets.

Everyone stood when they entered and the newcomers bowed and curtsied to the lady of the house. Then they all sat again, except for the men who stood slightly off the side of the furniture. Lady Findor sat in a chair opposite the fireplace and Lady Halbany took the open spot next to Emilia. Then Lavinia quickly introduced Lady Allard and Emilia.

"Thank you all so much for coming," Lavinia then said, who had chosen a royal blue dress of her own for today. "I've dearly missed you."

"It has been far too long," Lady Findor said.

"Yes," Lady Halbany agreed. "When you left for Empyria we didn't know if we'd ever see you again."

"Well we're all here at last," Lavinia said, smiling.

Lady Findor and Lady Halbany exchanged a look. "Well, not all of us," Lady Halbany then said, frowning sympathetically.

"Yes," Lord Halbany spoke up. "We were very sorry to hear of Eleazar's passing."

"We all were," Lady Findor said.

"Eleazar was very well liked by everyone at the Council," Lord Findor added. "It is a shame."

"Then why are you the only ones he trusts?" Emilia said. The sympathy they extended to Lavinia was fine, but the initial small talk was already getting on her nerves. She had never had a taste for it, not even in Empyria.

"Excuse me?" Lord Findor asked.

"Emilia," Lavinia scolded quietly.

But Emilia couldn't understand why they were wasting time on pleasantries like this. Lord Urbane had already confirmed his faith in these people. It was time for them to prove it. "If he was so well liked, then why are you the only ones he trusts?" she elaborated.

"My dear, you speak as if he were still here," Lady Halbany said lightly.

Emilia smiled. "Exactly. Because—."

"Emilia," Lavinia said, more sternly. "Could you find Mr. Brandstone and have him check on the tea?"

"What?"

"I'll come with you," Lady Allard stood up and hurriedly pulled Emilia up with her, not letting go of her hand until they were out of the room.

"What are you two doing?" Emilia asked. "We brought them here so Lord Urbane could—."

"I know, I know," Lady Allard said in a hushed tone. With everything she knew about what was happening in Empyria and the fact that she had endured the long trek across the mountains to flee what was happening there, they had decided that Lady Allard could be trusted enough as well with Lord Urbane's secret. "But there is a gentler way to do it."

"Is there a gentle way to say someone's come back from the dead?"

Lady Allard raised a scolding eyebrow at her. "Lavinia has a plan. Just follow her lead and be pleasant, alright?"

Emilia sighed. "Fine."

Lady Allard nodded and the two of them walked back into the room.

"Ah, I was just about to inquire about Miss Tamsin," Lady Findor said. "We heard rumors of an engagement while you were away, but nary a word since your return."

Lavinia smiled nervously. "The past few months have been hard on her. We felt an engagement would be in poor taste. She's currently visiting some relatives by the sea."

"There's nothing better than seaside air to calm the nerves," Lady Findor said.

"I agree," Lady Allard said politely, taking a seat again. "I'm originally from Alstair and there is truly nothing more calming than a light breeze off the waves."

"And how are you liking the countryside?" Lady Halbany asked, looking between Lady Allard and Emilia.

"It's lovely. And quite refreshing," Lady Allard said.

Emilia smiled tightly. "Yes. There is so much, um, green here."

"It is something one takes for granted, I suppose," Lady Halbany said.

While Lavinia was giving Lady Allard a grateful nod for diverting the conversation away from her missing daughter, Emilia noticed the two men exchange a look when the attention was turned to Lady Allard and herself. She wondered suddenly if it had been a mistake for them to be here, if her and Lady Allard's presence only raised questions about the others who were missing, namely her parents and Lord Allard. Or if they already knew what was happening in Empyria and were choosing to remain tight-lipped about it.

"Perhaps we would like to take our tea outdoors today?" Lavinia suggested. "It is such a pleasant day after all."

"That's a wonderful idea," Lady Findor commented. "I have missed your gardens myself, Lavinia. They are truly the best in Jalsai."

Lavinia dipped her head in thanks. Then, "Gentlemen, if I could impose on you to wait for Mr. Brandstone and inform him of our change, I would be most grateful."

"Of course," Lord Halbany said. "Anything we can do to help."

The Ladies then all stood up and Lady Halbany hooked her arm with Lavinia's. "Take your time, gentlemen. We'll need at least two turns through the gardens to catch Lavinia up on all the latest gossip," she said conspiratorially.

"The latest gossip indeed," Emilia said under her breath.

Then they walked out of the parlor and down the hall to the back patio doors. Emilia lingered behind, hoping to steal away back to the parlor to catch Lord Urbane's grand entrance, but Lady Allard hooked her arm and pulled her away. And even once they were walking the wide paths of the gardens, she kept her arm secured around Emilia's.

"It's best to let Lord Urbane talk to them alone," Lady Allard whispered to her as they followed in slow footstep with the others, who were chatting brightly together a few steps ahead.

"I hate not knowing what's going on in there," Emilia said, glancing back towards the large house.

"It is between Lord Urbane and the other lords now. It is our job to support him in the best way we can."

"You mean by getting out of the way. By literally being on the outside," Emilia huffed. "All the important decisions are being made by the men and we're just supposed to go along with whatever they decide."

Lady Allard tugged at her arm, stopping her for a moment, and turned to face her. "What is really the matter?" she asked.

Emilia glanced away, not wanting Lady Allard to see the pain behind her frustration. "I was kept in the dark my whole life about who I truly was. About whom I belonged to. And now I'm just as powerless. My father is dead. Lord Regoran is dead and there is nothing being done about it."

Lady Allard patted her arm sympathetically. "There will be justice for your father. You have to trust Lord Urbane."

But Emilia realized she didn't know if she did trust Lord Urbane yet. He had kept his affair with her mother a secret. He had kept his identity a secret as well until she had found him out. His character and discernment had perhaps kept him alive, but at what cost to others? What cost had been exacted on the relationships with those around him?

"Did you trust Lord Allard? Is that why you left?"

Lady Allard took a quick breath, her sympathetic smile replaced by a stony composure. "I left because Madame Corinthia needed my help. The tide of power was shifting and we would've ended up on the wrong side of it had we stayed. Madame Corinthia, and her baby, are safe because I did what was in my power."

"I'm sorry," Emilia said, dropping her gaze.

Lady Allard sighed, softening again. "It may not seem like much, but you are never *powerless* my dear." She glanced over at the other ladies. "Go. I'll tell them you went to check on Madame Corinthia."

"What?"

"Go, before I change my mind," she said, slipping her arm out and striding towards the other ladies.

Emilia spun and headed back towards the house without wasting another breath, trying not to appear too much in a hurry, but she was already worried that she had missed too much. She fleetly ascended the steps and went back into the house, going through the library this time where she could eavesdrop from the adjoining door to the parlor. She weaved through the furniture in the library as if she were trying to avoid a bee, but then slowed when she heard voices coming from the next room. She tip-toed over to the large wooden door and carefully pressed her ear against it, trying to hear what was being said. But the door was thick and muffled the voices beyond her discernment. She thought about just barging in, but she knew it could potentially halt any progress Lord Urbane was making.

She sighed and backed away from the door, finding one of the chairs to set herself down in, and resolved to be the first one Lord Urbane spoke with when they emerged rather than returning to the gardens. She glanced around the room, glossing over the multitudes of books that filled the shelves, wondering if half of them had ever been read or were just there to adorn the walls, sitting silent and still with knowledge that would never reach human eyes.

She stood up slowly, an idea starting to form, and crossed over to one of the shelves. Lady Allard's words came back to her about never being powerless. Her fingertips brushed the titles as she moved along the wall, not knowing exactly what she was looking for, but believing she would know when she saw it. Being born into a Lording family meant she had grown up with a special education that included reading, writing, history, art, dancing, and several other additions that suited a well brought-up lady. But she wondered: what did the men learn with their education? Geography? Diplomacy? Politics? Law? The basic structure of society was known to all, but the knowledge of its intricacies was reserved for those who had shaped it to favor themselves. The laws that governed society were meant to favor the ones with the most power. But what if Emilia could find a loophole that would grant her access to that power? What if she could find a way, within the laws themselves, to make sure she was never on the outside looking in again?

She scanned the shelves voraciously, like a bird who had found the only fruit tree within a hundred miles, and began pulling promising titles out of their place and piling them on a small end table. And when she had devoured all the shelves within reach she went over and pulled the sliding ladder over to reach the upper levels. She found a particularly large volume near the top, but when she pulled on it another came out with it and went tumbling to the floor. She froze, having forgotten for a moment in her excitement of the tense discussions taking place in just the next room.

The door to the parlor swung open then, and Lord Urbane came in looking quite stern. Lord Findor and Lord Halbany followed suit, though the perturbed looks on their faces had nothing to do with Emilia.

"Sorry," Emilia stuttered. "I was just—."

"Please, Emilia," Lord Urbane said. "Go back outside with the others."

"No need for that, Eleazar," Lord Findor said. "I think—I think it's time we took our leave. Come Phineas, let's fetch the ladies." He started walking to the other door.

Lord Halbany gave a comforting pat to Lord Urbane's shoulder. "We'll be in touch," he said and then followed Lord Findor out of the room.

Emilia climbed slowly down the ladder, but she dared not utter a word at the look of seething tension in Lord Urbane's eyes. He said nothing either, and the two of them stood in awkward silence for a long minute. Then the sound of footsteps and doors shutting were heard beyond the library. A moment later, Lavinia and Lady Allard came walking in, but the other two ladies were gone.

"How did it go?" Lavinia asked cautiously.

Lord Urbane finally broke his agitated stillness and sighed. "Halbany took it well, but Findor—I don't know if it was too much of a shock or he's already on the other side. How did it go with the Ladies?"

"They took it better than I had hoped," Lavinia said. "It was a good idea to split them up."

"Wait," Emilia interrupted, "you told them? I missed everything?"

"This is not about you, Emilia," Lavinia said.

"Does anyone here think I'm incapable of screwing things up?" Emilia continued.

"Emilia," Lavinia warned.

"No, don't answer that," Emilia said, pointedly dropping the book she had held loudly on the floor. "Just make all your plans without me." And she marched out of the library and went up to her bedroom, determined not to care if they all thought she was just getting in the way. She was not a stranger to having decisions made without her. Her mother had been particularly skilled at planning Emilia's calendar with barely a minute for Emilia to schedule something of her own. This had no doubt fueled her rebellious tendencies and need to escape, but now that she was free, Emilia found that she was still living on the outskirts of her own life. Living in a new city, with a new family should have been emancipating, but Emilia felt more like an outsider here than she ever felt in Empyria. And what was the worst, as she treaded this emotional isolation, was not knowing if it was freedom she craved more or connection.

She skipped dinner that night and declined a tray of food brought to her room. She waited until the noises of the house had quieted and the lights had all been put out before lighting her own candle. She intended to go back to the library, but when she opened her door she found a stack of books piled neatly in the hallway. She picked them up and saw they were the ones she had selected earlier. She bit her lip, wondering if Lord Urbane had done this.

She brought them into her room and set them down on the desk by one of the windows. She lit another candle and arranged them so she could see better, then took the top book and opened it. But something caught her eye out the window before she could begin reading. A single person was quickly approaching the house, cutting across the circular drive on foot holding a single lantern, headed towards the front door.

Emilia grabbed a candle and rushed out of her room and down the stairs. The earnest pounding against the door began just as she reached it and she flung it open, surprising the young man there. He couldn't have been more than fifteen, wearing a dark, woolly jacket and a circular cap. He didn't try to come in, but pulled a thick letter out of his pocket and handed it to her.

"For the master of the house, Miss," he said. He tipped his hat and then jogged back across the drive.

Emilia stepped back and closed the door, having not a chance to say anything to the young messenger. She inspected the letter and saw that it wasn't even sealed. She looked around, but everyone had gone to bed and it seemed no one had been disturbed by the brief knocking on the door. The boy had said it was for the master of the house, but she had no idea where Lord Urbane had gone off to.

She unfolded the letter and scanned its contents under the dim light of her candle, her stomach tightening with each line, though she had barely reached the end and she was already running back up the stairs. She flew down the hallway towards Lavinia's room and started pounding on the door, the letter gripped tightly in her thumping fist.

"Lavinia!" she shouted. "Wake up! Lavinia!"

The door swung open and Lavinia's silhouette shadowed her as light from the fireplace inside spilled out into the hall. Lavinia's hair was let down and she was in her night shift, but there was no sleep in her eyes.

"Emilia? What—?"

"A letter arrived, just now," Emilia interrupted her, thrusting the letter towards her. "They're coming for Lord Urbane. Where is he?"

And then Lord Urbane stepped into her view behind Lavinia, not yet in his night clothes. He took the letter and began reading it.

"Who's it from?" Lavinia asked.

"There was no seal or signature," Emilia said.

"It's from Findor," Lord Urbane said with certainty as he finished the letter. He went over to the fire and tossed the letter in.

"Lord Findor? But I thought—," Lavinia started to question.

"I was wrong," he said. "Halbany's betrayed me. Guards are on their way here." He rushed out of the room and started down the hall, leaving Emilia and Lavinia to follow nervously. "Brandstone!" Lord Urbane bellowed, as he trotted down the stairs.

"Eleazar, wait," Lavinia pleaded as they hurried after him. "What are you going to do?"

Mr. Brandstone appeared through one of the doors then, holding a lantern. Lord Urbane bid him to follow as well and they made their way into the retiring room. He started gathering papers and scrolls and told the butler to get them to the horse master. Those letters needed to get to Lord Findor.

Then there was a loud bang against the front door and everyone froze for a moment.

"You need to go," Emilia said.

But Lord Urbane shook his head. "I'm not going to run this time."

"What? They'll arrest you if you don't."

"And they'll arrest the rest of you if I do," he replied.

The banging repeated itself and Lord Urbane urged Mr. Brandstone to hurry.

Emilia realized then he was right. His existence was out there now, witnessed by more than a few, and the corruption within the Council held enough power to twist the perception of his allegiance. If he ran, then they would either arrest Lavinia and herself and maybe even Lady Allard for their ties to Empyrian "traitors" or use them to flush Lord Urbane into the open again. Either way, he was protecting them.

"I'll stall them," Emilia said. "Buy you as much time as I can."

Lord Urbane nodded gratefully as he and Mr. Brandstone continued to gather the letters that were the evidence of the atrocities happening in Empyria. Lavinia still did not look pleased and started to fluster as Emilia left the room.

She walked through the massive entryway as the banging on the door intensified. This time it was followed by muffled threats of forced entry if no one was to let them in. She noticed Lady Allard at the top of the stairs, rubbing sleep from her eyes, and put a finger to her lips before forcefully waving her back to her room. Taking the cue, Lady Allard hurried away.

Emilia finally reached the door and took a deep breath, waiting as long as she could before opening it. She flung it open, surprising the guard who had his fist raised to pound it against the door again but lowered it when he saw her. There were at least a dozen guards, fully armed and attired, some holding lanterns. But the one she was surprised to see was the one who stepped forward.

"Ah, Miss Regoran," Commander Garz greeted her with an amused smile. The lantern light reflected starkly off his bald head and gave his already chiseled features a more grievous look. "I wondered if I would see you tonight."

His presence took her by surprise and for a moment the same feeling of needing to flee that she had had when she had last spoken to him took hold, but she tightened her grip on the door and resolved to keep her feet rooted to the floor for as long as she could.

"You could see me in the daytime, when the hour is more…agreeable," she offered.

"I do apologize for the lateness of the hour, but I have business that could not wait."

"Then I would question the nature of your business," she replied coldly.

Commander Garz pressed his lips into a thin smile and took another step forward. "My business is between myself and Lord Urbane, who is in fact alive and in this very house. But this is not news to you, is it?"

Emilia held her ground and her gaze.

"And I believe that we had an agreement, the last time we spoke, did we not? You were to come to me if anyone from Empyria tried to contact you, and yet, here I am on your doorstep, instead of you on mine." He raised an eyebrow, taking another step closer.

"I've never been good at following orders," she said, tilting her chin up defiantly. "And you never said 'please'."

He narrowed his eyes at her and she knew he was losing his patience for the banter. "You will step aside, Miss Regoran, or I will be forced to move you."

"Again, no 'please'?"

His patience ran out and he grabbed her arms, pushing her back into the house. "Search the house," he called back to the guards, who began streaming into the house.

"Let her go," a voice boomed from across the room and Lord Urbane came walking in. Despite his noticeable limp, he looked formidable in the vast room, commanding the shadows that roamed from the lantern light. "I'm right here."

Commander Garz smiled and released Emilia. She backed away and pressed into one of the walls, her heart beating with distaste for the man. She saw Lavinia slowly come out of the shadows behind Lord Urbane, her hands clasped together tightly over her chest. The Commander wasted no time and ordered his men to seize Lord Urbane. He didn't struggle as the guards took hold of him, but his expression was full of resistance. They marched him past Commander Garz and out the door. Lavinia looked like she wanted to run after him, but she held her place.

Commander Garz ordered the rest of his men out of the house, but before he left he looked at Lavinia and then at Emilia again. "Guards will be posted around the perimeter at all times. You are not to leave the house. Is that understood?" At Emilia's glare, he chuckled. "You would do well to remember our agreement, Miss Regoran. I remove people who become…useless." Then he followed his men out and closed the door behind him, taking the light of the lanterns and Lord Urbane with him.

Chapter Four

Tamsin crept around the twisting limbs of the statues inside the cavern, caution determining her slower pace, though she knew she was getting closer to the exit with each step. This emboldened her to keep going, despite feeling like each of those steps was being watched by the immobile stone creatures. Lifeless as they were, their presence was eerily assertive and Tamsin found herself glancing at each one she passed, feeling as if she were treading on open water and if she looked away she would fall in and be consumed by the shadows lurking beneath the surface.

She heard a scratch against the floor and the hurried rush of movement nearby and stopped. She crouched down and gripped the handle on her sword at her waist, slowly drawing it out. She heard the sound again and held her breath so the sound of it wouldn't distract her from pinpointing its location. She slid her eyes back and forth, trying to make out anything in the darkness. The sound grew closer, like the bristles on a brush striking a piece of parchment.

Tamsin raised the broken half of her sword and was just about to lunge when the sound transformed into a dark figure before her. She stopped herself just in time and let out a quick breath, lowering her sword again.

Enrik froze at the sight of her blade, his eyes bright against the faded stone around them, but then relaxed slightly as she lowered it.

"I thought you were—," she started.

"I know," he said. "I'm sorry for scaring you. I didn't see you at the canyon so I came back."

"I'm not scared," she said. "You saved me back there. I'm grateful." She walked over to him and gave him a hug, having to stretch on her toes to reach her arms around his neck. She released him and was about to thank him, but then she paused, a new feeling pushing her gratitude away like the wind blowing a dead leaf off a tree.

"Tamsin?" Enrik asked, noticing the change.

Tamsin shoved him as hard as she could and he staggered back, surprise and guilt battling for dominance over his face. She wanted to shove him again, to keep shoving him until all the anger over losing Samih was gone, but she stopped herself. Instead, she clenched her fists and let out a frustrated cry. "How could you, Enrik?! Do you even know what you've done?"

His mouth fell open wordlessly, his bottom jaw trembling in the absence of an explanation.

"I'm so angry with you, I can't even look—." But she did look at him then. She really looked at him and for the first time she saw the dark circles under his eyes, the vertical streaks over his cheeks of unwashed tears, the slump of his shoulders, and the haggard way his clothes fell over his body. But what she noticed most of all was the dull glisten of his eyes, the hopeless glaze of desperation. A look she had seen on Haven, in the cells of Empyria. "Oh, Enrik."

"Tamsin, I'm so sorry," he said, his voice breaking under the weight of his sorrow. "I never meant to hurt anyone. I didn't know what I was doing. That man—he—he's dead, isn't he?"

Her silent stare was the only answer she could give, or she risked breaking herself.

Enrik shook his head. "I'm so sorry. I'm so sorry."

"Why?" Tamsin asked, still finding it difficult to quell her anger.

Enrik wiped his nose with his wrist. "Those creatures killed all the men. All of the soldiers. Monstran caught me trying to escape. Then he took me to the Master and I—it was like I was walking in a nightmare. He has this control, this ability to—it was like a fog and anytime I even thought of disobeying the fog turned to chaos and destruction, screams and—." He shook his head again. "I was a slave in my own mind, Tamsin."

Tamsin let her hand tighten on her sword handle. "Are you still under his control?"

"No, but if we don't get out of here he might do it again."

"Do you know who he is?" She had little time to piece it together after talking with the amon'jii. The Master was their leader, but beyond that she had yet to work out his identity.

Enrik's eyes were pits of fear. "He's not of this world, Tamsin. He's something...else."

"What do you mean? He's not an amon'jii? One of the creatures?"

"No, but he's not human either. He—he's trapped. I followed Monstran and spied for weeks and I think all this time he's been preparing Haven somehow to be a—a host, so the Master can come back into the world. I know it doesn't make sense."

"You've seen Haven? Where is he?"

"I don't know anymore."

Tamsin tried not to let her frustration consume her. "Do you know where the Master is? If you take me there maybe we can find Haven and get him out."

Enrik's eyes widened. "No, we can't go there. All he needed yet was that stone, and now Haven's...not himself. He's a slave too."

Tamsin's lip curled, her anger bubbling again like boiling water. "And you gave it to him."

"Tamsin, please, I—," but he was cut off as a high-pitched shriek cut through the air. It was some distance away yet, but close enough to make them both jump.

"We need to go," Enrik said.

"Wait. Do you know where the firestone is? If we can get that back, then Haven would be free to come with us, right?"

"Tamsin, it won't be that simple."

"The choice is simple enough," she said, trying to ignore the fear rising in his eyes. "You can come with me or you can go."

He didn't have the chance to answer though, for a snarl slithered out of the darkness only feet from them, followed by the gleaming fangs of an amon'jii from around one of the statues.

"Tamsin! Ru—." His warning was cut off as the amon'jii leapt at them.

Tamsin was able to quench its fire before it could burn them, but she was knocked sideways before the rest of her could react. She slammed into one of the statues and fell to her knees. She grabbed her broken sword as she heard Enrik cry out. She charged at the dark shape and plunged the jagged blade into the amon'jii's side. It let out a wail and tried to whip around to confront her, but Tamsin slashed again, this time connecting with the creature's exposed neck. Its shriek faded into the stream of blood pouring out of it and it collapsed to the ground. Tamsin shoved its twitching claw out of the way and grabbed Enrik's arm, pulling him out from under the amon'jii's convulsing form. He staggered clumsily to his feet and the two of them rushed towards the wall where the hazy gray light from the outside made the exit known.

The smell of fresh air should have been pleasant as they crossed the threshold into the canyon, but the air was heavy with stagnant smoke and ancient decay. They stopped when they came to a sunken ledge off the narrow path and slid down onto it, crouching under the little overhang that the edge of the path created. The hidden alcove gave them the chance to catch their breath and Tamsin her first look at the Ravine. The other side of the canyon wall rose well above them and yet she couldn't see the bottom through the blurry patches of mist that hovered between the walls, almost like clouds that had fallen in and never found their way out again. The opposite wall was etched with shadowy crevasses and alcoves just like this one, with pointed outcroppings piercing the mist, but none were long enough to bridge the gap between the two sides.

"Haven where are you?" she whispered into the air.

"Tamsin, please, we have to leave," Enrik panted.

"I'm not leaving without him," Tamsin resolved, turning back to look at Enrik. "You can go if you wa—," she started, but then her mouth fell open.

Enrik leaned back against the rockface, his eyes glazed over as if he was asleep, though they were wide open. "I don't think I'm okay," he said, his eyes moving slowly to his hand, which had turned a glossy red. Across his stomach was a wide strip of blood, dripping slowly across his trembling fingers.

"Oh lords," Tamsin breathed, realizing their close call had been a lot closer than she thought. She froze, the shock of the sight rendering her mind useless for a moment. All she could see was Samih and that horrible moment when everything had turned to ash before her eyes. And she had not only been powerless to stop it, but had been blind to the threats around her, like a horse that could not see the wolves at her side because she couldn't take off the blinders on her bridle.

Enrik's eyes returned to hers, seeming to study her until his blank stare transformed to one of devastated awareness. "Oh lords," he echoed her. "I'm—I'm going to die here, aren't I?"

His question punctured through her shock. Had she forgiven him enough to save him? As angry as she was with him over Samih and stealing Haven's firestone she couldn't let him die here. Though for a horrifying second she thought if she did leave him here, to bleed out among the rocks, then she could go save Haven. But it would cost Enrik his life, and she had the power to help him right now.

Two hot tears slid down her cheek, one for her shame at her selfish thought of abandoning Enrik here, and the other for actually abandoning Haven, though it melted the last of her icy binds. "No, you're not going to die here," she told him. She closed the gap between them, trying to see the extent of his injury. She was no healer, but she knew if she didn't stop the bleeding, it wouldn't matter what she did. There was too much of it coming out too quickly.

She grabbed her pant sleeve, ready to rip off a piece to tie around the wound, but paused, and realized she had a better solution. She had done it once before, so she knew she could do it again. Even if it had hurt like the seven hells.

"Enrik, I'm going to help you, but I need you not to scream, okay?"

His eyes widened for a moment and then he nodded.

"Okay," Tamsin said, taking a deep breath. She placed her hands on the wound, feeling as gently as she could until she found each end of the gash.

Enrik whimpered underneath her touch, but pressed his lips together in a hard white line.

Tamsin didn't relish what she was about to do, and she wondered if this might kill him as easily at it could help him. She met Enrik's gaze and she knew she had to try. "No fear," she told him, nodding.

He nodded back.

Tamsin took another deep breath and focused her power on the wound, feeling a brief burst of heat beneath her hands as she squeezed the edges as close together as she could. Despite her earlier request, Enrik let out an anguished cry, drops of sweat budding on his forehead as the smell of burnt flesh filled their noses.

"There, it's done," Tamsin said, but Enrik's eyelids fluttered and he sagged forward. Tamsin caught him and managed to hold him up. "Enrik? Enrik?" She feared he was dead for a moment and then heard the rasp of his haggard breath. Relief filled her, but it was cut short by the sound of another cry, from somewhere deeper in the tunnels.

The amon'jii were coming again.

"Enrik, Enrik," she repeated more frantically this time.

He mumbled something incoherent as she shifted under his weight. He was even thinner than he had been back in Empyria, but he was still a good distance taller than she was and she knew she wouldn't be able to carry him out of here on her own.

"C'mon, I know it hurts, but you have to help me," she said, dragging him out from under the alcove. "We have to get out of here." She maneuvered his arm around her shoulders to prop him up against her and then lifted him up to stand, gritting her teeth from the effort.

A soft chuckle bubbled from his lips. "That's exactly what I told Haven."

"What?" Her head shot up to look at him.

Enrik groaned and hunched forward, but Tamsin held him up, groaning herself under his weight. She knew she had to keep him talking. She needed him to stay conscious. "When did you talk to Haven, Enrik?"

"I tried to get him out," Enrik panted. "We were so close."

Tamsin swallowed the lump in her throat and coaxed him to walk. "Well we're going to make it, okay? Just one step at a time." She looked around them, searching for a way out, and saw the ledge angle down around the corner and knew that was her only option. There was no way Enrik would be able to climb anything, so down was the only direction available to them. Down into the canyon. Down into the Ravine of Bones.

"Father, can you tell me a story?"

"It's late, Haven. You should be sleeping."

"I'm too afraid."

"Afraid of what?" His father's large form shuffled over to Haven's sleeping mat. His legs, like two large reed canoes, bent down so his face was more visible to his son. But the passage of time had made the memory blurry around the edges and all Haven could see was his father's dark beard.

Haven bit his lip, debating if it would be braver to confess or just go back to sleep. His father was a warrior, first sha'diin to the Kazsera and could intimidate even the fiercest of enemies to cower before him. But he was also a protector, a defender.

"The dark," Haven finally said, his lower lip trembling.

His father made a sound in the back of his throat. "And why does that scare you?"

"Kellan said he saw a Watcher. He said they take kids at nighttime and take them to Ib'n. And they never see their family again."

His father made another sound and scratched his chin. "Kellan, huh? And who told Kellan this?"

"His brother, Mai'ko."

His father pressed his lips together and nodded in thought. "I will tell you a story, Haven. But you'll have to do something for me when it's done."

Haven nodded quickly, willing to agree to anything to hear it.

"It's about your mother's grandsire. His name was Iikan. He was a Watcher. There's a story about him, about a time when he went searching for Ib'n's lost heart."

"Ib'n's lost heart?"

"Do you remember the story of when the Lumierii defeated Ib'n at the Great Battle?"

Haven nodded.

"Do you remember that it was Baat, the goddess of the sun and sky, that ripped out his heart?"

He nodded again, eyes wide and glossy as the imagined scene played in his mind.

"Well, it's said that Baat gave the heart to one of the Lumierii and told him to hide it somewhere where it would never be *found. He took it and vowed to Baat that he would never let it see the light of day again. He traveled for many days and nights. He went into the desert waste. He went to the tallest mountains. He saw the Endless Water that reached beyond the edges of the world. But every time he went to bury the heart or toss it into the deepest canyon or throw it into the Endless Water to carry it far away with its current...he stopped. He couldn't do it."*

"Why not?" Haven asked.

His father shrugged. "Some believe that he felt guilty for betraying his creator. That even though Ib'n had brought chaos into the world, he had still created something beautiful with the Lumierii. But there are some who think that Ib'n's heart still had power. That he had not been vanquished, only separated from his mortal body, and when the Watcher took it, that power consumed him and compelled him to betray Baat and the other Lumierii. He took the heart and was never seen again.

Either way, the heart was lost, and your great grandsire, Iikan, decided to go looking for it, for it was rumored to be the root of all evil and discontent and fear in the world. Iikan had a family before he was turned. He loved them and would do anything to keep them safe. He couldn't bear the idea of one of his children becoming like him, so he did what he thought was the best thing he could do: he left."

"He went to go find the heart," Haven breathed, his little hands clutching the edges of his blanket. "Did he find it?"

The shadowy image of his father's beard shook back and forth. "He never did. And you know why? Because it is only a myth."

Haven's eyebrows scrunched together, trying to work out the meaning of the story. "So what happened to him?"

"He eventually fell to the sun curse, as it happens to some Watchers. But do you know why, Haven? Why I told you this story?"

Haven shook his head.

"Because Iikan took the story of Ib'n's lost heart and tried to make it true. Iikan thought that fear and evil belonged to one thing and if he could destroy it, then he could destroy all the bad things in the world. But fear is part of this world, Haven. It is as natural as the wind blowing through the reeds. But the one thing about fear, Haven, is that you have the power to destroy it."

"I do?"

He nodded and pointed to Haven's chest. "You have the power to tell fear 'No.' It will come and go like the rains, but when it does come, you must be stronger than it." He put his hands on his knees and then pushed himself up. "Come with me, son."

Haven scooted out from under his blanket, wondering what his father had in mind next. He followed him out of the muudhiif and into the humid night air. His father stopped at the edge of their mud flat and put his hands on his hips, surveying the surrounding reed beds and mud flats. The wind gusted up every few breaths, bringing with it the tidings of an impending storm that would break through the thick air. Lightning illuminated the clouds in the distance, answered by a low gurgle of thunder.

Haven felt his father's hand pat the top of his shoulder. "You must learn to overcome the fear, Haven. You'll stay out here tonight. If you're still here at dawn, I'll know that you've learned the lesson." Then he turned and walked back into the muudhiif.

Haven stared at the retreating form of his father, caught somewhere between terror and shock, but he dared not move. A crack of lightning made him jump and he turned back to look at the reeds bending in the wind. His arms were straight as oars by his sides and his lips pressed firmly against one another, but it did nothing to stop the rest of his small body from trembling. A thousand terrifying scenarios raced through his mind: scaly-skinned creatures clawing their way up the mud flat from the water, the shadows between the reeds transforming into horned demons, and—

A cackle of lightning broke up the darkness again and the shape of a tall, darkly clothed figure flickered in the light across the water on the opposite reed bed. A Watcher. He stood still among the swaying reeds and a wide-eyed Haven knew he was watching him.

"No, fear," he whispered with hitched breath. "No, fear." He shut his eyes and several tears escaped down his cheeks. "No fear."

Haven opened his eyes. The jagged black edges of his cell surrounded him. He sat on his heels with his back pressed against the wall. The chains that had once held him hung motionlessly on either side of him. There was a screeching creak from the door as it opened on the opposite side of the room. One of Monstran's human servants quickly skulked away again, making way for Monstran himself to enter. Monstran's purple robes flowed effortlessly around him as he stopped in the middle of the room, indicating he had been walking with more vigor than his usual to get here.

Haven cocked his head to the side, watching him. Monstran was excited about something.

Monstran smiled, his teeth matching the brightness of his silver hair. "Haven, I have something for you," he said. He snapped his fingers and the skulking servant rushed in again, carrying something in his arms. Monstran took the bundle and held it out. "New robes for you."

Haven slowly got up and took the pile of clothing. The fabric was mostly black, though the edges revealed swaths of crimson and silver hiding within the folds. At Monstran's nod he began putting the robes on, his hands awkwardly navigating the different ties and straps as if he had not gone through the same motions a thousand times in another life. When he had finished everything else, the last thing that remained was the hood. He grabbed the edges, pulling them up and over his head until he was completely engulfed within the shadow it created. He looked up until Monstran's approving gaze appeared just beneath the edge of the hood.

"Extraordinary," Monstran said.

The servant reappeared and placed a pair of knee-high boots in front of him.

"Walk with me, Haven," Monstran said.

Haven slipped the boots on and followed him out of the cell. He walked next to Monstran as they made their way through the tunnels of the Ravine. As long as Monstran was with him the amon'jii would not harm him. They were loyal to him he said, but their patience and self-control was limited to the fullness of their stomachs. Bats and mountain goats were hardly a thing to keep an army fed with. Haven could feel their hunger, their ravenous lust for blood pounding through the walls like drums. But he was not afraid.

"Very soon," Monstran said, "your purpose will be fulfilled and Ib'n's children will rise once more."

Haven kept along silently until they reached an opening in the cliff and stood upon a narrow ledge overlooking the canyon. The wind blew up from the dredges below and ruffled the edges of his hood. It smelled of rotten wood and Sulphur.

"Yes, very soon," Monstran repeated, taking a deep, pleasure-filled breath and sighing heavily. "Everything I have done.

Everything you have endured. It has all been to serve the one true Master. And because of you, his reign will be omnipotent. At last, he will break free of his prison. Your sacrifice, Haven, will be forever hailed as the greatest deed the world has ever seen. If I could take your place I would, but alas I do not have the blood and power of the Lumierii running through my veins. Has all of your strength returned yet?"

"Most."

"Well, it won't be long now. You've been reborn Haven, stronger than you ever were. Just as the Master will be."

Haven...

Haven twitched ever so slightly at the sound. He looked at Monstran, but the silver-haired man was still gazing triumphantly across the canyon with no indication that he had heard anything. Haven let his gaze roam over the canyon walls, but aside from a nesting bird there was nothing.

Haven...where are you?

This time he felt a tiny tremor in his chest, like something had shaken his ribcage. He took an involuntary step back. This, Monstran noticed.

"Perhaps you've had enough today. Let's get you back."

"No need. I will go."

"Very well." Monstran motioned to his attendants, who remained in the shadows of the tunnels yet, to follow him.

Haven turned and left Monstran there. He flexed his fingers at his sides, trying to shake off whatever it was that had just happened as he made his way back to his cell. He had spent a long time coming to terms with his presence in this place and convincing himself that the events of his past had been a pitiful—

You don't scare me, a woman's voice whispered, almost teasingly.

Haven stumbled, clutching his tunic over his chest. What was happening?

"Are you alright mister?" one of the attendants inquired.

Haven straightened and nodded, resuming his walk. If the attendants told Monstran about this it would delay the happening and the Master was already quite impatient to begin. Haven needed to be strong to face what was next. He was the master of his pain and whatever this was would not control him.

The worst is over, Haven. It's all in the past now. I'm going to get you out of here.

He entered his chamber and stood near the wall. "Put them back on," he growled and waited patiently while the attendants looked at each other uncertainly and then finally replaced his shackles. Once he was secure again, they took his empty bowls of food and closed the door behind them.

He could remember before. When his chains hung from the ceiling and the pain enveloped him like a second skin. He used to have visions of a girl. Sometimes she came to him as a child and sat with him and hummed songs to him. Other times the girl was older, with honeyed skin and long hair cascading down her back like a river. She would whisper encouragements to him. But she wasn't real. A manifestation of his tortured mind. An echo of an unattainable life. So he told her to go, to leave him alone.

This wasn't like the other times, though. The voice was...the voice was the same, but this felt strange. Like a numb limb finally coming back to life or like something he had buried deep trying to dig its way back out.

Remember what you used to tell me? Do you remember?

The pull on his chest intensified. The veins in his arms and neck bulged as he clenched his fists. No, the Watcher was gone. He only existed in dreams now.

No fear...

"AhhhhhHHHHHH!" Haven roared until he feared his chains would snap and the walls would cave in.

Chapter Five

Making their way down into the canyon was easier than going up, but even that was a challenge. Tamsin was covered in sweat and rock dust after only an hour and every muscle screamed from the effort of supporting Enrik. But she pressed on, pausing only in brief intervals to let Enrik breathe and find their next path. She tried to stay as close to the outer wall as she could, only venturing back in when there was no other option. Their best chance of surviving now was avoiding the amon'jii at all costs and so far she had seen no traces of them near the canyon, probably because the paths were too narrow for the large beasts.

"Tamsin," Enrik murmured, the pain making him groggy. "Stop, please…"

Tamsin removed his arm from around her shoulders and helped him sit against the rock face. She untied her water skin from her belt and helped him drink. He rested his head back when he had finished and closed his eyes, his breath coming out in ragged pants.

"Rest for a minute," she instructed, before getting up and walking a little further along the path by herself. She glanced back, worry etched into her features, for Enrik, and for herself. He should not be moving with his injury, but they couldn't stop for long. And she wondered how long she would be able to support him before she collapsed from exhaustion herself. One of them would fall before they ever found a way out. And the thickening mist didn't help. There were some sections where she could hardly see three feet in front of her.

She kicked at a stone before stopping to crouch down and rest her legs. She hung her weary head for a moment, hearing the *crick-crack* as the stone skipped along the path.

Her head shot up as she had an idea. Her hands scrambled over the ground until she found another loose stone about the size of her palm. She gripped the stone in her hand and stood back up, her legs shaky with fatigue. Then she tossed the stone into the mist, losing sight of it almost immediately.

*One...two...*she counted...*thr—*

Then the sound of rock hitting rock echoed from below and she let out a breath in relief. She rushed back over to where Enrik was still propped up against the wall. "Enrik, we're close to the bottom. We're so close." Then she wrapped his arm over her again and hoisted him up, pressing her lips together against the effort, but she was renewed with new conviction now that the bottom was near.

They walked for another ten minutes, the slope getting steeper every minute, but finally they made it below the mist and Tamsin could see where their descent leveled off and expanded into a rocky plain. Stepping onto the flattened terrain was like a cool breath of air, even though the musty scent of the Ravine still lingered. Persistent clumps of dirt and grass pressed up through the ground in sporadic patches, adding some welcomed softness to the hard rock. And even though the ground was still uneven, it was a relief to not have to brace against the downward slope of the path.

Tamsin kept her eyes and senses alert as they inched along, trying to ignore her own increasing pains. The ache in her side from the wound inflicted by Mowlgra at the Duels was telling her to stop, as she was sure Enrik's wound was telling him, but she feared what would happen if she did. Putting as much distance as she could between them and the amon'jii was paramount, as was finding a way out. And the deepening shadows within the Ravine told her the afternoon was quickly fading, though it was hard to tell through the ceiling of fog above them how late it actually was. Spending the night here, with a hoard of nocturnal creatures that now wanted her dead, was the last thing she wanted.

Something crunched underneath her boot and she stopped for just a moment, sliding her foot away to see what it was. Dirty splinters of white bark lay in her footprint in a broken line. She dug her toe into the dirt some more and more of the white bark cracked under the disturbance, this time in a circle as if she stepped on a piece of glass, sending the cracks out like spiderwebs.

Her breath caught in her throat as she realized it wasn't tree bark she had stepped on.

"What's wrong?" Enrik panted.

Tamsin shook her head and shuffled them forward once again, though this time noticing every unnatural shape or color protruding from the dirt. The Ravine of Bones, the Ma'diin called this place. And now she knew why.

"Do you know any way out of here?" she asked him as a desperate pit began to take hold in her stomach.

"I've never been down here before," he said, looking around through squinted eyes. "I'm sorry."

"Don't be sorry. The canyon has to end at some point, right?"

"I don't know about ends, but look," he said, lifting his hand to point ahead of them.

Tamsin followed his gaze and saw a massive opening in the rock face ahead. They limped towards it together and when they reached it they could see it wasn't a cave at all, but a tunnel. The opening could have easily fit her whole house back in Jalsai and she wondered if the amon'jii used this tunnel.

"Do you think it's a way out?" Enrik asked.

"There's only one way we're going to find out," Tamsin replied, trying not to think about the bones behind them and how they had ended up there. "Wait here," she said, depositing him next to the wall. She walked a little ways in on her own, stretching out with her senses to see if she could feel any amon'jii hearts within the tunnel. The sense was blurry, but she didn't think any were in their direct path, rather it felt like she was hearing the echoes of their fiery heartbeats through the walls. She knelt down and felt the ground here, rolling the soft dirt between her fingers. It reminded her of wet sand, like the kind she had felt just after escaping the mangroves.

She walked back to Enrik, who looked up with a pained, but hopeful expression.

"I think this might connect to the anasii hada," she said. "I think there was water here once."

"The what?" Enrik asked.

"Where the Empyrians built the dam," she explained.

"If we can get there, they could help us," Enrik said, trying to get back to his feet.

Tamsin hurried over to help him, hoisting him up once again. All the color was gone from his face, but he seemed more alert, more determined now.

They walked into the tunnel, staying near the wall so they wouldn't be so exposed in case there was anything lurking in the dark down here. And the light from the canyon vanished quicker than Tamsin expected, hastening her desire to reach the end of the tunnel as soon as they could. Enrik was groaning with each step, but he too seemed bent on outrunning the dark.

"We can do this, Enrik," Tamsin encouraged him, feeling him lean more on her the further they went. "Just keep—."

She was cut off as the ground suddenly crumbled under her foot, sending them both crashing to the ground. Luckily, Enrik had a tight hold on her and pulled her away from the edge that had suddenly appeared. Falling rocks echoed down below as they lay on the ground, panting heavily. Tamsin rolled over first, touching Enrik's arm.

"I'm…alright…" he mumbled, but his face was drawn tight with pain.

Tamsin then propped herself up to her knees and carefully began feeling across the ground with her fingers until they closed over the edge that had just given way. It was too hard to tell in the dark how far it went, both across and down. She clenched her hands for just a moment and then returned her attention to Enrik. She helped slide him back and to the wall so he could rest for a minute without fear of falling in. Then she rested too, leaning her head against the wall and closing her eyes.

But then her eyes snapped open almost immediately again. She turned around, feeling the wall with her hands until they closed on the tuberous branches that climbed it. She moved her hands further over the wall, coming across more thick vines clinging to the nooks in the rock. She stepped back, not sure how far the vines extended through the tunnel, but hoping her idea worked.

She took a deep breath, tapping into the energy where her power lay and sent it out to the wall. Instantly, the vines exploded with flames, sizzling up the rock wall and over the ceiling, crisscrossing and diverging, sparking more snake-like trails of fire along the walls. Her body was already overwhelmed from the trek through the Ravine, but she grimaced and pushed the flames further until the inside of the tunnel was alight like a trellis covered in fireflies.

"Tamsin?" Enrik breathed, his eyes wide with fearful wonder.

Tamsin took a few steps forward, the edge of the pit now visible in the orange glow surrounding them. It was deep, deeper than the light could illuminate, and stretched across like a black lake. But on the other side of the tunnel, encircling the cavity, was a walkway that sloped up and around to the other side.

"There," Tamsin said, pointing to it. "Come on." She lifted Enrik up and they skirted the edge of the pit to the walkway. It was wide enough for at least two wheelhouses to traverse, so they had no fear of falling into the dark hole, but the incline stretched their strength, making it impossible for Enrik to ask more questions and Tamsin to answer any. When the walkway finally leveled off a bit, Enrik gripped her arm suddenly.

"I remember this," Enrik said. "When we first got here, this is where we came in. There," and he pointed in front of them.

A large archway was carved into the rock just a few yards ahead, encasing two wide doors with metal bars running up them.

"That leads inside," Enrik said as they paused to look through the bars. The tunnel beyond was pitch black and neither one of them lingered long to try and decipher what was on the other side.

"And the way out...?"

"It's just up ahead," he said.

They struggled on, putting the dark pit and the metal gate behind them as the light began to fade in the tunnel from the burning vines. They burnt out quickly, even as Tamsin ignited new ones as they went along and released the ones that broke and fell to the ground. But Enrik was right; very soon the burning vines were no longer needed and Tamsin released them all in lieu of the light coming from the outside.

Sunset was not far off when they finally emerged, as the sky above was already shaded with the blue hues of night and a few stars could already be seen, but the light brought a bittersweet taste to her mouth. She and Enrik had made it out with their lives, but she had failed to get Haven out.

She wiped the corners of her eyes. "Which way, Enrik?"

"Um..." Enrik looked back and forth. In front of them was a wide wall that broke their view of the world beyond. It was not nearly as high as the canyon they had just left, but high enough to make climbing it out of the question. The same vines that had clung to the tunnel walls cascaded over the edge, anchoring themselves in the crevasses and cracks in the rock. But running through this new canyon was a path, one going towards the setting sun to the west, the other going away from it.

Tamsin could guess which way led to the desert and the anasii hada, but she was unsure if their odds were better with the Empyrians or the Ma'diin.

But neither of them had the time to choose, as just then a hissing shriek echoed between the walls behind them.

Wordlessly, the two set off on the path towards the sunset, hurrying as quickly as they were able. Tamsin didn't care where they were going now, as long as the sunlight bought them a little more time against the nocturnal creatures. But the sound had been close, too close, and as the sun set, the shadows deepened in the canyon.

Tamsin saw a pile of large boulders up ahead and when they reached them, she helped Enrik onto the first one, cupping his boot in between her hands and lifting him up. He groaned and fell on his side, wincing heavily on top of the rock.

Tamsin knelt on the ground for a moment, catching her own breath. The pile of boulders rose about halfway up the wall; the rest they would have to climb. But if the amon'jii had caught their scent, then they were out of time. They would never outrun the beasts through the small canyon.

A snarl snapped her head up and she pulled the handle of her broken blade out just in time to see an amon'jii emerge from the large tunnel they had just come out of themselves. The creature had already spotted them and stepped carefully into the shadowy crevasse.

"Enrik, start climbing," she urged him. "Now, now!"

She could hear his groans behind her as he shuffled over the stones, but she never took her eyes off the amon'jii as it continued to approach them. So far it was the only one, and she wondered if its caution was because of this fact. She felt its heart pumping eagerly and she immediately crushed the fiery power building within it, but the creature was not deterred. She made a decision then and turned around and leapt at the boulder, scrambling to crawl up it. The creature shrieked as it realized she was getting away and stabbed at the ground. She heard the scrape of the amon'jii's claws behind her and swung her broken sword around. The amon'jii's head snapped back, missing the bite of Tamsin's blade, but it struck with one of its massive legs. Its claw missed her ankle, but punctured her boot enough to pin her down. She fell hard against the rock as the amon'jii pulled back, ripping her off the boulder. On the ground again, she rolled away, but was a second too slow as the amon'jii clawed at her again. She screamed as she felt her skin tear just below her elbow. She swung her broken blade, but the amon'jii bit down on it and tore it out of her hand as if it were ripping off a chunk of meat.

Then the amon'jii staggered sideways, hissing in surprise as a rock pelted it, then another and another. It whipped around to face its new foe, but then a spear struck its hind leg. The creature wailed and twisted back and forth until it ripped the wooden shaft out.

Tamsin used the distraction to dart away, hardly able to believe she was still alive. She climbed back up the boulders, staining the stones red with the blood seeping out of her arm. Enrik had vanished so she kept going until she reached the top of the pile. Then she grabbed onto one of the vines that had forced its way into the rock and began to climb. It had withered from the harsh conditions, but its tuberous fibers held together under her weight. She heard the amon'jii shrieking below and there were shouts coming from above, but she could focus on neither of them. Her heart pounded in her ears, blending with the roiling anger she could feel from the amon'jii, as the vine creaked beneath her fingers. She was so close and yet her exhaustion chose this moment to make her limbs tremble and her thoughts slur.

A hand was thrust over the edge, appearing right above her. And then a man's grizzled face followed it, his eyes urgent. "Take my hand, girl! Reach!"

Chapter Six

The world snapped back into focus as this new hope flooded Tamsin's vision in the form of a wild, bearded man, his cheeks red and puffy. She tightened her grip with one hand and then reached up with the other, stretching as far as she could. His massive hand engulfed hers, locking onto her wrist, and in one giant heave pulled her up onto the plateau. She had no time to catch her breath, however, as the man hauled her to her feet, nearly dragging her as he pulled her away from the edge. She did notice, however, they were not alone. Several more men were standing near the edge, hurling stones and whatever else they could find at the amon'jii below. And two more were supporting Enrik between them, already hurrying away.

"Let's go!" the bearded man yelled and Tamsin was prodded into a run along with her band of rescuers.

They traced the path down the plateau, charging headlong as if they were being pursued. The sun was close to setting and the shadows were stretched out long over the rocky terrain and Tamsin knew the reason for their urgency. They veered off into the wild, stumbling over crumbling rocks and logs so old they were as grey as ash, but didn't slow down until the shadows had grown so dark they could hardly see.

Breathing hard, they finally stopped near an outcropping of rock that from the north looked like it dropped straight down, but the landscape curved down and around the side and Tamsin saw that underneath it actually opened up into the ground underneath it. It didn't go back far, but enough to shield them from the elements.

She crumpled to the ground once they were all inside, not caring if the others saw her trembling. Everyone seemed to be too busy getting air back into their lungs to notice anyway. The pain from Mowlgra's wound throbbed mercilessly and her arm still bled freely from the laceration there. She leaned back against the cave wall gingerly and observed the men that were slowly getting back to their feet. She had lost her water skin, her knife, and her broken sword, but these men didn't seem to be faring much better. They all seemed to be in their forties or fifties; most of them sporting beards that hadn't been cut in a while. Their clothing was similar to what she had seen the sha'diin wear, made up mostly of vests, straps, and shortened trousers, but they were quite worn. Some of them had cloth wrapped around their hands and wrists with leather cuffs. It reminded Tamsin of how she and Haven had looked after the sandstorm; their clothes in sand-caked tatters like they had been in the desert for years instead of hours. Only half of them seemed to carry actual metal weapons, but the others possessed spears and other crude hand-made weapons. One man had a whip looped around his belt.

  She caught the eye of the man who had rescued her; he was watching her too. He started speaking to the others, telling them to gather wood, get a fire going, and delegating other various tasks.

  "I don't think a fire's a good idea," Tamsin said, "unless you want that amon'jii to find us."

  The others looked at her too then and then back to the man that was clearly their leader.

  "The meat was left at the other camp," one of them said. "A fire would do no good."

  The leader nodded. "We'll go salvage what we can in the morning. We'll go hungry tonight. Nothing we're not used to."

  Tamsin did feel responsible for their current situation, but she could do nothing about it now.

  "Settle in," the leader said. "It's going to be a long night." He walked over then and crouched in front of Tamsin, propping his elbows up on his knees. He had a full beard and thick curly hair that was dappled gray. His face was friendly, but his warm brown eyes were pinched at the corners like he was figuring out the best way to approach a feral cat.

  He spoke in a perfect Ma'diin accent, albeit a little gruff. "I don't even know where to start with you, *lu'ashiipena*, so maybe you can tell me which question to ask first." He held a small knife in between his palms, spinning the point into the ground.

Tamsin made no attempt to smile at the title he had given her: little woman. Though she was grateful for their help, she wanted to be left alone to lick her wounds. She was exhausted and still reeling from her encounter with the amon'jii. It was hard enough trying to puzzle out how she was able to speak to the beasts, and now she had to contend with these strangers.

"You saved our lives, so I want to trust you," she said, "but if you don't know who I am, then I'm afraid I can't."

One of the other men was too late subduing a chuckle and the leader looked back at him with a raised eyebrow. The other man's chuckle turned into a cough.

The leader turned back to Tamsin. "Forgive me girl, but as you said it was us who rescued you, I think we deserve an answer for sticking our necks out for you."

"You deserve my gratitude, and you have it," Tamsin replied, shifting in discomfort. She was already making plans in her head to leave as soon as possible though. She had to get back to the Ravine. She would make sure Enrik was cared for, take a couple weapons and then take the first opportunity to leave.

The leader rocked back on his heels until he was sitting completely. "You were fending off an amon'jii in the Ravine, protecting your friend, so I don't know whether you are extremely brave or extremely foolish, but we've got the whole night ahead of us and since your friend has seen better days it looks like you and I get to chat."

Tamsin glanced over towards the back of the cave where two of the men were hovering over Enrik.

One of the others chimed in. He had a long scar that ran across his right eyebrow and down the bridge of his nose. "You don't want to play that game with him, girl. You won't win."

Tamsin glanced at the knife still in his hands and then up to his unwavering gaze. They wanted her imagination to pick up what they were insinuating, but whether it was true or not she couldn't discern. Her mind played back to waking up in the Ma'diin's camp at the Hollow Cliffs. What would've happened if she had trusted them then? If she had stayed and not run off?

"Aren't you worried the amon'jii will come here looking for us?" she asked. "You sure you want to stick around?"

"It's going to rain soon. I'm not worried about the amon'jii," the leader said, though his eyes betrayed him. They were all worried. They would be fools not to be.

As if on cue, rain started spattering the ground outside, lightly at first and then in sheets. Whether Tamsin wanted to be or not, she and Enrik were stuck with them for the time being.

"You have no reason to worry about us, girl. I've never hurt a woman in my life. I don't plan on starting now."

The way he said it, she believed him. And they wouldn't have helped her with Enrik if they were just planning on hurting them.

"Are you hurt badly girl?"

"Not as badly as my friend, but I would like to check on him."

"He's in good hands for the moment," he said. "We've learned a trick or two out here about how to survive. The others can see to him until we're done."

It wasn't a request. She would have to talk until his curiosity was satisfied. She nodded to the man that was tending to Enrik. She had noticed the man walking with a limp before. "And what about your men?"

The man must've overheard her. He looked over his shoulder for a moment. "It's an old wound. Shouldn't have been running on it, but I'll be fine."

"That's Enok," the leader said about the man with the limp. "Treygan (the one who had chuckled earlier), Hronar (the one with the scar)," he continued to name each man and pointed them out. "And my name is Ardak."

These men looked like Ma'diin and spoke like Ma'diin, but there was something different about them. Compared to her life in the Cities, and even Empyria, the marsh lands offered a rugged and tribal way of life, but these men took the concept to another level. Almost as if they had been wandering the Ma'diin wilderness for months if not years.

She decided to test her theory. "Which Kazsera do you answer to?" she asked.

Ardak narrowed his eyes at her. "If I tell you ours, will you tell us yours? Because I'm having trouble seeing how any Kazsera would let her sha'diin go to the Ravine alone."

"That's fair," Tamsin conceded. She took a breath, curious to see how they would react. "I have no Kazsera."

She caught more than a few raised eyebrows and some of the men stopped what they were doing. Ardak, though, surprised her when he let out a laugh.

"We have one thing in common then," he said. "Neither do we."

It was Tamsin's turn to raise her eyebrows. "But you are Ma'diin."

Ardak nodded, looking at the ground for a moment. "And that is where our similarities end. Your friend is certainly not Ma'diin and you may look it, but your accent gives you away. You're not from here either. So how is it that you know so much about the Ma'diin?"

"I'm half Ma'diin," Tamsin said, waiting for the next round of questions that inevitably followed a confession like that.

But it never came. Ardak's eyes widened for a moment, followed by something else, but Tamsin didn't know him well enough yet to discern whether it was disbelief or disgust. Either way, she was glad when Enok called Ardak's name. Ardak looked over, then looked at Tamsin and then nodded towards the back of the cave, that same mysterious look still lingering in his eyes. Tamsin got up and went over to where they had Enrik laying on a blanket. He was covered in sweat, but his breathing was strong and steady. She waited until Enok had left to get fresh water before she spoke.

"How are you doing?"

"Who are these men?" he asked instead of answering her question, his voice hoarse.

She looked back to where Ardak, Enok and Hronar were talking quietly with their heads close together, trying to hide their glances towards them. "I'm not sure yet," she said. "But I don't think they'll hurt us."

"Thank you," he said weakly, "for not leaving me there."

Tamsin turned back to him and swallowed thickly, trying not to think of what it may have cost her. "Don't thank me," she said quietly.

"I tried to get Haven out. I did, but Monstran found us. He killed—he had killed everyone. The other soldiers. But he kept me."

Tamsin was starting to put the pieces together from what he had said earlier and what she had gleaned from the amon'jii. Monstran was cruel. He didn't keep people alive without a purpose. She realized that after she had found Haven in the catacombs of Empyria. She pressed the memory and the emotions that came with it away. "Don't worry about that now. You should get some rest while you can."

Enrik took a few shaky breaths. "I wasn't as strong as Haven. I was so weak. Haven was there for months and it took the Master only a day to break me open and infiltrate every thought, every feeling." He opened his glassy eyes then and looked at her. "If you somehow free him Tamsin, he won't—he's not—." He took a deep breath. "The Master has him. It's not Haven anymore."

The look in Tamsin's eyes mirrored the storm brewing in her thoughts. She wouldn't accept that she was too late. Her mouth felt dry as she asked, "Do you know why this is happening? Why they need Haven?"

"Because he's one of them, one of the night men. They're stronger than others. And Haven has survived where others had died. The Master, he—it sounds crazy, but he's not…alive, yet. He needs someone like Haven, someone strong to come back."

Enok returned then with fresh water and some clean cloth, cutting off Enrik's chance to reply. "He needs to rest," Enok said gently. "Have no worries. I will watch over him tonight."

Despite her burning questions, she agreed, so she left them and found an empty space by the wall away from the others. The rain at the entrance spattered near her feet as she leaned back against the cold rock, but not near enough to get her wet. She rested her head back and closed her eyes, letting the sound of the rain fill her mind.

Several hours later, Tamsin awoke from a dead sleep to the sound of thunder directly above them. Startled, she shot up, ignoring the protest from her side. It took her several moments to remember where she was, and who she was with, but seeing the sleeping forms of the men scattered in the cave brought everything back quite quickly. It was still pouring rain out and a waterfall-like curtain had formed at the mouth of the cave. Lightning crackled overhead in sporadic bursts, turning the curtain of rain into a glowing white sheet. The thunder answered almost simultaneously, making Tamsin question the integrity of the cave they were in. She shook her head at the Ma'diin men's ability to ignore it as they continued to sleep, some only shifting slightly. Then she noticed the cloth wrapped around her arm, only a slight red line staining it. One of the men must have wrapped it while she slept. And she had not noticed a thing.

She got up gingerly and walked over to the back of the cave, stepping around the still forms of the Ma'diin. Enrik was deep in sleep as well, his breaths even and his face relaxed. He seemed alright, which made her hopeful that everything they had done for him would turn out. These Ma'diin men had done more than Tamsin could thank them for, but now she had a decision to make: trust them even further and leave Enrik with them or stay and make sure he was alright and figure out how to get him home. She went back over to her little spot in the cave and sat down on her heels, trying to sort out her thoughts from her fear. If she tried again, would she even make it to Haven, now that the amon'jii knew about her? And if Enrik was right, would Haven even come back with her?

The lightning burst through the sky again, illuminating the sheet of rain at the entrance and—

The blood drained from her face and her spine stiffened like a frozen pine. It was impossible…the amon'jii abhorred water…

The lightning surged through the clouds again and this time the dark shape of an amon'jii beyond the curtain of rain was unmistakable.

Tamsin jumped up, quickly looking around for a weapon. Hronar's spear was the closest thing to her, leaning up against the wall, so she grabbed it and pointed the end at the entrance. She tiptoed forward until she could feel tiny droplets spattering on her skin. Only the lightning revealed the beast beyond the sheet of water, but otherwise she was in total darkness. She thought, just for a moment, that her fear had conjured up the image, that she wasn't completely awake, but then she reached out with her senses and felt the hot heartbeat pulsing only feet away. Her rapid breathing seemed to echo in the dark chamber and despite the strangeness of the amon'jii being out in the rain, she hoped that it was oblivious to their presence there. She could wake up the others, but if any of them made a sound, then they would be found.

"Come back to the tunnelsss and we won't kill thessse men."

Tamsin jumped at the sound, still unaccustomed to hearing the amon'jii's language. But it was unmistakable and so was the fact that the amon'jii knew exactly where they were. *"You want me to come back?"* she replied.

"The Great One will only ask once."

The Great One. He knew she had been there. *"You tried to kill me in there. How can I trust you?"*

"Trussst. There isss no trussst. You will die here or you will die there. Choossse."

Tamsin's heart beat heavy in her chest, overpowering the sound of the rain as it pummeled the ground. This could be it: her final chance to get in the Ravine. As much as her legs trembled at the thought of going back there, she knew she wouldn't choose to stay. No one ever got a free pass with the amon'jii, let alone two. And she wouldn't waste it.

She crouched down and set her spear on the ground. She stood back up slowly as another burst of lightning crackled over the rain, illuminating the ominous silhouette of the amon'jii just outside the cave. She took a step forward, the water splashing on her boots…

A hand shot out of the darkness and grabbed her arm. She whipped her head around and saw Ardak next to her, his eyes wide and dangerous as he put a finger to his lips to keep her quiet. Then Hronar stepped closer, picking up her discarded spear. Ardak looked at him and made a quick little motion with his hand, then let out a high-pitched whistle. Almost immediately the cave was vibrating with movement as the rest of the Ma'diin were snapped out of their sleep and grabbing for their weapons. Ardak let go of Tamsin and he and Hronar jumped through the curtain of water as a more sinister sound rumbled from the amon'jii's throat.

"Wait!" Tamsin shouted as more of them followed out into the rain. But they ignored her so she darted out after them, not even getting the chance to wipe water out of her eyes, before something slammed into her, sending her rolling until she collided into a large boulder. She scrambled to her feet, but another blow landed on the back of her shoulder and sent her staggering. Someone grabbed her arm just before she fell and hauled her back towards the cave, but a vicious snarl interrupted their path. It was hard to see who was who through the dark and rain, but the black mountain in front of them, its fangs dripping with water, was unmistakable. It lunged at them and the man holding Tamsin shoved her away and swung his spear at the beast.

Tamsin managed to stay on her feet and shook water out of her eyes, surveying the scene as best she could. There wasn't just one amon'jii, but two, and as quick as the Ma'diin were, the amon'jii were faster. The Ma'diin tried to surround them, thrusting with their spears and knives, trying to shout coordinating attacks through the rain, but for every spear that got close the amon'jii seemed to swipe two away with their jagged claws.

I have to help, Tamsin thought, but she didn't know what else to do. She was already keeping the amon'jii's deadly fire contained, but it wasn't enough. She had no weapon and hiding was out of the question, but if she didn't do something then the Ma'diin would be dead within minutes.

She ran towards the fighting before her instincts had a chance to balk, shoving past the ring of men around one of the beasts. The amon'jii whipped around, the skin around its nose and fangs twitching with rage. It raised a claw to strike her...

"STOP!" she shouted in the creature's own language.

There was just enough force behind her command to make the amon'jii pause, and even the Ma'diin stopped for a moment, staring at her in confusion.

"Just. Stop," she said. Her limbs trembled uncontrollably from a chilly mix of fear and rain, but she held her ground, holding her hands out to stop each side from doing anything. She knew speaking to the amon'jii would stir up more distrust with the Ma'diin, but she couldn't stop that now. *"I'll go with you,"* she said. *"Just no more killing."*

The amon'jii blew a quick puff of air through its nostrils. It put its claw down and took a step toward her, bringing its face within inches of her hand. For a moment, Tamsin thought it had worked, but then a high-pitched scream ricocheted off the raindrops. They all turned to see the other amon'jii lying on the ground with a spear in its neck.

"No!" Tamsin yelled, but it was too late. Enraged, the amon'jii in front of her barreled into her, knocking her to the ground with one of the huge, swirled horns on its head. Before it could finish her off, the Ma'diin descended upon it, stabbing at it with their spears and knives. The amon'jii shrieked and crashed through them, snarling and snapping. Tamsin turned her head and its gaze fell on her for a brief second and Tamsin could see the betrayal there as clear as if she had been looking into a pair of human eyes. Then it turned and fled into the darkness.

Tamsin rolled gingerly on her side so she wasn't choking on the rain, breathing heavily. The others were breathing heavily as well, but they all helped each other back into the cave. Enok was limping again and Treygan had a nasty looking gash over his right temple, but besides that everyone was still alive and able to make it inside. Once through the curtain of rain, Tamsin sunk to her knees, holding her ribs.

"Two of them," Treygan gasped. "There were two of them together!"

Hronar stumbled over to Tamsin, the look in his eyes murderous. She tried to get up, but he gave her a powerful kick to the torso and she fell back, the taste of blood and dirt filling her mouth. He shoved his foot on her chest and put his full weight on it, effectively sealing her to the ground.

"Hronar...?" she gasped. She lay still, not daring to provoke him any more as she felt the tip of his spear against her throat.

"Hronar!" Ardak bellowed. "What are you doing?!"

"She was speaking with them Ardak! Speaking with the beasts!" Hronar cried.

"Look what you are doing! Put down your spear, Hronar."

"So she can run back to the amon'jii? I don't think so." His spear pushed deeper against her skin.

"We don't know anything yet," Ardak said, inching forward with his hand on his sword. The others watched them nervously, though had yet to move.

"Exactly!" Hronar exclaimed, glancing at Ardak. "We don't know who they are or—"

The momentary lapse was all Tamsin needed. She grabbed his spear and pulled, sending him sprawling. She rolled away as he tried to regain his balance, coming up to one knee. Ardak jumped in between them, forcing them to stay apart.

"I am not with the amon'jii," she hissed through gritted teeth. "I don't know how I can speak to them, but I can." Her vision blurred and she put a hand on the ground to keep from tipping over.

Hronar looked at her suspiciously. "It sounds like *jiin* work to me."

Tamsin glared at him, her blood boiling at the thought of being accused of that again. "I'm not *jiin*. Without me doing that you'd be dead right now."

Hronar's expression was still defiant. He ignored Ardak's extended hand to help him up and walked a few paces away, but didn't make any more advances towards Tamsin. The others stood quietly as the water dripped off them, forming small puddles on the cavern floor.

"Why were you at the Ravine in the first place?" Enok asked, his tone more curious than suspicious.

"I went to rescue someone."

"And the amon'jii got your scent and followed you here," Ardak said, though he didn't make eye contact with her.

"Even so, the amon'jii never come out in the rain. Never," Enok said.

"What did they say?" Ardak asked Tamsin.

"They offered to spare you if I went with them."

At this Ardak turned to look at her, but Tamsin couldn't read his expression in the dark.

"It doesn't make any sense," Enok said. "They've never shown anything above basic instincts before. But language, negotiations, adapting their hunting patterns, tracking a particular person—this changes everything. I mean, we should have been incinerated back there."

Ardak held up his hand towards him impatiently. "Let's focus on one thing at a time."

"No, Enok's right," Treygan, said, dabbing at the gash on his forehead with his sleeve. "If they're coming out in the rain now, it's not safe here anymore. We should leave now."

"I agree," Hronar said. "And leave them here. If the amon'jii are after her, let her deal with them."

Ardak held up a hand in warning. "We're not leaving anyone here."

"Why didn't they use the demon fire on us?" Enok asked, still circling around the newfound knowledge they had just acquired.

"The rain?" Treygan offered, but the others were silent. Apparently they had written it off as luck.

Ardak narrowed his eyes. "You're not a Watcher," he said to Tamsin.

Tamsin shook her head. "No, I'm not."

Enok limped over to them. "That was you?"

"What do you mean?" Hronar asked him.

"She stopped them from burning us," Ardak stated.

Tamsin's head started to spin from the barrage of conversation, so she simply nodded in confirmation of Ardak's assessment.

"The amon'jii in the rain. Girls talking to them," Treygan muttered. "The marsh lands aren't the same as they used to be."

"Who are you?" Hronar asked.

Tamsin wiped her forehead with her sleeve and winced. She hadn't wanted to give away her identity before because she didn't know how trustworthy these men were, but considering they just risked their lives again she probably owed them that much. "Lord Urbane of the Cities is my father and Irin of the Ma'diin was my mother. I am Tamsin, Kaz'ma'sha of the Ma'diin."

Murmurs spread throughout the cave as looks were exchanged. Ardak was the first to step forward. "That is quite the title for someone so small," he said, raising his spear. The others did the same, raising their own weapons.

Tamsin stood up, still clutching her ribs. Hronar's stunt had elevated the pain from a manageable throb to a tight fist clenched around her lungs, but if more was coming then she would defend herself on her feet. "I may be small, but if you attack me again—."

"No, no. You misunderstand girl," Ardak said. "I mean, Tamsinkazsera." He lowered his spear to the ground and flipped his fingers over his hand in the sign of respect. The others followed suit and laid their weapons at her feet.

Now it was her turn to be confused. She tried to shake the water out of her eyes, but a blurriness remained. She staggered sideways and Ardak caught her under the arms and held her up. "Who are you?" she asked them.

Ardak smiled, the whites of his teeth contrasting sharply against his dark beard. "A long time ago we all made a choice to avenge our Kazsera's death and by doing so we became exiles. Our Kazsera was your mother, Tamsin."

Then everything went dark.

Chapter Seven

"You're going to faint right into those books if you do not look up and eat something," Sherene said.

Emilia had not even heard her come in, but she looked up from the desk and saw the day maid holding a tray by the door. "I didn't think that would concern you." She and Sherene had yet to have a pleasant conversation since they arrived. And since learning of Emilia's true parentage, Sherene had decided to keep her distance. She may have been loyal to the Urbanes, but so far that had not included Emilia.

"One bed-ridden woman in this house is quite enough," Sherene said, speaking of Madame Corinthia.

"Fine," Emilia conceded, though she returned her gaze to the open book in front of her. "Toss me a biscuit."

Sherene scoffed. "Toss me a biscuit? This house may be in crisis Miss Emilia, but it is not an excuse to behave like a farmyard pig." She set the tray down loudly on the end table and then began tidying up the room, smoothing the blankets on the bed and picking up discarded clothing strewn about the floor.

Emilia tried to ignore her and instead focus on the book in front of her as she had for the last day and a half since Lord Urbane had been taken. She had thrown herself into her research, looking for something, anything that could help them and Lord Urbane. They had had no word of his whereabouts since Commander Garz had taken him, but were reminded of the incident by the guards that patrolled the grounds outside. And Mr. Brandstone said that he had delivered the evidence to the horse master, Raolo, but he had not returned either.

Sherene stopped by the window and peered outside. "It's a shame they weren't here when that awful Brunos fellow barged in."

Emilia snorted. "A shame? They probably would've let him in the front door."

Sherene rolled her eyes and continued about the room. "At least that man is in a cell somewhere and not roaming about anymore."

Emilia sat up straighter, looking up from her book for a moment, an idea starting to take shape in her mind. "I need to go see him."

"Have you lost all sense?" Sherene asked, stopping once again to stare at Emilia in bewilderment. "I would think that would be the last place you would want to go, if you could indeed leave."

That was the tricky part. With guards patrolling at all hours it was impossible to leave the Urbane manor. But Brunos had been in Empyria. He had to have seen something that would condemn Cornelius Saveen. He was mentioned in the letters that were now hopefully in Lord Findor's hands, but beyond that she didn't know the details. Lord Urbane had hinted at a fourth party in play, someone Brunos and Mr. Monstran worked for, but if Brunos had no direct loyalty to Cornelius, then he could possibly be turned and used as a witness.

"Of course I don't want to go," Emilia said, "but he could help us free Lord Urbane. He's the only other person that could confirm what's in those letters."

"I want Lord Urbane's safe return just as much as you, but that would not only be an impossible task, but a foolish one." She crossed over to the desk where Emilia was. "I don't know what you've been reading, but it's filled your head with ridiculous ideas." She started snatching the books off the desk then.

Emilia lunged for them, ripping them back out of Sherene's hands. "No. NO," she said forcefully, clinging to them like Sherene had tried to set her favorite childhood dolls on fire.

"Young lady," Sherene started, putting her hands on her hips.

But Emilia shook her head. "No," she said again, though this time her voice trembled, surprising Sherene and herself with its vulnerability.

"Miss Emilia?"

"I know you don't like me and you think me selfish and vexing, but I want to help. I've done some terribly stupid things in the past, but I have to try and make up for them. And if I just sit here and do nothing, well, that would be worse than doing the wrong thing." She looked up from under her brow, breathing heavily.

Sherene's countenance softened after a moment. She walked over to the bed and slowly sat down on the edge of it, then motioned for Emilia to join her.

"Yes, I find you selfish sometimes and your lack of self-control vexes me beyond measure, but I do not *not* like you, Miss Emilia," she said as Emilia sat down next to her. "You have stepped into the space that was reserved for someone else. And I'll admit, I did resent you for it, for being here instead of Tamsin, who I have known her whole life. But if I am being honest, it's because I love her and I miss her and not knowing if she's safe scares me to death. And seeing you here, was only a reminder that she is not." Sherene took a deep breath, taking the pause to regain her emotions. Then she took Emilia's hand and squeezed it tight. "I haven't taken the time to get to know you, and that's my fault."

"You sound like Lord Urbane," Emilia said, remembering her talk with Lord Urbane after she had confronted him at the Council building.

"Well, for all of his faults he does have a good heart. His past has not been the straightest, but like you he knows when to change course to rectify any bends in the road."

"Was I a bend in the road?"

Sherene raised her eyebrow. "Do not twist my words. I would say his ignorance of you was the bend. I would also say he wants to change that. But he may never get the chance if we are divided in our own house."

"So you'll help me then?"

Sherene tilted her head. "Yes, as long as it does not put you or anyone in this house in harm's way."

Emilia smiled. "Then I'll leave you out of the dangerous plots and only include you on the proper ones."

Sherene snorted. "Lords help me." Then she stood up and smoothed out her skirt. "Tell me you have a better idea other than visiting that Brunos man."

Emilia stood up as well and crossed back over to the desk. She picked up a book and handed it to Sherene. "I won't go see him if I can find a way to get in."

"Get in? Where?"

"The Council. I need a seat at the table. They might be trying to silence Lord Urbane, but they will not silence me."

"That is a lofty goal," Sherene said, both her eyebrows raised up to her hairline. "Women do not hold seats of power in the Council."

"Not yet."

Hours later, the stack of books they had gone through had risen considerably, but neither one had uncovered anything that could be useful. Pieces of information, tidbits of law that outlined what a lord or lady had rights to during their lifetime of governance only reiterated what Emilia already knew. Women were excluded from all Council sessions and had no authority or input during voting sessions. Even Lavinia, had Lord Urbane really been deceased, only had temporary stewardship over the Urbane seat at the Council. As did her own mother, Lady Mary, over the Regoran seat. If Emilia and Tamsin both died without any sons, then the hereditary membership ended and a new lord would be appointed from the pool of relatives.

But looking for a loophole or a way around the exclusion of her gender was proving to be a challenge.

"Can you read me that passage again?" Emilia asked, putting her fingers to her temples.

Sherene cleared her throat and flipped a couple pages in the book she currently had. *"If a Lord is unfit or unable to perform his duties as set to him by the Council of Lords, then a steward may be assigned in his place if no direct living descendant of age exists to fulfill the role."*

Emilia shook her head. "It wouldn't be enough. It wouldn't even get me in the room. I'd be a placeholder."

"What if we could get Lord Findor to present the letters to the Council, bring you in as a witness?"

"I'm hardly a witness and we don't know if the letters even made it to Findor."

A knock sounded on the door frame then and they both looked up to see Lavinia standing there. Sherene got up immediately and went over to her, asking if she needed anything, but Lavinia waved her away. She was dressed in her evening wear, but she looked weary, as if she had been awake for days.

"Are you not coming to dinner again?" she asked, looking at the piles of books and papers strewn about the room.

"I'll get a tray sent up," Emilia said, glancing over to the one still untouched that Sherene had brought up earlier.

"I think you should join us tonight. I have something important I want to talk to you about."

"But we—."

Sherene interrupted her. "I'll help her get dressed for dinner, my lady."

Lavinia nodded gratefully and disappeared from view, but Emilia waited until the rustle of her skirts could no longer be heard before she turned to Sherene with a betrayed expression.

"A united house, Miss Emilia," Sherene reminded her.

"Whatever she has to say cannot be as important as this," Emilia said, pressing her hands on the book in front of her. But the mention of dinner had awoken her empty stomach and it announced its displeasure with a loud gurgle.

"Maybe, maybe not," Sherene said. "Come. Get changed. Get something to eat and some fresh air and I'll be here when you return."

Emilia finally conceded and went to change, picking out a deep blue evening dress that was relaxed enough around the middle to accommodate her appetite. She went downstairs to the dining room and found Lavinia and Lady Allard already seated and waiting around the decorated table. Lady Allard made some compliments about Emilia's dress and the beautiful flower arrangements adorning the table, but it wasn't until after the second course had been served that Lavinia actually spoke.

"I have something to give you, Emilia," she said, lifting up a piece of parchment that had been sitting next to her napkin on the table. "Eleazar suspected what you were up to, with your books," she explained, "and he wrote this the night he was taken away." She handed it to Emilia with a pinched expression.

Emilia took it and unfolded it. Then she gasped as she read what Lord Urbane had written.

"What does it say?" Lady Allard asked.

"Is this real?" Emilia asked Lavinia. Even though it had Lord Urbane's signature and seal on the bottom, she couldn't quite believe it.

"Yes, it's real," Lavinia replied without a hint of a smile. "From this moment on, you are the heir and Lord to the Urbane family."

Lady Allard's eyes went wide, though her expression wasn't filled with the same dismay as Lavinia's. "Is that possible?"

"Through the Law of Exigency, yes it is possible," Lavinia said, taking a sip of wine.

"Law of Exigency? I've never heard of it," Emilia said.

Lavinia put down her wine glass. "It is an old law, one put down by the founders of the Council during the Golden War. It was meant to protect the new Council, to keep it alive even if the new lords or their sons died on the battlefield. In those times, things had to be decided quickly. They didn't always have time to vote new lords in, so they wrote a law that said any lord could bequeath his title and all its responsibilities and power to someone of his choosing. After the war was ended and peacetime began, the law was phased out in favor of the vote should no hereditary heir exist, but…" Lavinia took another sip of wine, "…the law was never officially abolished."

"But I'm—I'm a woman," Emilia said. "Everything I've read says—."

"Eleazar told me that this law does not discriminate against gender or rank. He could've picked you as easily as he could've picked Mr. Brandstone."

"Then why didn't he pick you? Or Tamsin?"

"Those would be the obvious choices, wouldn't they?" Lavinia's disdain dripped from her lips like her wine had gone sour.

Emilia tried to ignore it, her mind already racing with the bigger implications of this move. Yes, there would probably be no chance at a peaceful relationship with Lavinia anymore, but Lord Urbane had done this for a reason.

"What will happen to you?" Lady Allard asked Lavinia.

Lavinia stared at the wine in her glass, tipping it around in a circle. "My stewardship was never really real, since Eleazar's been alive all this time, but if he ever returns, his lordship will be in name only." She looked at Emilia. "You are the Lady and Lord of this house now." Then she pushed back from the table and walked out of the room.

Emilia and Lady Allard sat in silence for a long moment until finally Lady Allard politely cleared her throat. "Congratulations, Emilia. But I should…"

Emilia nodded, understanding. "Go ahead."

Lady Allard removed her napkin from her lap, setting it on the table. Then, "Don't judge Lavinia too badly. We're all going through our own trials now," she said before excusing herself from the room to go after Lavinia.

Emilia sat at the table a minute longer, staring at the piece of parchment, still not quite believing that Lord Urbane had chosen her and that everything she had been searching for the last few days was right in her hand. Though, she admitted to herself, she had probably been searching for this far longer than she realized. The fate of the entire household was in her hands, not that she had any ill intentions towards them, but more importantly, her own fate was finally freed from the web she had been stuck to her entire life.

But there was someone else who still needed freeing and that would take precedence above everything else.

She shoved back from the table, knocking her chair over as she fled the dining room and back upstairs. She burst through the doors to her room, surprising Sherene who was still pouring through books. Emilia held up the parchment triumphantly. "I have what we need."

Chapter Eight

Georgiana waited until Tomas had made an appearance down in the rebels' new hideout within the caves of the Hollow Cliffs before enacting her plan to see Reynold. She had told Aden that she would talk to Tomas about it, but she had decided the less people that knew about it the better. So when Tomas came down to see off the man that had volunteered to go to the Cities and plead their case, Georgiana slipped quickly and quietly back down the long tunnel that stretched underneath the desert sands and emerged into the depths of the Allard compound.

The hour was late so she had no fear of being noticed when she stepped up into the pantry room of the Allard's kitchen, but she made sure to cover the hatch in the floor with the rug in case anyone came down while she was out. Getting to the wall, however, was trickier. Guards patrolled the compounds and the streets even at night and making it to the wall felt like a risky game of seek and hide. But she finally got to the section she was familiar with, the section where she and Enrik had gone dozens of times before. The part that overlooked the Elglas. But that wasn't why it was important. It was important because this was Reynold's area to patrol. And unless his orders had changed, this was where he would be.

But the longer Georgiana waited, the more she began to worry that his patrol had changed. No one else was here and no one else came. She climbed down the stairs, wondering if maybe she was already too late and that it wasn't his patrol route that had changed, but he had been caught for helping her. He had warned her of the list of names at the Armillary and perhaps he had already been found out for doing so.

Then she had another idea and she scoffed at herself for not thinking of it sooner. Reynold was notorious for his love of ale and tonight wouldn't have been the first night he cast his patrol duties aside for a pint. She rushed off, careful to avoid the guards that hadn't forsaken their posts and made her way to the nearest tavern. There weren't many on this side of the river, under the scrutinizing gaze of the compounds, but she knew of one that the guards sometimes frequented. She knew it was dangerous, but she didn't want to go back without an answer one way or another.

The tavern was lit on the outside by a single hanging lantern that had opaque green panes encased by black metal hinges. She waited until no one was around before she crossed the street. The hazy emerald glow was dim enough to conceal her, but once she opened the door and went inside, there was nowhere to hide. Not even her cloak could completely mask all of her golden hair. But luckily, her appearance did not turn many heads, and the tavern was quite full. The sight of so many men in uniforms made her stomach lurch, but for the most part the guards seemed happily engrossed in their own drinking and boisterous talk.

The rest of the lanterns inside had a mix of green, blue, and yellow panes, giving the establishment a heightened vibrancy that wasn't found anywhere else in the desert. Swaths of glittering fabric, detailed with complex patterns, hung in great drooping curves from the ceiling and between the lanterns. A large fireplace crackled along the far side of the room, sending its warmth across the well-swept floor. Several servants skittered around from table to table, bringing food and mug after mug of ale. Georgiana hadn't been in here in a while, but she didn't remember it being so grand. Even the other taverns couldn't boast such extravagance. One was lucky if they got a table that didn't wobble or a single candle to see the person sitting across from them. She wondered if this was something sanctioned by Cornelius, a way to keep his soldiers loyal and happy.

She threw her gaze around the room as she walked slowly over to an empty table in the corner and sat down. The barkeep came over and poured her a cup and she smiled, but only swirled the liquid around after he left. She scanned the patrons, but she did not recognize Reynold's face among them. She didn't want to ask for him for it would only invite questions, so she resolved to wait. And listen.

But it wasn't long before a group of men burst through the door, laughing and hanging onto each other's shoulders as they stumbled inside. Clearly it was not the first tavern they had visited tonight, but it didn't stop them from hollering for more ale. One voice in particular stood out and Georgiana craned her neck to see around the other customers.

It was Reynold and as he clinked his glass against his comrades' his eyes caught sight of Georgiana. His eyes popped in surprise and he froze for a moment. Then he took a big swig from his glass and his eyes darted around the room before settling on Georgiana again. He mumbled something to his friends and slowly, but directly walked over to the table where she was seated. He grabbed an empty stool on the way and sat down on it at the end of the table instead of sitting across from her. He glanced once over each shoulder and then propped his elbows widely across the table, as if to block her from view.

His face scrunched together tightly for a moment and then he pressed his palms against the table. "What in the seven hells are you doing here, Gia?"

"We need your help, Reynold."

"We?"

"The rebels and I. We need someone—."

He held up his hand quickly to silence her. "Are you kidding me, Gia?" he hissed. "You're still with them?"

"What else would I be doing? After what Cornelius did to my father. After what he did to Lord Regoran. How could I do anything else?"

Reynold downed the rest of his glass. "I know what he did, Gia. But I thought you'd be smarter than that." He rapped his knuckles on the table. "You should get out of here before someone recognizes you."

"I came to ask for your help and I'm not leaving until I get it."

Reynold grunted in disapproval and reached for Georgiana's still full cup, but she clasped down on his wrist before he could drink.

"Reynold. We need you. If we are to have any chance of taking control of the Armillary we need you to help us."

"The Armillary? Lords, Gia. I stuck my neck out for you once and now you want to drag me down with you? I shouldn't even be talking to you."

"But you are," she whispered intensely. "And you did before too. You saved a lot of people, Reynold, because you helped me."

He rubbed the back of his neck. His eyes were glassy, but hadn't lost their focus yet, so Georgiana knew he wasn't completely unable to make an informed decision.

She decided to press him further. "You know what's happening is wrong. That's why you helped me before. That's why you'll help me again."

"Dammit, Gia!" He slammed his fist against the table, causing some of the other patrons to glance over. "Do you know how dangerous this is? Do you want to end up like your father, tossed in a ditch somewhere out in the Sindune?"

Georgiana was worried that some of the others might come over soon, but she froze at the mention of her father. "Why would you say that?" she asked, each word feeling heavy in her mouth. "My father was sentenced to the mines back in the Cities. He told me."

Reynold made an irritated growling sound in the back of his throat. "He lied to you, Gia. He's dead."

Georgiana felt paralyzed. She wanted to yell at Reynold, to tell him he was the one lying, that her father wasn't dead. But she couldn't move or speak and that incapability came from the same pit that told her a drunken man was an honest one. As ugly as it was, alcohol loosened the truth from one's lips, not falsehoods. All this time she had believed her father had been sent to one of the prisoner camps to work in the mines and all this time he had been dead. There was no hope of one day freeing him. No hope of being reunited. She was truly alone.

"Ask Lord Allard, if you don't believe me," Reynold continued, finally snatching Georgiana's cup and taking a swig. Then he seemed to notice Georgiana's detached stare and he sighed. "I'm sorry, Gia. I can't help you."

Georgiana blinked a few times, shaking off the frost, but unable to rid herself completely of the numbness. "You've done quite enough," she whispered and then slid out from her seat. She walked over to the door in a cold haze, everything and everyone beyond her focus. She wasn't filled with the hot rage that had consumed her after her father's imprisonment. All that anger had suddenly cooled and hardened, as if it had been a piece of molten metal plunged into water. No force of water or fire could change her now. She was crystallized as she was. A rebel. An orphan. Daughter to no one but iron determination.

A hand on her arm stopped her before she got to the door and she turned back to see Reynold. His eyes were apologetic and his mouth opened and closed a few times, but nothing came out.

Georgiana just shook her head. "Let me go."

The door opened behind her and Reynold's eyes glanced up. They went wide for a moment and then he pulled her closer, putting his arm around her shoulders. "Shh!" he hissed at her before she could say anything and started walking her back to the table.

Georgiana looked back towards the door and saw another group of guards making their way in, only this time they were accompanied by Cornelius Saveen.

The air in the tavern stilled as one by one the soldiers present recognized him and even the civilians and servants stopped their drinking to take notice. Cornelius glanced around the room, soaking up the nervous silence for just a moment before putting his hands up like he was sorry for disturbing them. But the truth was he very much wanted to. Maybe when he was just a Captain his presence here wouldn't have caused such a disruption, but now that he was a Lord, *the* ruling Lord of the city, it was like seeing the sun in the middle of the night.

"Please, don't stop on my account," he said, "but…while I have your attention anyway, I suppose I can tell you now." A smile slipped over his lips as he took a few more steps into the room. He knew this tavern was popular amongst the men, not only for its high-end atmosphere, but for its high-end ale. And it was the only one that he allowed to carry Arak. Therefore he knew it would be crowded and the perfect place to make his announcement. "We must stay vigilant in protecting our walls from enemies outside and within. But, in one week's time, the gates of Empyria will be re-opened again. However," he added, as the excited murmurs quieted down once more, "they will only be open for one day as we restock our supplies of food, weapons, and of course…ale!"

Boisterous cheers erupted around the room and cups were lifted up in triumph as if they had just won a great battle. The men that had come with him joined the crowd, except for Captain Pak, who remained at his side.

"It was a clever move, my lord," Pak commented beneath the cacophony of renewed drinking.

"Of course it was." Cornelius had designs to reopen the gates, but not in a week. He would tell his men later that the shipments had been delayed, but not until after his trap had been sprung. If there were any rebels or sympathizers here tonight, word would surely spread of the incoming supply. And it would be too big of an opportunity for the rebels to ignore.

A woman bumped into his shoulder on the way towards the door and another man quickly grabbed her and pulled her away, apologizing for her drunkenness.

"Reynold, isn't it?" Pak asked.

"Yes sir," Reynold said, looking a bit flushed himself. "Have a good night sir, my lord." Then he took the girl's shoulders and directed her out the door.

"One of your men?" Cornelius asked and Pak nodded.

Soldiers talked. Servants talked. It was only a matter of time now.

The bait was laid and in a week they would know if the fish had bit.

He is not ready…
He is, Master. He is yours.
He is in torment…he hears whispers…
He has relinquished his past. He has regained his strength so once you join him you too will be strong. He awaits your arrival as a faithful and eager servant. And then you will wipe out the faithless and their unpardonable sins.
Hmm…

And then your power and reach will know no limits. You will join the world once more as the rightful god-king, and you will build an empire so great that none could rise against you ever again. You will bury any resistance like a tidal wave—

SILENCE! *The girl...she invades his mind...she is watching...she is WATCHING!*

Tamsin's eyes shot open and she gasped for air as the feeling of a crushing darkness released itself. She rolled onto her side, holding herself steady by pressing her hand into the ground, though she felt anything but steady as her whole body continued to heave.

Blurred footsteps hurriedly approached her and helped her sit up. A water skin was pressed to her lips and her body's thirst quickly blunted the edge of the shock she felt. She took a long, deep drink and her vision began to clear as the water worked its natural magic, bringing her senses back to the waking world. Several men surrounded her and she pushed the water skin away, looking at each of them not with embarrassment, but like they were her anchors, each one rooting her to this place.

"Are you alright, girl?" Ardak asked, gently putting his giant hand on her shoulder.

Her eyes darted back and forth, though she saw nothing except the memory of the darkness closing in. She had heard his voice, Monstran's voice, but it was the other voice that sent chills down her spine. And that voice had known she was there, listening. It had turned on her, suddenly and it filled her with such a terror that she could not quite believe how she was still alive. "I—I have dreams," Tamsin said, not wanting to elaborate further.

Ardak and Enok exchanged a look.

"I'm sorry," Tamsin said, noting the look. "It is not your burden to carry."

"It is no burden to help you carry whatever it is that torments you," Enok said.

Tamsin looked at them again as nods of agreement echoed Enok's statement. "Why?" she asked. These were the same men that had rescued Enrik and herself, but they looked different now, aged by their connected past, but alight with that same knowledge. These were the Exiles. These were the ones who had left their homeland behind to follow her mother, Irin, to Empyria. The ones who had been banished to the desert waste for massacring the men who had gone on the initial expedition.

"Don't answer that or she might pass out again," Hronar said, who was sitting against a rock, fiddling with a long piece of grass several yards away.

"Ignore him," Ardak said. "He's feeling guilty for the way he treated you before."

Hronar grunted and tossed the grass aside before getting up and walking away.

Tamsin followed him with her eyes for a moment and then noticed their surroundings. They weren't in the cave anymore. Patches of dirt and long grass pocketed the area and the sun shone on large, wiry bunches of dried brambles that made her feel like she was in a giant bird nest. "Where are we?" she asked.

"Near the smoky lake," Ardak said, as if that explained everything.

"You woke up just in time," Treygan said, bringing over a bowl of soup from the small cooking fire.

The aches in the rest of her body were slowly starting to make themselves known, her bruised ribs not the least of them. She felt nauseous and waved away the bowl, but Ardak took the bowl anyways.

"It has herbs in it that will help with the pain," he said, holding it out to her.

She grimaced, but she knew he was right. She took the bowl, but then had another thought. "My friend, Enrik, where is he?" She had not seen him among the men.

Ardak held up a pacifying hand before she could question him further. "He is alright. Jorviis took him down to the lake to better clean his wounds."

The others got their own bowls, which resembled small cups rather than actual bowls, and settled in around the fire. Ardak, however, stayed with Tamsin.

A few minutes passed with only the sound of quiet eating filling the air, though Tamsin's stomach still hadn't steadied itself yet so she held her bowl in silence until she had sorted through her thoughts. "You should have let me go alone Ardak," she then said softly.

Ardak raised an eyebrow, but didn't seem confused by her statement. "We couldn't. Enok suspected who you were. He's always got his ear to the ground. It's why we were in this region in the first place."

"You don't owe me anything. In fact, you saved my life more than once now. It's I who owe you."

"I don't think you truly fathom the loyalty these men harbor. As do I."

You were loyal to my mother and you were exiled for it, Tamsin couldn't help but think. "You still should have let me go," she said.

There was a long silence, long enough that Tamsin thought their conversation was finished, but then Ardak asked, "Why do you want to go back into that hellish place so badly? I hope it wasn't just to chat with those beasts, something I suspect you want to talk about as little as I."

Tamsin *hmphed* in agreement.

"You rescued your friend already, so what else is there?"

Tamsin swallowed the painful lump in her throat as her dream trickled back into her thoughts. "I didn't rescue everyone."

Ardak sighed through his pursed lips. "It would be foolish to go back there, girl."

Tamsin put the bowl down. "The man I love is there. He was taken prisoner and I'm going to get him back."

"Do you realize, now that we know who you are, we can't let you just walk back into danger? You are too important."

"And *he* is important to *me*." It was Tamsin's turn to sigh, feeling the familiar frustration of the cage her heritage brought beginning to build. But then she had an idea. "As Tamsin Irinbaat and Kaz'ma'sha of the Ma'diin, I release you from your oaths and sentence of exile. You are free to go back to your homes."

She expected some kind of cheer or clapping or exultation of some kind, but the Exiles continued to sit motionless, staring blankly at her. Finally, Ardak reached up and touched her arm. "Girl, oaths are easily broken by words, but not so when they are carved into souls."

Tamsin furrowed her brow. It wasn't these men's fault. These men had saved her and before her they had sacrificed their whole lives for her mother with a loyalty as fierce as if for one's own family. As much as Tamsin had been integrated into Ma'diin society, she still struggled with that sense of unwavering devotion. She didn't trust it, she realized. The Exiles had lost their homes, their families, everything they had known. Did they harbor no bitterness? No resentment? Was she still an outsider looking in, unable to grasp the idea of this unbreakable bond Irin had inspired? But then she realized they were saying the same thing. She loved Haven. They loved Irin. And this love extended to her. Despite any pain or suffering the love caused, it remained.

Enok stood up, leaning on his staff. "Your mother's death released us from our vow to her, but our loyalty does not release us from our vow to avenge her."

"But did you not take your vengeance all those years ago when you killed the Empyrians?" Tamsin asked, amazed that these men could hold guilt and grudges for nearly two decades.

Treygan thumped his fist into the dirt. "Those men attacked us first."

"They boasted about their alliance with us," Hronar said gruffly, walking back into camp without looking at Tamsin. "But they had no intentions of keeping it. They made us believe we were welcome. That we could lay down our weapons. That our Kazsera didn't need protection." He looked around the camp at the others, but no one, not even Ardak, met his eye. As if they had all heard him tell this story before, and they all still carried the guilt of letting their guard down. "We got complacent. We got soft. We trusted the northerners with *our* Kazsera. And our weakness gave them the opportunity they were waiting for."

"They blamed us and we blamed them," Enok explained. "But we still don't know for sure what happened."

"Our failure to protect her will not happen again," Hronar's voice rumbled like trees bending to a strong wind.

"So our vengeance is not to kill more men in her name," Ardak said. "It is to help and protect you."

Tamsin was stunned and overwhelmed by their passionate devotion and need to remedy their shame. Her voice was strained when she spoke again, feeling the weight of their sentiment. "Do you not know how she died then?" she asked, barely able to get her voice above a whisper.

Their confused stares were laced with hesitation and Tamsin did not relish what she was about to tell them. For eighteen years these poor men had thought it their fault. They felt responsible for letting Irin out of their sight. But it wasn't. She knew the details; she had read the letter from Lord Saveen to her father a hundred times. She had to take a few breaths before she could explain how her mother had really died. And who was really at fault.

When she had finished, she sat back and hugged her knees to her chest, feeling as if she had just stabbed each of them in the heart. The looks on their faces ranged from horror, to shock, to rage, and to numbness. But the silence was the worst.

Ardak put a consoling hand on her shoulder, but even he could not find any words to say. Where there should have been relief of guilt and a release from their burden, there was only a heavy emptiness.

Finally, Tamsin looked up. "I am sorry my family has caused you all so much pain." She could feel the tears about to spill over so she stood up swiftly and started walking away. She didn't know where she would go, but she could not bear the sight of their wasted years etched into their faces.

She did not get far however, for suddenly a hand gripped her arm and forced her to turn around. Hronar's red, grizzled face stared back at her.

"You test us so soon, Kazsera?"

Her confused look prompted him further. "I said we would not fail to protect you like we did your mother."

"But did you not hear me? I—."

"We heard you, girl," Ardak said, stepping up next to Hronar. "You have given us our honor back by telling us the truth. We will not betray that gift by turning our backs on you."

"Then I will give you one last choice. I meant what I said about releasing you from your exile. Will you return to your homes? Or will you come with me to the Ravine?"

Hronar crossed his arms over his puffed-up chest and turned to face the others. In a loud voice he said, "Is anyone else tired of sand in their shoes?"

An amused murmur of agreement went through the camp.

"Then sharpen your spears, boys. We're going hunting."

There was something that lightened in the air after that, almost as if their lungs had been filled with dust from the past and now it had suddenly cleared and they could all breathe again. At least for the Exiles. They talked into the morning, discussing the near future while they sharpened their weapons and prepared to go back to the Ravine. The energy the Exiles displayed cheered her some; she felt a camaraderie with them. She was Kazsera to them, but they treated her like one of their own. And their lightheartedness made her feel good about their newfound purpose. Roaming the desert waste and living just to survive was a wearisome existence, but now they had a path. They had something to look forward to. Even if that something was as dangerous as going into the Ravine.

Tamsin just hoped it would not be to their deaths.

She noticed that all the Exiles were looking at her in silence. She didn't know how long she had been wrapped up in her thoughts, but she brushed them away now. Some of them seemed amused by her absentmindedness, though Ardak's look betrayed that he knew her mind was anything but absent. She tried to go back to sharpening the knife Enok had given her, but she could still feel Ardak's gaze upon her. He had been silent all morning. She knew he had his reservations about going back to the Ravine; she did as well. It made her sick to think of putting anyone else in danger, especially in that place. And she was sure Ardak didn't want to see any of his men hurt either.

Enok came over to check on the wound on her arm then, gently reminding her that she should not move it too much, but before he could chastise her further Ardak called him over and said something too quiet for Tamsin to hear.

"It will only add an hour, maybe two," Enok whispered back to Ardak. "We'll still be able to make it to the channel before nightfall."

Ardak nodded and patted Enok on the shoulder appreciatively before he went over and continued packing up their supplies.

Tamsin sidled over to Enok. "I thought we were going straight to the Ravine," she said.

Enok took a breath, and then realizing Tamsin had overheard, let it out with a sigh. "It is not much out of our way."

"What isn't?"

"It is a place that marks the boundary between the Ma'diin and the amon'jii. Some people call it the shaman stones."

Tamsin felt her stomach clench at the name and she took a sharp breath. "Why would we go there?" she asked, unable to keep the alarm out of her voice.

Enok squinted his eyes slightly. "You've heard of it?"

She nodded. "I have." The Havakkii had almost brought her there to be 'cleansed,' but had chosen the mangroves instead. "Why are we going there?" she repeated more firmly.

"It is…important to Ardak," Enok said. "And it will be safer there for your friend than it will be with us. That is all I can tell you."

"Can? Or will?" Tamsin challenged.

Enok paused to study her a moment. His eyes remained focused on her as if he were waiting for her to reveal something and not the other way around.

Tamsin turned away from his scrutinizing gaze, not wanting her apprehension to reveal itself any further. She trusted them, and her gut told her she could, as they had already risked their lives for her. She decided then that she would go with them, but she would be on her guard. She would be ready for whatever waited for them there.

The afternoon sun was waning quickly when they reached a small glade of dried-up bushes, delicately preserved by the surrounding boulders and rock outcroppings that formed a protective barrier against the wind. There was a narrow path that led down into it, flanked on either side by gray walls of stone. They had to walk single file to get down into it, for it seemed more like a pit to Tamsin than a glade, but as Enok explained, it made for a safe refuge from the amon'jii for they could not traverse the narrow way. But once there, they were afforded a little more room and could easily stretch out without being too close to each other.

Tamsin noticed a small ring of stones near the center of the glade, built up only slightly wider than the length of her arm.

"This is it?" Tamsin asked, moving cautiously closer to the ring. "These are the shaman stones?"

A few chuckles bubbled through the group and some amused looks were exchanged until Ardak silenced them with a look.

Enok leaned a little closer to Tamsin. "It is only a fire pit," he said. "The real shaman stones are down just a bit further."

Tamsin flushed with embarrassment and then a thought popped into her head. "You have been here before."

Enok nodded. "Every year we pass through here. It's not Ma'diin land yet, but we only make camp for a day or two before moving on."

"I won't be long," Ardak said. "We'll be moving again within the hour." He moved past them as the others settled in for a break. He had a cold, determined look on his face, as if he was about to do something equally unpleasant as it was necessary.

"Wait," Tamsin said, "I want to come with you."

Ardak turned back to her a moment. "This doesn't involve you, girl," he said in his usual gruff voice, but there was an added edge to it whether he meant it or not.

"Tamsin," Enok warned.

"No. I'm coming. The Havakkii were going to take me here, but chose the mangroves instead. I want to see them."

Ardak's lips twitched at the mention of the Havakkii. The general rustling of the others quieted and Tamsin could feel their eyes on her. Nobody was chuckling at her expense now.

"The Havakkii?" Hronar asked. "Why on Mahiri's earth would the Havakkii have taken you there? They haven't taken anyone to the mangroves in over fifty years!"

"It seems things have changed since we left," Enok said.

"How did you escape?" another asked.

"Enough," Ardak said, then after a moment. "You can come." Then he turned away and headed back through the narrow pathway.

Tamsin quickly followed him before he could change his mind.

"You owe us a story!" Hronar called after her.

Tamsin smiled a little then went back up the path and around and down past the boulders that made up the glade's perimeter. There were more dead thickets once the ground leveled off and they followed a winding path through them, for they were too thick and tall on this side to be brushed aside to make a straight path.

Once they were far enough away, Tamsin asked, "Why did you change your mind? Why did you let me come?"

Ardak, who had remained silent the entire way, said, "The Havakkii use the stones to scare people. You want to face that fear. It is not my place to stop you from doing so."

"Is that why you come here?" Tamsin asked. "To face your fear?"

Ardak paused for a moment to look back at her. "In a way."

"Should I be afraid?" Tamsin asked.

"If the Havakkii had taken you, then yes. The stones are at the edge of Ma'diin territory. The amon'jii sometimes wander down from the Ravine this way and find a way through. The Havakkii would have left you here for a night to the mercy of any amon'jii that would've come. But with me, girl, you are safe." Ardak then continued through the thicket, pushing branches out of his way as he went.

Tamsin shook her head and pressed her lips together slightly, her thoughts tied up in the past. She remembered the pleasure the Havakkii seemed to take from such cruelty. But not anymore. Never again would they be able to do such a thing. Oman had seen to that.

She suddenly realized that Ardak had disappeared. She froze, listening for the creaking of branches, but she heard only silence.

"Ardak?" she called out. She kept going straight, pushing the thorny branches out of her way with her forearms. Only a few footsteps further then she stumbled out into a clearing as the branches snapped back to their original place behind her.

She looked around, getting her first look at the shaman stones. It was as if she had crossed over into a time that had frozen in one moment. There was only one other place she had seen that looked like this: the graveyards of Ireczburg. Low, near the base of the mountain that towered over the northern city, there had been a snowy field of rectangular stones and etched into them were the names of the warriors that had fought in the Golden War. And guarding these stones were a dozen or so gray statues resembling these warriors. Some had spears or spiked helms carved above their heads and others had swords and shields held up with pride. All looked regal. Honorable. Proud to have died and fought for their city. Peaceful even, as the snow fell quietly around them.

But the statues that Tamsin saw before her now were anything but peaceful. Scattered around the clearing were dozens of statues of men. Of Ma'diin men. Only a few were standing, some were lying down, and others were kneeling in the dirt. But each was different, as if the sculptor had wanted to depict a scene of some kind, though Tamsin couldn't figure out what. She took a few steps closer to one that was lying down on its back. His hand was clenched over his chest, as if it had been holding something, but nothing was carved there. The statue was light gray, though darker than the stones that made up the nearby glade where the Exiles waited, but green moss had begun to creep over the cracks that spread over the surface like a spiderweb. The statue's face was worn, but its expression was startlingly exquisite. It was not of calm, but of pain. And its eyes were a lighter shade of gray, nearly white, as if they had been painted to distinguish them.

Tamsin moved away from the statue, wondering why the carver had portrayed the statue this way. She looked at another, who knelt on the ground with one hand raised towards the sky. A similar anguished expression had been carved into this one's face and as Tamsin weaved her way through the statues she realized that they had all been made this way. She cringed at the ones with the more contorted postures, but she couldn't look away. It was an endless garden of frozen fear, as if each of these men they were meant to portray had suffered some terrible fate.

Something touched her shoulder and she gasped, spinning around quickly.

It was Ardak.

Tamsin let go of her breath shakily, embarrassed that he had startled her so easily.

But his eyes told her he understood. "This place…it gets under your skin a bit," he said.

"I understand why the Havakkii would bring people here," she said. "It's unnerving. Are they the ones that carved them?"

Ardak's eyes narrowed under his bushy brows. "The Havakkii? No."

"Then who? And why? I didn't think the Ma'diin were skilled at stonework."

"We can go back now," Ardak said, ignoring her questions.

But Tamsin's questions burned more fiercely. Perhaps it was the painful energy filling this place or perhaps her tolerance for being kept in the dark about things had been shaved thin. "If you want to keep why you came here a secret, then fine. But you chose me as your Kazsera. You did not have to do that. I know you've only had yourselves to answer to for a long time and I won't force you to keep any promises to me, but if you still wish to follow me then I only ask that you are honest with me. Do not keep me in the dark like so many others have tried to do. Don't hide things to protect me."

"Protect you?" Ardak's expression was pained, the lines around his face deepening. "I do not tell you things to protect *myself*. If I tell you the truth about the stones, then you'll know why I come here. For I have known another shame, other than failing your mother."

Tamsin's intolerance ebbed a little at seeing the usually stoic oak of a man rattled by his own guilt. "If you are worried that I will think less of you for whatever it is you think you have done wrong, I assure you it won't. You saved my life. I will not judge you for what happened in the past. I've had my own share of failures as well."

Ardak sighed deeply. "You are right. You deserve to know the truth." He sighed again and looked around at the statues. "Do you know what 'shaman' means?"

Tamsin blinked a few times, scrunching her eyebrows together. "In the northern tongue there is a similar word. It means someone who has special abilities to commune with the gods. But that was all before the war. Before religion was banned. Does it not mean the same here?"

"No," Ardak said. "Even in the Ma'diin tongue it is hard to define exactly. Shaman is shortened from sha'ma'niihadharakru. Its closest translation is 'the frozen death of the seeing man.' But it is more complex than that. The emphasis pairs 'death' with 'frozen,' not with 'man.'"

"Implying that death is the thing that is frozen," Tamsin said.

"I fear that is the best I can explain it."

Tamsin thought about it for a moment. "So these sculptures are meant to capture the moment of death, to immortalize it to instill fear?" she asked, looking at the anguished expression carved into the one standing next to them.

But Ardak's expression was even more pained than before, as if she had missed the point entirely.

"Tamsin, these stones, these *sculptures*, as you call them, were not made."

"What do you mean?" she asked warily, his tense expression making her uneasy.

"The stones are—were—Watchers."

Chapter Nine

"I don't understand," Tamsin said, but even as she did she took an involuntary step back away from Ardak, away from what his words implied. That the shaman stones used to be real people. That they used to be...alive. "How is that possible?" If it were true, and Ardak's expression was far too stricken for it not to be, then it meant that each of these statues, these men, had been turned to stone. And from the expressions frozen on their faces it had happened at the moment of their death.

"This is the curse of the Watchers," Ardak said. "This is what happens when—."

"When they're exposed to the light," Tamsin finished breathlessly. She turned around, looking at the stone figures encircling them, feeling as if they were spinning around her. Watchers. They had all been Watchers. Just like Haven.

She put her hands up to cover her nose and mouth. There were so many of them. She could almost hear their horrified cries, their tormented wails calling out to the gods for mercy as their limbs cracked and lurched to a final, frozen state of immobility. Gasps for air filled her imagination, echoing around her skull in a sickening tide of desperate breaths.

Then she realized that they were her own and her knees buckled, crumpling beneath her like ashes. She caught herself on a rock, breathing heavily.

Ardak was beside her in a moment, asking if she was alright.

"This place," she breathed, once she had enough air to fill her lungs. "I don't know why it's affecting me this way."

"Tamsin, you're bleeding," Ardak said, his forehead scrunching together in concern.

Tamsin touched her hand to her nose, seeing the red stain on her fingers as she pulled it away. And then, beyond her hand, her eyes focused on the rock she had caught herself on. But it wasn't a rock. It was one of the stone Watchers, her blood smeared over his chest.

She pulled her other hand away abruptly, feeling like an intruder. Then, slowly, she replaced her hand to touch the cold stone as a different feeling came over her, something closer to pity or responsibility. She leaned closer. "I'm sorry this happened to you," she whispered. She looked closely at the stone Watcher's face, thinking how unfair it was that his sacrifice was captured in his worst possible moment. That his lifetime of defending and protecting his people had ended like this. Cold and alone.

Heat radiated through her palm, her power building through her emotions, and she thought if she could do anything she would at least make it not so cold so she released the energy into the stone until it felt warm underneath her fingers.

"Come, Tamsin, I should get you out of here," Ardak said.

Tamsin nodded and stood up, but before she went to follow Ardak she paused. "Ardak," she called to him softly. "Did you know one of these men?" If that were true, it would start to make sense why he would come here every year. It was like visiting a grave.

Ardak stopped. He opened his mouth to speak, but then they heard a sudden, violent crash at the edge of the clearing.

"Ardak! Ardak!" a voice bellowed.

Tamsin and Ardak hurried through the broken web of statues towards the voice and saw Hronar standing at the edge of the thicket with a heap of scattered branches all around him.

"What is it?" Ardak asked when they reached him.

"We've been ambushed," Hronar said, breathing heavy from running.

"The amon'jii?"

Hronar shook his head. Other than a few twigs sticking to his clothing and hair he seemed unharmed. "The Ma'diin."

"Where are they now?" Tamsin asked.

"In the gorge," Hronar said.

"We have to hurry," Tamsin said, "before something happens."

Hronar put his hands on his hips and bent over slightly, still breathing heavily. "You know, I've done more running in the last week than I have in the last ten years."

Ardak rolled his eyes. "Come on."

The three of them rushed back through the thicket and up the rocky path back to the gorge where the Exiles had made their temporary camp. Tamsin could hear them before she saw them and they stopped on the far side of a boulder, just out of sight. There were a group of about ten Ma'diin standing armed with spears and swords at the mouth of the secret glade as the Exiles sidled out of the narrow pathway into the clearing. One of the Ma'diin was shouting and the Exiles threw down their weapons in a pile as they came out. As far as she could tell no one had been hurt, but from the aggressive energy the newcomers were displaying Tamsin didn't think it was far off. She had to do something.

"They're probably here looking for me," she whispered.

"And if they're not?" Ardak whispered back.

"Look," Hronar said.

They did and saw Enok limping out of the pathway. Walking right behind him though was another figure, cloaked all in black and even through the dark layers of clothing it was plain that he was holding himself back, as the tip of his sword was never further than an inch from Enok's neck.

"You didn't say there was a Watcher with them!" Ardak hissed.

"I didn't know!" Hronar hissed back.

Before either of them could say anything else or try to stop her, Tamsin jumped out from behind the boulder and started towards the group.

"Stop!" she shouted. "Everyone, stop!"

The heads of the newcomers and the Exiles turned and some weapons were redirected towards the sound of her voice.

"Who says so?" the one closest to her blurted out and started advancing towards her, his spear raised.

The Watcher moved in quickly and grabbed the man's spear, hurling it aside. "Your Kaz'ma'sha," he growled, and the man shrank back from the venom in the Watcher's voice.

Tamsin stopped. She hadn't expected to be facing him so soon, though she should have known he would come after her. And from the sound of his voice, she assumed Kellan would have some choice words for her.

Kellan didn't waste a beat and in three long strides was directly in front of her. She raised her chin to meet his gaze, but his n'qab was up and she wasn't as good at reading his facial cues yet so she just stared into the darkness of his hood and waited for him to speak first.

It did not take long as Kellan was not known for his patience. "We've been searching everywhere for you," he said. Then he reached his hand up as if to touch her face and Tamsin instinctively flinched back. He froze and then slowly moved his hand and unhooked his n'qab, revealing his bright mahogany eyes. They locked onto hers for a moment and then wandered over her body, stopping at her hands. "You're hurt," he said.

Tamsin looked down and saw blood smeared across the back of her hand. She had almost forgotten what had just happened at the shaman stones. "No, I'm fine," she said. "It's not—."

"Say the word and these men will face the end of our swords right now," Kellan said, his other hand tightening around his sword handle.

"You will not touch them!" a gruff voice bellowed from behind her.

Tamsin turned and saw Ardak and Hronar slowly making their way towards them, their swords raised and pointed forward.

Kellan's mirrored theirs in an instant. "Take one more step and you'll wish you hadn't," he warned.

"We're not afraid of you, Watcher," Ardak said.

"Enough!" Tamsin barked, shoving Kellan's sword away from her. "Put your weapons down," she said loudly so everyone could hear her. "We're all on the same side. Kellan, these men rescued me."

"Rescued you?" Kellan's brown eyes were still fiery.

"It's a long story. I'll tell you everything later."

Kellan slowly put his sword away, but he still watched Ardak and Hronar with distrust. "Who are they?"

"Ardak, Hronar, and the others were once part of my mother's tribe, long ago. They've sworn to help me," she said, hoping to ease some of the tension.

But if anything, Kellan's eyes grew more intense. "Part of your mother's tribe? They are the ones who were exiled?"

"You know about that?"

Kellan stepped slowly around Tamsin towards Ardak. "They shouldn't be here," he said.

"I've released them from their exile," Tamsin said.

"Still, they should go back to whatever sand dune they crawled out from," he retorted.

"We've made a new oath," Ardak said. "To protect Tamsin."

"You left before. Who's to say you won't again?"

"Kellan."

Kellan stopped at his name, heeding the warning in Tamsin's tone.

"You shouldn't speak of things you know nothing of, boy," Ardak's own tone rising. "We never abandoned our Kazsera."

"I wasn't speaking about her," Kellan hissed. Then he turned back to Tamsin, sheathing his sword. "We should leave this place," he told her. "Get as much distance between us and the Ravine as we can before nightfall."

"We aren't going back," Tamsin said. Kellan's mahogany eyes sparked like embers being prodded in a fire, but she continued. "I won't go back without him."

Kellan's frustration was teetering on the brink of control and he lowered his voice. "I will use force if I have to."

Tamsin curled her hands into fists, but refrained from hitting him. She would not be threatened into changing her plans. Instead, she withdrew her broken blade from its holder. "So will I," she said.

Kellan stared at her for a few moments without so much as a twitch, displaying an unusual amount of discipline. Then he withdrew his own sword again. "A duel. You win, we go to the Ravine. I win, we go back to the Ma'diin. Agreed?"

Tamsin could feel the tension rise around them as the sha'diin and the Exiles looked between the two, but Tamsin was confident and determined in her decision.

"Agreed."

The others gave them a wide berth as Tamsin and Kellan circled each other. There was no ring to step out of like at the Kapu'era, nor were they using *tiika* sticks. Their steps were careful and their eyes never wavered from each other. Each was taking this as seriously as if it were a real life or death duel, for each believed the other would not concede lightly.

Tamsin's patience ran out first and she was the first to strike, ignoring the echo of Haven's training about letting one's opponent reveal their weakness first. But she felt the whips of time moving her forward, guiding her broken sword towards her goal. She didn't want to hurt Kellan, but she had bested him in training before and she knew she could do it again. This time was different though. It felt different. Kellan wasn't here to help her get better; he was an obstacle.

The fire in Kellan's eyes hadn't dimmed, but it had refined itself until all of his emotions were no longer controlling his actions, but bolstering them. As he parried Tamsin's blows, she could see the feral cat that he often portrayed disappear and transform into a lethally focused hunter. It seemed easy for him and she realized she had made a mistake when he finally went on the offensive. He had been silently studying her; he already knew she was hurt, but now he knew where. How she moved, what parts she favored; it all told him how to win.

Her lapse in judgement boosted her anger and though it helped her repel his first few advances, it wasn't enough and she quickly found herself outmatched as each block became harder to hold. His attacks became faster and she knew if she didn't do something soon, then she wouldn't be able to keep up.

Kellan struck again and this time their blades locked, but only for a moment and then Kellan released one hand from the handle and grabbed Tamsin's arm.

Tamsin cried out as his fist tightened over the wound the amon'jii had made and she dropped her broken sword, realizing as it clattered to the ground that she had lost.

Kellan had the end of his sword pointed at her before her own had even stopped falling, but he let go of her arm. His mahogany eyes flickered apologetically for a moment, but the steel in them remained until he was satisfied Tamsin would surrender.

"Haven sacrificed his whole life to protect the Ma'diin," he said. "Do not abandon them when they need you the most. And they do need you, Tamsin."

Tamsin didn't want to listen to him; she already felt bad enough for leaving and she didn't want to believe she had done all of it and come all this way to leave empty handed.

"He is right, Tamsin," Ardak spoke up. "We should go with them, gather our strength, and come up with a solid plan." He walked over to her and put a hand on her shoulder. "Then I swear to you we will return. And not a moment later."

Tamsin was surprised by his show of solidarity with Kellan for a moment, but the rough conviction in his eyes begged her to see reason. Then she realized she may not have gotten Haven, but she wasn't going back empty handed. The Exiles were under her care now as much as everyone else and they deserved the chance to go home too. She looked around at their faces, tense and anxious as they waited for an answer from their Kaz'ma'sha. She exhaled slowly and nodded.

Kellan lowered his sword and a palpable sigh of relief went through the others. He snapped a few orders to the sha'diin as the Exiles picked up their weapons and belongings again. Tamsin picked up her broken blade, feeling deflated and embarrassed, but within the minute they were all marching away from the rocky hideout. Kellan waited until everyone had sidled past before following at the tail of the group. Tamsin didn't know whether it was in case the amon'jii decided to follow them, he wanted to make sure Tamsin didn't run off again, or he just didn't want to talk to her. Either way, she was relieved to find herself next to Enok as they followed the sha'diin towards the setting sun, for she found his presence growing on her as a calming one, even when he didn't say much.

"Are you alright," he asked her, glancing at her arm.

She nodded, though she wanted to talk about anything other than her failed duel. "Are you nervous about going back?" she asked him instead.

He took a deep breath into his chest. "A little, I admit. We've had only each other for company for so long and none of us thought we'd see our homeland again."

"But won't you be glad to see your families? Your tribesmen?"

"It's been so many years. There are some who might remember us." He glanced back to look at Kellan for a moment and then turned ahead again quickly. "But I fear we might be strangers to them now."

"You'll get to know each other again, I'm sure of it," she said reassuringly, though she glanced back at Kellan, who was several paces back, following silently.

The evening shadows began to blend together as night descended and the sha'diin called for a stop to make camp. Everyone started pitching their buurdas and setting up supplies for the cooking fire. It was a little awkward at first, but everyone seemed to be glad to have something to do. Food was prepared: a light meal of padi, but there was twice the amount of mouths now and still being so close to the edge of amon'jii territory made everyone cautious about going out to hunt after dark. Everyone except Kellan, but he never went more than a few paces out of the firelight, circling the camp just outside of the buurdas to make sure nothing was going to creep up on them in the middle of the night.

One of the sha'diin who had come with Kellan approached Tamsin as everyone was eating with a stack of blankets in his arms. He bowed his head before speaking. "Kaz'ma'sha, the Watcher Kellan wanted me to tell you that you may use his buurda tonight, as he will not be needing it. These," he lifted up the blankets, "I can cover the front with, if you wish privacy."

"Yes, thank you," she replied sincerely.

The sha'diin bowed again and left to secure the blankets as he had said. Tamsin waited a moment as the smile slowly disappeared from her lips. She wanted to be grateful for Kellan's offer, but she couldn't appreciate it when she was uncertain about the intent behind it. She couldn't keep going with this fog between them. She had to clear it away. She finished eating and decided that she would wait until everyone had gone to sleep and then go find him.

It was not long before everyone was asleep in their buurdas or on blankets on the ground and Tamsin was able to softly walk away from the fire. She crept past the sleeping forms and into the darkness beyond the buurdas, fastening her sword belt just in case. She looked out around her, hearing only the sound of bugs chattering and clicking nearby. Then movement to her right caught her eye and a shiver of caution ran up her arms and neck instinctively at the dark shape quickly approaching her, but then in a space of a breath the shape outlined itself in a familiar way and she relaxed a little. But only a little.

"What are you doing out here?" Kellan said hotly, as he came closer.

"I wanted to talk to you," she said, noting his tone. "Did you think I was trying to leave?"

"If I did you couldn't blame me for it."

She lifted her chin a little, though she knew he was right. She bit back her reply and instead said, "I wanted to apologize for that. I know I didn't make a good decision at the time—."

"You let that witch woman manipulate you," he interrupted her. "You risked everything without even a thought of what it might do."

"I risked my life and my life only by going," she said, trying her best not to let his words pierce her. "I had a chance to get Haven and—."

"Chance? What chance? And you risked everyone by going. Did you think no one would follow you? And if you had died do you think the Kazserii would stay united long enough to handle the northerners and the dam on their own?"

Tamsin felt the heat rising to her cheeks. "Of course I thought about it. And I'm not dead. And I know it may have been wrong at the time, but I don't think it was wrong now. I never would have found Ardak and the others if I hadn't gone."

Kellan scoffed. "The Exiled ones should have stayed away."

"How can you say that?"

"Easily. If you knew who they are—."

"And you do?"

"More than you!" Kellan took a deep breath then, glancing over to the camp, but it looked as though no one had awoken. He stalked a few paces further into the darkness and Tamsin followed him.

Kellan stopped when they were out of earshot of the camp and turned back to face Tamsin again, but Tamsin spoke first. "I know you're angry with me, but don't take it out on them, or Haven."

"Haven? Why would I be angry with him?"

"Because I love him…and not you. Not that way anyway."

Kellan's mahogany eyes glowed more intensely than she had ever seen before with a brightness that rivaled the sun, but she could not look away. She could only stare back and allow the heat to bore a hole through her.

"At least I don't let my feelings destroy my judgment," he said evenly. "Even if you had managed to get him out of there, what future could you have with him? You're the Kaz'ma'sha and he's a Watcher. A broken one. It would be doomed."

Tamsin could feel her patience crumbling like dried earth with each word he spoke. "Have you forgotten that you're a Watcher too?"

"Not for a moment. But I'm here." He reached down and grabbed her hands, holding them tightly in his own.

She wrenched her hands free, taking a step back. "And if someone would just help me Haven would be here too. But—." She took another step back as a horrible thought crept into her mind. "But you don't want him here, do you? If he was here, then nothing would ever happen between us."

There was a low rumble in the sky above them; the only sign that a storm was approaching for the clouds were invisible in the darkness, but it may as well have come from Tamsin's very core.

"You won't even deny it," she said incredulously.

Kellan's chin shifted slightly, his lips pressing together repeatedly. "You have to choose, Tamsin."

"Choose? Between you or Haven?" Tamsin couldn't believe she was having this conversation. "You are supposed to be his friend aren't you? His oath-brother! How can you be so selfish?"

"No," Kellan said, the tension in his voice echoing her own. "You have to choose between him or your people. You are their leader now. They are looking to *you* to lead them. Even if they did follow you to the Ravine, do you really think that is the best thing for *them?* I have spent years of my life protecting them from the amon'jii and you would lead them right into their nest? For one man?"

Tamsin could feel the pressure burning in her skull from her power. It was always made worse when she was angry, but she ignored it this time. She was so angry at Kellan that she didn't even care that the power building within her was making her head pound and her fingertips tingle. The very air around her seemed to pick up on her rage. The wind whipped through her hair and cloak and the clouds awakened with tiny bursts of lightning, swirling in slow spirals above them.

"You're a coward," she hissed through the brewing storm. "You're hiding behind the Ma'diin to avoid your own shame."

"You don't know what you're talking about," he hissed back.

"I see him in my dreams, Kellan. I know he's alive."

"And that doesn't scare you? Why would they keep him alive, Tamsin? Didn't you see him in your vision? Wasn't he fighting against us?"

"It wasn't real!" Tamsin shouted back. "There's still time to get him back. He's not lost to us yet."

But his words struck through her anger, hitting a nerve of truth. They were nearly out of time. She was afraid she would have to make a choice. But she was only one person and her battles were multiplying.

Kellan lifted his arm up to his face trying to block out the wind. "Tamsin," he said, softer now, but making it hard for her to hear him. "He was lost to us long before you met him."

A flash of new anger pierced her just as lightning crackled overhead, illuminating the violent emotion contorting her face. Before she knew what she was doing, her sword was in her hand and she was swinging it at Kellan. He jumped back, avoiding her first swing, and then drew his own just in time to block her second. But her fury would not relent so she pushed him back, each strike more ferocious than the last. "How dare you!" she screamed at him. "How dare you give up on him! I will go through the northerners, I will go through the amon'jii, I will even go through you!"

Kellan tripped over a small boulder sticking out of the ground behind him, but rolled off to the side just as Tamsin's sword came crashing down upon the rock.

She let out a furious cry, releasing the power that had been organically building with each word and arc of her sword, but fire did not shoot up the length of her sword, nor did Kellan's cloak catch on fire. In less than a moment, there was an eruption of white-hot light in front of her and a blast of thunder as if a drum had exploded inside her skull. The force of it threw her several yards back, sending her rolling over the rocks.

She lifted her head up when she had finally stopped moving, though the ground still felt shaky underneath her. She staggered up to her feet, pressing the heels of her hands into her head, but it did nothing to lessen the deafening ringing in her ears. She looked around, trying to get her bearings. There was a dark hole in the ground where they had just stood, with pieces of the boulder scattered in every direction. And then she saw Kellan. He was a few yards away, lying face first in the ground, unmoving.

Seeing his still body propelled her forward as she stumbled over to him. She called out his name, but she couldn't even hear her own voice, drowned out by the ringing. She dropped to her knees when she reached him and grabbed his shoulders, pushing him over onto his back. She shook his shoulders and screamed his name again.

His mahogany eyes fluttered a bit then and his mouth opened in a desperate attempt for air.

Every ounce of anger she carried towards him vanished and was replaced with relief, but it was momentary. Yes he was alive, but his face twisted in pain. She tried asking where he was hurt, but he either heard the same ringing she did and couldn't hear her or he was in too much pain to answer. His chest moved up and down quickly and his eyes fluttered again, but he made no move to get up.

"Help!" Tamsin yelled, hoping someone could hear her. Her hands fluttered over him, trying to locate the source of his pain, but it was dark and he was covered in his cloak.

Someone grabbed her shoulder then and she looked up to see Enok and behind him several others were running over to them.

"He's hurt! He needs help!"

Enok said something back to her, but she could only shake her head and point to her ear. He shouted something to the others and then tried to pull her away from Kellan. She shook her head again. She could not leave him. Especially when she had the horrible feeling that she had somehow done this. She looked up to the sky, seeing the lightning still crackling through the billowy dark clouds, though it was not nearly as intense now as it had been a minute ago.

Enok waved his hand in front of her face, drawing her attention back. Others were there now, Ardak and Hronar included, and Enok signaled for her to go with him. When she refused again, Hronar came and wrapped his massive arms around her and lifted her off the ground. She cried out, but she found she did not have the strength to fight him or to even be mad. He carried her away and soon she was surrounded by concerned sha'diin.

She shut her eyes, but neither that nor the constant droning noise in her ears could drown out the aftermath of what had just been unleashed.

Chapter Ten

The night was a silent blur for Tamsin, as she seemed to be stuck in a storm cloud of her own making. The sha'diin had fretted over her for a time until she finally pushed them away, frustrated by her inability to help or even hear what was going on. The ringing in her ears had lessened but her hearing had yet to return. Ardak and Enok attended to Kellan in his buurda, which Tamsin knew was extremely generous of them, for she knew firsthand how powerful and dangerous Watcher blood could be, though whether or not Kellan was injured like that she had no idea. She could only pass the time by standing, pacing, sitting, and trying to read the occasional glances of the sha'diin towards his buurda.

She didn't realize she had dozed off until she felt someone gently shaking her awake. Her heavy lids resisted at first until she realized it was Ardak who sat next to her. She blinked away the last tethers of sleep, noting that most of the others were asleep too.

Ardak's lips moved in the dimmed firelight, but she shook her head and pointed to her ear. He frowned and stood up, motioning for her to follow him. He led her over to Kellan's buurda, holding up the flap that the sha'diin had originally placed for her privacy so she could enter. There was not much space so she knelt down next to Kellan. His eyes were closed and in the faint light from the fire Tamsin couldn't tell if he was merely sleeping or if…

Her lower lip trembled and then she felt Ardak's hands close around hers. He moved them over to Kellan, pressing her palms lightly onto his chest, and after a moment she felt it rise and fall. Her breath hitched in relief. She nodded in thanks to Ardak, grateful for his and Enok's help, then removed her hands from Kellan's chest as a cloak of guilt wrapped itself around her. She got up and walked back outside before Ardak could see any of it on her face.

She had let her emotions consume her. Everything she had said to Kellan had been true, but she had abandoned her control. Each of them had said what they needed to, though Kellan didn't deserve to be lying unconscious in a buurda for it. She had told herself last night that they needed to clear the air between them. She knew Kellan had feelings for her, deeper than she could reciprocate, and she had gone out there with a veil over her eyes hoping he wouldn't see that she knew exactly how her abandonment would have affected him. Their confrontation had left them both bare though, revealing their ugly truths as clearly as if they bore black tattoos along their skin. If it meant gaining Tamsin's affection, Kellan would forsake Haven, his own brother. And Tamsin would forsake everyone else to save him.

And circling around the fringe of these thoughts like a shadow was the sense that she was the reason Kellan was lying in that buurda. Not because she had forced him to be in the wrong place at the wrong time, exposing him to the storm's fury, but exposing him to *her* fury. Somehow she had struck him. The storm inside her had united with the storm in the sky and all of her rage, all of her betrayal, had manifested into that white-hot spear.

The greyness of the morning was emerging, bringing the shape of the world back into focus as the darkness receded. Small shrubs and grasses took form once again, adding texture and depth to what had been a black maw beyond the circle of firelight. And then the colors grew, though they were dull and muted as the sun had not properly shown herself yet. But even without crisp morning rays, the sha'diin soon began to stir as well, rolling over on their sleeping mats, yawning and stretching, their bodies governed by the same force that pulled the sun up every day. Some of them seemed surprised to see Tamsin up and alert, albeit looking a little afflicted, though they gave her the sign of respect off their hands as they rose and began to move about the camp. Tamsin walked away from the camp though, with no destination in mind other than some distance.

"Girl."

Tamsin put her hand up to her ear, but she hadn't imagined it. She turned around to see Ardak approaching her again and for a brief moment, underneath the wild hair, wrinkles, and years of having to form a tough exterior, she saw a vulnerability that leaked through. And seeing it displayed on someone else gave her the mirror to see her own cracks. Like a cork that was too dry and was starting to crumble away as the screw turned, she could feel the bitter wine swallowing her up. And in that sticky syrup was every doubt, fear, frustration and prick of guilt. She was too tired to swim through it. She was exhausted from holding back the tide of fear, trying to pretend like she wasn't terrified to face the Ravine again, terrified to lose Haven if she didn't go back, and terrified of what would happen to everyone else whether she went or not.

Ardak seemed to sense this and rushed over, foregoing what he had planned to say and did something that caught Tamsin off guard: he wrapped his arms around her and hugged her.

He did not say a word and it only took Tamsin half a breath to unfreeze from the unexpected motion. It was an act of compassion, soaking up all the turmoil that was spilling out of her, and he would not let go until she had relinquished it. He reminded her of her father, a great man with the stoic presence of a bear, able to comfort her with the simplest gesture of strength and kindness. Even though she was not Ardak's child, she could not contain the stifled sobs that escaped into his chest as she gripped the front of his shirt. His giant arms provided her with the safe space she needed to release her desperate feelings, without feeling shame or embarrassment for their existence. She knew she would still have to face everything, but for these few minutes, she could just be Tamsin, a girl whose world was under siege.

When the force of the sobs had subsided, he gently led her back over to the camp and sat her down near the cooking fire the sha'diin had erected. Normal sounds started to return to her: the crackle of the flames, shuffling feet over the dirt and light chatter between the sha'diin. And after a short time, Ardak presented her with a bowl of hot padi, though he still didn't say anything. Tamsin ate her food in silence and watched the others grab their own bowls, though she didn't notice Ardak had disappeared until after she had finished. With her belly full, her exhausted bones urged her to find a quiet place to curl up and get more than an hour's worth of sleep, but she wanted to find Ardak first and thank him for his kindness.

But she did not see him anywhere in the camp and as she wandered around, she noticed some of the other Exiles were missing as well. Perhaps they had gone hunting. She saw Enrik underneath one of the buurdas and Enok was next to him, so she grabbed two more bowls of padi and brought them over to them. Enrik still looked weary, but he was able to eat on his own, which was a good sign. Enok accepted the other bowl gratefully.

"You did not go hunting with the others?" she asked him.

Enok gave her a funny look. "Ardak did not tell you?"

"Tell me what?"

"Ardak and the others—they are going back to the Ravine."

Tamsin felt a hole open up in her stomach. "What?"

Enok's lip twitched uncomfortably. "He wanted you to be free to make the decision that needed to be made. You can go back to the Ma'diin, without the guilt of abandoning your man. They are going back for him."

Tamsin was beyond words. She thought she had no more emotions left this morning, but hearing this ignited a whole new clash of hope and raw fear. And a debt that could never be repaid. But one thing was absolute: they would either return with Haven, or they would not return at all.

"Did they buy it?"

Sherene nodded quickly. "Yes, the midwife is on her way."

Emilia smiled. "Good. Are you ready?"

Sherene nodded again, though with a hint of nerves this time.

"You'll be fine," Emilia assured her. With herself, Lavinia, and Lady Allard under careful scrutiny and the whole estate being guarded, they had to come up with a clever ruse to smuggle Sherene out long enough to get word to Lord Findor. They needed him to summon an emergency Council session, one which Emilia would show up to. She had her own plan to escape the estate, but she needed the Council members all in one place.

After a few minutes, the crunch of carriage wheels turning over the gravel drive could be heard until they stopped in front of the main doors. Then Mr. Brandstone welcomed the midwife into the house where Emilia and Sherene were waiting. Emilia escorted the woman upstairs, explaining that Madame Corinthia was experiencing pains. With the impending arrival of her child, it made for an easy excuse. Once she showed the midwife to the room where

Madame Corinthia and Lady Allard were waiting she crept back to the top of the stairs and signaled to Sherene.

The day maid nodded and went out the front door where the midwife's carriage was still being held. Emilia went back to the room where the midwife was talking to Madame Corinthia, but slowly sidled over to the window where she had a view of the front drive. She could see Sherene talking to one of the guards and though she couldn't hear, she knew exactly what she was saying: telling them that the situation was more severe than the midwife had thought and she needed more supplies. Sherene and the guard talked for another minute and Emilia began to doubt whether Sherene's fervent act would pay off or if their plan was about to be cut off at the knees. But then she saw the guard step aside and Sherene climb into the carriage.

"Yes!" she cried as the carriage pulled away once more. Then she realized everyone in the room was looking at her and she cleared her throat. "Sorry, I think I need some air," she said and stepped out of the room, pulling the door closed behind her. Now all Madame Corinthia and Lady Allard needed to do was keep the midwife occupied until Sherene got back.

"Emilia."

Emilia jumped and turned to see Lavinia standing behind her.

"Did I see the midwife here?" Lavinia asked.

Emilia nodded. They had decided not to include Lavinia in their plans as an act of kindness. Lavinia had been withdrawn ever since Lord Urbane's removal and Lady Allard suggested they leave her out of anything that would cause her more stress.

Lavinia went to go inside, but Emilia stepped in her way.

Lavinia raised her eyebrows. "Step aside Emilia. If Madame Corinthia isn't feeling well, then I—."

"I'm sure she's fine," Emilia insisted. "Cerena is with her right now. But there's something I wanted to talk to you about. Would you walk with me?"

Lavinia squinted her eyes for a moment, then finally nodded and they made their way outside into the gardens. Guards patrolled outside here too, but they wouldn't bother them as long as they didn't stray too far from the main paths.

Blinking against the morning sun, Emilia finally turned to her. "I wanted to talk to you about Lord Urbane's will," she said.

Lifting her face up to the sky, Lavinia stared up into the clouds for a moment, seemingly unaffected by the bright rays or the warmth of it on her skin. "You own this estate now, plus several others. All I ask is that I can still choose where to go once things are settled."

"That's not what I—," Emilia shook her head. "I would never force you to leave. In fact, I have no interest in running the estate. My purpose is elsewhere."

"Power can often be mistaken for purpose, my dear."

"What do you mean?"

"It's the blindness that comes with both those things. We think we have control, but it's quite the opposite. We may have the best intentions, but sooner or later, what we intended is not how things turn out at all."

Emilia wondered if perhaps Lavinia had been wounded more deeply by Lord Urbane's trail of betrayals than she had let on. Lord Urbane's letter declaring Emilia as the heir to the Urbane name was just the latest, but Emilia had no intentions of taking the running of the estate away from Lavinia. Her status as a Lady would remain the same as would all of her responsibilities. But as she looked at the matriarch of the Urbane family, she realized that all of this shifting of power, all of the revelations about Lord Urbane's affairs, even if they had been before Lavinia married him, was shredding the pillars of her life. And her despondency now was not correlated with her defeat, but with her mind's attempts to fortify herself against these assaults. Lavinia was not a weak woman, but her strength was being tested right now. And once all of this became public and the gossip started to circulate, she would need that fortitude.

"I would never do anything to cause you more pain," Emilia said, hoping Lavinia believed her.

They heard shouts then and looked back towards the house to see Lady Allard waving. Emilia thought for a moment that maybe the midwife was leaving and Sherene was not back yet, but then she heard what she was yelling: the baby was coming. The two women picked up their skirts and rushed back to the house and inside.

"Cerena?" Emilia asked Lady Allard quietly as they made their way back upstairs.

But Lady Allard could only smile and lift her hands up helplessly. "I think the baby wanted to be included in our plans too."

Emilia laughed and they followed Lavinia into the room. Madame Corinthia was lying in the bed, looking surprised and slightly fearful as the midwife organized her supplies on a nearby table.

"Is it true?" Lavinia asked as she went over to the side of the bed.

"Yes, my lady," the midwife answered.

"But she's not due for another month," Emilia said.

"You've traveled recently, no?" the midwife asked and Madame Corinthia nodded. "That may have speeded things up, but there is no need for alarm. We will take good care of both of you."

Then Lavinia told Emilia to go find Sherene so she could assist the midwife. Emilia and Lady Allard exchanged a quick look, but Emilia nodded and left the room. She hurried down the hall and found another maid, telling her to fetch more supplies for them, but instead of going back she went downstairs. She went to one of the front windows, anxiously watching the guards pacing back and forth and waiting for Sherene to return.

Finally, she saw the carriage turn around the front hedge by the gates and into the drive. She rushed over to the front door and, not waiting for Mr. Brandstone, flung it open. She ran out to meet Sherene as she climbed down from the carriage. The maid was carrying a brown satchel and held it close to her chest.

"Well?" Emilia asked.

"Inside," Sherene replied, ushering her back into the house before the guards could get too close. Then once the door was closed, she gave the satchel to Emilia. "I made it to Lord Findor's estate," she said, "and he gave me these."

Emilia looked inside and saw all the letters from Empyria stuffed in there. "Why would he give them back?" she asked. "Is he refusing to call on the Council?"

"The Council's already been called, by Lord Halbany. And there's guards at Findor's estate too; he can't get away."

"When is the Council?" Emilia asked.

"In an hour. Findor thinks Halbany is going to persecute Lord Urbane for conspiracy against Empyria and the Cities."

"Without these letters, they'll get away with it," Emilia said. "And with Lord Urbane imprisoned, there's no one to challenge it. I have to go, now."

"Do you want me to come with you?" Sherene asked.

But Emilia shook her head, telling her they actually needed her in Madame Corinthia's room. They would fill the rest in, she assured her. Then she went back up to her room to grab one last thing before she enacted her own plan. She grabbed Lord Urbane's will and put it in the pocket of her dress. Sherene's news hadn't changed anything except moving up their timeline a bit and making Emilia the lead in the case against Cornelius. Lord Urbane's will was more important than ever now; it would've been enough to have a seat in the Council and a vote on Lord Urbane's side, but now everything rested solely on making sure Emilia was in the room. Lord Urbane was out. Lord Findor was out. She would have to plead the case for all of them.

She went back downstairs and out the front door once more. Instead of avoiding the guards, this time she marched right up to one of them. The man held up his hand to stop her and asked her what she was doing.

"I have information for Commander Garz," she said. "I need to see him right away."

"We have orders to keep you—."

"Commander Garz told me that if I had any information regarding Empyria or Lord Urbane, then I was to give it to him personally. If you want to go against those orders, then that's fine. We can stay here and listen to the sounds of a woman giving birth. The screaming should start soon."

The guard's cheeks twitched as he contemplated Emilia's offer and glanced at the house with uncertainty. Finally, he whistled over to one of the other guards and called for a carriage. Within minutes, one was brought around to the front and Emilia stepped in and sat down opposite the guard. The driver shook the reins and the two horses began taking them down the drive and away from the estate.

Emilia tried not to let her little triumph show as they made their way to the Council building, for the guard's grim expression hadn't changed and she knew he was still weighing the possible outcomes of their course of action. But as the Council building came into sight, it was her turn to grow nervous. She had rehearsed her lies, but Commander Garz was just as formidable as the stone building and now that everything rested on her shoulders, it was much more imperative that she succeeded. The carriage came to a stop outside and the guard escorted her out and up the steps. He led her inside and through the building, but she remembered the way. As they walked through, she saw a large group of men going through some doors on the other side of the main hall. The men were dressed in black robes, but each had a uniquely colored sash pinned to one shoulder. She had seen her father's council robes many times and she knew these were the other lords. They were starting their session. She had to hurry.

But before she could change course, another smaller group came walking up to them. And this one was led by Commander Garz. Surprise flashed across his face and then irritation.

"What is she doing here?" he demanded of the guard who had brought her.

"She said she had information for you. That she was to bring it to you immediately," the guard explained.

Garz looked at Emilia and raised an eyebrow. "Hmm. Take her to my office. Wait there until after the council meeting."

"I have information about the rebels," Emilia blurted out before the guard could escort her away. "And Lord Urbane. You were right. I have been in correspondence with Empyria."

"Sir, the council is about to start. We—" one of his officers whispered next to him, but Garz held up a hand to silence him.

He took a step closer to Emilia. "What information?"

Emilia held up the satchel. "Letters, confirming Lord Urbane's plot against the Empyrian lords."

A victorious gleam creased the edged of his eyes, but he still stared at her with a note of suspicion.

She had lied to him before and he had known they were lies, but now she had to do everything in her power to make him trust her. Just enough to get her in the room. "I don't want to be…useless," she said, echoing his words from the other night. Those words were true enough.

He stared at her a moment longer, then motioned to one of his officers who then took the satchel away from Emilia. "Come with me," he then said and proceeded to tell her not speak unless spoken to as they made their way to the Chamber of Lords. They walked into the same room where she had just seen the other lords go into.

Upon entering, Emilia found the room split into two large sections by a grand staircase that descended into the middle of the room. Every few steps down, the staircase divided into a walkway on either side that circled around the room and met again on the opposite side. Interspersed along these walkways were seats made of stone, made slightly less rigid with plush, red cushions. The uppermost walkway was sectioned off by a banister and was layered with pillars that rose up to grasp the ceiling, mirroring the ones outside. But the main difference here was there were no flags of any kind to differentiate between the lording cities. Here was where they all came together under the unified banner of Delmar. Their sashes were the only thing that identified them individually. The chamber was large enough to seat a hundred men comfortably, but only about twenty-five seats were filled near the center circle of the room. Each of the seven ruling cities had no less than three ruling lords to govern it, but most had more and had at least one of those lords as a permanent envoy in Jalsai to represent their city's interests at the Council. Some had aides or scribes with them, but these men wore no sashes.

Emilia was ushered onto the top walkway and left to wait with two of the officers as Garz made his way down the stairs to the center of the chamber. In the center was a large dais that had a painted map of Delmar on it. A man was already standing there addressing the other lords. It was Lord Halbany and he was in the midst of explaining why he had summoned this meeting when Garz reached the platform.

"Ah, glad you could join us, Commander," Halbany said, though he was clearly anything but glad about Garz' interruption. But then his eyes glanced up the room to where Emilia was. "What is she doing here?" he asked, recognizing her from the other day when he and the Findors had met at the Urbane manor. "You know very well women are not allowed—."

"I am aware, my lord," Garz said as the other lords looked up as well. "But you were just informing the lords of the crisis brewing in Empyria and its perpetrator, Lord Urbane. Miss Regoran, a former citizen of Empyria" he said, gesturing towards Emilia, "has just brought us evidence that condemns Lord Urbane of these crimes."

A murmur went around the chamber and Emilia knew this was her moment. She had to act before she was either kicked out of the chamber or the lords were manipulated by Garz' and Halbany's words. "That's not entirely true," she spoke, loud enough for the chamber to hear. Garz whipped around, anger flashing in his eyes, but Emilia didn't stop. "The evidence I have condemns Cornelius Saveen and the conspiracy against the other lords and people of Empyria."

"Remove her!" Halbany shouted and Garz started climbing back up the stairs as the officers next to her each grabbed one of her arms.

"It is against the laws of the Council to remove one of its members while a session is ongoing," Emilia said.

"Lording ladies are not members of this Council," Halbany rebuked.

"I am not a Lording lady," Emilia said, struggling against the officers. "I am Emilia Regoran and by my father's decree under the Law of Exigency, I have a seat on this Council."

Another murmur went through the lords, louder and more fervent this time. Some seemed confused as they consulted with others, but even more looked stunned.

"I have the will to prove it!" she said as the guards tried to force her off the walkway.

"That's impossible," Halbany proclaimed. "Lord Regoran is dead. There's no way he could've—." But then he stopped as the chamber became silent and all eyes turned to him. His mouth opened and closed several times, but no words came out as he looked at his fellow lords and he knew he had slipped up.

Emilia hadn't known how deep Halbany's involvement went, but she did now. The other lords lack of knowledge of her father's death said it all.

One of the other lords stood up. He had gray hair, but it was neatly cut around his chiseled face. "Lord Halbany," his voice boomed across the silent chamber. "Please step down. Miss Regoran, come forward."

Garz whipped around on the stairs as he reached Emilia. "Lord Taul, I must insist—."

"Commander," Lord Taul's steely blue eyes cut through the space as loudly as his voice did and did not dare to be questioned. "You will stay silent or you will be removed from your position."

Garz pursed his lips, but he did not argue again.

Emilia knew he was seething underneath that uniform. The guards let her go and she walked past Garz and down the stairs, taking the satchel with her, knowing his eyes were boring into the back of her skull. But she didn't care. She was out from under his thumb now. She reached the center circle and went over to Lord Taul, handing him the satchel and then pulling Lord Urbane's will out of her pocket. He took the letter and scanned its contents with a focus so intense Emilia knew if there was one word out of place he would find it.

After a minute he looked at her, but she could not tell if he was pleased or not. Then he held up the letter for the other lords to see. "The Law of Exigency has not been used in many years, but this is indeed a legal document proclaiming Miss Regoran as Lord and heir…to the Urbane seat. Now," he held up his other hand to silence the lords as they voiced their questions, "we were all under the impression that Lord Urbane had died in the desert, but as Lord Halbany just informed us before your arrival, we know he is alive."

"He is," Emilia said. "He was arrested by Commander Garz a few nights ago."

"Why did he not return to the Council?" Taul asked.

"Because he didn't know who he could trust," Emilia said, looking directly at Lord Halbany. "He revealed himself to Lord Halbany and Lord Findor, but Halbany betrayed him."

"Why?"

"There is a conspiracy going on," Emilia confirmed, "but it is not led by Lord Urbane. Cornelius Saveen has seized control of Empyria and is consolidating his power with help from Lord Halbany and Commander Garz. He murdered my father, Lord Regoran, and is murdering anyone who stands against him."

Lord Taul leaned over to his aid and ordered him to find Lord Urbane and Lord Findor. Then he turned back to Emilia. "If what you say turns out to be true, Lord Saveen will have to be removed from his lordship."

"That is why Lord Urbane needs your help. Why *I* am asking for your help now." Emilia turned in a circle to look at each of the lords. "Cornelius will not let Empyria go without a fight."

It was dark by the time Emilia returned to the Urbane manor. She was exhausted, but happy to notice that the guards had all gone. They were once more free to leave the estate as they wished. There was a strange, covered carriage parked outside the front, but the midwife's was gone. The candles were still lit inside, indicating the household was still awake so she went in search of Sherene and Lady Allard, but she didn't have to go far. Sherene appeared at the top of the staircase, pausing when she noticed Emilia.

Emilia grinned and bowed. "You are looking at the newest member of the Lord's Council," she said, thinking Sherene would be ecstatic knowing their efforts had paid off.

But the day maid's expression was lined heavily with fatigue and sorrow as she came down the stairs.

"What's wrong, Sherene? It worked. Everything we did—." She was cut off as the sound of a baby crying echoed upstairs and she gasped. "She had the baby?!"

Sherene nodded. "A baby boy. But—Madame Corinthia didn't make it."

Emilia felt all the elation of the day's accomplishments slip away like a shadow sliding across the sand. "She what?" She remembered the strange carriage outside and suddenly realized what it was for: to take bodies away.

"The baby is healthy, but the delivery was too hard," Sherene explained.

Emilia took a deep breath. They hadn't been great friends, but Madame Corinthia had barely been older than she was. And within the span of only a few hours, she was gone. She walked upstairs and went to Madame Corinthia's room. She turned the knob and opened the door a few inches. It was dark inside, but she saw the silhouette of a white sheet on the bed, unmistakable what it was covering beneath. She took a step back, accepting that she did not have the stomach to go any further. She knew she should pay her respects, but she could do so at the funeral. This felt too intimate somehow. But then she wondered what kind of funeral she would actually have. She didn't even know if Madame Corinthia had any relatives in the Cities or back in Empyria. Her now orphaned child could be the only tether to the living world, the only evidence that she existed at all.

The thought sent chills right through her bones and she turned to go back to her room, but stopped as she saw firelight flickering brightly from another room down the hall. She went over to it and saw Lavinia sitting in a chair, gently rocking the bundled baby in her arms next to the fireplace. Emilia stood there for a minute, just watching them, perplexed by the serenity she saw on Lavinia's face. It was not the same woman she had talked to in the gardens earlier that day.

Finally, Lavinia noticed Emilia standing there. "Emilia, where have you been all day?" Her tone wasn't scolding, but rather, soft, as not to disturb the sleeping infant.

"Bringing your husband back home," a deep voice replied and Lord Urbane stepped around Emilia and into the room.

Lavinia's face melted into shocked relief, but she took a deep breath, remembering to keep her composure as she held the newborn. Lord Urbane crossed the room and knelt down in front of her, tenderly putting his hands over hers. They didn't say a word to each other, but were content just to be in each other's presence once more.

Emilia backed away and started down the hall, deciding to let them have their moment. They had achieved a victory today. Lord Urbane had been freed and Lord Halbany and Commander Garz had been arrested. Emilia had been given a seat on the Council and they had voted to act on Empyria.

But they had also been dealt a loss and Madame Corinthia's death was a warning Emilia would not ignore. Emilia vowed that she would not be forgotten when her time came. But she would have to work for it if she wanted a legacy. Becoming the Council's first female member was a good start, but her legitimacy hung by a thread. The real work started now.

Chapter Eleven

Tamsin didn't know how well her return would be received and the closer they got to the Ma'diin army's camp the more she found herself having to banish those thoughts. But they swirled around to the forefront again and again, joining the already restless flurry of thoughts circling her mind, the Exiles not the least of them. She took it as a good sign that the sha'diin that were leading them back still treated her like the Kazsera, but she also knew there were much stronger personalities waiting for her. Their little caravan moved quickly, having turned two of the buurdas into makeshift litters for Kellan and Enrik that could be carried with relative ease. Enrik was doing better, but Kellan had yet to wake up. Enok had modified his litter with a cover to protect him from the sun, for which Tamsin was grateful, but every time she caught a glimpse of it, it reminded her of why he was there in the first place. Dark clouds seemed ever present on the horizon, but no other storms had made an appearance on their journey. Tamsin still doubted the weather was solely to blame for Kellan's current state and she eyed the rolling sky with a wariness, feeling like the eye of a hurricane, whose winds were only waiting to be called upon again.

"Are you thinking of the path ahead or the path behind?" Enok walked up next to her, keeping in step with her even though he limped.

"Is it that obvious?" Tamsin responded.

"I've walked thousands of miles, Tamsin, and I know when one's thoughts are not where the feet are."

This stirred up a memory. "My mother used to say that walking should always be done with a partner, for it was good for the tongue, but could stir up fog in the mind. My Empyrian mother," she added, feeling unsure about talking about the woman who raised her in front of someone who had been devoted to the woman that should have raised her.

But Enok was gracious enough to take it in stride. "She sounds very wise," he said.

They walked together in silence for a little while then and Tamsin found that Enok's presence alone was quite calming. He had a refined temperament, for a Ma'diin, and it reminded her of things neither before nor behind her, but rather of a more stable, ordered time.

But the respite was brief and soon enough the sights and smells of the large Ma'diin camp emerged, breaking up the dry landscape with colorful activity. Their small group was spotted by several sha'diin on the outer edge of the camp; some ran over to greet them and within moments the news of their arrival spread like the movement of the sea. Wave after wave billowed over the Ma'diin, each fold bringing a new shell of information. The Kaz'ma'sha was alive…they had captured a northerner…there were strange sha'diin with them…the Watcher Kellan was wounded…

Tamsin realized very quickly that she had many vulnerable facets in their group and if she did not make it very clear that they were all under her protection then things could get out of hand before she had the chance to reassert herself. She didn't know what she was walking into, if the Kazserii had decided to strip her title in her absence or not. She ordered several sha'diin to find Numha and Oman as they continued into camp. She tried to read the faces of the people they passed and there were many, perhaps more than had been at the Kapu'era. But these were not the dueling grounds. They had traveled west since their flight from the Ravine, but they were not on any tribal land that Tamsin recognized.

Until she saw the muudhiif, separated from the thousands of buurdas and small tents strewn over the ground with its towering reed pillars and green canvas tapestries hanging over the sides. It was the very first muudhiif she had seen upon coming to the marshes, though the marshes now were dry with cracked dirt and the ladder-like planks that had connected the mud flat to the others covered only small puddles. It was where the Ysallah'diin had taken refuge after their own territory had been destroyed.

This was Hazees' old tribal land.

Next to her, Enok was still, but his eyes betrayed his anxiousness at being surrounded by so many of his former people. Enrik had propped himself up to his elbows on his litter, his head darting back and forth as more and more Ma'diin gathered around them.

Tamsin's own trepidation at returning was gone. There was something about the sight of Hazees' muudhiif that bolstered her purpose. Hazees had killed Ysallah and had tried to kill Tamsin, more than once, and had she allowed Hazees to take over the Ma'diin then the repercussions would have spread like a flood, suffocating anyone Tamsin had touched.

"Thank you, Ardak," she whispered into the wind.

Tamsin's eyes turned to several women who emerged from the muudhiif: Isillah, Lam, and Zekkara. The latter looked surprised, but Isillah looked like she had swallowed a sour grape. She stared at Tamsin and Tamsin stared back. Isillah had been Hazees' former ally, and though she had pledged her tribe to Tamsin like all the others, there had remained a sliver of rebellion in her demeanor. If anyone were to use Tamsin's absence to sow discord and reach for power, Tamsin guessed it would be Isillah.

A familiar voice called out to her and Calos emerged from the crowd, a delighted smile spread across her face. K'al was close behind, though her joy was contained behind her curious eyes as she beheld the Exile next to her Kaz'ma'sha.

A solid ring of people had formed around them, though no one seemed bold enough to make the first move before the Kazserii.

Tamsin decided it would be her. With all eyes on her, she moved to the muudhiif and yanked one of the green strips from the wall. No one moved, but just watched as she dragged the heavy fabric back to the center of the circle where she dropped it before Isillah's feet. Almost before it had completely settled on the ground, the fabric ignited, sending blooming flames into the air.

Many gasped or took a step back, but Isillah held Tamsin's gaze.

"Your Kaz'ma'sha has returned," Tamsin said. "What do you say to that?"

Isillah held her gaze for a few moments more then dipped her head and flicked her fingers over her hand in the sign of respect. "I say…welcome back."

Numha and Oman showed up shortly after with R'en, who had to shove through the crowds of people wishing to greet Tamsin. Smiles surrounded them, though one tight-lipped man came up and offered Tamsin a water skin without meeting her eyes. He wore a thick, black cord around his neck, but that was all Tamsin could make out until the crowd moved in and he disappeared.

"Thank you!" she called out, hoping he had heard, and then took a long, cool drink.

Oman, with some help from the sha'diin, took Kellan away. Poma showed up as well and Tamsin asked her to take Enrik to her family's muudhiif. Enok offered to go with them and Tamsin obliged, not only trusting him to see to Enrik's health and safety, but because she could see Enok was in need of some breathing room. As comfortable and collected as he had been in the wilderness, he was two steps away from being utterly lost here.

Out of everyone, Numha seemed the most relieved by Tamsin's presence, though she didn't say much until the swell of greeters had dispersed. Then she directed Tamsin into the large muudhiif and ushered everyone else out save for Tamsin, R'en and herself. They exchanged hugs, but when Numha stepped back Tamsin could see the question burning in her eyes.

"Ask me," Tamsin said, ready for whatever interrogation was coming to her.

"The Alamorgrian woman, Mora, told us you left willingly to go to the Ravine." Numha's freckled green eyes were warm, but her tone belied the betrayal she felt. "Did she lie to us?"

"She told you the truth," Tamsin said.

Numha nodded silently, though Tamsin knew she was doing her best to reign in her emotions. Numha was reliable in that way, always able to keep her eye on the bigger picture, but Tamsin knew too that she was probably the one who felt the sting of her disappearance the most.

"You look worse than when you left," R'en commented, circling around Tamsin with a scowl. "Though that probably works in our favor."

"How so?"

"Most of the Ma'diin think you were kidnapped by the same person who killed Samih. We thought so too until we talked to the witch woman."

Tamsin could guess which ones thought otherwise. But she didn't really care. What she needed to do was make sure Enrik was safe. The fact was he had killed Samih and once word spread of his identity there would be calls for retribution. Tamsin herself had wanted it, but she knew it was not Enrik's fault, and he had saved her in the Ravine. She explained all this to Numha and R'en, who agreed to post guards around Poma's muudhiif.

"Who was the other man with him?" R'en asked.

"His name is Enok," Tamsin said. "He will need our help as well." Then she launched into the details of what had happened at the Ravine, the Exiles finding them, and the events that had happened after Kellan found them.

The two women could not conceal their shock. Numha cupped her hands around her neck and R'en started pacing, quickly forming a figure eight of her footprints in the ground.

Finally Numha said softly, "We will help Enok find any family members that are here. And *when* the others return, we will do the same for them."

"I just can't believe it," R'en said. "All this time. And now they're going back to the Ravine. They're as mad as you are, Tamsin."

"They're devoted," Numha said, smiling. "And not to Irin. To you."

Tamsin shook her head. "Sometimes I still don't know how I ended up here. The Ma'diin, the Exiles, you. You all follow me and I can't make sense of it."

"A leader isn't chosen based on logic, Tamsin. We choose to follow you because we can feel it, here," Numha said, tapping her fingers to her chest. "We know we pushed you into this, but you have become…extraordinary." Her eyes were proud, but touched by a hint of sadness, and Tamsin couldn't tell where it came from, if it was still the hurt over Tamsin leaving or something else.

Tamsin took a deep breath. Extraordinary or not, she couldn't rely on that now that she was back. She was the Kaz'ma'sha, but she felt the rope on which that title hung had thinned since she left. She needed to be caught up on what had happened here while she was away if she was to be any use. She asked for K'al and Oman to join them, to get an idea of where the Kazserii and the Watchers were at. She didn't want to waste any more time, for she could see for herself from the brittle reed patches and dried waterways they had passed to get here that the dam's reach was spreading.

The state of the Ma'diin army was filled with palpable energy. Never before had such a large force come together, but despite the excitement, Tamsin found that the Kazserii and her kazsiin had managed to keep things somewhat organized. Food and water were already being rationed. Patrols were constantly coming and going, leaving no edge of their camp unwatched. More Ma'diin were filtering in every day, either bringing in fresh supplies from their tribes or offering themselves in service. Scouts had been sent ahead to ascertain the northerners' position and the best location for their next campsite. Without the waterways to navigate, the anasii hada was just about a day away, and moving thousands of people would probably require two. The Kazserii had been convening, coming up with plans to deal with the northerners when they arrived, but the question of the dam still remained.

K'al suggested meeting with the other Kazserii as soon as possible to finalize their plans, but a tiredness had descended on Tamsin that she felt all the way through her bones and it did not go unnoticed by Numha, who suggested she rest.

Tamsin had one more thing to do before she did. She asked for everyone to leave except for Oman and once they were alone she took out her broken sword and offered it to him, explaining what had happened. Oman had given it to her, as a symbol of the Watchers' loyalty before she set off for the Duels. It had once been a beautiful, curved blade, inlaid with stones, but ten seconds into her first fight with an amon'jii and it had been reduced to five inches of metal.

"I'm sorry I could not take better care of it," she said, knowing the sword had belonged to Oman's past mentor. "Can it be mended?"

Oman turned it over in his hands. "Without the other piece—no, and even if it was reforged it would not be as strong as it once was. But even a broken blade can still be useful," he said, handing it back to her. "It fits you better now," he added with a slight upturn of his lips.

She was grateful for his graciousness, but there was more and she caught the moment his expression changed. "What's wrong?"

"I had to make a deal with the witch woman, Mora, to find out what had happened to you."

"What kind of deal?" Tamsin asked.

"Her information…for your blood."

Tamsin initially balked at the idea, but then she remembered all the vials she had seen in Mora's home in Empyria. Vials full of Watcher blood. And her talk with Mora before she left for the Ravine had confirmed it. The others called her a blood stealer, an Alamorgrian. She was from a race that lived in the Ravine before the amon'jii came and would lurk in the marshes, waiting to steal blood from wounded Watchers so they could use it for their visions. It was a grotesque practice and Tamsin wondered what Mora wanted with hers, since she was no Watcher.

"I offered her my own," Oman said, "but she wouldn't accept it."

"No, it's okay," Tamsin said, realizing the position she had put Oman and the rest of them in when she had left. She lifted up her broken blade and hesitated for only a moment before slowly slicing it across her palm.

Oman moved quickly over to her, holding up an empty water skin under her hand.

Tamsin grimaced as she squeezed her fingers together, feeling the red liquid stream down her hand. But it was only for a few moments and then Oman replaced the water skin with a bandage and helped her wrap her hand.

Tamsin stared at her hand, and though the sting of it was still vibrant, there was something else on her mind that pained her more.

Oman was quick to pick up on it. "What is it?" he asked.

"I think Kellan is hurt because of me." Then she explained the fight they had had, the sudden storm and what she had felt when the lightning struck. The surge of power had been so strange and so deliberate that it felt like she had willed it to be there.

Oman did not seem overwhelmingly surprised by this though. "The sha'diin with Kellan have loose tongues. They're already spreading the word of what the Kaz'ma'sha did."

Tamsin ran her hands through her hair. "But I don't know for sure it was me. I can't feel it or summon it like fire, I just know I felt...connected somehow."

Oman laced his fingers together thoughtfully. "The forces of nature are no longer controlled by the gods alone," he said, almost as if he were repeating words he had heard before.

Tamsin's power, if it was indeed manifesting, was manifesting dangerously. Oman had told her once that her greatest strength was her ability to adapt. Was her power just adapting as well? She didn't think she had ever been as angry as she had been with Kellan before and if her power was evolving to keep up with her emotions then she needed to reign herself in before anyone else got hurt.

"There's more," she said quietly, scrunching her eyebrows up. "The Exiles know, but I didn't tell the others," she started. "The amon'jii...I can speak to them." She raised her gaze to meet Oman's like she had been caught stealing a dessert from the kitchen, but the n'qab under his hood was firmly in place, making his expression intolerably indecipherable. Though by his silence she guessed this was something he had not expected to hear.

"You spoke with them," he said at last.

She nodded and told him everything she could remember from her exchanges with the amon'jii. How they were sodden with rage over the Watchers, that their curiosity about her ability to communicate with them was the only reason they hadn't killed her right away, and how they kept referring to their leader, the Great One, whose sole mission was to wipe out the Ma'diin. And how they had invited her back to the Ravine at the Great One's behest.

Oman's lip twitched and he turned away for a moment, digesting this new information.

"The sh'lomiin, Zaful, said that when a woman possessed a firestone it became unpredictable," she said, recalling the night the sh'lomiin had visited. "Did Irin possess this ability? Was it passed on to me?"

Oman turned back toward her. "If your mother could do this she kept it well hidden." Then he walked over to her and put a hand on her shoulder. "I hope you know not to speak of this to anyone else."

Tamsin knew. She couldn't help that the Exiles already knew, but based on Hronar's initial reaction she understood it was important to stay silent.

Oman nodded approvingly. "You've given me much to think about," he said. "I will find Zaful and see if he can shed any more light on this." He gave her shoulder a squeeze and then walked out of the muudhiif.

Tamsin looked down at the broken blade in her hands, her reflection cut off by the jagged edge. Half of herself visible, the other half hidden from her. If the other half became visible, would she like what she saw? Or would it destroy everyone around her?

150

Chapter Twelve

A darkly hooded figure wandered around the statues, reaching out every so often to brush one with his palm. Gently, lovingly cradling the stone beneath his hand. The statues had long, pointed claws extended out almost as if they were reaching back. Their frozen snarls echoed silently around the cavern. Thin trails of glistening blood followed the hand of the cloaked figure, staining the solid stone in the same hue of the crimson cuffs on his sleeve. Ancient words dripped from his lips, muttered quietly, but forcefully every time he touched one of the stone creatures. Words that sizzled like water onto a burning pan.

Be free, my children...Awaken...Hear my voice...Taste my blood...

Do you think it will really work, Master? They have been asleep for so long.

The figure paused, but only for a moment.

Your doubt will be your undoing, Alhexander...

Forgive me, Master. It is an honor to behold your power.

The rhythmic chanting continued, over and over throughout the cavern. Until finally, he stopped and a low rumbling took its place as the air shuddered. Soon, the afain'jii would awaken. And they would be hungry. They would have a longer journey than their wingless cousins, the amon'jii, but they would be rewarded for their efforts.

Do you feel that...she is here...

The dark figure turned around and his icy blue eyes stared directly at her with a hatred so clear that it seemed to pull her towards it at the same time that it lunged at her.

Tamsin woke up abruptly, beads of sweat dotting her skin. She looked around and saw a small fire crackling in the center of the muudhiif with Numha next to it, gently prodding it with a long stick. Numha looked up as Tamsin stirred and came over to her with a cloth and water skin. She patted the sweat away from her forehead with the cloth and then helped Tamsin sit up. No light filtered through the roof or walls and the shadows cast from the fire were long and dark.

"I must've fallen asleep," Tamsin said, trying to shake away the images of her dream. Images that very much looked like the statues she had encountered in the Ravine. "I'm sorry, I don't even remember…" She pressed her hands to her forehead. The dream had a strange, foreboding air that tugged at her gut to do something, but she had no idea what and the sinister turn it had taken towards her left her pulse reeling.

But Numha's expression was too serious. Something was wrong.

"Tamsin," she started, "someone put *haava* in your water." She held up the water skin. "Who gave this to you?"

Tamsin could hardly think, between the terror of her dream and the heaviness of her eyelids that both lingered like smoke. "Umm, a man. When we first got back. I don't know him."

Numha tossed the water skin aside and untied her own from her belt, offering it to Tamsin. "Only mine or R'en's from now on, okay?"

Tamsin nodded, taking a small sip.

"Kep'chlan and Siinsha are outside right now. They'll make sure nobody gets in."

Watchers guarding the Kaz'ma'sha's muudhiif. "You think someone wanted to hurt me? While I was asleep?"

Numha shrugged. "I don't know. But you won't be alone, not for a second, until we figure out who did this."

But Tamsin already had an idea. If Isillah had been bold, she would've challenged Tamsin as soon as she got back, but from what she knew Isillah wasn't that daring. Poisoning her water, now that was something Tamsin could imagine her doing. It was the last thing she needed right now. She handed Numha's water back and rubbed the last bits of sleep from her eyes.

Numha's gaze was still concerned, however. "Are you still having nightmares about Haven?"

"Yes and no," Tamsin said. "The last few have been different. He—he knew I was there."

"Haven?"

Tamsin shook her head. "No. The Master. He's—he's also in Haven's mind and he knew I was watching. This last one though..." She shuddered as images of the dream came back. The dark figure walking around the cave of statues, the same cave Tamsin had been in, and the feeling that something terrible was about to happen. But the worst of it was when the figure had turned around to look at her. The face under the hood...the eyes...it was Haven. But the hatred, the darkness he emitted was something else. It was the same look she had seen on him during the Red Sight when she had her vision of the great battle. When he had turned against the Ma'diin. When he wanted to destroy her.

"Kaz'ma'sha! Kaz'ma'sha!" shouts were heard outside.

Numha crossed over to the door while Tamsin stood up. She took a shaky breath, feeling sick. She wanted to blame it on the *haava* root still lingering in her system, but she knew this last dream had been a turning point. She had tried to avoid the events of the Red Sight by going to the Ravine alone, but she had failed to get Haven, and now she feared she had failed to prevent what she had seen. Enrik had warned her that Monstran and the Master were using Haven, twisting him into something else, and even if the Exiles succeeded in finding him, it was now too late.

Numha came back in, followed by a red-faced sha'diin. The boy couldn't have been out of his teen years, but breathed quickly as if he had been running.

"What is it?" Tamsin asked.

The boy remembered to make the sign of respect and then made his explanation for his late-night interruption. "The Kazserii—they're meeting on the other side of the camp."

Tamsin exchanged a look with Numha, both women thinking the same thing: perhaps the *haava* incident hadn't been to harm Tamsin at all, but rather to keep her out of the way while Isillah summoned the Kazserii to sway them into a coup.

"Take us there," Tamsin ordered and immediately followed the young sha'diin out of the muudhiif. Most of the Ma'diin were sleeping, but some had awoken to the sha'diin's shouting and those that recognized the Kaz'ma'sha began to follow her, curious to find out the purpose of the brisk walk. Kep'chlan and Siinsha, who had been guarding her muudhiif followed as well, creating a good buffer between Tamsin and her followers. The coolness of the night air did nothing to alleviate the pit in Tamsin's stomach as they meandered quickly through the tents and buurdas.

Finally, they came to a large tent, nearly as big as a muudhiif, but made up of many different layers of overlapping canvas. Several kazserii from the other Kazserii were standing around outside it, but made no move to stop them. Tamsin walked to the tent, with Numha on her heel, and threw open the door flap, before her nerves could trigger any hesitation.

The tent was nearly full; all of the Kazserii were there and some kazsiin too, all seated around a small fire in the center that gave off just enough light to make shadows against the walls. They all looked up as she entered and the conversations quieted until only the subdued crackle of flames could be heard.

Tamsin looked around at the gathered faces, unable to determine their judgment because of the shadows flickering across their features from the jumping firelight. She straightened her back, forcing her own face to display courage and not the trepidation she really felt knowing her actions may have cost them everything.

"If you have assembled here tonight," she said, feeling her inner defenses working their way to the surface, "because you have decided to select a new Kaz'ma'sha, because you do not agree with my actions or believe I am up for the task—." She paused as she noticed the barely concealed smirks from some of the Kazserii and it made her anger rise.

Her bristling temper must have been visible for K'al stood up before she could say another word. "Kaz'ma'sha," she said, bowing down gently and flicking her fingers off the back of her hand. "This is not what you think."

Then, one by one, everyone stood up and made the same sign of respect to Tamsin.

"Then what is it?" Tamsin asked.

"This is your war council," K'al said, grinning.

The word 'war' made her breath hitch and though all eyes were upon her she hoped no one noticed. Suddenly it was like her first day of training again with Oman and Kellan, just a small naive girl going up against the masters of swordsmanship. But they were all still behind her. They still saw her as their Kaz'ma'sha and this thought tempered her nerves.

"There is a place for you here," Oman's low voice next to her interrupted her awe. She hadn't noticed him, but now he stood next to her shoulder. His hand pointed to the empty space for her in the circle, but his tone implied a deeper meaning to his words. He could see her lingering anxiousness and was trying to assuage it.

She nodded in thanks and took her place among the others, still trying to erase her disbelief that the rest of them hadn't decided to depose her. She looked around the room at the different faces assembled there and noticed the range of emotions reflected there: some looked nervous, eager, proud, awed, or stoically brave in the shadow of the days ahead. She realized that all those years she spent traveling with her father to the other Cities had left her wholly unprepared for her present circumstances. All those years, while her father negotiated with other lords and dignitaries behind closed doors, had been preparing her for a future that was gone. The little she did learn about what was said in those rooms she learned from the other lording ladies as they entertained each other over afternoon tea. But those years had not been in her control. The weeks she had spent with Oman and Kellan had given her the piece of knowledge she needed now: that her greatest asset was her ability to adapt. And right now, she had control. She didn't need years of training to prepare her; she just needed to believe that she already possessed the abilities she would need. She needed to trust herself. She had already survived so much since she first left the Cities because she was able to adapt. The only thing that she couldn't adapt to, the only thing that stopped her in her tracks, was losing Haven.

The sobering thought brought her back to the tent. She sat down and they rest did the same, with only the sound of rustling clothes to break the silence as everyone settled in again. Numha was seated to her right and Oman to her left. She was slightly surprised that the Kazserii had agreed to include the Watchers, but pleased to know that they at least agreed the Watchers were an integral part of this. Perhaps more progress had been made in her absence than she thought. R'en also joined them, slipping in quietly from outside, though she remained standing behind Tamsin.

Isillah stood back up and made the sign of respect to Tamsin, though she looked stiff, as if her next words were going to be uncomfortable. "We stand with you, Kaz'ma'sha," she said. "We all know what you have faced since coming here, mostly because of our own superstition and bigotry, and though some of us would like to think we would have overcome the same, it's not true. But what is true is that the Ma'diin are stronger with you, not without. I—I want to apologize for not realizing that sooner." Then she bowed her head.

Tamsin was stunned for a moment. Isillah had been her most vocal opposition thus far since Hazees' passing. "Thank you," she said, not knowing what else to say, and Isillah sat back down. Her apology seemed genuine enough, but Tamsin was not entirely convinced of her authenticity yet. Perhaps Isillah hadn't poisoned her water, perhaps it was one of the others, but no one stood up to refute Isillah's words. Maybe it was all an act to throw them off Isillah's trail. Tamsin glanced at Numha, whose expression seemed to mirror Tamsin's own misgivings. Numha glanced back with a slight nod and Tamsin knew she would be watching everyone with careful scrutiny.

K'al stood up next, a warm smile on her face. She too made the sign of respect before speaking and looked around the muudhiif proudly before landing on Tamsin. "We are all glad that you are safely back with us, Kaz'ma'sha. It is a gift that you have been brought to us and an honor that you choose to fight with us."

Tamsin took a steadying breath, "I want to tell you that I am grateful for each one of you and the honor you have shown me. I know our future is challenging and uncertain, but I know that we are stronger together. I may be young and inexperienced and not have a clue as to what I'm supposed to say in a Ma'diin war council, but I have risen up against everything and everyone that has tried to shove me down and the trials I have experienced have shown me that it is incredible what you can stand up to when others stand with you." Tamsin sat up a little straighter, her nerves finally giving way to what her instincts were picking up on. The energy in the tent, the support and show of loyalty, was all pointing to one thing. "You have a plan."

K'al's smile widened. "You are our first move in the war to come."

Though K'al spoke with hope and optimism, her words settled on Tamsin like an autumn frost. Despite the bright eyes and eager smiles around the tent, it felt like the Kazserii had already decided Tamsin's fate and whether they won or lost what was to come, from this point her future was sealed. She risked another glance at Numha, but the young woman's gaze was just as curious. Tamsin realized that this would be her first time hearing of it as well.

"What is the plan?"

Chapter Thirteen

The tent was quiet as K'al finished explaining the plan the Kazserii had come up with.

"You can't be serious," R'en said abruptly, stepping into the circle as if to put herself between Tamsin and the Kazserii's ideas.

"Be quiet, R'en," Tamsin told her.

"You can't actually be considering this," R'en said. "If the northerners found out—."

"Be quiet, R'en, or leave."

R'en bristled for a moment, but returned to her place behind Tamsin.

"I know you only want to protect your Kazsera," K'al said, addressing R'en, "and it seems that we would give her up to the enemy, but she is not *their* enemy. Not that they know of. Tamsin's northern blood will be their undoing. And our salvation."

Tamsin's thoughts churned over and over like an endless wave, envisioning the numerous ways this would play out. After hearing the Kazserii's plan, though, this was the one that would work. She could feel it. "Whose idea was this?"

"It was my idea to draw the northerners out away from the wall," Calos, the Kazserii's newest and youngest, said.

Tamsin gave her an encouraging smile. "It is a good plan."

Calos smiled back, proudly and bowed her head. "It wasn't just me though. Isillah had the idea to send you in to convince them to come out."

She could nearly hear R'en's teeth grinding as she fought back her objections. Even Numha shifted uncomfortably next to her. Before they could say anything, she turned to them directly. "This is what you trained me for." Then she turned back to the Kazserii. "I'll do it."

Even if it had been Isillah's initial idea, it didn't deter from being the best plan they had managed to come up with. If Isillah had an ulterior motive, then Tamsin would just have to be extra vigilant. If the Kazserii wouldn't depose her, then maybe the northerners would do it for her. But either way, using Tamsin to infiltrate the northerners' camp, under the guise of an escaped Ma'diin prisoner, to lure them out to face the Ma'diin army while finding out how to undo the dam was a stroke of genius.

"But what about the amon'jii? And the other Ma'diin too young or old to fight?" Numha asked.

"By being on the western border of the anasii hada," K'al said, "we will be putting our distance between us and amon'jii territory. We'll have more scouts on the eastern border to alert us of any attack. We know what you saw when you had the Red Sight. We won't let an ambush happen."

Tamsin glanced at Oman, to gauge his reaction to this, but he remained still, his hands tucked into his sleeves.

"And the elders will take the children to the dueling grounds," Calos spoke up. "It's the highest point in the marshes."

Tamsin shook her head. "That won't be good enough." She didn't want to think this way, but she had to. As a leader it was her responsibility to prepare for all outcomes, especially with everything hinging on her. If she succeeded, then the marshes would be flooded and in that case the dueling grounds would be perfect. But if she failed, then those very grounds were too exposed to both the amon'jii and the Empyrians if they decided to come south.

"There's nowhere else for them to go," Calos said with a frown.

But Tamsin caught K'al's eye and it gave her an idea. "There is another place," she said. "I want someone from every tribe to go back and take anyone left in the villages to the K'al'diin."

There were confused looks from the other Kazserii. "But, Tamsin," K'al said, "even though I am willing to open our mudflats, we do not have enough to—."

"They won't be staying there," Tamsin interjected, already knowing K'al's concern. "I need your sha'diin to take them through the mangroves."

The confused looks turned to nervous murmurs, which Tamsin had been expecting.

"But the mangroves aren't safe," Calos said.

"You barely made it out of there yourself," Numha added.

Oman shifted slightly next to her. "Can you trust them?" he whispered knowingly.

She turned to him, remembering the night she had met him. Not only had he guessed who she was, but that she had help escaping the mangroves based on the wooden canoe she had acquired from the Islanders.

"Completely," she assured him.

"Wait, trust who?" Numha asked.

"There are tales of the mangroves," K'al said, her eyes squinting with curiosity, "and rumors of ghosts that wander the trees, their spirits bound to the forest, but they are not ghosts are they?"

Tamsin shook her head. "There are people that live beyond the mangroves, on islands in the sea." She could see the awe and disbelief on the faces around her, but she had to keep them on track. "K'al, have Rashu take the elders and the young to the place he and Oman found me. Just beyond that is an inlet into the mangroves. They will keep going west until they reach the sea. Someone from the islands will meet them. Ask for a man named Saashiim and tell him the Kazszura'asha needs his help."

K'al nodded and motioned with her finger and one of her kazsiin stepped forward from the shadows behind her. The other Kazserii motioned to their kazsiin as well, instructing them as Tamsin had bid and then ushering them out of the tent to put it in action immediately.

Even with the Havakkii and Baagh the tiger gone, the journey through the mangroves would be difficult, but once they reached the other side they would be safe. Much safer than the rest of them.

She took a deep breath. "And now about the amon'jii." The Red Sight still pulled at the back of her mind and whether it was a glimpse into their future or not, the idea that the amon'jii would be lying in wait for them while they engaged the northerners did not sit well in her stomach. "I have an idea, but I don't think you're going to like it. I—." She noticed several eyes dart towards the door and she looked to see another figure standing there.

"With your permission," Enok's voice flitted through the tent. "I would like to stay and hear the rest."

A murmur went through the Kazserii and even Tamsin was aware that this was highly irregular. Enok was a man, a sha'diin, and an Exile and just one of those things would be enough to bar him from this meeting, but Tamsin also trusted him. "Of course, Enok," she said, nodding.

He echoed her nod, flicked his fingers in respect, then took his place.

Tamsin turned back to the Kazserii, but Enok's presence seemed to have ushered a new air of foreboding as they waited to hear what she would say next. "The amon'jii are amassing in the Ravine of Bones. They have a leader and are just waiting until he gives the order to attack us."

"You make them sound intelligent," Isillah said disdainfully. "Like they are capable of making a coordinated attack."

"They've done it once before," Oman said.

Tamsin nodded. "And they're going to do it again in greater numbers. But instead of waiting for them, why not us pick the time and place?"

"You want them to attack us?" Calos asked.

"Not quite. If we succeed in breaking the dam, we have the chance to take out two enemies instead of one. If it works, we'll never have to worry about the amon'jii again."

"You want to lure the amon'jii out so they're right in the water's path when the dam breaks," Numha said.

Several hushed whispers went around the tent, reacting to the idea.

"Yes," Tamsin said. "If we wait for the amon'jii to attack us at a time of their choosing, we won't stand a chance. Even if we post sentries we won't have enough people to defeat them. And if they choose to come at night it will be even worse. There are not enough Watchers to protect everyone. They would be killed first and then the rest of us would be next."

"How many amon'jii are in the Ravine?" Calos asked.

Tamsin glanced at Oman. "Hundreds. Maybe more." She scanned the room to see what their faces gave away.

Finally, K'al asked, "Watcher Oman, what do you think?"

All eyes turned to the silent hunter, his expression hidden under his n'qab, and there was not one of them who would speak before him as he processed this idea. He leaned forward a little, his elbows resting on his knees and his hands in his lap.

"You warned us we would not like it," he said and made a deep humming sound in the back of his throat. Then, "You have proposed to us a way to make the marshes safe, perhaps for a very long time. It is something no Watcher has been able to do for thousands of years. What you are offering…is peace. And I believe that it is worth the risk." Then he leaned back and was quiet again.

"Thank you, Oman," Tamsin said. She knew the Watchers already supported her but having them support her plan against the amon'jii was a welcome validation.

"How do you plan on luring the amon'jii out?" someone asked.

This was perhaps the part that intimidated her even more than the thought of facing an amon'jii hoard. She would have to face their master.

"I will need to discuss that with the Watchers."

Numha narrowed her eyes a moment and then addressed the Kazserii. "With the waterways gone, we are about three days away from reaching the western edge of the anasii hada."

"We've already sent teams of scouts ahead to find a good place to make camp and also to make sure the way is clear of any lingering amon'jii," R'en added.

"Then we'll prepare our tribes and you can discuss with the Watchers further your plan for the amon'jii," K'al said.

Tamsin nodded and then one by one the other Kazserii and their kazsiin left the tent, each making the sign of respect to Tamsin as they did. And then it was only Tamsin, Oman, Enok, Numha, and R'en left around the crackling fire.

"Now, how do you propose on luring the amon'jii out of the Ravine?" Numha asked.

Tamsin took a deep breath. "When I first held Haven's firestone, back in Empyria, something happened. There was a…presence inside it, screaming. Haven told me it felt like someone else was trying to take control away from him. I believe now that same person is the same one that is leading the amon'jii."

"The one from your dreams," Numha said.

There was a slight rustle as R'en took a step forward. "Someone tried to take control of his firestone? How?"

Oman held up his hand to silence her. "You think you can reverse the contact," he said, "and send a message back to their leader."

Tamsin nodded. "If it works, I will show him our army. Lure the amon'jii out of the Ravine and to the mouth of the river." She had already made contact with the Master, she was sure of it from her last dream, but even then it was as if she was a bystander, a shadow. She was convinced that if she wanted to communicate, then she would need to use a firestone.

"Tamsin," Oman warned, "using the firestone like that...is dangerous."

"I know," Tamsin said. "And I won't force any of the Watchers to risk themselves for this. When Haven tried to describe what it felt like...he was clearly shaken by it."

"I wasn't talking about us."

"How long would it take the amon'jii to reach the mouth of the river from the Ravine?" Numha asked.

Oman thought for a moment. "Two nights, maybe less. But Tamsin..."

"Do you think it will work?" Tamsin asked earnestly. "You know more about the amon'jii, about the firestones than I do. Do you think it can work?"

"There are stories, old stories of Watchers using the firestones to communicate with each other, but that knowledge, if it were ever true, is lost to us."

"But Tamsin has already shown she can do extraordinary things," Numha said. "She has gifts that go beyond even the Watchers."

"And Enrik told me that Mr. Monstran is in possession of one, another other than Haven's. Maybe that's how he communicates with the amon'jii leader."

Oman was on edge about it, that much was clear. "I have sent for Zaful already. Don't do anything until we speak with him, okay?"

Tamsin didn't want to wait very long. If she could draw the amon'jii out, it would give the Exiles a better chance of making it in and out alive without the beasts roaming the tunnels, if they weren't there already. But she nodded, knowing it would take precise planning to time everything out just right.

The others eventually sidled out of the canvassed tent, but Tamsin asked Enok to stay behind for a moment. He had remained quiet after his late entrance and though it was not out of character for him to be so, she wanted to know why he had wanted to be there at all.

His answer wasn't what she expected, however. "Before we left the marshes," he said, "I was training to become one of the sh'lomiin."

"You were a story keeper? You know Zaful then?"

"Yes, I knew him. He's been a sh'lomiin for a very long time."

"And what about you? You're back now. Do you want to resume your training?"

Enok's eyes twinkled warmly as he smiled. "I never stopped. I may not know all the stories of my people yet, but I do have new ones to add. That's why I wanted to be here. It may not seem like it to you, but these are important times we're in, difficult, yes, but important. And I think someone should be there to hear it all."

Tamsin had never thought of it that way before, about what they were doing as someday being a part of the Ma'diin's history. But it would be, whether they won or not. She felt the weight of it start to settle on her, as if their future history was waiting to know, along with the rest of them, what would become of them.

"Do you think it could work, Enok? Do you think the firestones can be used?" She was aware of history's gaze upon her now, watching her every decision.

"I have seen stranger things happen," he said. "And if it is possible, I would put our best chance with you. Though Oman is right. It could be dangerous." He leaned in then, studying her face as if to ascertain the thoughts behind it. "But that doesn't deter you, does it?"

Even with history's judgement looming over her, she wasn't about to change her mind. If she was to be remembered, it was going to be for her actions, not for the wheels of doubt that churned in her mind, resurfacing like a full moon. "You said these are important times. If I don't take risks now, then when?"

Chapter Fourteen

Tamsin looked at her untouched bowl of padi and pushed it away. Hunger eluded her midst Numha's insistence that she eat something. But Tamsin knew she wouldn't be able to until Oman came back with Zaful. Using the firestone to make a connection with the amon'jii leader was pressing more and more on her mind.

Numha sighed at her. "If Kellan is what's troubling you, I have news."

Tamsin looked up. It had been several days since Kellan had taken that blow of lightning and he had yet to wake up. The Watchers kept her updated on his condition, but it hadn't changed, and they were running out of time before the entire camp moved and made its way to the anasii hada.

"What news?" she asked.

"Oman told me if Kellan does not wake up by tomorrow, there are some sha'diin who are willing to take him and catch up with the others headed to the mangroves."

Tamsin knew Oman didn't want to lose any more fighting men, but they couldn't take Kellan with them in his condition. She knew he would be safer with the others and though she wished she could have spoken to him again she didn't want to be worrying about him when she needed to focus the most.

"Thank you, Numha. That does help a bit."

Numha nodded and went over to the muudhiif door just as R'en came in. R'en stopped her and the two spoke in hushed tones for a moment, just long enough to peak Tamsin's interest.

"What is it?" Tamsin asked.

"There is a man outside," R'en said. "I do not know his name, but he's been lurking around the camp."

"Is he Tamsin'diin?"

"He is a *kriiva*," Numha said with a frown.

"What is that?" Tamsin asked.

"He wears a black cord around his neck with two knots hanging down the front. It means his family is dead," R'en said.

Tamsin breathed in sharply. The man was a widower. "But Poma lost her husband and she wears no cord."

"Women do not wear them," R'en said. "Women can mourn their husbands, but they will find another. It is not so with the men. They must show their devotion to their mates even beyond death."

The Ma'diin's customs on marriage and courting made the Delmarian way seem like a stroll through the garden, Tamsin thought. "Will you bring him to me?" Tamsin asked. "I don't want any of the sha'diin to be afraid of me, especially if they need help." She knew rumors had already spread about what happened to Kellan. Maybe their new Kazsera could summon lightning at will and would strike anyone down who opposed her.

"A little fear is never a bad thing," R'en said.

"R'en," Tamsin said, reproachfully.

"I'll find him," R'en replied and she and Numha left the muudhiif.

It wasn't long before R'en returned with the man and Tamsin instantly noticed there was something strange about him. Outwardly he appeared as many of the other sha'diin did. He wore loose pants and an open vest that displayed a body that worked hard for his living. His dark hair fell in several braids that brushed the tops of his shoulders. Though looking closer, Tamsin could see the frayed strands that escaped, as if they hadn't been re-braided in quite some time. But that wasn't what felt strange about him. Maybe it was the way he stared at her, unblinking with deep brown eyes set under a heavy brow. Or how still he stood.

"Would you like me to stay?" R'en asked, seeming to sense the same thing Tamsin did.

But Tamsin shook her head no, her eyes returning to the cord that hung around the man's neck. She didn't want to judge the man before she knew his story.

R'en nodded and slowly left the muudhiif. Tamsin knew she wouldn't be far if she needed her.

"What's your name?" Tamsin asked him.

"Ko'ran," he replied, his voice as intense as his gaze.

"And who is your Kazsera?"

"You are."

She allowed a small smile. "Before me."

"I was Ysallah'diin."

"Oh, I am sorry," she said.

"And then Hazees'diin after Ysallah passed."

"Then I am even more sorry," she said. It must have been hard enough to lose one's Kazsera and then be forced to join another, let alone Hazees'. Though none of this answered her real questions. She wondered if his family had been lost before all this took place or because of it. "If there is something I can do to help you, Ko'ran, please tell me," she said in earnest.

Ko'ran then flicked his fingers over his hand in the sign of respect, and only then did Tamsin realize he hadn't done it upon entering the muudhiif. Another strange sign.

"It is what I can do to help you," he said, bowing his head and finally breaking his intense stare. "I wish to offer myself to you, as you are now my Kazsera. It is your right to claim me."

Tamsin's forehead rippled together. "Claim you? I don't think I understand." His offer puzzled her. She thought back to the rules of the Kapu'era that Numha had explained to her; perhaps it had something to do over her victory of Hazees. But if he already thought of Tamsin as his new Kazsera, why was he coming to her now?

His eyes looked up. "I offer myself to you, Tamsinkazsera, as your kazsiin."

"Kazsiin?" Tamsin was even more confused for a moment. "Wh—?" And then it hit her. Numha had told her that a man was only asked to be a Kazsera's kazsiin if she was romantically inclined towards him. "Oh seven hells," she breathed, feeling her face flush. "Um, I'm sorry, I appreciate your offer, but I—I do not require that of you."

Ko'ran bowed deeper. "I am sorry to have offended you Kazsera."

"No, I'm not offended," Tamsin said quickly. "I just don't understand...why?"

Ko'ran looked up again, his features softening a little. "I was kazsiin to Ysallah for seven years. We had a child together, a little girl." His hand drifted up to the cord around his neck. "But she died.

And then when Ysallah passed Hazees took me for one of her own kazsiin. It was her right to do so, but she didn't do it because of that. She did so because..."

"She was cruel," Tamsin finished, finding her loathing for Hazees growing even beyond her death.

Ko'ran nodded and Tamsin couldn't help but feel pity for the man for he had lost his child, his Kazsera, his tribe, and then been used like some kind of trophy in Hazees' power games.

"I thought if I offered myself to you first, it would be easier and you would be inclined to show mercy instead of malice."

"I am not cruel like Hazees was," Tamsin said, "nor do I wish to replace what Ysallah meant to you." But something else prodded the back of her mind. "Why would you need my mercy?" But no sooner had the question left her lips than she knew the answer. He had been there the day they got back. He was the one that had given her the water skin. The one that was laced with haava. "You're him, aren't you?"

Ko'ran looked like she had just slapped him, but he was not surprised by her deduction. "I am so sorry, Kazsera."

"Why did you do it?" she asked.

"I was approached by—." His eyes squinted together. "There is one who does not approve of your reign." He spoke as if he was afraid to say the name.

But Tamsin could guess who he was speaking of. "You don't need to fear retribution from me, or from her," she said.

Ko'ran's countenance became less rigid, less intense as her words seemed to fill him with relief. "Everyone says you are a powerful Kazsera, but I see you are a compassionate one as well. I will not give you reason to doubt me again."

Tamsin smiled, moved by the man's obvious remorse. Whatever Isillah had done to manipulate or coerce him was not his fault. Tamsin had left, and by doing so she had left room for dissension to grow. She felt sorry that Ko'ran had been used like this. "Would you like to sit? I have food if you are hungry," she picked up her bowl of untouched padi and offered it to him.

He nodded in thanks and sat down across from her. "I would be honored," he said, accepting the bowl.

Tamsin waited until he had a few bites before diving further and she took the minute to study him closer. He looked strong, but was on the leaner side and his eyes had dark circles underneath them. But being this close she could almost feel the protective wall he had around himself, held together like an aging muudhiif, start to disintegrate. She thought she understood now where his strangeness came from. She understood the layers it took to protect oneself from grief, and then even more to pretend like the world couldn't hurt you.

"Can I ask you something, Ko'ran?"

He nodded.

"Did you and Ysallah love each other?"

He put down his spoon. "Yes. For a while. She was a bit older than I, but that didn't matter. But after our daughter died we grew apart. I did not handle the loss well. Ysallah, though she grieved, was able to use her sorrow to fuel her strength. She made it her mission to destroy every enemy that crossed her."

"Which is why she was the one who went north, to Empyria," Tamsin said, thinking back to those first days after the Ma'diin had arrived.

Ko'ran nodded again. "Our tribe lands were affected the most by the northerners' wall. Without water, more amon'jii would come and more of her people would die. I sometimes wonder if I had gone with her if I could have changed her fate. If she would still be alive."

Tamsin knew the 'if' game all too well and she knew it was a steep cliff that led to more guilt and blame. "Ysallah fought for her people, for what was right. We can't help her anymore, but we can still fight for those she left behind. We can finish what she started."

Ko'ran sat up a little straighter as if to shake off the dust of the past that was weighing him down. "I will do this. For Ysallah. For Lu'sa."

"Lu'sa. Was that your daughter's name?" Tamsin asked.

"Yes," he said, absently touching the cord around his neck again. Two knots, one for Ysallah, one for Lu'sa.

Tamsin noticed something then around his wrist. It was some kind of bracelet made from old leather and beads. There was nothing special about it, other than the fact that it looked—.

She inhaled sharply, feeling the bite of the past nipping at her and the absence of another particular bracelet. "Ko'ran, your bracelet, can I ask who gave it to you?" She held her breath, unable to take her eyes off of it. It looked identical to the one Haven had. He had given it her and she had lost it, after promising to keep it safe.

Ko'ran looked at his bracelet, his eyebrows scrunching together. "Lu'sa did. She was only four years old, but she was so giving. I could not part with it. Why?"

Tamsin blinked. "I'm sorry, it just, it looks like one that was given to me. I said before I would take no other kazsiin because there is someone else. He's the one that gave me a bracelet just like that."

Ko'ran looked at her again, that intense stare returning. "Do you have it?"

Tamsin closed her eyes for a moment, still filled with guilt about losing it. "No, I lost it."

"He gave it to you," Ko'ran said, though he wasn't speaking to Tamsin anymore, more like he was thinking out loud. "He gave Lu'sa's bracelet to you." He stood up suddenly, his chest heaving with each breath.

Tamsin jumped up too, her hand by her hip, ready to draw her blade. But Ko'ran made no move against her. He seemed agitated, but under control, for the moment.

"Ko'ran...?"

His eyes found her again. "Where is he? The one who gave you the bracelet?"

"He's not here," Tamsin said cautiously, unsure again of Ko'ran's intentions. "Wait, do you—do you know him?"

Ko'ran's eyes were bright. "Lu'sa made two bracelets that day. One she gave to me. The other she gave to my friend. He was like a second father to her. She loved him. She gave him the bracelet the same night she died."

Tamsin's own breathing intensified. Ko'ran knew him. Ko'ran knew Haven. And Lu'sa had been the one to give Haven the bracelet that he had given to Tamsin. *Everything that is important is with you now,* he had told her.

"He gave it to me the same night the northerners attacked us," she said. "He wanted me to keep it safe. I—I think he didn't think he was going to survive." Her mind darted back and forth through the memories of that horrible night with a new perspective. She had to be sure though. "Ko'ran, tell me your friend's name."

"Haven."

Tamsin swallowed thickly. "And is he still your friend?"

Ko'ran took a few breaths, the muscles in his neck stretched tight. "That is why I need to find him. Where is he?"

"Tell me what you plan to do first," Tamsin said, her hand hovering over her blade handle again.

Ko'ran noticed this and instantly flicked his fingers over his hand, this time as a genuine gesture. "I do not intend to harm him, Kazsera. I need to tell him that he is not responsible for her death."

"What?" Tamsin asked, relaxing her hand.

"Haven was there the night Lu'sa died. The amon'jii attacked our village. Haven saved her from the amon'jii, but she drowned. Haven survived and before he had even recovered he vowed before me and Ysallah that he would avenge her. Months went by before we saw him again and when he returned it was with the hearts of a hundred amon'jii he had killed."

"He said there were stories about him," Tamsin said. "That's the reason why." There had been moments in Empyria, Tamsin recalled, when she had thought Haven had someone else, a lover maybe, back in the marsh lands, from little comments he made or looks that had crossed his face. But it was all because of a little girl and her tragic end.

"Haven is renowned in the marshes for what he did," Ko'ran said. "But I don't think even slaying a hundred amon'jii will temper his guilt. Which is why I need to see him. Please, will you grant me this favor Kazsera, and tell me where he is?"

Tamsin's nostrils flared and she had to take a deep breath for speaking. "He's back there. In the Ravine."

Ko'ran's eyes were glassy with horror. "He went back?"

"Not willingly. He was captured in Empyria and the one who controls the amon'jii now has him in the Ravine."

"Do you think it's for all the amon'jii he killed? They are seeking their own revenge?"

She shook her head, closing her eyes, feeling the weight of everything she had to do.

She felt hands touch hers and she opened her eyes, but it wasn't Ko'ran's hands that held hers. She gasped as she saw the long, slender fingers of the Blue Lady cradling her own. She looked up and saw the woman she had seen only a few times before looking comfortingly down at her. The Blue Lady's sapphire skin shimmered like the sea underneath a midnight moon.

"You are not alone," the Blue Lady said softly. And then she let go, and as a wave comes upon the shore and wipes the sand clean, a rustling breeze floated through the muudhiif and the Blue Lady disappeared.

Tamsin blinked several times, wondering if she had really just seen her again. Then she looked at Ko'ran, who was staring at her with his mouth open and tears streaming down his cheeks.

"Did you see that too?" Tamsin asked hesitantly. "Did you see the Blue Lady?"

Ko'ran dropped to his knees. "Blue? No, Kaz'ma'sha. It was my Lu'sa. My little girl. I—I saw her. You are truly blessed, Kaz'ma'sha."

Tamsin was confused for a moment and then she remembered what Saashiim had told her about the Kazszura'jiin, that she appeared to some in the form of loved ones. Ko'ran had seen Lu'sa and Tamsin had seen someone else. But still none of it made sense. She didn't know who she was or why she kept appearing at strange times. The first, when she was little, on her birthday. The second, when she was lost in the desert beyond the Hollow Cliffs. The third, in the muudhiif with the Hazees'diin, leading Hazees to think she was possessed by jiin. And now, with Ko'ran. None of it made sense. What was the pattern if there even was one? What was the reason? And up till now, no one else had seen her.

"Please, take this," Ko'ran said, and he bit at his wrist until the bracelet came off. Then he offered it to her.

But Tamsin held up her hands. "No, I couldn't. It's too precious to you."

"The Q'atorii have given us a sign," he said. "Even the dead are with you. Please." He stretched out his hand again.

Even the dead are with you. The phrase made Tamsin shiver. What kind of enemy would she be facing if even the dead were supporting her? But she found herself holding her wrist out and Ko'ran tied the bracelet around her. Then he flicked her the sign of respect, tears still cascading down his cheeks. But he was smiling.

"I will be your sword and spear. We will avenge our loved ones and wipe this earth clean of our enemies. Command me, Kaz'ma'sha."

Tamsin looked at this new man before her, for he was not the same one now as when he came in. How such a transformation could take place, and so quickly, confounded her, especially when she was left with more questions, more uncertainty, than before. She didn't know why the Blue Lady kept appearing to her, but what she did know was that she would do whatever it took to protect the ones she loved. She was as lost as she had been in the desert, and then all she had known was to put one foot in front of the other until she couldn't anymore.

So that's what she would do.

Even the dead are with you.

"That man you met with is telling everyone you can talk to the dead." Numha and R'en walked into the muudhiif. Tamsin had invited them and the Kazserii for supper, but the latter had yet to arrive.

"Not with the dead, but I can't say that death herself has been silent," Tamsin said, thinking grimly of the Blue Lady's cryptic visits.

R'en narrowed her eyes then looked to Numha. "I can't tell if she's serious," she said.

Numha just shook her head. "Whether it's true or not, the people are believing it. Combine that with the rumors that you took down a Watcher and they'll be ready to sacrifice their firstborns just to be in your presence."

"I didn't 'take down' Kellan," Tamsin said, irritated that some would see it that way. "What happened was—wait, what did you say?" She stopped tightening the straps on her wrist guard.

Numha smiled. "All I'm saying is they love you, Tamsin. The Ma'diin don't actually sacrifice children."

R'en raised her hand. "I still don't know how I feel about her talking to the dead."

"What did that man want anyway?" Numha asked, continuing to ignore R'en's one-sided commentary.

"Nothing really," Tamsin said, not wanting to subject Ko'ran to R'en's wrath once they found out he had contaminated her water. Ko'ran had freely admitted to his mistake and even before seeing his daughter Tamsin believed he was on her side. And she wanted to deal with Isillah herself.

The others started to arrive then and quiet chatter filled the muudhiif as sha'diin flitted in and out with food and drink. Soon everyone was settled down around the fire, seeming to enjoy the mood that came with having a concrete plan going forward. Even Numha seemed relaxed, who was discreetly monitoring everything that was set forth before Tamsin.

Tamsin remained quiet, choosing to watch and listen to the others. Before the meal was over, however, she decided it was time to break the upbeat atmosphere. She had thought it through carefully and she knew this was what she wanted to do.

"Isillah!" she called out over the conversations like a sharp whip.

Everyone quieted and looked back and forth between the two. Isillah, who was seated across the muudhiif, met Tamsin's gaze.

"Can you tell me what would happen to a Kazsera if she was caught trying to poison another?" Tamsin asked, pushing her bowl aside.

Isillah's lip twitched, but she kept her mouth closed.

"You don't know?" Tamsin stood up and took a few steps closer to the fire. "Maybe I could ask your friend, Ko'ran, since he's already explained so much."

Isillah looked like a trapped animal ready to gnaw her own leg off rather than stay caught, but she held Tamsin's gaze across the flames.

"He is under my protection, by the way," Tamsin continued. "If he is harmed, I will know who to hold accountable."

"It was hardly poison," Isillah muttered through her teeth.

Numha and R'en both jumped up, but Tamsin held her hands out to prevent them from doing anything further. She already knew what to do. She took a few more steps until she could feel her skin sizzling from the heat of the fire and then with a simple thought, parted it. The flames peeled away from each other, spreading out wide like the petals of a rose until there was enough space for Tamsin to walk through without getting burned, straight to Isillah. She knew it was an unnecessary spectacle, but she wanted it to serve as a reminder. She wanted the display to be fresh in their minds.

"A single person should not have so much power," Isillah whispered with a lingering sliver of contempt as she looked up at Tamsin's fiery silhouette.

"I agree," Tamsin said, "which is why I do not use it often or lightly. Tell me, Isillah, is this one of those times? Before I killed Hazees, I gave her the option to join me. She refused and look where she is now. I'll tell you what I told her: what's happening is bigger than all of us. But I will only ask you once. Can I trust you?"

Isillah finally dropped her gaze, defeated. "Yes," she said softly.

Tamsin had the experience to know that even though Isillah agreed, she may go back on her word, but she also had a gut feeling that Isillah wouldn't betray her, now that she had been exposed in front of everyone. She might be bitter, but she wasn't vindictive, like Hazees had been.

Tamsin looked down at her for a moment more, then released the flames behind her until they were crackling normally again. She turned to look at each of the Kazserii present. K'al seemed undisturbed by the situation, Calos was smiling proudly, and the others were caught somewhere between surprise and judgmental distaste towards Isillah.

"Good," Tamsin said. "Let that be the end of it then." With that said, she went back to her place and sat down.

The others looked unsure of where to go from here, but they didn't have a moment to think about it before a sha'diin entered and announced that Oman was waiting outside. Tamsin motioned to let him in and subdued the fire a bit.

Oman's shadowy form loomed large over the seated Kazserii and kazsiin as he stepped into the circle.

Tamsin knew immediately something was wrong and she offered to speak privately with him, but he shook his head.

"No, they need to hear this too," he said gruffly. "I spoke with Zaful, the sh'lomiin, about what you had learned from the northern boy in the Ravine. The leader of the amon'jii; they call him

'The Great One.' His human followers call him 'Master.' Zaful remembers a time when he was called 'The Assassin's Eye' and before that 'The Enslaver' and many more before that. But they are all one being. We know him as Ib'n."

Murmurs and questions went around the muudhiif, spinning together in a quick blur for Tamsin, but she could not take her eyes off of Oman. Even though his n'qab was in place, she knew he was looking right back at her with those silver eyes.

"We are dealing with a god."

Chapter Fifteen

Tamsin paced back and forth outside of Kellan's buurda in the early morning light. The camp was already awake and moving as the Ma'diin made their preparations to leave for the anasii hada, though Kellan had yet to wake up and would therefore be joining the others headed for the mangroves in just a matter of hours. But in the wake of Oman's news, Tamsin's idea to use a firestone to lure the amon'jii out by communicating with their leader had been pushed to the forefront of her mind, even though Oman had now strictly forbidden the idea. She had felt Ib'n's power through Haven's firestone already, though she hadn't known what it was at the time. And she believed in her own power now. If Enrik was right about the firestones being used to communicate, then she had to try. But it was also Enrik's words that made her hesitate, remembering what he had said about the Master's power, how he had broken into Enrik's thoughts and manipulated him into killing Samih and stealing Haven's firestone. And she remembered Haven telling her how it had felt like someone was trying to take control away from him when the connection had been made with Ib'n. If she tried to use Kellan's, would Ib'n try to control Kellan? Would Kellan be strong enough to withstand it while he was unconscious?

But she had her own power and she was stronger now than she was before. And she believed if Kellan was awake, he wouldn't hesitate to let her try.

She stopped pacing and walked over to the buurda, her mind made up. Her hand reached for the flap, but stopped when she heard shouts not too far away. She couldn't tell if they were in excitement or warning, but they sounded urgent and a moment later her name was thrown into the loud calls.

She drew her hand back, wondering if fate had just intervened on her behalf. But fate or not, she knew she couldn't ignore the cries so she made her way towards the commotion. A large gathering had formed near the edge of the camp and as she got closer people started to recognize her.

"Kaz'ma'sha! Kaz'ma'sha!"

"They're back!"

"Quickly! Let them through!"

A whirlwind of voices bombarded her as the crowd parted for her, revealing a smaller group of men in the sea of Ma'diin. Tamsin stopped in her tracks and her mouth fell open slightly. Her eyes darted from one face to the next, though each held the same weary weight, with dark circles under their eyes and a hunch in their shoulders, as if they had been traveling through the night without pause.

The Exiles had returned.

But she noticed that neither Haven nor Ardak was with them. Her eyes finally settled on Hronar and her heart pumped heavily as her head tried to work out what this meant.

Hronar stepped towards her. "My Kazsera," he said, his voice scratchy from lack of sleep, though he could not seem to find any words to follow as the crowd quieted to hear what he had to say.

More were starting to gather around them, but Tamsin hardly took notice as she tried to interpret his body language, his tone. A part of her wanted him to just blurt it out, but the other part, the part that was starting to disintegrate at the thought, wanted him to stay silent forever.

Numha stepped up next to her then. "Did you find him?" she asked, intervening before her Kazsera's fear could take over.

Hronar rubbed the back of his head. "That's the thing," he said. "We found…nothing."

Tamsin's icy hold broke. "Nothing?"

"The Ravine was empty when we got there. Deserted. Everyone and everything in it are gone." Hronar briefly explained what they had seen, or rather hadn't seen, on their mission. The tunnels, caves, canyon…they were all bare save for a few items the humans living there had left behind. And there were no tracks or clues as to where they had gone. They hadn't seen any amon'jii on their return either.

Tamsin and Numha exchanged a look. There was a god on the loose and now he was on the move. And so was his army. Tamsin called for some food and water to be brought for the Exiles and sent out messengers to the other Kazserii. The Watchers as well. They had all spoken last night after Oman's news and despite the gravity of Ib'n's return they had all agreed to move forward as planned with their attack on the northerner's stronghold and the dam. Even now, Tamsin wouldn't change their plans, but the Kazserii and the Watchers needed to know this. They all needed to be prepared.

The people dispersed, spreading the news and clearing up the camp's supplies with newly infused urgency, but Tamsin remained with the Exiles.

"Where is Ardak?" Tamsin asked Hronar.

"There is a muudhiif not far from here—he is there."

"Is he coming back?"

"I don't know. He thinks he has failed."

"How far is this place?" Tamsin asked.

"Tamsin, you can't go," Numha said, already knowing where her Kazsera's thoughts were. "We are hours away from leaving."

"Hronar?" Tamsin asked, ignoring her.

"We could catch up before midday."

"Good. Take me there," she ordered.

"Tamsin—," Numha tried stopping her again.

But Tamsin was already set. "I will not leave him behind thinking he has failed me."

The determination burned in her voice and Numha finally took a step back, relenting. "Alright."

Ko'ran came forward then. "May I come, Kazsera? I think I could help."

Tamsin furrowed her brows, not knowing why he would want to, but nodded anyway. Then the three of them departed, not wanting to waste any more time.

The waterways were gone, so they traveled on foot, walking through the paths once marked by water but now hollowed canals winding through the dry reed beds. But even so it was not long before Hronar told them they had arrived. They climbed up onto a clearing, disrupted only by a couple broken clumps of reeds and what looked to be an abandoned muudhiif. There were holes in the walls and roof and splintered poles crossed over the entrance. But it was alone; there were no other muudhiifs surrounding it, no wooden bridges connecting it to other flats. No evidence of farming or any kind of use of the land around it. The dirt was a strange color as well, mottled with black patches.

"I've been here before," Ko'ran murmured.

"Whose muudhiif is this?" Tamsin asked. She thought Ysallah's had been the closest to the Ma'diin's border and this muudhiif had no colored banners or anything to indicate who it belonged to.

"It belongs to the Watchers," Ko'ran said. "It is called the '*cav'iif.*'" *The house of fire.*

Tamsin took a few more steps closer to it, eying it with a caution she couldn't explain. No one had mentioned this place before, not even Kellan. If this was where the Watchers turned their young proteges into night hunters like them, she wondered why Ardak would want to stay here. Though he had taken her to the shaman stones as well. Someone he knew was a Watcher. Perhaps this was where her mother was turned. It made sense then for him to be here, but Tamsin couldn't let him stay here, not in this place of misery and pain.

"You should go," Hronar said then, motioning towards the door. "You may be the only one he'll listen to."

She took a deep breath and nodded, then walked over to the entrance. She quietly opened the tattered door flap and stepped inside.

Ardak was standing in the middle of the room with his back to her. It was dark, save for the couple streaks of sunlight that filtered through the holes in the ceiling. There was a reed mat on the floor and several pouches hanging from hooks on the wall, but other than that the muudhiif was deserted, as if it had not been used in some time.

"Ardak?" she said softly.

Ardak didn't move or turn to look at her. He knelt down next to the reed mat and gently brushed some dirt away. Then he picked something up that looked like some kind of dried branch. He twisted it his fingers for a moment and then set it back down. "This used to be a *shavenna* plant," he said. "My wife used to make an oil with it and rub it on our son's chest at night. He used to get quite ill as a baby."

"If you come back with us, I promise I will help you find them again," Tamsin said.

A sad smile flitted across his face. "No, girl. My wife died before we left the marsh lands."

The silence lingered a few moments as Tamsin hesitated to ask the next question. "And your son?"

Ardak stood back up, slowly, as if he were trying to lift a fallen tree. "My son—he died here and was reborn here."

"Your son became a Watcher," Tamsin said, her heart aching for him. Ardak had been through more than any one person should have to in his life.

"It is why I go to the shaman stones every year. To see if he is among them."

"But he's not, is he? Come back with me," Tamsin said. "Oman will know him, surely. We can find out where he is." If they could find Ardak's son, then she believed that at least some of the guilt that was clearly consuming him would be lifted.

Ardak walked over to her, but his face still harbored the pain of the past. He lifted his hands and slowly put them on either side of her face, then kissed her forehead, as a father would a daughter. "You brave, brave girl," he said, when he finally pulled away. His eyes were alight with emotion, with his failures of the past, but there was also a flicker of something else too, something akin to pride.

"He was my best friend," Ko'ran said, walking into the muudhiif. He looked around as Tamsin and Ardak both turned to him, his own memories of this place coming forth. "He had been getting sick so my mother made cavast and told me to take it to him. But when I got there, the Watchers were taking him away. His mother just sat there and cried and I couldn't do that. I couldn't leave my friend. So I snuck off during the night and followed them."

"They took him here, but I was too scared to go inside so I watched through a hole in the side. He was so weak, he just laid there, didn't fight back, but his eyes were glassy with fear. They were sharpening their knives and saying they didn't know if he would survive it, if it would be more merciful to let him die. Another man came in with a sack. It dripped blood from the bottom. He whispered something to him, but I couldn't hear. Then they took one of the knives and dug it into his chest. He didn't even cry out. His eyes rolled back into his head and then he was still. One of the men reached in and pulled out his heart. My friend was dead."

Tamsin didn't need him to say the name. She knew who he was referring to.

"I don't remember picking up the rock, but suddenly I was charging into the muudhiif, screaming, ready to bash their heads in. But one of them grabbed me by the neck and held me like I was a wild snake, yelling and thrashing about. Murderers I called them. But then the one pulled the amon'jii heart out of the bag, still bright and bleeding and I could only watch in awe. He said some kind of prayer and pushed the amon'jii heart into Haven's chest. One started stitching him back up and the other that had Haven's heart held it in both of his hands. He closed his eyes really tight and stayed like that for a long time. When he opened his eyes again, he opened his hands and I saw Haven's heart. But it wasn't the round, wet muscle. It was slowly turning to stone. Orange and red and fiery and hard."

"His firestone," Tamsin breathed.

"Before the man had even finished stitching him up, Haven opened his eyes and started screaming. They weren't the screams of a boy. I heard the screams of a water buffalo that was on fire once, and that was more human than what I heard that night. I got sick then and blacked out. When I woke up, Haven wasn't screaming anymore, but he looked different. He was still pale, but he looked strong. I told him to come back with me. I could get him out of there. But he said 'no,' that he didn't belong there anymore."

"What did you do?"

"I left. The Watchers wouldn't let me stay anyways."

Ardak made a sound in the back of his throat, like he was choking on the emotion clearly marked on his face. "I'm sorry I couldn't save him then and I—I couldn't save him now. I failed him."

Tamsin's eyes widened slightly in confusion, but then the air caught in her throat and a crescent of tears lined her vision. "Your son...?"

Ardak pressed his lips together for a moment and the hairs on his beard quivered as his chin trembled.

Tamsin felt the tears spill over the sides of her cheeks, realizing why he had gone back to the Ravine and why he thought he couldn't come back to the Ma'diin. Ardak was Haven's father. He had left his son for a cause that would end in tragedy. Then when the chance came to redeem himself and save his son, it was too late. But it was not his fault. She pressed her hands over his and squeezed them tightly. "You did not fail," she said earnestly. "Your son saved my life more than once. He is strong and brave and fiercely protective. And he is gentle and kind. He is just like you."

Ardak, fighting to keep his emotions in check, leaned over, touching his forehead to Tamsin's.

"I refuse to let any more time be taken from us," Tamsin said. "We will find him. We will get him back."

They stayed that way for a long moment. Ardak did not cry or make a sound, but his quiet shaking was enough proof of his overwhelming feelings that Tamsin knew she now had another reason to get Haven back. Haven had only ever spoken of his father once and it had not been with great fondness, but she hoped if they all came out of this alive, then their reunion would be a happy one.

When Ardak finally pulled away, he took a deep, steadying breath. "I had no idea when I pulled you up from that ridge of who you were or why you were there," he said. "But you love him. You love him unconditionally. My son and my Kazsera."

"Are you getting soft on me Ardak?" she asked teasingly, but only because his endearment made her heart ache.

"With my Kazsera, never, but with my new daughter, yes."

Chapter Sixteen

Georgiana was ready. They had planned for days and she had even sent up a prayer to whichever old gods were listening because it was now or never. Today was the day the shipment was arriving from the Cities. And the rebels were going to intercept it before the Empyrian soldiers even knew they were there. Their plan was to create a diversion, not far from the city's main courtyard at the gates, which would hopefully pull away some of the soldiers meant to receive the shipment. At the courtyard, Tomas would lead a group to overcome any remaining soldiers, commandeer the supply wagons and drive them to the abandoned Urbane compound. Once night fell, the supplies would then be transported in secret to the Allard compound where they would then be taken through the tunnels to the rebels' hideout.

Her meeting with Reynold had not gone as she had hoped, but they had gained this information from it, which was even more valuable. With more food and weapons they would be much better equipped to deal with the soldiers and could afford to take their time to plan out their attack on the Armillary, which Aden assured her was still their main objective. She had not seen or heard from Reynold since that night at the tavern and he had escorted her back to the Allard compound. But she didn't mind so much that he had decided not to help them. She didn't care at all really if she ever saw him again. She knew that was unfair of her, to attach the anger of her father's death to him, especially when she knew who was really responsible, but his revelation had shocked her and would always be linked to him.

She put him out of her mind as she pulled on her boots and brushed the sand off her clothes. She headed out from her little alcove and joined the group that was gathering in the main cave.

Tomas, Aden and several others were busy giving instructions and distributing what weapons they did have. Fishing spears and scaling knives mostly, which was why it was so crucial to intercept this shipment. The Empyrian guards' weapon of choice was the crossbow and the rebels wouldn't stand a chance of taking the Armillary without a few of those themselves.

Aden caught her eye and started walking over to her, but Tomas stepped in the way, giving Georgiana a frustrated glare. He had not taken the news of her secret outing to meet Reynold with much pleasure or approval, despite the news she had returned with. She had hoped it would have earned her the right to be involved with more of the activities, proving she could be discreet and gain useful knowledge, but the look on Tomas' face told her the opposite.

She marched over to him, intent on arguing for her place among them. "I'm coming with you," she said loudly, before she had even reached him. Several others looked over at them, but quickly looked away, not wanting to be a part of the inevitable fight.

"No," Tomas said flatly.

"You wouldn't even be going if it weren't for me."

"Don't be petty."

She scoffed. "I'm not the one being petty. Just because I'm a woman doesn't mean I can't help."

"I never said that. And you can help. By staying here and looking after everyone while we're gone."

"They don't need looking after. They're not children."

The space between them had diminished with each word until they were nearly nose to nose, waiting for the other to break first. But it was Aden that finally pulled them apart.

"This is not the time for this," he scolded both of them. "Gia, you're not coming with the main group, but—" he added as she was about to protest again, "we do need someone at the Urbane compound to receive the supplies."

"Agreed," Georgiana said without hesitation.

They both turned to Tomas, waiting on his final word. Finally he agreed and went back to organizing the others.

Georgiana grinned. Waiting at the Urbane compound wasn't nearly as bad as waiting here in the Hollow Cliffs.

But Aden shook his head at her. "Don't look so happy. He's only trying to protect you, you know."

"I'll be as happy as I want," she rebuffed him. "And I don't need anyone protecting me."

Aden patted her on the shoulder, knowing she had been taking care of herself for a long time, even before her father's death.

"Let's go everyone," Tomas shouted. "I want to get there before the solders do."

Everyone grabbed their supplies and shuffled into the tunnel leading to the Allard compound after him. They didn't know what time the shipment would be arriving, but it was agreed beforehand that they would leave before the servants were up at the Allard compound so they could slip out unseen and then get set up before the soldiers had a chance to enter the courtyard. They lit the tunnel with torches, but when they climbed up into the kitchens of the Allard compound, the halls and rooms were still dark. They then crept along silently through the underbelly of the compound, not risking it all by making unnecessary noise. Tomas led the main group out of the compound then and beyond the walls, but Aden hung back for a moment with Georgiana.

"Go to the Urbane compound now. Look towards the courtyard. When you see the diversion smoke it will only be a few minutes. Hang this over the wall by the gate so we know the way is clear." He handed her a folded-up piece of fabric then, but in the darkness she couldn't tell what color it was. "*Be careful,*" he added.

She nodded and then watched him hurry after the others for a moment before setting off by herself.

The Urbane compound was a quiet, two-peaked mountain when she arrived, looming up into the sky as the grayness of the morning light began to settle on everything like ashes. The building was solid and unchanged by the desertion of its inhabitants, much like a mausoleum, and Georgiana quickly felt the weight of the emptiness around her as she stepped into its chambers. The last time she had been here was the last time she had seen her father. Tomas and Lord Regoran had shown her the secret tunnel from Tamsin's old room to the catacombs beneath the Armillary, where her father had been imprisoned. There had been guards still wandering the compound then, but she didn't see any now, so she made her way up the stairs to the tallest level, to Tamsin's room. She took a look around, but there was not much to see. All of Tamsin's things had been taken back to the Cities and all that remained was an empty bed frame, a cold, free-standing fireplace in the middle of the room and some aged paintings imprinted on the walls. She ran her finger over the crack in the wall that opened up to the tunnel, the crack that lined up perfectly with the painting next to it. The painting of a women holding a golden rope in one hand and pressing the other along the seam of the door. On the other side of the seam was another figure holding a silver vase, though the figure had faded beyond recognition. She wondered if the artist had painted the woman after the tunnel had been created and the golden rope was a clue as to what one would find down below.

She knew she couldn't dwell on this though, as she was reminded of her task by the weight of the fabric she held in her hand. Even as small as it was she still had a part to play and she would not let the others down. So she went back to the doorway and fixed her eyes on the courtyard in the distance.

The sun had barely made it to mid-morning when a large pillar of smoke rolled up above the cityscape. This was it. Georgiana gripped the fabric in her hands and raced down the stairs of the Urbane compound till she made it to the small courtyard. From there she climbed another set of stairs to the wall that encircled the compound and threw the fabric across the top so it draped over the stone next to the gate. A few minutes, that's what Aden said it would take after the decoy smoke filled the air. A few minutes and the others would be rolling up to the gate with their desperately needed supplies.

She waited eagerly on the small parapet, glancing at the alleys between the nearby buildings, wondering which one they would be using. She waited, but no wagons were forthcoming, nor could she make out the distant grind of wheels against the packed ground. She ran down from the wall and back to the main structure, racing up the stairs to get a better vantage point. The veranda on the third level encircled the entire building from which she could see in multiple directions. She shielded her eyes from the sun and looked out, but still she saw nothing.

It had only been a few minutes, she reminded herself. Perhaps they had to take another route to get here. She paced back and forth along the veranda, trying to dispel her nerves through the constant movement. She did this for a few more minutes, and then a few more, until she noticed something: the decoy smoke had disappeared.

She stopped, frantically scanning the horizon with her eyes, but the sky above the city was once again clear.

The feeling that something was wrong pulsed through her body like thundering hoof beats and she knew she couldn't wait any longer. She fled down the stairs once more and out of the compound, the sense of urgency propelling her faster as she raced through the city streets. The only thing that slowed her down was the sight of people gathered around as she neared the courtyard. People clogged the alleys connecting with the open space and she had to dart down a few side streets to find an opening where she could get a better view. She covered her golden hair with her hood and peered between two people who were watching the spectacle from one of the surrounding alcoves.

Next to the dry fountain in the middle of the courtyard was a wagon pulled by two horses. But the wagon was filled with empty barrels. And kneeling on the ground in a tight cluster, with their hands behind their heads, were the rebels. A contingent of no less than fifty soldiers surrounded them, their crossbows aimed evenly at them. A couple bodies lay on the ground, motionless, nearby, with dark stains in the sand around them, but the soldiers paid those ones no attention.

Georgiana could hardly breathe as she searched through the faces of the remaining rebels. Only when they were ordered to stand and start walking did she see Aden and Tomas. Aden had one eye shut as blood dripped down from his eyebrow and Tomas walked with a limp, his lips sealed in a grim line. One by one they were ushered through and placed in metal shackles.

The crowd whispered amongst themselves, but Georgiana slowly backed away, unable to believe that their plan hadn't worked. It hadn't worked…it hadn't worked…unless…

They had been set up. The wagon had been empty, which meant the shipment of supplies had been a lie. A ruse to lure the rebels out.

Spurred by this realization she raced back through the city streets, back to the Allard compound. She had to tell the others what had happened. They had to start planning a way to rescue the others before it was too late.

She turned the corner just before the Allard compound and skidded to a stop, hurriedly backtracking until she was hidden behind the building. Another contingent of soldiers was huddled around the gates, effectively blocking her way into the compound. She took a couple steadying breaths and then peered around the edge. Her feet had stopped racing, but her heart had not, and it quickened even more when she saw what they were doing: escorting people out of the compound in a single line. And they weren't the compound's servants; they were the rebels. The guards had found their hideout.

Georgiana pressed her back against the wall, squeezing her fists and eyes shut. She was powerless. In less than an hour, everything they had worked for and sacrificed for had vanished. It was as if a great flood had come and swept her feet out from under her. She was alone at sea. She couldn't go back to the Hollow Cliffs now. She couldn't go back home. She was adrift, watching everyone else sink below the surface, wondering when the waves would take her down too.

And the worst part was she was the one that had made it rain. All of this was her fault.

Tamsin followed Ko'ran and Ardak out of the Watchers' muudhiif, only to find that Hronar, who had been waiting for them outside, was not alone. Oman was standing next to him, cloaked arms crossed over his chest. He did not look pleased and judging from Hronar's perturbed scowl it seemed he had already received the blunt end of Oman's discontent. The elder Watcher rarely let his irritation show, but Tamsin suspected it wouldn't be pleasant when it did rear up.

Oman waited until they had all walked over before he spoke. "What are you doing here, Tamsin?" he asked, his voice eerily cold.

Hronar grunted. "I already told you, Watcher."

"Not you," Oman said. "Tamsin."

"I couldn't leave Ardak behind," Tamsin said firmly. "I didn't know this was the Watchers' muudhiif when I came, but Ardak is Haven's father, Oman."

"I know who he is," he said, his hood turning slightly in Ardak's direction. "If he wants to stay here, you should let him. Your place is with the Ma'diin right now."

Tamsin was a bit baffled by Oman's stone demeanor. "You're starting to sound like Kellan," she said.

Ardak held up his hand. "It's alright, girl. I'm grateful you came here, but he's right."

"If a single water buffalo strayed from the herd, would you go after it or would you stay with the group?" She turned to look at each of them.

"It's your responsibility now to care for the group," Oman said.

Tamsin shook her head. "Ardak was the one who needed me right now. The others can look after themselves until I get back."

Oman took a step forward and even Tamsin had to stop herself from taking a step back from his intimidating presence.

"I know how you feel about Haven," he said, "but that does not mean you owe Ardak anything."

Ardak took a step closer as well, almost as if to put himself between Tamsin and Oman. "She doesn't owe me anything, you're right, but she shows just how great a Kazsera she is by coming here. And I am still Haven's father and I care very much about him."

Oman turned to face Ardak, though most of his face was hidden by his n'qab. "I am more of a father to him than you ever were!" he said vehemently, pointing a finger at his chest. "I watched that boy suffer more times than I can count. I was there for him each time he fell. I was the one who taught him how to stand on his own. I—." He stopped himself, though his body continued to tremble with the force of his anger.

Tamsin finally understood why Oman was so upset. She put a steadying hand on his arm. "We're all on the same side here," she said softly. "We all want him back."

Oman slid his arm away. "Do you think it's been easy for me, knowing he's been trapped there? But I still do my duty, Tamsin." He turned quickly and walked away.

Tamsin watched him go for a moment, feeling each emotion that he left in his wake like the ripples that followed a ship at sea even after he had wandered out of sight. Hronar and Ko'ran shifted uncomfortably, but Ardak was the first to suggest that they follow him and head back to the Ma'diin, even as stricken by Oman's words as he still looked. They all silently agreed and walked back, with barely a look or a word between them until they caught up with the rest of the group.

Tamsin sought out Numha right away and asked about Oman, wanting to speak with him again and try and mend some of the scars that were still wounding him. The presence of the Exiles had shaken awake the past and though Tamsin realized she would never fully know the history of the men and women she had come to know, it was her hope to forge a future that was not overshadowed by pain and regrets.

Numha pointed through the tide of walking Ma'diin, but Ardak put a hand on Tamsin's arm before she could go.

"I would like to speak with him first, if I could," he said.

"Ardak, you don't—."

"I do," he said. "He's not wrong, about a lot of things." His gruff tone was still riddled with guilt, but there was also an acceptance to it. He patted her arm and then walked away.

"What happened out there?" Numha asked.

Tamsin sighed. "Twenty years happened."

The moon was shrouded in gossamer white strokes and surrounded by pastoral tufts of clouds as the evening light painted itself across the sky. The Ma'diin army was still finishing up setting up camp for the night as Tamsin wandered among them.

"Did you talk to Ardak?" she asked softly.

He nodded, but still didn't look at her. "I am sorry for my outburst earlier," he said. "I—." He stopped splitting the reed stalk then. The passion behind his words earlier may have been subdued, but he seemed to be still very much in turmoil over the issue.

Tamsin knelt down next to him.

"I'm losing them, Tamsin," he finally said. "Haven, Sakiim, Samih, Kellan... and countless more before them. The sun is setting on the Watchers and I can do nothing to stop it."

This wasn't like Oman. The very air around him seemed to sense his defeat.

"That's not true," Tamsin said, furrowing her brow.

At this, Oman turned his head. "Is everyone so focused on the northerners that we've forgotten what's coming? We've set ourselves up against a god, a powerful and malicious one. Ib'n has awoken once again. The end of my people has begun."

Tamsin felt the insurmountable sadness that radiated from him wrap around her like a blanket, but she also felt a stubborn defiance rise up to ward it off. "This is not my teacher talking," she said. "This is fear talking."

Oman shook his head. "Maybe. But the Watchers have already been thinned out. Our chances become slimmer with each one that falls."

"Don't focus on our chances," she reprimanded him. Seeing him like this unnerved her more than she wanted to admit. "Focus on the men that you've trained. That you've *raised*. The only reason we stand a chance at all is because of you." She moved closer to him. "I know you don't want to lose anyone else. But I believe we can still save them."

Oman unhooked his n'qab to reveal his intense silver eyes burning starkly against the pink and cobalt evening sky.

"What is your gut telling you?" she asked. "Not your fear, your gut."

His eyes narrowed for a moment. "That I should trust you," he said. He reached down and pulled on a string by his waist, releasing a small, leather pouch. He opened it and pulled out his firestone.

Tamsin's eyes widened. Oman had told her that using the firestones to contact Ib'n was too dangerous, but now here he was, offering his own. "Are you sure?"

He handed it to her and nodded. "We won't save them by doing nothing."

Tamsin looked at the firestone in her hands. It was similar to Haven's, but not identical. The same glossy black covered the broken surface, but the glimpses of color beneath were like silver snowflakes crackling through the darkness within. It was warm in her palms and she remembered the hypnotizing way the darkness seemed to deepen just as the familiar, hollow sound began to pulse in her ears.

It was happening again. But this time she had to be ready for it.

The world around her began to dim as the stone pulled her in closer, coaxing her away from the reed bed she kneeled on, away from Oman, away from the pastel colors of the evening. It lulled her into the abyss, into the darkness that was as alluring as it was mysterious.

She waited for the screaming to start, that high-pitched wail that sounded like it erupted from the pit of the earth, but the abyss was eerily quiet. She turned to look around, or thought she turned, but she couldn't see her body anymore, as if she only existed in her mind now. All around her was just an endless landscape of darkness. Even the hollow pulsing began to fade.

The silence was broken then by a deep, slow laugh, though she couldn't tell where it was coming from.

She-hunter...

Tamsin whirled around, but the owner of the elusive whisper wasn't there.

You are brave to come here...

Tamsin turned again, hearing the voice right next to her ear, but the darkness was absolute. She didn't need to see though to guess whose voice it was. A voice that left a frost on her skin like the first day of winter.

Brave, but unwise...

The frost began to harden as the darkness seemed to press in against her, making it harder to breathe and think.

Tamsin! Another voice cut through from farther away, but much more urgent, more desperate.

Tamsin spun around, desperate herself at the sound of Haven's voice echoing around her.

Tamsin, get out of here!

She started running, trying to find him, though the voices sounded no closer no matter which direction she went. But the blackness around her started to thicken, as if the frost was now pulling at her feet, creating a quagmire in which she would soon fall into.

Kazsera...Tamsin...come back, Oman's voice drifted through the dark.

She could feel herself sinking, though there was nothing to grab onto, nor could she see what was consuming her.

Tamsin! Haven's voice warned her. *Go!*

Kazsera...Kazsera! Oman's voice shouted, closer now.

I'll see you soon, she-hunter...

She fell forward, plunging into the emptiness as easily as if she were falling into a pool of water, but just before she succumbed to the disorienting freefall she felt something grasp her arm.

She gasped for air as the reedbed flooded her vision once more. Her eyes darted around until they finally landed on Oman who was kneeling in front of her, gripping her arm. He was breathing heavily and his silver eyes explored hers with worried questioning. The firestone lay on the ground between them, dull and silent once more.

"Thank you," Tamsin breathed, not knowing how, but knowing Oman had pulled her out of there.

He nodded, helping her sit up straight.

"Did you...could you...?" Tamsin started, but she didn't know quite how to ask if he had heard or felt any of what she just experienced.

The pink traces of evening had faded into the darker hues of night, allowing a few stars to emerge on the horizon. It seemed like so much light compared to the utter blackness she had just left.

"Just whispers," he said, glancing at the firestone. "And I could feel you starting to...slip away."

"You were right," she said. Oman had been against this idea, even without knowing the extent of the danger that resided within. Had she tried this on her own, she didn't know if she would have found her way back.

"We had to try," he said.

The breeze rustled over them, bringing with it the cooler undertones that the night promised. It reminded her of the frost. And the last words she heard in that place.

"Oman," she murmured, "He's coming."

Chapter Seventeen

It was the morning before they were to set their plan in motion; the morning when she should be preparing and going over every detail in case there was a flaw, but Tamsin had been woken up by Numha in the infant hours of the morning and told to just sit. So Tamsin did, and watched the drifting storm clouds over the marshes outside her muudhiif. They hovered mid-way over the swaying reeds, pushing the wind through them as if they were strands of stray hair. The grayness of the morning was just covering the night stars, slowly fading them to make way for the lush golden hues of the sunrise to dance between the storm clouds and the earth. It was much different than the darkness that had haunted her sleep.

She didn't turn around when she heard soft footsteps approaching, but she could sense who it was. "How do you capture something so beautiful so that you never lose it, Numha?"

Numha sat down beside her and was thoughtful for a moment. Then she sighed wistfully and said, "I wish I had the answer for you Kazsera, but I fear there is none. Either the beauty changes or we do. Even our memories get soft and hazy with time."

They sat there for a few moments, each lingering in their own thoughts and the evanescence of the sunrise before them.

"Beauty can sometimes be found in loss though," Numha finally said. "It makes us stronger, more grateful, and brings us clarity to see what is really important."

"Your age does not match your wisdom," Tamsin said.

Numha gave a slight smile. "Loss can also make you wise."

Her words stole Tamsin's attention away from the horizon.

"The last time I saw K'tar alive was on a morning like this, and he stared at the sunrise just like you do. He had his cloak and n'qab of course, but I was really good at reading his lips, his cheeks, even the speed of his breath. And that morning he was...sad. As if he would never see the sun rise again. He didn't speak, he just stood there and watched until..." Numha lowered her gaze. "And then he got in his canoe and left. And I never saw him again. And I don't think I ever will."

Tamsin reached over and took Numha's hand, her friend's hand. It was the first time she had shared anything like this and Tamsin realized they had more in common than she had known. Amidst everything going on it was easy to forget that everyone had a past, everyone had people that were important to them.

Numha squeezed her hand back gratefully, then closed her eyes and shook her head, banishing the painful memories. "Whatever K'tar faced out there, Tamsin, he faced it alone. I want you to know that *you* do not."

Tamsin's throat tightened a little and she found she couldn't even get a thank you out. Numha squeezed her hand again, understanding.

"Would you like to know now why I woke you at such an hour?" Numha asked.

Tamsin nodded, clearing her throat. "As beautiful as this was, I could have used another hour."

Numha smiled. "I know, but there is something we must do." Then she got up and motioned for Tamsin to follow her.

Tamsin did and followed Numha back into her own muudhiif. There were two women standing there in the center with small, respecting smiles.

"This is Eha and Shirii," Numha said, introducing the two women before her. "They will be helping with the *rahdiishii* this morning."

"The what?" Tamsin asked.

"The painting," Numha said. "Do you remember the ceremony at the Duels? When the Kazserii were marked with the colored powders?"

"Yes."

"That ceremony comes from another tradition. Before a battle, it was custom for the Kazsera to be painted, or brushed rather, with the color of her tribe. She then took a walk through the tribe and it was good luck to anyone who touched the painted Kazsera. They used to say in older times that battles were won by the tribe whose Kazsera was touched by the most sha'diin. It was the only time many of them ever got the chance to do so," she said, speaking of the Ma'diin's incredible reverence to women and their Kazserii in particular.

Tamsin then noticed the clay jar in Shirii's hands. "Won't the northerners find it strange if I am painted a different color?" Tamsin asked.

"We'll bathe you when your walk is done," Eha said encouragingly.

"It is tradition," Numha reminded gently. "And it will give the Kazserii a chance to officially pledge themselves to you."

Tamsin realized this was probably in reaction to Isillah's previous actions. If anything malicious befell Tamsin by the hands of one of the Kazserii, then the others would now have a true and legitimate reason to take action. "Alright," Tamsin acquiesced.

Eha and Shirii began the painting process then. Shirii removed the lid off the jar and Tamsin glimpsed the same shimmery blue powder she had seen at the Duels. Eha unrolled a long leather satchel with a couple narrow brushes inside.

"Where does it come from?" Tamsin asked about the powder.

Eha dipped her head respectfully as she laid the brushes out. "It used to be gathered from the pla'naii flower, long ago," she said, her voice light like a drifting song despite her age. "But that was even before my time," she joked at her own expense. Shirii seemed a few years older than Tamsin, but Eha could have been Tamsin's grandmother. Her hair was more silver than brown and the wrinkles around her hands and face mapped out a lifetime of stories and hard work. "What is in the jars is the last of it."

"Why is that?"

"Because the pla'naii only grew in the north, in your country, before it was your country. Before the Great Waste came upon it."

The Great Waste. She remembered how Haven had spoken of the desert around Empyria, of how it had been a lush, green landscape once.

Then Shirii approached her, a timid smile on her face, and Tamsin realized she was waiting for her approval.

Tamsin nodded and Shirii began removing some of Tamsin's clothing to expose her arms, legs, and midriff. She took a short brush made of oxen and carnii hair, dipped it in the pot of blue powder, and then lightly brushed a streak on the back of Tamsin's hand. "It is custom for the reigning Kazsera to be brushed in the sacred color of her tribe before going into battle."

Like war paint, Tamsin thought grimly. She was suddenly struck by a memory of the blue woman as she stared at the back of her hand. Both times she had seen her now she had been covered in the shimmery sapphire dust.

"Wait," Tamsin said suddenly, staring at the deep, velvety blue color. Her breath caught in her throat as a shiver ran up her arms where the brushes had touched her.

"Is everything alright, Kazsera?" Eha asked.

But Tamsin didn't know. She stared at the powder, unable to bring her gaze away as the world seemed to condense to that single hue that was as complex as the midnight sky. The look on her face must have been one of horror because Numha was suddenly gripping her elbow.

Tamsin nodded numbly, though her mind had never seen more clarity. The blue woman had been a Kazsera of the Ma'diin. Of *her* tribe. "I'm fine. Who was the original Kazsera of our tribe?" she asked, pointing at the pot of blue powder.

"The sh'lomiin would have that answer," Eha said. "My memory only goes back to your grandmother, and before her I know only a couple names from our history."

"Why are you asking, Tamsinkazsera?" Numha asked inquisitively.

Tamsin was not keen to divulge yet another oddity about her, especially one that had already landed her in hot water with some of the Ma'diin. *Well,* she thought, *maybe not hot water, but enough to try and drown her.* But at this point she didn't know if it even mattered to keep it a secret.

She sighed. "When I was with the Hazees'diin and the Ysallah'diin after I first came here, I had a...vision. We were sitting in the muudhiif at the evening meal and I saw a woman transform herself from the fire. A woman that was painted blue." Her eyes darted between their faces, looking for reactions, but Shirii was the only one to show a glimmer of surprise. "It's partially why they summoned the Havakkii to take me. But it wasn't the first time I saw her. Once, as a child, she came to my bedroom and spoke to me.

Then, when I came to Empyria, she appeared in the desert before Haven found me. And then yesterday, when I spoke to Ko'ran. He saw his little girl, but I saw the Blue Lady again."

"Ko'ran has been telling everyone about what he saw," Numha said with a smile. "You are growing more godlike to them with each passing day."

But Tamsin did not wish to be godlike. She did not wish to have the power that she possessed. Powers that got her friends hurt, that got her kidnapped by zealots, and allowed her to speak to barbaric creatures that would love nothing more than to see her blood spilled on the ground.

Eha seemed to sense her discomfort. "We must finish our work," Eha said, ushering Numha out of the muudhiif.

Tamsin felt shaky at best, but she knew she had to get over it.

"I have an idea," Shirii spoke up softly, "that I think could help."

It was the first time the girl had spoken. Tamsin nodded her consent.

Shirii whispered something to Eha, who nodded, and then Shirii disappeared out of the muudhiif, leaving Tamsin to wonder what her idea was. She turned to Eha instead.

"Why are you not with the others, Eha?" she asked.

"Others?"

"The ones headed for the islands beyond the mangroves."

"And miss the chance to paint the Kaz'ma'sha? I have been painting Kazserii since before your parents were born, but this is the honor of my life."

Tamsin was speechless for a moment. She hadn't realized just how important this tradition was. "Will you go once this is over? A lot of people could get hurt soon and I don't want—."

Eha smiled and patted Tamsin's hand, interrupting her. "I have never left my Kazsera's side before a battle. And I am too old to do things differently now."

Even as Kaz'ma'sha Tamsin knew she wouldn't argue with the woman. "Alright." Then she had another thought as Eha went back to arranging the brushes. "Eha, did you ever paint my mother?"

"Yes," she replied. "Several times."

"And did she—was she ever—?" Tamsin didn't know quite the right words to ask. Here Eha was, delighted to be painting the Kaz'ma'sha, and Tamsin's stomach was in knots thinking about what was to come.

But as Eha had said, she had painted many Kazserii and she had seen every emotion there was. "Scared? Yes, she got scared. She never, never let anyone see it, but I could always tell."

Tamsin mulled this over. She didn't know if she would ever be as brave as her mother. Every story, every comment she heard only added to the mountain that was the figure of her mother. Impervious, frozen in time as this great Kazsera, a leader unparalleled by any other, followed by those who vowed to never follow another even after death.

"I've never seen a battle before," Tamsin confessed. "I've seen little fights and the Duels, but nothing like what's going to happen. Nothing like what I've seen in—." She stopped herself, not knowing who all had heard of her risky experience with the Red Sight.

But Eha nodded knowingly anyway. "What you have seen has caused you to doubt yourself. But I will tell you something. Something that has been true for every Kazsera, from the first to the very last. Every single one has doubted themselves at some point. When you are responsible for others' lives, every choice can seem like it's balanced on the edge of a knife. If you let doubt rule you, you will get cut every time. But if you let those lives in, if you allow yourself to feel them here," she said, pointing to her chest, "then the choice ceases to be a choice anymore. It becomes a path."

"But if there are lives balanced on both sides of the knife," Tamsin said, "how can one be chosen over the other?"

"Who says the paths do not converge?" Eha said with a slight smile.

Shirii came back into the muudhiif then, followed by several others, each carrying a clay jar of their own. "These are the painters from the other eleven tribes," she said. "I thought, since you are the Kaz'ma'sha, that you might want to wear all of the colors." They laid twelve clay pots in a semicircle before her, each representing one of the twelve Kazserii that the Q'atorii originally ordained when the Ma'diin were created. The lids were lifted to reveal colorful, shimmering powder. Eha named the original Kazsera that belonged to each color, a virtue she embodied or an honorable deed, and then the name of the living Kazsera that held that title.

Tamsin felt her eyes water and her throat tightened a little. She nodded quickly, unable to loosen the words out of her mouth. The women converged on her then. Jars were opened, more brushes were laid out and the next half of the hour was a delicate flurry of hands and color, all caressing her with soft restraint and intricate detail. Eha directed them where to go: blue and gold on her arms, intertwining like vines, red and orange down her chest and midsection, green, purple, and more blue down her legs, swirling around her like a storm, black streaks around her eyes with pristine white circles dotting them. As they painted, Eha began to sing:

"Her light will be born under the watchful eyes of the stars.
Her heart will break against the rocks.
Her tears will replenish the dry earth.
Her iron will ring through the darkness so all will know
That the sun has risen again.

Hers will be the fury.

Her blood will bind the roots of all that grows.
Her song will rally the weary.
Her people will fall to their knees.
Her strength will embrace them and send them to the water
Where all began and all will end.

Hers will be the judgment.

Her sword will carve the truth.
Her voice will travel the world.
Her allies and enemies will succumb to the fire.
Her ashes will soar higher than the heavens to the place
Where darkness and light collide.

Hers will be the fury.
Hers will be the judgment.
Hers will be the choice.

Hers will be the tide that changes the forces of the earth and moves Gods and queens."

"That is what I used to sing for your mother," Eha said when the melody had ceased.

Then she and the others finished their painting as Tamsin continued to be entranced by the song, feeling more connected to the past, *her* past, than she ever had been. The words took her back in time and she imagined another woman being painted by a younger Eha, as she summoned the courage and conviction to face the world beyond the walls of the muudhiif. To face the untold adventures that waited for her. Tamsin finally emerged from the muudhiif, Eha, Shirii, and the others beaming behind her. She looked at Numha and R'en and the other faces gathered. Some stood up slowly as others dropped to their knees, but she could not gauge if her painted self was being received as well as she had hoped. She had trusted Eha and Shirii to know what they were doing per the tradition, but she wondered now if maybe she had insulted them all.

Then Numha broke into a wide grin. "Kaz'ma'sha," she said, flicking her fingers over her hand. "Follow me."

Chapter Eighteen

*"Spirits of the gods, fill our eyes with your presence.
We need your light.
Spirits of the gods, fill our lungs with your presence.
We need your strength.
Spirits of the gods, fill our blood with your presence.
We need your courage.
Spirits of the gods, let your presence fall upon us.
Turn the stars to rain."*

These were the words Tamsin heard over and over again as she walked through the Ma'diin. Some uttered it quietly as she passed, some were more vehement with the prayer, but soon it all became a continuous, endless stream of voices, filling the air around her with energy. It was earnest and at first a little unnerving, weaving through the people like a fever, but then it became more song-like, waxing and waning and giving instead of taking. Whether it was their words being fulfilled or the sight of the new Kaz'ma'sha walking among them in all her painted glory, Tamsin began to notice a change in their tones and faces. She knew the news had spread that Ib'n had awoken and was designing the destruction of their world once more, but she didn't see the fear of doom in their eyes. Instead, she saw hope and trust and bravery. The stakes were high for every single person and every one of them was rising up to meet them.

She knew what the people believed, but she was still hesitant to embrace it herself. Could it really be a god? She'd lived her whole life thinking that gods and religion were just stories that people believed to make the world make sense. But the world made sense to her without it. Good and bad, everything was a consequence or reaction to something else. People made choices and created things and the world was constantly shaped around that. There were no ascended beings that lived outside of those rules, outside of what could be perceived by the senses.

Everything in her world had made sense...until she came to Empyria. Until she met the Ma'diin. Until she had unlocked powers within herself that transcended what any ordinary, and extraordinary, person could do. She was no superior being, but she was living outside of those rules. Elements responded to her will, not the other way around. She could communicate with creatures as no one had done before. The world was not as simple as it was before, or perhaps, it never had been and she was just finally catching up.

She felt footsteps next to her, silent and weightless as they walked alongside her. She only had to glance slightly and see the blue shimmer of the veil to confirm who it was. Tamsin kept on walking, taking a few paces to compose her thoughts, but then she realized she only had one question.

"Why do you keep appearing to me?"

The Blue Lady kept in step with her, though none of the others seemed to be able to see her. "Is it not obvious yet?"

"I suppose it is," Tamsin said. "I can do things the others can't. And you knew, even before I did, when I was a little girl."

The veil shimmered as she nodded. "I knew, but that's not the only reason," her melodic voice cascaded over the Ma'diin's chanting. "You have one more question, little one, but you're afraid to ask."

Afraid or not, Tamsin had the feeling the Blue Lady already knew what the question was. "Am I making the right choice?"

"Only time can answer that, not I."

"But you're a god too, are you not? Or spirit? Don't you know how this will end?"

"I've been known by many names by many people, but what I am cannot influence the destiny of this world, Tamsin."

"But you can influence its people."

The Blue Lady chuckled, the sound floating across the wind like chimes. "The gods created people to shape this world's destiny. I only come here when that ability is being threatened. There is one who is already close to doing so. And you know his name."

Tamsin knew and yet she stubbornly wanted to refute it. "Why do the other gods not interfere? Can they not lock him away, like before?" She knew it should feel absurd; she was having a conversation with a woman who was neither dead nor alive about gods and destiny and the fate of the world, but she was strangely calm, as if for the first time she was exactly where she was supposed to be.

"He is not playing in their realm anymore. He found a loophole, as you are now aware."

Haven was that loophole. Ib'n was coming back into the world through him and away from the gods' reach. "And are you a loophole for the other gods? By appearing to me?"

"You are," the words caught the wind like a ship's sail and disappeared into the sea of people.

Tamsin turned around, but she was already gone.

"The scouts have seen them there and there," R'en said, pointing out the locations in the distance. "Their hunting groups go out from the western edge of the anasii hada; one goes north and the other goes west. The latter usually return first, just before midday. If you leave within the hour you should be able to intercept them on their way back. Are you sure you want to do this?"

Tamsin nodded. She had bathed and been washed clean of the ceremonial powders from the day before, but had been preparing for her endeavor for several hours already by sparring with the sha'diin. Not only did it tire her out, but she allowed them to land a few blows that sent her into the dirt. If she wanted to sell her story to the Empyrians, then she needed to look the part: weary, dirty, and desperate. Numha thought it was a bit excessive and kept a disapproving eye on things from the sidelines, but she didn't stop it. After they had finished and eaten a meal, Tamsin, Numha, and R'en had set out to a near outcropping of rocks where the scouts had been waiting for them. Tamsin had already said her goodbyes to the Kazserii and she didn't want her departure to be a huge spectacle, since she planned to return in a couple days.

"Alright," R'en said, "then it's just the final touches."

Tamsin handed over her broken sword, knife, and took off her boots and handed everything over. She held out her hands and let R'en tie her wrists together with some braided carnii hair while Numha undid Tamsin's own hair so it flowed freely around her to the whims of the wind. She had already traded her nicer clothes for some basic garments that looked as if Poma had allowed her children to piece together and then drag through the reed patches.

"Has there been any word from Ardak?" Tamsin asked. She had wanted to see Ardak before she left, but he and the other Exiles had been absent all morning.

"Oman summoned them early this morning," R'en said.

"All of them?" Tamsin raised her eyebrows. She had hoped Oman and Ardak had repaired things between them or at least come to a mutual understanding, but neither one had said anything to her. Though Oman wanting to speak to all of the Exiles made her wonder.

R'en shrugged, indicating she knew just as little as Tamsin on the matter.

"Do you want to go over it again?" Numha asked.

Tamsin wasn't sure if she was asking for Tamsin's sake or her own; she'd never seen Numha this nervous before, but she agreed it wouldn't hurt to go over the plan one final time before she left. "I'll meet the hunting party on their way back. I'll say you took me prisoner and I've escaped. They'll think they're rescuing me and take me to the anasii hada where I'll be able to see exactly what we're up against."

"And then?" Numha asked, even though they had gone over this a dozen times.

"I will convince them there is an army coming in two days and their best chance of survival is to negotiate, which they will need me for."

"Then you'll be able to tell us what you've learned," Numha said. "And depending on their numbers, we'll either take them hostage to draw the rest of the northerners out or—."

"Or we bring the second half of the army up behind them and cut the head off the snake," R'en finished and gave the binds around Tamsin's wrists one last tug. Between the three of them R'en seemed the most confident. But she was always one eager for a good fight.

Splitting the army up into two groups had been Oman's idea. One would approach from the west and the other would come up from the south against the edge of the anasii hada. This way they could surround the majority of the northerners once they had left their fortress and keep an active watch over their eastern flank for any amon'jii. Sha'diin had been assigned to communicate between the two groups. And once the way was clear, Oman himself would lead a team into the fortress to break the dam with whatever Tamsin had learned.

A hint of a grin crept over R'en's face. "I think it's missing something," she said, studying Tamsin's ensemble.

Both women knew what she was talking about.

"R'en, between the Duels and her run-ins with the amon'jii I think she sufficiently looks the part," Numha said.

"Do it," Tamsin said. "I'll just return the favor later."

R'en chuckled, then without any further pause raised her hand and struck Tamsin across the face.

Tamsin fell back on her elbows from the blow. Her anger instinctively rose up, but when she touched the back of her hand to her lips and they came away red with blood, she smiled. "That'll do I think."

Numha groaned in irritation and then helped Tamsin back to her feet. "I'm not happy with either of you right now," she mumbled and Tamsin and R'en exchanged amused smiles.

But then no one said anything and the playful, painful moment was over. The three looked at each other with varying degrees of gratitude and determination and they knew that it was time to part ways.

R'en squeezed Tamsin's shoulder and then beckoned for the other scouts to follow her away. Numha took a moment longer, but she looked like she was struggling to find the right words to say. So Tamsin simply nodded and then flicked her gaze towards the others' retreating forms. Then she turned away, before Numha saw how hard it was herself to leave again.

Tamsin dug her bare toes in the ground, listening to their fading footsteps for just a moment, and looked up at the clouds floating across the wide sky. She remembered the words the Ma'diin had chanted when she had walked among them, asking the gods for light, strength and courage. She bit her lip and took a deep breath.

"I'll try to be all those things for them," she said, "But if you have any left over, I could use a little."

Then she started walking towards the anasii hada with only the sound of the wind to accompany her.

Chapter Nineteen

It was like she was running through a memory, *her* memory, of the first time she had woken up under a buurda and had run away into the desert. But it seemed so long ago that it almost felt like someone else's memory, that she was merely witnessing it. She had been so naive and scared that all of her decisions had been based out of fear. She was still afraid, despite Haven's words ringing in her ears: *no fear...no fear...no fear*. With each step closer to the anasii hada the question of how Haven could live by this mantra grew in her mind. How could he completely sever fear's icy hold? How could he banish it from his heart? Even if it was not so much fear for herself anymore, but fear for the others she left behind, it was still fear that kept her running.

She stopped to catch her breath, wishing she could stretch her arms out, but they were still uncomfortably secured around her wrists. As she breathed heavily and more air entered her lungs, her thoughts began to focus again and she wondered: maybe it wasn't the absence of fear that Haven meant. Maybe it was actually saying "no" to fear. As if fear was a person one could talk to.

The sound of hoofbeats breaking over the rocky plain disrupted her thoughts and she refocused her attention to the direction they were coming from. There was maybe a dozen of them, trotting steadily east back to the cliffside still a good distance away.

She had misjudged the distance. Or they had taken a route further north back to the anasii hada. Either way, she had some ground to make up, and quickly, if they were going to see her. She started running again and shouted, trying to get their attention before they passed her.

"Hey! Over here!" she cried and then cursed under her breath as she realized she was shouting in Ma'diinese. "Help!" she shouted, this time in the common tongue. Though she had started speaking in the common tongue with Enrik again, it was still awkward, as if that had become her second language, its place usurped by Ma'diinese. She couldn't make any mistakes like that among the Empyrians, for she knew they would see right through her. She would have to play the part perfectly if this was going to work.

"Help! Please! Help me!" she shouted again, waving her bound hands up in the air as she continued to run towards them.

She saw several heads turn her way and then a fist was raised up in the air by one of the riders, signaling to stop the horses.

Tamsin ran a few more yards towards them before she pretended to stumble and then collapsed to her knees. Five riders broke away from the main group then, heading straight for her at a speedy canter. There was no mistaking they had seen her now. She didn't try to get up, but watched them closely as they drew nearer. She noticed some had one hand on the reins, the other on their weapons, but none were drawn yet. Even if they did think she was Ma'diin it was a good sign that they weren't just going to cut her down as they rode by. But she knew even when they found out who she really was she had to be careful. After the massacre at the dam, she didn't know if the Urbane name would be well received here. Some had tried to kill her father while others had tried to protect him. It all depended on who was left in charge.

The riders slowed their horses as they reached her, encircling her in a flurry of hooves. The ensuing cloud of dust made her eyes water, but she let it, hoping it would add to her disheveled and desperate appearance.

One of the riders dismounted from a large, black horse and approached her slowly. His brown eyes were wary, set under a cautious brow, but his sword remained at his hip.

Setting an example for the others, Tamsin hoped. She guessed from the uniform he was low-ranking but an officer, for his was the only one still buttoned all the way up to his collar. The desert heat could be unforgiving and glancing at the others, whose jackets were all unbuttoned at least halfway or tied around their saddlebags, she suspected the officer cared little for the usual dress code here, at least not as much as she knew higher ranking officers did. The others glanced nervously at Tamsin, then back to their commander, then around them as if they were expecting more people to jump up out of the ground. But the officer kept a steady gaze on Tamsin.

"Please," Tamsin said, allowing her vulnerability to seep into her voice. "Can you help me?"

The officer blinked in surprise. "You speak the common tongue?"

Tamsin nodded. "I'm not Ma'diin," she replied. Then, before the officer could ask, said, "I'm Tamsin Urbane. Daughter of Lord Eleazar Urbane."

The officer's eyes widened in shock, and even the horses seemed to pause their anxious hoof stamping. The other riders exchanged glances, but Tamsin focused on the officer, trying to gauge his sympathies through the surprise.

"You are Lord Urbane's daughter?" the officer asked slowly.

Tamsin nodded. "Did you know him? Before he died?" she added, hoping the knowledge of his death would add to her credibility.

It seemed to work. The shock the officer felt seemed to be broken by the oddity of having a conversation with a Lord's daughter in the middle of this barren landscape.

"I did not," he replied. "I was stationed here after the tragedy at the dam." He blinked a few times, finally seeming to take in Tamsin's bedraggled appearance. "Forgive my astonishment, my lady," he said hastily, kneeling down next to her. He took a small knife from his belt and sawed away the ropes binding her hands, then offered his own to support her. "Can you stand?"

Tamsin nodded and let him help her back to her feet. She grimaced a little as she stood, though only to hide her smile knowing she had secured his sympathy.

"Thank you…I'm sorry, I don't know your name."

He cleared his throat a little. "Lieutenant Farrows," he replied, keeping a steady hold on her elbows, as if he expected her to topple over again at any moment. "How is it that you came to be here, my lady?"

This was it. "We were going back to the Cities, but our caravan was attacked and I was taken captive. The Ma'diin brought me here, where I've been their prisoner." She blinked a few times, as if she'd lost her bearings. "Where is here exactly?"

"We're not far from our outpost, where the dam is," Lt. Farrows replied, almost offhandedly. "How long have they held you prisoner? How did you escape?"

Tamsin let a fearful expression cross her face and her eyes dart around past the others. "I can tell you later, but we have to get out of here now," she said quickly. "They'll come looking for me and I can't—I can't go back there," she said, letting each word become a little more frantic than the last. She took a step and let her knees buckle, but Lt. Farrows hold on her was sure and he kept her upright. She looked up into his concerned brown eyes. "And I couldn't forgive myself if they found you because of me."

"Your chivalry rivals the best of us," he replied.

"We're not afraid of those mud-loving savages," one of the other riders said and an echo of agreement went around the circle.

Tamsin did her best to freeze her expression.

"Stand down, Parsons," Lt. Farrows said, his training starting to override his curiosity. "Protecting Lady Tamsin is our priority now, not picking a fight. Go tell the others to make haste to the outpost and then ride ahead to tell the Commander of our coming."

Parsons nodded and then dug his heels into his horse's sides and they shot away like an arrow back to the main group.

"Can you ride?" Lt. Farrows asked Tamsin.

Tamsin nodded. "I'll do my best." She really wanted to ask him who the Commander was, but she didn't want to risk sounding curious too soon. She still had to play the victim in distress part.

Lt. Farrows pulled his horse closer and then helped Tamsin mount, lifting her up and over the withers with ease.

Tamsin slid her fingers into the horse's mane. It was an odd feeling, being so high off the ground, after having been without a horse for so long. It was both exhilarating and unsettling.

"Don't worry, my lady," Lt. Farrows said. He put his foot in the stirrup and climbed up behind her. "We'll protect you with our lives if necessary. Keep your eyes open men," he then told the others. "Form up!" He grabbed the reins and spurred his horse forward as the others formed a semicircle behind him.

The horses responded to their riders with eagerness, as if they were privy to the importance of their new mission.

Lt. Farrows wrapped an arm around Tamsin as his horse's speed increased. Tamsin tensed and swallowed a gasp at the pressure on her still healing ribs, trying to hide her discomfort. She felt Lt. Farrows' arm shift slightly in response, though it now shadowed her wound she had received from Mowlgra at the Duels. She gritted her teeth together and tried not to be frustrated by the fact that she still had to suffer the consequences from that experience. Instead she focused on the landscape leading up to the ever-growing ridge before them. It might be a short ride, but she still had a long way to go once they reached the cliff.

The Empyrians had done well hiding their entrance to the outpost, disguising their series of switchback paths up the cliffside with bolstered edges. Only the riders themselves and the horses' heads were visible above it and once they reached the halfway point, Tamsin saw the soldiers nested against nooks in the inner walls. Some were armed with crossbows, some with spyglasses and others with trumpets. Not enough to fend off a large attack, but enough to hold the winding path while an alarm was sounded. The path itself was wide enough to accommodate four horses riding side by side or a small wagon carrying supplies. The anasii hada was not as tall as the Hollow Cliffs, but the wind still whipped Tamsin's hair around her face as they ascended. She tried to see over the walls to locate the area she had instructed R'en to take the small group of Ma'diin, but everything blended together in a mess of brown and beige rock.

They rode all the way to the very top, or very nearly, for once they emerged out of the wide channel the path leveled off into a sunken plateau, completely exposed to the sky. Nestled along the plateau that, as far as Tamsin could tell stretched to the river's edge, was a forest of Empyrian tents and soldiers. The outer edges of the plateau were built up like the sides of a bowl and contained dark entrances to tunnels leading into the anasii hada, which were framed by stone blocks as wide as Tamsin was tall. This was not some temporary camp to abandon as soon as the dam was complete. This was a stronghold, one that the Empyrians could hold indefinitely.

Lt. Farrows guided his horse deftly through the maze of tents, ignoring the stares and curious murmurs from the other soldiers they passed. With each tent they went by, Tamsin felt more and more exposed, like everyone could see that she was an enemy trotting into their territory. She didn't realize until after they stopped that Lt. Farrows hadn't asked her a single question during the entire ride. She wondered if during that time he had grown more suspicious of her, somehow doubting what she had already told him. But after he dismounted, he immediately turned and helped her slide off the horse and didn't let go of her even after her feet were firmly on the ground.

The horse blocked her view on one side and a large tent on the other, but what Tamsin could see through the gaps looked much like what they had just ridden through. There were some crates stacked in a pile next to the tent and a short wooden table and chair next to a cold fire ring. The smell of wood combined with horsehair and leather saturated the air around them. The bold concoction was enough to set her memory nerves ablaze.

Parsons came jogging over to them through the gathering crowd. "Captain Tarney's been informed," he said. "He's gone to fetch the Commander—apparently there's a situation at the dam, but he should be here soon."

Lt. Farrows nodded. "Good. Now go and find Mr. Brennan. She's as white as a sheet."

Only then did Tamsin notice her hands were shaking. Her pride flared, knowing she had been through much worse than an uncomfortable horseback ride, but the more she tried to still them the harder they shook.

"I'm sorry the ride was rough, but you're safe now," Farrows said, leading her gently over to the tent.

Tamsin realized Farrows hadn't spoken to her the whole ride because he was concerned for her, not because he was suspicious of her.

"I'm alright," Tamsin said, grimacing as her entire torso protested that statement. "I've been through worse."

But her words seemed to have the opposite effect and the look of concern on Farrows' face deepened even further.

"Your bravery is admirable," he said, "but someone like you should never have to say those words."

Tamsin paused to look at him as a surprising wave of guilt washed over her, reminding her of what she was supposed to be pretending to be here. This man had known her for less than an hour and was genuinely concerned about her. And she was about to send him, and all the others starting to gather around the tent, straight into the Ma'diin army that was seven-hells bent on their defeat.

She turned to look at the other soldiers forming around them, all with varying degrees of curiosity and confusion. They were just soldiers. Men and boys, some about Enrik's age, just following orders.

Farrows followed her gaze and immediately gave them all a warning look. "Jameson!" he shouted, recognizing one of them. "Bring us some food and water and a clean blanket." Then he walked Tamsin inside the tent and pulled on some ropes, allowing Tamsin a little privacy as one of the flaps unrolled to the ground. "You'll have to excuse them," he said. "We don't often get visitors. And when we do they're never as pretty as you." He gave a quick smile and then offered her a chair.

"I'm sure I look quite a mess," she said distractedly, unable to keep from staring at the chair. It was just a plain wooden chair, but seeing one after having gone without for so long seemed such a simple thing. She was so used to sitting on the ground that she hadn't even registered its absence until now. She took a moment to look around the large tent. There were a few long cots along one of the walls and a desk and cupboard on the other side, separated by a standing partition. On the desk was a pitcher and a wash basin.

"Do you wish to lie down instead?" Farrows asked, motioning to one of the cots.

"No, it's just—it's been a long time," she said, brushing her fingers over the back of the chair.

"How long have the Ma'diin had you?"

"I don't even know," Tamsin said quietly. And it was the truth. "The days and nights all become gray and there's no beginning or end to them."

"I understand how that feels. I've been here three months and sometimes it feels like it's been years. Some days I can hardly picture my daughter's face."

"You have a daughter?"

"Yes. She turned five this year."

Another wave of guilt crashed into her, this time bringing with it a sickening pit of nausea in her stomach. She had underestimated the true impact of what would happen if she succeeded. Men and women on both sides would lose their lives in battle and leave behind a wake of orphans and widows. But the dam had to be destroyed, she reminded herself.

Another man entered the tent then and Farrows introduced him as Mr. Brennan, their healer. He didn't look much older than Farrows, but the mop of dark hair tied loosely at the back of his head and a beard that hadn't been shaved in weeks gave him a more weathered appearance. The one Farrows had called Jameson followed him in with an armful of the items he had requested. Jameson left immediately after setting the things down on one of the cots, but Farrows remained, grabbing a blanket and wrapping it around Tamsin's shoulders.

"Thank you, Lieutenant, but you may go now," Mr. Brennan said.

"Maybe I should stay, in case—," Farrows started to say, but Mr. Brennan cut him off.

"That stallion outside isn't going to unsaddle himself," he said with a stern eyebrow.

"Alright," Farrows said, "but if you need anything," he turned to Tamsin, "I won't be gone long."

Tamsin nodded and thanked him and then Farrows ducked out, though still clearly not too keen to leave.

Tamsin turned her attention to Mr. Brennan. "You don't look like any healer I've ever seen before."

Mr. Brennan was in a beige tunic and dark brown trousers covered by what looked like a leather blacksmith's apron. His sleeves were rolled up and his boots were covered in tan dust. "That's because I'm not one," he said. "Technically speaking anyway. I was the horse master until Mr. Athers passed away. Then the Commander asked me to step in. Taking care of horses and taking care of people aren't too different. Begging your pardon, my lady."

She waved away the remark. "I'm sure you're doing a great job, but why did they not send for a new healer?"

"We did, but our messenger returned and told us Empyria was completely closed. No one in or out."

Tamsin shifted slightly. She'd had no news of Empyria or the Cities since coming to the marsh lands, but it hadn't seemed strange up until now.

Mr. Brennan went over to the desk and washed his hands in the basin then dried them with a towel before coming over to Tamsin. "My father was a healer from Alstair. It's funny how we end up shadowing our parents, even when we choose a different path."

"Yeah," Tamsin said, thinking about her own father's journey to the marsh lands, wondering how much of it mirrored her own. Then she cleared her throat. "Though I don't think my path has been quite the same."

He chuckled. "You have me there," he said. Then his face grew serious as his eyes pinpointed the cut on her lip where R'en had struck her. He knelt down in front of her. "You don't have to tell me what happened," he said, "but if you're hurt, you don't have to be afraid to say so."

Tamsin's eyes unwillingly welled, unable to look away from the amount of compassion in Mr. Brennan's face. "Don't you even want to know who I am?"

"My lady, I've already heard a dozen rumors just on the walk over, but I don't need that to see what's right in front of me: a brave young woman who looks like she's been through the seven hells."

Tamsin's breath was shaky at best as she was in danger of unraveling before the kindness of these men. Of course the Ma'diin's mistreatment of her was all a lie, but she had been through a gauntlet of horrific events, things she could have never imagined six months ago. And all it took was a little kindness from these men to make her feel like a child who skinned her knee and needed a hug. Pretending was a lot harder than she thought it would be, as it was starting to scrape at the tough layers she had built. She knew she would have to be vulnerable if they were to believe her, but she felt like she was teetering on the edge of something, some unnamed truth she wasn't ready to face. Maybe she wasn't strong enough or maybe she was surprised at how quickly she felt stripped of the identity being the Kaz'ma'sha gave her. Brave or not, Mr. Brennan's assessment felt closer to her core than any title she'd received. Though she had a feeling the seventh hell was still waiting for her.

"Your ribs," Mr. Brennan continued, "are they broken?" Then at Tamsin's confused look he explained, "The way you're sitting, favoring your side."

Tamsin hadn't even realized she had been and she instinctively sat up a little straighter. She had been seen by healers before, but none had seemed quite so intuitive. Considering that horses couldn't talk, and as the former horse master, she imagined Mr. Brennan had to be more perceptive than the average person to ascertain his ward's condition. But she also feared for a moment that her injuries would give her away, as if he would be able to read her history from her scars.

But Mr. Brennan's warm brown eyes remained sympathetic and he was nothing but respectful as he waited for her.

Finally, she said, "Bruised, maybe, but not broken." She let the blanket that Farrows had given her slide down and then she lifted up the bottom of her tunic, revealing the true reason for her discomfort: the scar on her side left by her duel with Mowlgra. Her other bruises from the Duels had faded, but this one had never had the chance to properly heal. She had decided to go to the Ravine on her own before giving it the chance and the subsequent burn mark over the wound when she had attempted to speed up the process blazed an ugly trail across her skin.

"May I?" Mr. Brennan asked and at Tamsin's nod touched his fingers around the mark, pressing lightly in places.

Tamsin knew he was scrutinizing every flinch, every sharp breath, but she would rather have him see her wince than see the memories the physical pain recalled to the surface.

Mr. Brennan raised an eyebrow. "This isn't just a burn mark," he commented, though he stuck to his word and didn't pry for details.

"It was weeks ago, but I had to...*cauterize* the wound myself," Tamsin offered. She had to stay as close to the truth as she could.

His other eyebrow rose to join the first, but before he could reply, footsteps sounded outside and then several men entered the tent. Farrows was there along with two others and they all stopped at the sight of Tamsin with varying degrees of controlled surprise. Mr. Brennan quickly drew Tamsin's tunic back down to cover the scar and stood up to greet them.

"Commander. Captain," he said, acknowledging the newcomers.

Farrows cleared his throat. "Lady Tamsin, this is Commander Ruskla and Captain Tarney."

"It's true," Captain Tarney murmured. He was short in stature with golden blond hair and a round face that looked as if he was constantly out of breath.

Tamsin stood up to meet them, but was almost pounced on by all four of them as they urged her to stay. She slowly sat back down, then the Commander stepped forward. He was an imposing presence in the tent, built like a tall bear, and the numerous silver medals pinned to his jacket matched his close-cropped hair. Though his most striking feature were his light blue eyes, stunningly sharp as if they could pierce through ice without even trying.

"I'm not quite sure where to begin," he said, his voice surprisingly soft. "So I'll start here: Lieutenant Farrows has filled me in on the circumstances surrounding your…being here. And I guess my first question is…"

Tamsin held her breath. So far she hadn't sensed any malice towards the Urbane name, but she still didn't know who or how far up the chain of command the attack at the dam had gone or if any of the guilty members were even still here.

"… are you okay?"

Tamsin hadn't been prepared for that and all she could do was nod.

"I want to assure you that whatever you've endured is behind you now. Nothing will hurt you within these walls."

"Thank you, Commander," Tamsin said, finally finding her voice. "I'm sure you have other questions as well, but there's one thing in particular that is most urgent."

"Of course." He made a motion with his hand and Captain Tarney grabbed another chair for him. He settled down across from Tamsin and then nodded, encouraging her to continue.

"The Ma'diin are coming," she said bluntly, though she laced her eyes with fear.

"We know," he said as if Tamsin had just told him yesterday's weather.

"You do?"

"Yes, our lookouts have seen several of them sneaking around lately. Scouts of their own we imagine."

"We knew the chances of them sending another raiding party here and we're prepared," Captain Tarney added.

"Another raiding party?" Tamsin asked.

Captain Tarney suddenly looked uncomfortable and Farrows shot him a look.

Tamsin knew what he was referring to, but she wanted to see their reactions. "Like the one where my father died."

"Yes," Commander Ruskla said. "I believe it's in poor taste, Captain," he glanced back at Tarney, "to bring that up so soon after Lady Tamsin's incarceration."

Captain Tarney's already red cheeks brightened even more and he apologized.

"But Captain Tarney's right," the Commander continued. "We are prepared now. We all deeply regret the events surrounding your father's death, so we've made sure we will not be caught unawares again."

His words should have assured her that they had truly not been involved in those events, but Tamsin was not convinced. Perhaps he was truly sorry and he just wanted to move past the discomfort of a conversation like this, but that gave it the feeling he was glossing over the details on purpose. She would make a point to bring it up again, but for now she would continue to be cautious.

"I am grateful to hear it," she said, "but the Ma'diin aren't coming with a raiding party. They have an army."

"An army? How many?"

"It's hard to be sure, but there are hundreds, if not thousands, on their way here right now."

The light in the tent seemed to dim then as the shadows deepened over their faces.

The Commander was the first to speak again and his icy blue eyes now matched his tone. "How long until they reach us?"

Tamsin did her best to put a little tremble in her voice as she glanced down at her hands. "I—I don't know. Two, maybe three, days." The Ma'diin were in fact ready now, but they were waiting on her to gather what information she could first. "I do know they're angry." She looked back up, letting her eyes dart between each of them for a moment. "They, um, they—."

"It's alright," Farrows stepped over. "We should really let you rest."

"Of course," Commander Ruskla said. "We can discuss everything in further detail once you've rested. Communication with Empyria has been difficult lately, but we will get you home as soon as we can, I promise. But trust my men in the meantime. You are well protected here."

Tamsin finally nodded, consenting. "Commander, I want you to know that your men have been nothing but kind to me. They are truly extraordinary men."

"I couldn't agree more," he said proudly. "But I better be going. Lieutenant Riggs won't be able to keep the Inspector occupied forever." Then he ordered Farrows to see she was given everything she needed after Mr. Brennan was done.

"Commander, a word first?" Mr. Brennan asked, then Commander Ruskla nodded and they ducked out of the tent together with Captain Tarney right on their heels.

Tamsin's knuckles turned white as she gripped the chair, staring at the spot the Commander had left.

"My lady?" Farrows asked, picking up on her change in countenance.

But Tamsin couldn't respond. She could only feel the new weight the Commander's words had left on her chest. Lieutenant Riggs was here at the outpost. Enrik's *father* was here. And within days she would be sending him, and the rest of them, to meet their fate. But there was more to it: she remembered that night hiding down in the kitchens and overhearing a conversation between a man and Lt. Riggs and the day she realized Riggs was not to be trusted. She had told Cornelius everything she knew, but he had never told her what had become of him, or if he had confronted Riggs at all. But that seemed unlikely now, with Riggs being here. Cornelius had been behind the attack at the dam and if he had sent Riggs here to see it through it meant he was a threat. If Cornelius had told Riggs that it was Tamsin that had overheard him that night, then she was in possible danger. There was no way Riggs could be aware of her involvement with the Ma'diin…but he was in communication with the Master and the Master knew she was with them.

Her stomach clenched uncomfortably as she realized all this and she couldn't keep the realization off her face. She was dimly aware of Farrows gripping her shoulder and calling for Mr. Brennan, but her mind was swirling too violently to respond to him with words. When Riggs found out she was here, would he connect the pieces? Did his knowledge go that deep? Would he tell the Commander, or worse, the Master?

She felt suddenly like she had walked into a pit of snakes and it was only a matter of time before the viper found her. And once that viper struck, the others would join in. She couldn't let that happen or their whole plan would fall apart.

Mr. Brennan returned and she tried to wave them away, saying she was okay, but every time she said it she felt more and more alone. And that feeling made it harder to focus on what she needed to: finding a weakness in the dam. She would have to be stronger than that. She would play her part, get what she needed and see this through. She took a few deep breaths, for tomorrow would come quickly and she would need all of her skills to navigate the snake pit.

Chapter Twenty

Tamsin lurched forward, then gripped the edge of the cot to keep from tumbling off as she realized she was a foot off the ground instead of on her usual sleeping mat. She panted heavily, realizing she had just woken up and she was in Mr. Brennan's tent and not the dark cave that she had been dreaming about. As her heartbeat slowed down again, she thought about the dream and though she had been looking at the cave from the outside, she felt its cold stone freezing her insides. Like a dark prison, locking her within her own worst fears, unable to claw it out of her or risk losing the better parts of her along with the worst.

"Tamsin."

She flinched and looked over, only then realizing Mr. Brennan was right next to her, crouched down next to her cot. "How long was I out?" she asked, her voice feeling hoarse.

"Only a couple of hours," he said gently. "Are you alright?"

She nodded. "I—." Then she realized what had happened. "I was screaming, wasn't I?"

He echoed her nod.

The fabric of the tent pushed in and out slightly from the breath of the wind and then the front flap whipped open as a large gust intruded, but it wasn't the wind. It was Lt. Farrows. He burst into the tent like he was charging into battle.

Mr. Brennan held up his hand. "Everything's alright, Lieutenant," he assured him. "She's alright."

Farrows still had a panicked look about him, but his shoulders seemed to relax a little as he looked at Tamsin and saw she was in fact unharmed.

"I'm so sorry," she said. "I—I have nightmares sometimes." She sat up on the cot, remembering how unnerved Samih used to get with her nightmares.

"Oh, lords no, don't be sorry," Farrows said.

Mr. Brennan brought her some water then and she drank. It soothed her dry throat, but the lingering coldness of it only reminded her of the cave.

"Are you hungry? Farrows could get you something from the Burrow," Mr. Brennan suggested.

"In a little while, maybe," Tamsin said, knowing she would probably be sick if she ate so soon after a nightmare like that. Especially knowing it was no ordinary nightmare. "What is the Burrow?"

"Our community mess hall," Mr. Brennan said, "or as close to one as we could make out here."

"Perhaps I could show you around," Farrows said, "when you are feeling up to it."

Mr. Brennan shook his head at Farrows, indicating his thoughts on the idea, but Tamsin saw her opportunity.

"I think the distraction would be nice," Tamsin said.

"That's what I'm afraid of," Mr. Brennan muttered, shooting Farrows a look.

Tamsin pretended not to know what he was talking about, though she realized that as the only woman in the outpost, she would be more of a distraction than the other way around. "You wouldn't keep a horse that had been abused locked up in a stall, would you?"

That got to him. Mr. Brennan begrudgingly consented, but sternly instructed Farrows to return with her at the slightest change.

Farrows nodded and helped Tamsin to her feet and she let him guide her out of the tent. He walked her past several tents as the sounds and smells of the outpost bombarded her. Many men stopped to look as they went by, but most were polite enough to nod or salute Lt. Farrows before remembering what their current task was.

They stopped in front of a small tent, not too far from Mr. Brennan's.

"I have something to show you," Farrows said and he held open the front flap with a smile.

Tamsin stepped inside. There was a cot against the far wall with a small stack of neatly folded clothes. On the side was a stool and next to it a round oaken washbasin that was about as wide as her arm and filled with water. On another small table was a stack of towels and a bar of waxy soap.

"You did this?"

Farrow's smile widened. "I thought you would like to freshen up, and not where the rest of us go," he added with a chuckle. "I'll be just outside. Take your time," he said and closed the flap, giving her some privacy.

Tamsin looked around the small tent again, feeling the stack of guilt starting to add up with each kind word and gesture from Farrows. But as she sat down on the stool and dipped her feet into the water, she couldn't help but relax, even just a little. The water was neither hot nor cold; Farrows must have warmed it after she had fallen asleep, but it had since cooled, though just the submersion of her bare feet and legs felt like a salve for her nerves. She grabbed the soap and a towel and started alternating scrubbing and rinsing before she let herself completely fall into the trap of peaceful relaxation for she was still eager to see the dam. When she had finished with her legs she removed her tunic and started on her arms and chest, careful of the just-healed cut on her arm from the amon'jii. She wiped the towel across her neck and shoulders, letting little streams of water run down her back. And when she felt as if she had scrubbed a year's worth of dirt and sand from her skin, she stepped out of the washbasin and dried with a towel. She saw the pile of clean clothes on the cot and eyed them with a twinge of wariness, though she couldn't explain why. She unfolded and inspected them; they appeared to be riding clothes, not the soldier's attire they wore on a daily basis. She decided to try them and though they were a bit large, they were clean and not so different than the riding clothes she was accustomed to in the Cities. The boots he had provided came all the way up to her knees, but they served to keep the beige trousers from pooling around her feet. She rolled up the sleeves on the white tunic and used the sash from her old clothes to cinch around her waist. She then dipped the rest of her Ma'diin clothes into the washbasin and scrubbed them with the soap, vowing to return to them as soon as they were dry. She rung them out when she had finished and then hung them up on the side of the washbasin.

Farrows was there waiting, as he had said, when she stepped out of the tent. He smiled again and apologized for their limited choice in clothing.

"It's alright," she said. "I'm rather impressed that you managed to find something close to my size."

Then they set off through the camp again and Farrows pointed out different things to her as they went. The Burrow wasn't a tent as she had imagined, but a portion of the wall that had been hollowed out and carved into a rectangular cave. There were wide stairs that led down into the Burrow, which was adorned with long tables and benches and several cooking fires dug even further into the ground. Past that was Mr. Brennan's favorite place: the stables. They used to keep them at the base of the outpost, Farrows explained, but after the raid they relocated them here. There were a couple of canvas tarps mounted on poles for shade, but most of the horses seemed content to stand where they were tied, their noses shoved into grain bags.

One of the horses perked up at the sight of them, his nose continuing to rustle around the bag attached to his halter as his eyes and ears followed them. Tamsin walked over and scratched the side of his wide cheek, recognizing the horse that Farrows had ridden earlier. He dipped his head and blew out a satisfied breath through his lips.

"You're the real hero, aren't you?" she murmured.

"And he knows it," Farrows said, walking up next to her and rubbing the horse's other cheek. "There will be no living with him now."

Tamsin grinned and continued to pet the horse for a minute. Then she asked, "Do you think I could see the dam?"

"Of course," Farrows said, only too happy to oblige. "I would have to clear it with Captain Tarney first, but I don't see a problem."

Tamsin nodded gratefully as Farrows walked a few feet away to relay the message to another. Tamsin turned back to the horse, enjoying the feel of the silky soft hair under her fingers. "You'll keep my secrets, won't you?" she whispered.

Farrows came back and said it would only be a minute and he was right. Shortly after, the messenger came back, but he wasn't alone. Commander Ruskla was with him.

"Lady Tamsin," the Commander said, as Farrows straightened next to her. "Are you feeling better?"

"Much," she replied.

"That is good to hear. I also hear you're interested in seeing the dam. I thought I would escape my desk for a moment and join you."

Tamsin breathed a quiet sigh, fearing for a moment that he had come to stop her. She thanked him and then took his proffered arm as Farrows fell in step behind them. They walked to the far end of the camp and as the tents began to thin, the amount of building supplies increased. Rocks were stacked in piles and wooden beams were interspersed with pickaxes and ropes. They descended another set of wide stairs that ran next to a smooth slope, used for wheelbarrows and wagons, the Commander explained. The stairs soon disappeared into a large tunnel with a curved archway above their heads, but it was still big enough to fit at least three wheelhouses side by side.

"The Inspector was very clear about every detail concerning the dam," Commander Ruskla said. "We had a lot of setbacks in the early stages with cave-ins and flooding, which was why the outpost was set up above everything." He continued to explain the construction of the dam, the difficulties of navigating the caves, and how that had led to the loss of dozens of soldiers, builders, and even a few cartographers. But the Inspector was adamant about the location and detail of the structure so they pressed on. The dam itself consisted of one main one, but since ninety percent of the river was underground they had to add several smaller ones to seal up some of the lower caverns surrounding it.

"Wouldn't it have made more sense to build closer to Empyria?" Tamsin asked. "Or divert a portion of the river instead of blocking it completely?"

"Your father said similar things when he was here," Commander Ruskla said. "But the late Lord Saveen was firm with his instructions, even if they were a little vague. Perhaps he was hoping to expand Empyria along the river and produce more fertile grounds."

"Did he not think the Ma'diin would find out?"

"I think he hoped to hide the dam within the caves here. The only other viable option would have been the Hollow Cliffs, but being so close to the city there was the risk of flooding."

There were several smaller tunnels leading off of the main one that retreated deeper into the anasii hada, but just past those, the tunnel narrowed slightly and then opened up to the sky over a long walkway. On their right was a stone railing that overlooked a drop-off into the now empty canyon. On the other side, rose a wall so high Tamsin thought it rivaled the height of the Empyrian compounds.

The Commander started detailing the specifics of the structure, noting its height and thickness in a proud manner, but Tamsin barely heard a word as she stared up at it. It stretched up to the exposed sky like a giant gate, crossed with the embedded pattern of a portcullis. But there was no lever or mechanism of any kind along the walkway to either lower or raise it. It was a solid wall, just like the Ma'diin said. A massive, impenetrable amount of stone and human engineering that held power over so many lives. The one idea, manifested into the great barrier before her, had altered the course of her life forever. And yet, the awe she felt for it overshadowed any anger that had accumulated in her thoughts whenever she thought about it.

She backed up, but Farrows stopped her just as she bumped into the stone railing on the other side.

"It's remarkable, isn't it," he said.

Tamsin nodded, recognizing the awe in his own voice, even after months of being here. She turned around and put her hands on the smooth, stone railing, stretching her fingers out across it. The railing came up to about her ribs and was the last barrier between the walkway and the dark chasm below. On the other end of the walkway though were two large doors, sealed by a single plank running across them.

"What's over there?" she asked.

But before either of them could answer, another soldier came walking up to them. "Commander, the Inspector wishes to see you. He's in your chambers."

The Commander sighed. "Alright, please escort Lady Tamsin back."

"I would actually like to meet the Inspector, if you don't mind," Tamsin asked. Perhaps she could glean more information from the man that had orchestrated the design of it.

"You have quite the interest in this project, don't you?" Farrows asked.

"I do. My father died trying to negotiate for it. I would like to learn as much as I can."

"Alright. Come with me then." The Commander then led her away from the dam and back through the tunnels until they emerged above ground once more. Several men stopped their daily tasks to nod or salute him as they walked through the rows of tents.

Tamsin walked next to him silently, ignoring the lingering stares from the soldiers. The eyes that watched her weren't shocked by her presence anymore, but curious. Nothing was a secret here and Tamsin was sure every single one of them knew who she was by now, but none of them would dare speak to her while the Commander was with her. Though with each step that took her further away from the dam there was an added heaviness. Her task to find a weakness in the dam was slowly solidifying as an impossible one in her mind.

They went through the two stone pillars that marked the Commander's chambers: a series of adjoining caves that allowed him the only true privacy in the entire outpost. Doors had been hinged to the rocky alcoves and the interiors had been decorated to Empyrian standards. The outer chamber had a desk, several bookcases, an oak table in the center and half a dozen high-backed chairs. Candelabras had been mounted into the walls for light, illuminating the tapestries hung between them that were embroidered with the blue and gold colors of the Empyrian High Guard. Pieces of parchment and metal cups littered the table, evidence of the constant stream of work and decisions that came the Commander's way.

Already seated in one of the high-backed chairs at the end of the table was the man they called the Inspector. His back was to the door as they entered and all Tamsin could see initially was the edges of his maroon-colored robe and the top of his silvery hair.

"I'm sorry if you've been waiting long," the Commander said, walking to the other end of the table. "I'd like to introduce you to our guest, Lady Tamsin Urbane."

"Oh my," that calm, slick voice came slithering out, coiling around Tamsin's memories. The Inspector stood up slowly. "There are not many things that take me by surprise, but your presence here, my dear, is quite the welcome one."

He turned to face her and Tamsin felt the air freeze in her lungs as she stared back into the face of the man who had taken everything from her.

Mr. Monstran.

Chapter Twenty-One

Tamsin couldn't breathe. A blanket of frost had settled on her skin. She felt exposed, vulnerable, as if the tiniest tap of an ice pick would send cracks ricocheting through her limbs.

"Yes, Lady Tamsin's presence here has indeed brought a ray of light and beauty to our dreary outpost," the Commander said. "Though the circumstances of her arrival are quite horrific, her bravery and perseverance have given us all a new sense of purpose."

"Oh really?" Monstran asked, his eyes alighting with sinister curiosity. "That would be a fascinating tale indeed."

"Those barbaric marsh dwellers took her captive and she has survived being their prisoner for the last six months until she escaped just yesterday when one of our hunting parties stumbled upon her."

"Prisoner, you say?" Monstran commented, unable to completely hide the humor from entering his voice. "As much as it amuses me to see you so completely fooled, Commander, I must tell you that Miss Urbane is the farthest thing from a damsel in distress that she would like you to believe."

The Commander's eyebrows knitted together. "Excuse me?"

But Tamsin had let the surprise of Monstran's appearance paralyze her long enough. "Commander, if you care about the lives of the men placed under your charge, you will arrest this man immediately."

The Commander's eyes darted back and forth between the two and held his hands up in an attempt to deescalate a situation that he clearly did not understand. "Now hold on a second. Do you two know each other?"

"Yes," the two answered in unison.

"Our past rendezvous are not your concern, Commander," Monstran added. "You will release her into my care after my inspection of the dam is complete. Until then you will keep her under close guard confined to this room."

"Commander, this man is more dangerous than you know," Tamsin said heatedly. "He—."

"Enough," the Commander barked. "Mr. Monstran. Miss Urbane. I do not care what history is between you, but in this outpost I am in charge and I will not have commands dictated to me like I'm some messenger boy. We will continue the inspection, Mr. Monstran, and until we can arrange transportation back to Empyria Miss Urbane will stay in our care."

A look of dangerous irritation passed over Monstran's face as if he had been pricked by a thorn and could not get the sliver out. "May I remind you, Commander, that it is Lord Saveen who commands you and your entire army here and it is his orders that I oversee operations here."

"And I am sure Lord Saveen would want me to ensure his fiancé's safe return."

"Ah," Mr. Monstran said, amusement returning to his face. "Still playing that game, are we?" He smiled at Tamsin.

"Lady Tamsin has endured much and has even provided us with crucial information regarding the Ma'diin's army. Even as we speak they are gathering on our western front so if we could please continue with the inspection, Mr. Monstran, I have much to deal with at the moment."

"The Ma'diin army? I'm impressed Miss Urbane. You've managed to fool almost everyone with your many masks. Prisoner, fiancé, ally. To the Empyrians you are their lady. To the Ma'diin you are their spy. But only I know where your true loyalty lies."

Tamsin's nostrils flared as she glared at him. "You know nothing, you wicked, vind—."

"Tsk tsk," Monstran said and even the Commander glanced at her in surprise. "That is no language for a lady."

"It is when the person deserves it. Especially when that man is nothing but a liar and a murderer."

"You try to wound me, Miss Urbane, but I'm not the one pretending here."

"That is quite enough, Mr. Monstran," the Commander said. "You're insinuating that Lady Tamsin is not who she says she is but that is not the case, I assure you. Several of my men have vouched for her identity and just before you arrived my scouts confirmed the presence of a Ma'diin encampment to the west, just as Lady Tamsin told us."

Tamsin's seething anger at Monstran was interrupted for a moment at the mention of the Ma'diin's encampment.

"Yes, I'm sure she told you that, but she left out the part where they let her come here. You see, we all have our armies, Commander."

The Commander was silent a moment, a third, cautious look creeping over his already impatient and confused countenance.

"He is trying to manipulate you, Commander," Tamsin said. "It's what he does best."

"You will note that she does not deny her involvement with the Ma'diin," Monstran said slyly. "You say she was their prisoner for six months. To use her own word, a lot of *manipulation* can happen in that amount of time."

"The Ma'diin have not manipulated me."

"No? So you betray your own people on your own accord then, by bringing your little army to their doorstep."

"I betray no one. You would see everyone but yourself destroyed, but the only blood that should be shed is yours."

"Spoken like a true Ma'diin," Monstran said. "If Haven were here he might just be proud, but he hasn't exactly been himself these days."

Tamsin jumped at Monstran, her hands grabbing the collar of his robe, and for a split moment there was a satisfying look of surprise on his face, but before she could do anything else the Commander's arms were around her pulling her away from Monstran.

"Enough! Both of you!" the Commander snapped.

Tamsin had to think quickly before all of their plans unraveled. The Commander had mentioned the Ma'diin encampment already which meant they were ready for her. And she couldn't give Monstran any more time with the Commander, especially alone, for she couldn't chance any more doubt being put in his mind. She didn't know if it would work from this far; she had hoped to be at the wall so she could at least see the Ma'diin's camp, but she had to try.

She squeezed her eyes shut, forcing her anger at Monstran to hold while she tried to picture her muudhiif: the canvas flaps, the reed poles, the fastenings, the colors, the textures, even the smell. She tried to get as clear an image in her mind as she could and then she mustered her power, bolstering it with her hatred for Monstran, and focused it on the image of her muudhiif. An intense pressure rippled through her mind and then broke and she gasped and opened her eyes again.

She was relieved to see nothing in the room had started on fire, but she didn't know if she had succeeded in getting her signal to the Ma'diin or not. All she was left with was a heavy exhaustion and the Commander and Monstran looking at her, the former with concern and the latter with suspicion.

"Are you alright?" the Commander asked, letting go of her. "You're as pale as a sheet." He called for one of the guards stationed outside of the door and told them to fetch Mr. Brennan along with the names of a few more guards.

While he was speaking to the guard, Monstran stepped closer to Tamsin and whispered, "What did you just do?"

"Take one more step and I'll show you personally," Tamsin whispered back.

Monstran smiled. "Since you like to play games, let's play a new one. Let's pretend I don't have an entire army at my disposal, nor will your Ma'diin be slaughtered when I order them to attack. You see, I knew exactly what was going on the moment you walked through the door. You can't fool me, Miss Urbane. You'll realize that when everyone else is dead and then you'll come with me willingly because I have the one thing you want."

"Mr. Monstran," the Commander said turning back to them, "your temporary quarters are—."

"Commander," Monstran interrupted, "I must tell you my patience is almost at its end. You will release Tamsin Urbane to me immediately or—."

"Or what?" the Commander cut him off. "This is my outpost and I will not tolerate threats of any kind." A few guards entered the room then. "You will both be confined to quarters until I can make sense of these accusations." He waved his fingers and the guards moved in around Monstran.

Monstran folded his fingers in front him slowly. "Very well," he said, nodding his head once. "I can wait for the inevitable." He cast a victorious look over Tamsin before following the guards out of the room.

"Please, Lady Tamsin, sit," the Commander said, sighing as if he had just broken up a fight between two children.

"Thank you," Tamsin said, though she didn't feel any better even with Monstran out of the room. "Commander, you have to believe me that Monstran—."

"Let's not waste any more breath on that man," the Commander said. "I do not care for him even though Lord Saveen has made it clear we are to defer to him on matters regarding the dam. However," he put a hand on her shoulder and squeezed just slightly, "if there is any truth to what he has said about you, the consequences would be severe, even for a Lording Lady. But if the Ma'diin are using you and you tell me now, I can help you. You're safe here."

Tamsin understood his tactics here, but she would not let him take her walls down and offer false security to get her to confess. "You don't believe me?" she asked, putting as much hurt as she could into the question.

The Commander's cheek twitched, clearly uncomfortable with the position he was in. "I can't imagine the conditions you were under during those six months. I—."

Before he could finish there was loud bang on the door again. "Commander!" a soldier burst through. "The scouts at the wall are seeing movement from the Ma'diin camp. They're coming this way."

The Commander's stance stiffened immediately and she could see his soldier's mentality returning.

"Alert Captain Dane and the First Squadron and ready my horse. And for lords' sake get someone to find Mr. Brennan."

"No need for that, Commander," Mr. Brennan said, walking through the door.

"Good. Check on Lady Tamsin and then see she gets back."

But Tamsin wasn't listening. Something didn't feel right. Monstran was arrogant, but he wasn't reckless with his words. He was calculated. When he said he could wait for the inevitable he wasn't referring to the Commander figuring her out. The inevitable was the Ma'diin and the Empyrians going to war. Suddenly it all clicked in place. The size of the pathway leading to the dam tunnel. The mysterious doors on the other side. It was just big enough. Monstran didn't have an army of men. He had an army of amon'jii. And while the Ma'diin and the Empyrians were fighting each other, the amon'jii would sneak through the back door and slaughter them all.

"Please, Commander, let me come," Tamsin said, a bit too hastily, but she couldn't let them go without her.

The Commander's eyes narrowed slightly.

"I can help. I can speak their language a little. I can help negotiate."

"It would take a massive amount of courage to face one's former captors and I do not doubt you have it, but I would not risk their wrath at seeing you with us, nor your safety. And if their intentions aren't to negotiate I can't have you in harm's way."

"The sh'pav'danya," she blurted out.

"What?"

"The sh'pav'danya. It's the Ma'diin's form of negotiation. It's what they did in Empyria and why they thought they could take me. It's an exchange. One of their men for one of yours. Neither is harmed while the negotiations take place. They might invoke it. If they do, I suggest you accept. At the very least it will buy you some time."

The Commander's expression was serious and Tamsin couldn't read if he believed her or not. "You understand that I will not jeopardize my men if I have even the slightest doubt of your word." Then without another word he turned and walked away.

It wasn't a choice between the Empyrians or the Ma'diin. It was choosing life over death. This, she was certain now, was what the Red Sight had been warning her about. That if she chose a side, any side, it would lead to everyone's destruction. It wouldn't just be seeing the trees through the forest; it would be ignoring the beasts hiding in the trees' shadows. The amon'jii, Monstran, the Master they were all working for...these were the real enemies. These were the ones that would choose death and destruction over life.

The amon'jii were planning on ambushing the Empyrians the same way the Ma'diin were. Only the amon'jii weren't planning on drawing them out; they were going to seal them in. Without the water stopping them, they could march right around to the Empyrians' entrance while at the same time attacking them through the dam tunnel. The Empyrians, not knowing about the deadly creatures, would all be dead before the sun came up.

If the Ma'diin and the Empyrians were too busy fighting each other, neither side would survive. And if the dam couldn't be broken in time she had to get them to fight together. But she couldn't wait for the Commander and his men to come back.

She would start with Lt. Farrows. As hard as it would be to admit everything had been a lie, if she had any chance of convincing anyone she would have to get him on her side. Then she would go to the Commander. She knew she had lost his trust, but not his sympathy so she still had cards to play.

It wasn't hard to slip out of the healing tent; all she had to do was shimmy under one of the side flaps and Mr. Brennan nor the two guards outside the entrance noticed a thing. From then it didn't take her long to find Farrows. She only had to ask a few people before one told her to look in the Burrow and no one seemed privy to the fact that she was supposed to be confined to the tent. The off duty gathering hall was sparse that evening and she located Farrows quickly. She walked over to where he was seated on a bench in quiet conversation with another soldier sitting across the table from him.

"Lady Tamsin," Farrows said, looking up as she walked over. "Please, join us."

Tamsin hesitated at the end of the table. "Actually, I was hoping we could speak privately."

"Of course." He nodded goodbye to his comrade and got up, escorting Tamsin to the other end of the hall, away from any of the others. "Is everything alright?" he asked, pulling out a chair at another small table so she could sit.

"I wish it were," she said as she sat down, Farrows doing the same, "but the truth is I need to tell you something, but before I do I need to know if I can trust you."

"Trust me? Of course you can. Why would you think otherwise?"

"Because my father trusted people here too, and he's dead now."

Farrows' brow was dark in the shadow of the torchlights hanging from the walls. "I wasn't here when your father came," he said. "But it was the Ma'diin that killed your father. The same ones that kidnapped you."

"It wasn't the Ma'diin," Tamsin said. "Cornelius Saveen ordered my father to be killed and he made it look like it was the Ma'diin to cover his own tracks and ruin the negotiations."

"That's quite a serious accusation to throw at a Lord," he said.

"It's the truth."

Farrows was quiet for a moment. Then, "I believe you."

"Thank you," Tamsin said sincerely.

He nodded, but his face was still burdened. "Why are you telling me this?"

"Because I need to tell you something else, something much harder than this, but I need you to believe it and believe that I'm trying to save people, not hurt them. And when I'm done telling you, I need you to remember that."

Farrows folded his hands in front of him. He looked as if he had swallowed a moldy piece of bread, but Tamsin had just finished confessing her involvement with the Ma'diin to him.

"You let me believe you had been kidnapped. That you had been their prisoner all this time. That they had beaten you and lords know what else they had done to you. But all of it was an act so you could get in here and you could spy on us for them? Unless…" he leaned in a little closer, that expression of concern creeping over the betrayal that was all too clear. "I saw the scars and what they had done to you. They couldn't be fake," he said. "Did they—did they do this to you to make you come here?"

She could see the anger building behind his eyes. Anger at the Ma'diin if they had tortured her into carrying out their plot.

Anger at being lied to if they hadn't. "The scars are real," she said. "But they're not all by the Ma'diin's hands. And the Ma'diin didn't force me to come here. I've earned and sacrificed for their trust and up until an hour ago I was working with them, hoping to find a way to destroy the dam and—"

"And destroy us too?"

"The Ma'diin aren't your enemy. And you're not the Ma'diin's. And I'm not either."

"Then what are you doing here?"

"I told you I'm trying to save people. Not just the Ma'diin or the Empyrians. Your daughter. My friends. The innocent people who have no part in this but will be hurt all the same unless we help each other."

"Some would call you a traitor for this."

"But do you?"

The question lingered in the air until he finally answered, "I don't know, my lady. I don't know."

"Please, Lt. Farrows. The man you call the Inspector is here, but he's not just here for the dam. He's here to make sure that his army of amon'jii can make it through and once they do your outpost will turn into a graveyard."

"Amon'jii?"

"They're creatures that hunt the Ma'diin. Some of my scars are from the amon'jii. I've gone up against them and believe me, your men won't win."

Farrows put his hands up to stop her from saying any more. "I can't listen to this. I want to believe you, but—."

"Then believe me," Tamsin pleaded.

Farrows sighed deeply and looked at her for a moment. Then he stood up. "I'm going to take you back to Mr. Brennan while I— while I figure this out."

"Lieutenant—."

"No. I should have you put in the brig, but in case the Ma'diin have manipulated you somehow, I don't want to subject you to more…unpleasantness. Please." He extended his hand.

Tamsin stood up slowly, but didn't take his hand. She was out of ideas and she said nothing as Farrows escorted her back to Mr. Brennan's tent. The guards looked shocked to see her, but she wasn't surprised by that. Farrows ordered more guards around the tent. Though they were confused, they obeyed his order.

Farrows gave her one last look before he walked away.

Lieutenant Isak Farrows walked through the rows of tents, acknowledging others' greetings with a half nod or a slight wave of his hand as he made his way to the Commander's quarters. The outpost seemed unusually busy at this time in the late afternoon, but he barely noticed as his mind was awash with revelations Lady Tamsin had told him. The plot against her father, the Inspector and the creatures that could annihilate them, and her own involvement with the Ma'diin. The lies and manipulation that swirled around the situation made things so murky that he didn't know who to trust. His military mind balked at the idea that the Empyrians were potentially aiding their own destruction by trusting a man like the Inspector, but his gut told him that Lady Tamsin would not have made something like this up. And the further he walked the more he doubted his own doubt about her, confessing to himself that maybe it was only because he was angry at being taken for a fool in the beginning, thinking he had played some heroic part in her rescue when really she had orchestrated the entire thing. But why did she admit the deception to him then when she had everyone believing the Ma'diin had wronged her? She could have kept on pretending until the Ma'diin had gotten what they came for, but she didn't.

He reached the Commander's quarters, but was stopped by one of the guards who held up his hand.

"The Commander's not here, Lieutenant."

"Where is he?" Farrows asked. "I need to speak with him immediately."

"You haven't heard?"

Farrows raised his eyebrows. "Heard what?"

"The Ma'diin are on the move. The Commander took the First Squadron out there. I would return to your own squadron if I were you."

"Of course," Farrows said. He was about to step away when he had another thought. "The Inspector, did he go with them?"

The guard shook his head. "No. He is confined to quarters until the Commander returns." He pointed down the wall to a singular tent not far from them.

Farrows nodded in thanks and walked over to the tent. It was larger than most of the soldiers' tents and the fabric was a dark color, odd for an Empyrian tent, but perhaps he wasn't from Empyria. Rumors floated around the outpost whenever he showed up and assumptions were made about the man, but if Lady Tamsin was telling the truth then the Inspector wasn't even from Delmar.

He slowed his gait as he approached, noting the absence of guards outside. If he was supposed to be confined to quarters then there should have been several. There was a glow coming from underneath the entrance flap and he heard a muffled voice inside. He looked around, but no one else was around. He crept over to the entrance and peeled back a tiny sliver of one side, just enough so he could see inside.

A shadow cut across the light and Farrows flinched, but the shadow passed and he saw someone carry an object wrapped in cloth over to another man who was partially hidden, but Farrows could see was kneeling on the floor with his back to him. The light from a lantern hanging from a rope on the ceiling illuminated the man's silvery hair and though Farrows had only seen him once, knew it to be the Inspector. The Inspector took the wrapped object and put it on a short table in front of him out of Farrows' sight. The attendant bowed and back away, his face concealed by a dark hood.

The Inspector unwrapped the small object and hunched over it slightly. Then he was still. "Master," the Inspector said. The word sounded like a hiss, but was amplified, almost like there was a wind stream carrying his voice through the tent. "The Ma'diin are here. Everything is in place for the attack."

Farrows furrowed his eyebrows. Who was the Inspector talking to? He tried to open the flap a hair more, but saw no one else.

"When?" the Inspector continued. "Very good, Master. There is one more thing…the girl. She is here."

He could only be talking about one person. The only girl at the outpost.

"Yes. I think she may try—no, I—." The Inspector kept stopping, like he was being cut off by someone Farrows could neither see nor hear. "Of course, Master. I will—of course. Send them now and—yes, she'll die with the rest of them."

The Inspector took a deep breath, putting his hands flat on the table for a moment, then re-wrapped whatever had been in front of him and handed it to the attendant. He stood up slowly, looking around the tent for a moment. "We're going," he said. "Leave everything and follow me."

Farrows jumped back and ducked around the side of the tent, just as the Inspector and three others exited the tent. They walked past him with a hasty gait, taking no notice of him crouched down in the shadows. He didn't know who the Inspector had been talking to, but he did know that Lady Tamsin, and the rest of them, were in danger. Lady Tamsin's story, as much as it humiliated and befuddled him, could not be discounted anymore.

When their footsteps had faded, Farrows crept out from around the tent and then bolted back across the outpost to Mr. Brennan's tent. But the closer he got, the more he began to hear shouts and calls for water. He ran faster, weaving between the tents and others running towards the commotion until he saw the great plume of smoke for himself.

Mr. Brennan's tent, or what was left of it, was engulfed in grey swaddles of smoke as a dozen men continued to launch buckets of water at it. The poles holding up the frame leaned precariously against each other and at least half of the fabric had burned way, but it was still too clouded to see what inside had survived.

"Tamsin!" he shouted. "Lady Tamsin!"

"She got out," someone called out and Farrows made his way over to the man.

He resisted the urge to grab the man by the collar. "Where is she?" he demanded.

"I don't know!" the man said. "She was right here and then…" But he didn't finish and could only look around helplessly.

Farrows' breathing slowed its panicked pace as his soldier's mindset kicked in. She had gotten out. She hadn't been caught in the fire. But where was she? He looked around too, though it was easy to miss someone so small in all the chaos.

He stopped, realizing that it probably hadn't been an accident and that there was one place that Tamsin would have gone.

Tamsin stared up at the slick wall, stretching up into the darkening sky like it thought it was the crown of the desert. Brought into being by man and now the lord over them.

"Some of the men call it 'The Guillotine.'"

Tamsin turned around to see Lt. Farrows standing there. She took a step away from him, but he held up his hands to show her he had not come to take her back.

"I'm sorry," he said. "I believe you now."

Tamsin wondered if she believed *him* now, but after a few moments of watching him, she concluded that she could trust him. They needed to trust each other if they were to save anyone from what was coming. She finally nodded, acknowledging him without the need for further details.

"They must call it that for a reason," she said, referring to his earlier comment. "There must be a way to raise it."

"They call it that because it—," he looked away for a moment, as if he was embarrassed, "—because it's a death sentence."

A death sentence for the Ma'diin. For anyone south of the anasii hada that depended on its water. Tamsin sighed. "There are no weaknesses. No floodgates. Nothing that we could move to get the water flowing again?"

"It would take weeks to even dismantle a small portion of it," Farrows said. "This rock is forty meters thick at its peak. It was designed to stand the test of time."

"We don't have that kind of time."

"I'm sorry," Farrows said. "Our best chance is to convince the Commander and see what the stonemasons can do."

Tamsin turned to follow him back, but stopped, as if her feet had been caught in a dune, just as she and Haven had been after surviving the sandstorm together. She felt as if the very air had become dense, holding her in place as if a force stronger than gravity commanded her attention. And it wasn't a painful sensation, but something had entangled itself in her senses, something she had felt before, something…

She turned back slowly to face the bridge running alongside the dam, to the darkness that she couldn't see that lay beyond the large, wooden doors at the opposite end. Her footsteps landed silently on the cold stone as she walked towards them, breaking her stillness like a woman sleepwalking. At first she could hear her own breath slowing down, then the sound of it disappeared as her heart echoed in her ears, warning her as she approached the doors. Then it was soon joined by another, then another until the something that had entangled itself became many somethings…a hundred somethings…until she could feel only the crescendo of thousands of fiery hearts. And there she was, in the neck of the hourglass that was the anasii hada, with armies of Ma'diin and Empyrians behind her and now one made of demonic creatures in front of her. The amon'jii were coming. Like tiny grains of sand they would come through and they wouldn't stop until the other end was buried.

Something touched her shoulder and she jumped, knocking her out of her trance-like state. She turned around and saw Farrows right behind her, looking concerned.

"Lady Tamsin? What's wrong?"

But she looked past him, up at the waning light from the clouded sky as evening descended. They had maybe an hour left before true darkness fell. An hour before the nocturnal creatures poured through the bridge like a plague. By sunrise, everyone would be dead.

Unless…

"Lieutenant, you have to go warn the Commander. Warn the Ma'diin. Get everyone out. The amon'jii are coming."

"The amon'jii—how do you know?"

"I can feel them," she said looking back to the door. "They're almost here."

"You're not going to stay here," Farrows said, horrified.

"I'm the only that can slow them down," she said. "It'll take too long to explain. You have to go. Now."

"I'm not leaving you."

"If you don't go, then everyone is going to die," she said forcefully. "I made a mistake before: I let the actions of a few evil men make me think the Ma'diin and the Empyrians were enemies. But if they don't fight together now, then the amon'jii will destroy everyone. Please."

Farrows looked at her, clearly torn. But the struggle in his eyes soon gave way to painful acceptance. "What if I'm too late? What if the Ma'diin don't believe me?"

Tamsin thought quickly and realized she still had a few cards left to play. "Then you have to convince the Commander. Take Lt. Riggs with you. The Ma'diin have his son, Enrik. He can confirm all of this. And tell the Ma'diin when you get there: *Iriita eya Kaz'ma'sha.*"

"What does that mean?"

Tamsin smiled. "Go," she said.

Farrows repeated the words and at Tamsin's nod of approval turned and ran back across the bridge to the outpost.

Tamsin's smile vanished and she turned around to face the wooden doors once more, letting her hands shake only for a moment. "No fear," she whispered into the empty, echoing air. She remembered when Samih had guided her through the anasii hada on their way to the marsh lands, a mile below her feet in the watery caverns. She remembered lying in the canoe, surrounded by darkness. If this was to be her tomb, then she would take as many amon'jii with her as she could. For Samih. For Ysallah. For Haven. For all of them.

250

Chapter Twenty-Two

Kellan stood perfectly still near Tamsin's empty muudhiif in the Ma'diin's encampment. The others shuffled around him, giving him and the large tent a wide berth as they went about their preparations for the assault on the anasii hada. Large clouds rolled ominously overhead, though they were still too dry to deliver any rain. The last time they had congregated like this was the last time he had seen her. They added just enough elemental presence to fuel his own feelings of anger. Anger that he had been sent away with the old and infirm. Anger that Tamsin had left, again. Anger that the Ma'diin hadn't stopped her. And anger that he hadn't been there to stop her either.

Amidst the flurry of footsteps around the camp he heard a pair stop next to him.

"We heard you came back," R'en's voice cut through his brooding with a cautious edge. "You alright?"

Kellan clenched his fists. "Are you going to tell me why you all agreed to let her go?" he asked, ignoring her question. It had taken him less than half an hour after waking up to find out what had happened, where they were going, and to head back to the outer marshes. His fury at being sent away had tempered his physical pain and driven him to rejoin the Watchers.

"So you know."

"Oman told me."

"It's not up to us. She is the Kaz'ma'sha and the other Kazserii agreed."

Kellan turned to look at her through his n'qab. "But you didn't agree."

R'en shifted her weight to her other foot, a subtle sign that he was right. "I do not like the thought of her in there, alone, surrounded by our enemy either, but we have to trust her. She's more powerful than any of us and she has a plan."

Kellan exhaled slowly through his teeth, trying to release his anger as he did. "So what is her plan again?"

"Tamsin will tell the northerners that our army is here. They will send a small party out to meet us, including Tamsin because she's the only one that can speak both languages. If she's found a way to break the dam she'll tell us."

"And then?"

"Then we attack." R'en said. "We draw out as many northerners as we can. Once they're out, Isillah will lead the second half of the army up behind them, cutting them off from the anasii hada and allowing the strike team to get inside and take out the wall."

"And what about Tamsin?"

"She'll meet up with the strike team inside."

"They won't leave the wall undefended."

"We know, but the team can handle it."

"Who's on it?"

"Ardak, some of his men, and a few sha'diin."

"She'll be well protected," Numha said, walking over to them carrying a large bundle wrapped in reed stalks. "Not that she'll need it. She was a force at the Duels."

"This won't be like the Duels," Kellan said. "She's never seen a battle on this scale before."

"Most of us haven't," Numha said. "But—."

Suddenly Tamsin's muudhiif burst into a giant ball of fire. Kellan, R'en and Numha all jumped back and there were shouts from others nearby as waves of heat rolled off the burning structure. The flames rose well above their heads, taking no time at all to consume every reed and beam as they snapped up towards the overcast sky, illuminating the shocked faces around them.

R'en started shouting at the sha'diin to clear out of the way and confirming no one was inside. But it was Numha who turned to Kellan.

"The Watchers?"

Kellan shook his head.

"Then wh…?"

They looked at each other at the same time with the same realization.

"Can you do something about this?" R'en shouted at him.

Kellan straightened his fingers and with a giant heave of power he extinguished the fire razing the muudhiif. A rolling cloud of dark smoke replaced it as the reeds and fabric holding it together collapsed into a heap.

"What happened?" R'en asked.

"Tamsin," Kellan and Numha answered together.

"What?"

"It was a sign. Something's wrong. Tamsin's trying to tell us something," Numha said.

"We're not waiting for the northerners to make the first move," Kellan said.

"Agreed," Numha said. "R'en, alert the Kazserii and send a messenger to the second army. We're going now."

R'en smiled and took off through the crowd, shouting orders at the sha'diin as she went. Suddenly the camp was ablaze with activity. Kellan had wanted to be on the strike team to go into the anasii hada, but he would have to figure out a way to get inside later. He would have to trust Ardak to see to Tamsin's safety, but if things were already going wrong he wanted to be the one to defend her.

It wasn't long before the army was assembled. They set out towards the anasii hada, eager and energized like a pack of wolves that caught the scent of a rabbit and all that was left to do was wait until it came out of its hole.

Kellan knew what they were feeling. He had felt it many times while hunting the amon'jii. The anticipation. He just hoped that what came out of that hole was indeed a rabbit and not something worse.

They halted their steady approach just beyond the range of the northerners' flying spears, though they were close enough to see movement along the wall where the northern men stood guard. Then after a few minutes of tense waiting they saw a group of northerners emerge from a hidden entrance at the base of the wall. Blue and gold banners whipped in the wind as they rode towards them atop their four-legged steeds.

Kellan and the other Watchers with the main group formed a semi-circle around the Kazserii at the front as they waited for their arrivals.

"I count no more than twenty," R'en said, who was standing next to them.

Numha made a motion with her fingers and several Ma'diin stepped forward and followed her a few paces away from the main group. Kellan followed her as did K'al and R'en.

The northerners slowed their animals as they drew near and stopped when they were several canoe lengths away. Three of them dismounted and took a couple steps closer, but all their weapons remained sheathed so far.

Kellan zeroed in on their leader immediately. A tall man with a shaved beard stood in the center with a steady, but sharp gaze that panned slowly over the Ma'diin in front of them. But as Kellan scanned the rest of the northerners, he felt his breath quicken slightly and he noticed the others next to him seem to have the same reaction.

K'al was the first to speak. "Where is Tamsin?"

A silence hung over them for a long moment as they realized she wasn't there.

"Do you think they found her out?" R'en finally asked.

"Shh," Numha said. "If they haven't we aren't going to do it here."

"They can't understand us."

"We don't know that."

"There's only one way to find out," Kellan said, losing his patience with the guessing game. If Tamsin needed help, then they couldn't waste any more time.

Numha took the hint and took a step forward. The northerner eyes all locked onto her. "Who speaks for you?" she asked them loudly.

There were a few moments of silence and then their leader stepped forward. He pointed to himself and said a few words, then pointed to the two next to him and uttered what Kellan assumed were their names. He said something else then, a question, and waited.

Numha answered with her own name and then introduced K'al, the Kazsera who had volunteered for this. The other Kazserii hung back with the main group, watching with the others.

K'al took another step forward. "We are here to give you the chance to surrender. Take down your wall or we will attack."

Kellan appreciated her directness. Whether the northerners understood her or not, her tone was not asking. And even though the northerners recognized men as their leaders, there was no question of the authority K'al held.

The northern leader squinted his eyes a little and then said something else, pointing back to his men and the anasii hada.

Perhaps to indicate their strength, Kellan thought, but without someone to translate they couldn't be certain. Without Tamsin these negotiations were pointless. Then that gave him an idea.

The northern leader started to say something else, but Kellan walked forward. The northerners' hands immediately went to their weapons and Kellan stopped. The northern leader put his hand up to calm his men, looking at Kellan with curiosity more than caution.

"Kellan?" Numha whispered to him.

But he ignored the others. He put his hand up to his hood and unhooked his n'qab, so the northerners could see his face. The overcast sky made it safe for him. Most of the northerners looked appalled or even frightened and even their leader blinked momentarily in surprise. Kellan knew the impact a Watcher's appearance could have on a member of the Ma'diin, and the northerners were no different. Normally it was something the Watchers tried to keep subdued, but he wanted the sight of his glowing eyes underneath his dark hood to unsettle them so they wouldn't have their walls up when he said what he was about to.

"Tamsin," was all he said.

Their reaction was just as he had hoped. The ones still sitting atop their animals all shifted uncomfortably, looking back and forth to each other with varying degrees of anger and outrage. The two next to the leader looked like they wanted to strike him down with their blades right there. It seemed as if Tamsin had played her part well. But it was the leader that remained the most composed. A slight twitch of his nose and a coldness clouding over his eyes was the only indication he gave that he recognized the name. The man said something, but Kellan had already gotten what he wanted. If Tamsin was in danger they wouldn't have reacted as they did, but there was still the question of Tamsin's signal fire. Why had she done it and why hadn't the northerners brought her with now?

The leader narrowed his eyes. He said something sternly and he couldn't hide the disgust in his voice.

But there was something else there too, something it took a minute for Kellan to pinpoint. Then he took a few, slow steps back until he was next to Numha, never taking his eyes off the leader.

"Tamsin has fooled them," Numha whispered to him. "See how agitated they are."

"Not all of them," Kellan said. "The leader is not fully convinced."

"How can you tell?"

"Tamsin isn't here," he said pointedly. "Either she is their prisoner now or something has happened."

"Either way, we need to see her," Numha said.

"So we draw them out, just as planned."

"There's another way," K'al spoke up. "The sh'pav'danya."

"They won't know what that is," Numha said.

"Yes they do," Kellan said, who hadn't stopped watching the leader. At mention of the sh'pav'danya, the leader's eyes had momentarily flashed in recognition. Tamsin must have told him. It must be what she wanted. "Say it," Kellan told her.

K'al nodded slightly, turning back to the northerners. "I offer the sh'pav'danya," she said, saying the word slowly. "If you accept, I will give you one of ours." She put her palm out towards Numha, who was about to step forward, but Kellan stepped in front of her, making it clear that if this worked then he was the one going. K'al raised an eyebrow at him, but continued. "If you deny, then you won't get one, you will get all." She made a tiny sign with her fingers and the Ma'diin hoard behind her raised their spears and simultaneously shouted.

Some of the northerners' beasts flinched and sidled sideways at the sudden noise, tossing their heads in displeasure. But the northern leader was not fazed. He began to say something, but was interrupted by another shout from the Ma'diin camp. One of the sha'diin surrounding the Kazserii pointed out past the northerners.

About halfway between the anasii hada and where they stood were two more northerners, riding furiously towards them on two of the four-hoofed creatures. Several sha'diin came forward to stand in front of K'al, their hands hidden in their cloaks, ready to pull out their blades, but the northerners seemed just as baffled by this late arrival as the Ma'diin. The leader barked something and two of the riders near him turned their beasts around and went out to intercept the newcomers. They slowed their beasts as the other two met up with them and after a brief exchange they walked over to the larger group together.

The wind blew up a little as they drew closer, as if to prepare the way for the ominous message the newcomers brought. The wind picked at Kellan's hood, whispering a hollow sound in his ear. Sometimes, he knew, nature was more privy to secrets of the world and if one could not learn to interpret the signs, then the truth would exact a harsh cost. He had never had the patience to interpret them, but if the wind was telling them anything now, it was that this time the truth would be demanding a payment in blood. And it was coming for them sooner than any of them were ready for.

The dryness in the air clung to his tongue like a burr, and Oman could not remember a time, even during the dry seasons, when a drought had permeated into the atmosphere quite like this, as if instead of releasing rain down, the clouds were pulling the dust and dirt up from the ground. He knelt down and brushed his hands over the brittle earth, the shadows blending together as the last hues of the evening light began to fade. He had been watching the skies and could see the clouds starting to gather together above, but they were not the tumultuous, water-bearing kind. If they did form rain it would not be in time. These were the kind that hastened night's cloak by creeping across the sunset, blotting out the tangerine rays like a swarm of shadows.

The Ma'diin would have to face the amon'jii without nature's help.

They were out there, Oman was sure. Tonight, they would face something beyond anything they had ever seen. Even the Watchers, who faced the nocturnal beasts regularly, had never had to go up against an entire hoard of them. One on one was challenging enough, but what was coming would test even the best.

The Watchers could slow them down, for how long he didn't know. Several had been tasked with strictly focusing on keeping the amon'jii's fire at bay while the others would be the first line of their defense. Keeping the second half of the Ma'diin army protected was their only goal until Tamsin found a way to break the dam. He just hoped they could persevere long enough.

He stood back up and walked through the shadowy pinnacles that were his brothers, waiting on the edge of darkness, their glowing eyes fixated to the east. Each one of them embodied the brotherhood of Watchers with remarkable bravery. Oman could remember each of their transitions, many he had performed himself. But it had been their determination to survive, their own strength of will that had forged them into the warriors they were now. They were the best. They had trained and fought and bled for years, but he knew they would all have to dig into a deeper well to find the courage this night would require of them.

"I can hear the call of the Green Mountain tonight," Kep'chlan stepped up next to him. "Edan is waiting for us."

"Probably," Ch'maen said, "But I will bury as many as my sword will allow before I go."

"You will need a bigger sword if you want to beat me," Kep'chlan responded.

A light banter emerged, each boasting a bigger number than the last of how many amon'jii they would take down before fate intervened. Normally Oman would discourage such talk. As innocent as it was, it drew their focus away from their surroundings. But tonight, he let them go.

Until his senses warned him something was off.

"Do you hear that?" Oman asked, putting up his hand.

Everyone was silent for a moment, listening to what he was hearing, but there was nothing but the wind. But that was the point. There were no distant bird calls. No frogs, no crickets. Everything was quiet.

"They're here."

Lieutenant Farrows dismounted from his horse and marched over to the small group of Empyrians gathered on the edge of the Ma'diin's army. He took a steadying breath, painfully aware that a truce depended squarely on what he did and said next. He tried not to think about how Lady Tamsin was faring back at the dam, or if he was too late.

The Commander stopped him with an outstretched hand when he got close, the look in his eyes torn between murder and concern. "You two had better have a good reason for being here."

"We do," Farrows said. "I need to talk to you and I need to talk to them," he pointed a finger at the Ma'diin. "Lady Tamsin has uncovered a plot and if we don't join with the Ma'diin everyone at the outpost will be killed."

"Lady Tamsin is not someone I entirely trust at the moment," the Commander said, his gaze darting back to the Ma'diin.

"The Inspector is the one who can't be trusted. He's on his way right now with an army. We need the Ma'diin's help."

"Don't let that pretty face turn your brain to sand," the Commander said. "She—."

"She told me everything," Farrows interrupted. "She was working with the Ma'diin. She was part of their plan to break the dam and she freely admitted it. But she also told me about the Inspector and how he's going to kill everyone with an army of beasts. I wouldn't have believed her, but I heard the Inspector. He spoke of an attack. And they're coming soon."

The Commander narrowed his eyes, but he didn't speak right away.

Farrows decided to press his advantage. If the Commander was already having doubts about the Inspector then Farrows needed to lean into that. They were running out of time. "Commander, I know you don't trust them, but trust me. We need the Ma'diin to be our allies. Otherwise both sides will be wiped out."

"Enough!" Riggs shouted, dismounting his own horse. "Those savages have my boy! They have Enrik!" He pointed a condemning finger at the Ma'diin. He started marching towards them, but Farrows and one of the captains grabbed him and held him back.

"What are you talking about?" the Commander asked.

"Tamsin told me the Ma'diin have his son. She said he could verify everything she said."

The Commander rubbed his forehead. "I need time to think."

"We don't have time," Farrows said.

"Yes we do. The Ma'diin invoked some kind of exchange. One of them for one of us. I'm going to take them up on it while I sort all this out. I am still the Commander here, though everyone seems to have forgotten that lately."

"Then use that to get Riggs' boy back and let me go," Farrows said. "I volunteer."

The Commander made a displeased grunt from the back of his throat, but he nodded. "Very well, but you will say and do nothing until we figure this out."

Farrows knew they didn't have time to figure it out, but he nodded, sensing he would have an easier time convincing the Ma'diin of what was coming than the Commander.

The Commander turned back to the Ma'diin, who had been patiently waiting while the whole exchange took place, though most looked on edge. "I accept your offer," he said, nodding at Farrows.

Farrows took a few steps forward until he was halfway between both, unable to suppress the dagger of intimidation pressing against his chest. He knew he had to do it, but facing down a hoard of strange, stone-faced warriors in the quickly fading light was enough to make his hairs stand on end.

For their part, the Ma'diin remained motionless, until one stepped forward. He was clothed in a dark cloak that hid his face and when the wind blew revealed gloved hands resting on the hilts of weapons.

"No," the Commander said loudly. "Enrik. We want the boy."

One of the women held up her hand and the dark-cloaked man stopped. Some of the other Ma'diin furrowed their brows and exchanged glances. The Commander repeated the name, but no one moved or said anything.

Farrows took a deep breath. "Iriita eya Kaz'ma'sha," he repeated the words that Lady Tamsin had told him.

The woman stared at Farrows and asked a question, but the man in the dark cloak threw up his hand and shouted something back to her.

"Iriita eya Kaz'ma'sha," he repeated, hoping that whatever he was saying was having the right impact.

The dark-cloaked man was right in front of him then, seemingly in one step, but he drew no weapon. "Tamsin?" he asked.

Farrows nodded, not knowing how much the man would understand. "Tamsin needs Enrik. The boy, like us," he said, waving his hand back towards the Empyrians. The—," he tried to remember the name she had used, "—amanjee. They're coming."

The dark-cloaked man shouted something back at the woman then with such intensity that she actually took a step back. Farrows thought he heard Enrik's name and watched as the woman ordered several of the others away.

"Farrows?" the Commander called out.

Farrows held up a pacifying hand. "I think they're getting the boy."

After a tense minute there was movement once again amid the ranks of Ma'diin and several men shuffled to the forefront.

"Enrik!" Riggs called out, recognizing the boy held up between two others.

The boy turned his head. "Father!"

Farrows noted that the Ma'diin weren't restraining him, but rather supporting him between them. He was bare-chested, save for the large swath of mossy bandages encircling his stomach.

The dark-cloaked man motioned for him and the Ma'diin brought the boy to him. He hooked an arm underneath the boy's to support him and the three of them stood in between the Empyrians and the Ma'diin. Up close he looked nervous, but he did not seem frightened to be amongst the Ma'diin. His face was pale, but his eyes were bright. Farrows took his other arm and together they helped him back towards the Empyrians.

Riggs could not restrain himself anymore and ran towards his son. "Enrik! What did they do to you? How did you get here?" He threw an accusing look at the dark-cloaked man as he took Enrik from them.

"I'm alright, Father. The Ma'diin took care of me. Is Tamsin with you?"

Riggs looked confused and slightly angry, though Farrows couldn't tell which news it was that conjured such a reaction.

But it was the Commander who stepped forward. "Enrik, what can you tell me about Lady Tamsin? It's important that you tell me the truth. Were you both prisoners?"

Farrows knew that their fate now lied in whatever words the boy uttered next. He seemed to realize something to this effect too for he looked at each of their faces, stopping on the dark-cloaked man with a look of trepidation.

"Tamsin is a leader among the Ma'diin. She was never their prisoner. I was, though not by the Ma'diin." Then he quickly explained how his squadron was sent to the east with Mr. Monstran, escorting a Ma'diin prisoner, and the events that followed. Monstran betrayed his whole squadron, allowing them to be massacred by the beasts that lived there. Then he used Enrik, enslaved him, to do terrible things. Tamsin rescued him, though he was injured in the escape.

"You see? Everything I told you, everything Tamsin told me, is true. The Ma'diin are not our enemy," Farrows said to the Commander.

Riggs shook his head and curled his lips. "There's more to it," he said. "But we should arrest Monstran now before the slippery snake has time to escape."

"I agree," the Commander finally said.

"Monstran is at the outpost?" Enrik asked.

"And she said the beasts are on their way," Farrows said.

"Then Tamsin is in danger." He turned to the dark-cloaked man, who had been listening to the exchange with silent focus. "Tamsin is in trouble. She needs you. Go!"

Whether he understood the words or not, the man certainly seemed to understand the urgency in Enrik's countenance and ran over to the Empyrians. Without hesitation he went over to the horse Farrows had ridden in on and jumped on its back. The horse squirmed a little sideways at the new, dark thing suddenly on its back, but the man stayed on and shouted something at the Ma'diin and then the Empyrians, and though each word was foreign, his meaning was unmistakable: let's go or he would go without them. The Empyrians responded with a flurry of activity, surrounding the Ma'diin man with their own horses while the Commander and his officers remounted theirs.

"C'mon," Riggs started pulling Enrik away, but Enrik shook his head.

"What did you mean, 'there's more to it?'" he asked. "Did you—did you know what Monstran was doing?"

"I had no idea you would be going to that place," Riggs said, shaking his head, as if the guilt of his involvement had finally latched onto him. "You don't understand—Lord Saveen—."

"*I* don't understand? I know what's coming!" Enrik stepped away from his father, holding his side. "I'm staying. I have to help them understand," he said, looking back at the Ma'diin.

"No, I'm getting you away from all of this, somewhere safe," Riggs said.

"No one will be safe if we don't stop Monstran and the Master," he said, stumbling back.

Farrows caught him, then caught the Commander's eye atop his horse.

"Riggs!" the Commander shouted impatiently, grabbing Riggs' horse's reins and riding over.

Riggs took a last, regretful look at Enrik and then remounted his horse. He dug his heels into its flanks and followed the Commander and the rest of his men back to the outpost.

Hands were around Farrows' arms instantly and he was pulled the rest of the way into the Ma'diin hoard as others helped Enrik back. They brought Farrows in front of a woman who had hair that matched the sunset behind them and sharp green eyes.

"We need Ardak!" Enrik shouted. "Ardak!"

The red-haired woman spoke a few words to the others.

"Who is Ardak?" Farrows asked Enrik.

"He can speak our language too," he said. "He can help us."

Suddenly people were shouting and pointing across the rocky plain towards the southeast, though the dark horizon made it difficult to see. Then Farrows saw a blazing speck of light speeding towards them over the terrain. The shape of a running man was soon silhouetted against the light from the torch he carried and many of the Ma'diin rushed out to meet him.

"What's going on?" Farrows asked, but Enrik shook his head, just as confused.

The woman with the red hair stood perfectly still and Farrows could see the firelight's reflection in her eyes as she watched the newcomer fall to his knees, dropping his torch in the sand. A dark trail of blood followed in his wake.

"Amon'jii," she said.

Chapter Twenty-Three

Kellan was met with every pair of suspicious and curious looks as they ascended into the northerners' outpost atop the anasii hada. He had not relished the awkward ride in, but he had refused to slow down for even a moment and by sheer force of will had not fallen off the bulky creature. He had understood enough of what the man outside had said to know that Tamsin needed him. And though the man's pronunciation was awful, Kellan knew he had also mentioned the amon'jii. Whatever was going on here, Kellan needed to know. Using the sh'pav'danya was not ideal, but nothing about this was ideal. And the other thing the man had said: Iriita eya Kaz'ma'sha. *Remember the truth of the Kaz'ma'sha.* This was a direct message from Tamsin for there was no way that man knew any Ma'diinese unless it came from her. The truth of the Kaz'ma'sha…She was the true leader of the tribes, the unifier of them all. They knew that already so why would Tamsin give that particular message? He hoped he would get the answer directly, but the others would have to figure it out for themselves.

They reached the top and rode through rows upon rows of tents, with the leader occasionally shouting things at the soldiers as they went by. They finally stopped when they reached a large tent and everyone slid down the sides of their animals. Some drew their weapons, looking unsure about the foreigner in their midst.

Kellan remained on the animal, looking at the nervous faces around him. "Tamsin!" he shouted, but this only served to increase their alarm. He shouted her name again. He would not stop until he found her.

Another man came pushing through the crowd. He wore some kind of long sash draped over the front of his waist over his regular clothes and he shouted orders at the others, but he didn't look like the other northern leaders he had seen.

"Tamsin?!" Kellan asked this new man.

The man eyed him seriously for a moment, as if deciding if he could be trusted or not, then pointed to the other end of the northerners' camp. He nodded to Kellan, offering his consent and approval with the simple motion. Then he yelled at the others some more and a path opened up. Kellan spurred his creature forward and ran it as quickly as he could through the maze of tiny dwellings. He jumped off the creature when he came to some wide stairs leading down into a tunnel. He looked around first, but he knew that was where she had to be and hurried down them, unhindered by the darkness that soon engulfed the tunnel.

Finally, the tunnel opened up and he caught his first sight of the wall. The sheer size of it stopped him in his tracks and he let out a quick breath. Nothing had ever made him feel so exposed, so vulnerably small, than this massive stone veil before him. Stretching out along the wall was a bridge and about halfway along it was a lone figure.

"Tamsin!" he shouted when he saw her small silhouette against the dark stone. He rushed across the bridge to her side.

She glanced over to him for a moment, then did a second double-take, clearly surprised by his presence. But she returned her gaze towards two large, wooden doors at the other end of the bridge quickly. "Kellan," she said, her voice a little raspy as if she were out of breath. "What are you doing here?"

"K'al invoked the sh'pav'danya. The man you sent is with them and I came here."

"No. You are supposed to be at the mangroves."

"I couldn't stay with them," he said, shoving aside the hurt that still lingered. "Not when I'm needed here. Tell me what's going on."

"The amon'jii are coming," she said, a line of sweat dabbing her hairline. "Monstran and his master, the ones who have Haven, are controlling the amon'jii and sending them here. They're not just going to kill the Ma'diin. They're going to kill everyone."

The northerners had caught up to them by now and the leader said something to Tamsin. She responded swiftly and authoritatively and though Kellan couldn't understand what they were saying, he understood now what she had meant. The truth of the Kaz'ma'sha was not that she was the unifier of the twelve tribes; she was the unifier of all. Ma'diin and northerners. And after everything the northerners had done to her, to Haven, and the Ma'diin, the only way she would help them was if something worse was out there.

One of the soldiers grabbed Tamsin and tried to pull her back from the bridge. Kellan drew one of his long knives from beneath his robe, pointing it at the man who suddenly stopped. There was more shouting from the others, but the break in Tamsin's concentration was long enough for Kellan to confirm exactly what she had said. He felt their flame-infused heartbeats. Hundreds of them. Maybe thousands. Like a flash of sunlight, the feeling slammed into him and he knew exactly what Tamsin had been doing. Why she had just been standing down here all alone.

He lowered his sword, turning slowly towards the doors at the end of the bridge. He took a few steps closer to them, the arguing voices behind him dim. Then the feeling began to fade, the fiery torrent subsiding to a flickering candle as Tamsin regained control. He turned back to her. The soldier had let her go, but she had the same look of constraint on her face as before.

"You have to warn the others," she said. "And get the Empyrians out of here."

"I'm not leaving you," he said firmly.

"They won't burn down the doors, but that won't stop them for long," she said. "I can buy you a couple minutes. Please."

Kellan took out another sword and offered the handle to Tamsin. "We will give them all the time we can. Together."

She took the sword from him and gave him a small smile. "Thank you for coming back," she whispered.

He nodded in return and faced the doors once more, filled with a steadiness that surprised him, especially with knowing what was about to come through.

Then the northern leader still huddled with the others behind them started talking to Tamsin once more. She responded in her strained tone, trying to convince them, Kellan knew, to leave. Let them, he thought. They would be useless against the amon'jii anyway.

A high-pitched wail shattered through the hum of the water on the other side of the wall then, stopping all conversation. It was answered by another, this one ending in a snarling gurgle that was much, much closer than the first.

Kellan caught Tamsin's eyes for a second. "They're here," he said.

Suddenly the tunnel on the other side of the doors erupted into a symphony of shrieks and growls, growing louder and louder with each moment.

Tamsin rattled off something to the northerners, who all looked stunned by the advancing sounds. The leader responded first and Tamsin replied, her last desperate attempt to get them to leave. The leader nodded slowly, then barked a few orders at his men. Some took off back the way they had come, but two of them stayed with their leader and drew their swords.

"What are they doing?" Kellan asked.

"They're staying too," Tamsin said softly. "The others are leaving."

"Very well," Kellan said, positioning himself directly between Tamsin and the doors. He glanced up at the high wall next to them, wrinkling his nose at it.

"I'm sorry," Tamsin said, noticing his gaze. "If I had found a way to break it, none of this would be happening."

"This is not your fault," he said sternly, refusing to allow the last words between them be of guilt. "The only thing you should be sorry for is striking me with that lightning bolt. I smelled like burnt hair for days." He turned and lifted his hood off so she could see the teasing in his eyes.

She smiled through the exertion of restraining the amon'jii's fire, the corners of her eyes squinting slightly. Then her eyes widened and she looked up at the wall. "That's it," she breathed. "Kellan," she said his name, her voice alight with hope.

He didn't understand at first, then his own eyes widened. "You can really do that?"

She nodded. "I think so. I just have to…" She closed her eyes and her fist around the sword handle went white.

The already dark sky above them started churning and a low rumble rolled through the clouds. But the amon'jii were getting close too, creating their own storm as their large bodies rambled through the tunnel.

Kellan closed his own eyes and concentrated. When he opened them he said, "Sixty seconds, Tamsin."

Tamsin gasped and staggered against the stone wall, her sword clattering to the ground. "It's too much," she said. "I can't summon it while I've got a hold on them."

Kellan grabbed her fallen sword, but didn't give it back to her. Her whole body shook against the rock and her face was as pale as the moon save for the tiny line of blood that had started to snake out of her nose. Even like this, she was perfect. "Then let me do it," he said calmly. "Let them go and do what you need to." He put his hand over the top of hers until he felt the shaking slowly stop. In its place burst the fiery hearts of the amon'jii and he grunted a little as he fought to suppress them. It felt like he was the wall holding back the flood as it tried to drown him and he could only imagine what it took for Tamsin to do it for this long. He knew he couldn't suppress all of them, but he could get her the time she needed. He took his swords back in both hands and walked over to the door.

Thirty seconds.

"Kellan!"

He glanced back and saw Tamsin's horrified face.

"What are you doing?"

"What I have to," he said, using the pommels of his swords to lift up the board that kept the two doors secured.

"Kellan! No!" She started stumbling towards him.

"I'll give you as much time as I can. I owe him that much." He opened one of the doors and ducked inside, pulling it shut and sealing himself in the darkness. He heard the board slide back into place behind him and raised his swords and turned to face the beasts that were charging through the tunnel towards him.

Ten seconds.

The end had always been a shadow. He knew it was there. He knew someday it would rise up and overtake him. But he had never known when. Until now. And now that he knew, the fear was gone. All that remained was certainty and a sense that he was fulfilling what he had been inherently charged to do. That sense filled him with strength for his final moments. He would make them worthy to remember.

Two seconds.

He took a deep breath.

Tamsin fell to her knees, her mouth moving, but no words came out. She was shattered and shocked, unable to comprehend what Kellan had just done. Seconds. He had sacrificed the rest of his life to give her mere seconds. The hope she had felt only moments before felt hollow now.

"What did that man just do?" the Commander asked. "What did he just do!?"

She crawled over to the door and banged her fists on them once, letting out a frustrated cry.

A series of pain-filled yelps were her reply, making her jump back from the door, but they were not human-made. Kellan was on the other side of the thick wooden doors, fighting for time. She couldn't waste it.

She scrambled back up to her feet and looked up at the dark clouds molding around and over each other in the early night sky. The power was up there. She just needed to focus it, to wield it as she would a sword. She pressed her hands to the cold stone wall and closed her eyes, concentrating on the chaos of the storm. Her emotions had always bolstered her power and right now she had plenty of that. But she didn't know how she had made the connection with the lightning the last time. She didn't know how she had harnessed it. She reached out with the same sense she used to feel the amon'jii and the Watchers, stretching it out like a fishing net, trying to catch something.

Something slammed against the other side of the door, but it didn't break open. It was followed by a series of shrieks and the sound of claws scraping against wood. The doors rattled and the scraping became more frantic.

Tamsin tried not to think about what was happening beyond the door. She had to block out the sounds. She had to focus. But every time she thought she found what she was looking for it darted away like a snake made out of smoke.

"Lady Tamsin!" the Commander shouted, reminding her that time was falling away from them.

There. She had felt it. Tamsin gritted her teeth and dug her fingernails into the rock. It was similar to the feeling of fire when she was looking to subdue it, though that was like catching a fish that was already floating at the top of the water compared to the slippery eel she was chasing now. But she had caught the tail end of a white-hot flame and would not let go, even as it writhed and jerked wildly with neither direction nor reason. She just needed a few more seconds to tighten her hold. As long as the door held and the amon'jii did not get through—

The door suddenly roared into flames and the splintered shards of the boards burst open as several of the beasts crashed through, shaking off embers as they zeroed in on their new targets.

Tamsin's concentration was broken and her eyes widened as she beheld what her mind could only imagine as one of the seven hells. Then she realized: if the amon'jii had used their fire, then Kellan's hold over them had been severed.

The sky overhead crackled with light and a booming clap echoed through the canyon.

"Run," she instructed the Empyrians, her tone dangerously low. She turned to face the amon'jii, putting herself in the middle of the bridge as her skin sizzled with unbridled rage. She would create her own hell for these creatures.

The amon'jii snarled and their skin glistened in the heat of the flames. Their mouths opened, ready to incinerate her until she was nothing more than a pair of ashy footprints on the rock beneath her.

But Tamsin wasn't interested in that. With a twitch of a thought, she forced the fire back until the beasts were choking on it. They gagged and clawed at their throats as more stumbled through the doorway behind them, clamoring and climbing over each other to get through to her. But she was just as relentless with their onslaught as they were. She wasn't going to let one ember get through their fangs. Only when they got close enough to her by sheer number of bodies did she turn her attention skyward.

It was now or it was the end.

Kellan. Samih. Ysallah. Her father. Haven. Their faces filled the clouds as she felt her power surge to join the raw energy in the sky. She let go of the amon'jii and as she felt the heat build around her, she felt a new kind of heat, one with enough force to break down the bones of the earth.

She wrapped her soul around it and struck.

A sound like a giant drum exploding ricocheted off the canyon walls just as a debilitating dagger of light saturated the air around them. At the same time Tamsin was sent crashing to the ground and the amon'jii staggered left and right as the bridge shifted underneath them with a violent shudder.

Tamsin lifted her head slowly, blinking against the white tapestry of light that lingered over her eyes. Jagged, dark lines now covered the wall like rose vines and were surrounded by glassy, black smudges. A faint, unfocused glow lingered on the eastern edge of the bridge where the doors had been, the smoke now pock-marked by rain drops. Though…

It wasn't rain. Tamsin realized the water spattering the ground wasn't coming from the clouds, but the cracks in the dam. The dam itself groaned like an old wooden chair, creaking as rock shifted over rock, sending fresh fans of water spraying down upon them. The burst of cold water on her skin helped spark her senses again just as the dam crumbled from the pressure of the flood behind it, though some of the crumbs were bigger than her muudhiif and shot out as if fired from a cannon.

Tamsin had less than a moment to scramble away as the boulders rained down, propelled by the water raging out behind them. She dashed forward as the amon'jii shrieked in terror around her, but neither she nor the beasts were fast enough to outrun the chaos that was now erupting all around them. She couldn't stay on her feet as the water rushed around her ankles and she slipped right into the massive body of an amon'jii. A boulder crashed down just inches behind them, splitting the rock underneath their feet and tossing large shards as if they were as light as leaves. Tamsin felt the ground heave and then she was sliding downward, caught in the watery avalanche with the rest of the fallout.

The hourglass had broken.

She thought she would be falling forever, over the edge into the very canyon she had looked into yesterday, but her body slammed against something hard as the water continued to swallow her and her descent was stopped. She grabbed for something, anything, for it was impossible to see in the churning darkness, until at last her fingers closed around a stable rock. She pulled herself closer to it just as the rocks beneath her gave way. Her legs swung wildly below, but she held onto that rock, using every ounce of strength she had left to keep the water from taking her. A cry broke away from her lips, but it was not of desperation or fear. She gritted her teeth together and forced her leg to come up until the heel of her boot was over the ledge. Then she pulled and dug her boot into the rock until her knee was up, then her thigh, then her chest, then she flipped over onto her back, breathing hard. She didn't know if it would last though so she rolled over again. Heavy from fatigue and water, she shakily pushed herself up to her hands and knees. The water roared down from the wound in the dam only a few feet away, pouring through the shattered remnants of the bridge that now only existed underneath the doorways on each end.

Tamsin looked across the water to the other side, noting the arch and the curve of the stairs that disappeared up and around the corner. And the man that was standing there dressed in Empyrian garb.

She was on the amon'jii side.

She exhaled all of the air out of her lungs slowly as she realized this. She had no sword, no knife, and barely the strength to stand up. A watery death lay to her west. And a fiery one to her east. Since the water had failed to take her, she would face the fire.

She gingerly climbed to her feet and, lifting her chin, looked into the tunnel. But it was deserted. The sound of the rushing water drowned out anything she might hear, so she reached out with her senses. She could still feel them, but they were far away and growing faint. The amon'jii had fled.

Something tickled the back of her mind. The sound of her name, trying to permeate the waterfall. She turned around and saw the Empyrian on the other side with his hands around his mouth, calling to her. She thought she could make out the countenance of the Commander as he started waving and motioning with his hands. She could barely hear him, but it seemed he wanted her to stay there, that he was going to get help and they would get her out of there.

Stay there, Tamsin thought, slightly amused. Where else would she go? Then an idea closed around her as tightly as a fist and she turned around to look at the deserted tunnel once more. Breaking the dam had been a victory, but her fight wasn't over.

Then, without looking back, she walked into the darkness.

Chapter Twenty-Four

Ever since the soldiers had captured the rebels, Georgiana had been living in a fog. Guilt and fear ran rampant in her mind as she wandered the Urbane compound like a ghost. It had been the only place she could think of where she could go and it had been the last decision she made after everything had gone awry. Food and water were scarce, but so was her appetite, so she didn't mind so much that the kitchens had been ransacked for their goods a long time ago.

But when she had woken up this morning, the fog had suddenly cleared, as if someone had lifted her up and told her that she was not useless. There was still more to be done. Hiding out was not helping anyone and even though she was the reason for the rebels' current imprisonment, if she stayed there and did nothing then she would have their deaths on her head as well. That thought alone was enough to blow away the mist and the crippling guilt. Whether she had a plan or not, she couldn't stay here any longer. She would go to the Armillary alone.

She climbed the stairs to the very top of the Urbane compound, to Tamsin's room, to the one way she was going to get in. Then, with only a torch and a knife she had taken from the kitchens, she descended the stairs beyond the secret door. Down into the depths she went, where the tunnel wedged itself between the walls and pillars of the compound, expertly designed to be invisible to its inhabitants. Down until it was free enough to weave through the natural underground below the city and it leveled off into a longer, wider tunnel. Then the familiar thrumming of the Elglas began to sound, telling her she was getting close. She entered the room where the large, metal grate occupied the middle of the room. She hung her torch on the wall and began unspooling the rope that was tied around the rock on one side. She checked the knot and then, with a bit of effort, slid the grate off the hole in the floor. She put a few new knots in the rope to make it easier to climb down (and back up, she hoped) and then tossed the end down into the hole. She gripped it tightly and then began to make her way down, carefully, and as quietly as she could. She dropped down the last foot and her boots splashed in a small puddle that had accumulated in the dark alcove. She stepped out of it and peered around the edge of the wall into the main tunnel of the catacombs. Torches were spread out sparsely along the walls, illuminating the many doors that covered the other alcoves, now turned into prison cells.

High-pitched clinking and distant scraping echoed from the far end of the tunnel with the occasional muffled voice accompanying the sounds, but it was beyond the bend in the tunnel. It sounded like miners, perhaps expanding the tunnel to create more cells, she thought. She crept out from the alcove, not seeing any guards, and tip-toed through some more puddles along the floor.

"Aden?" she whispered, looking through the checkered holes in the doors. "Tomas?"

"Gia?"

She stopped at the sound of her name, peering through the small slats in one of the doors. Several dark figures were huddled in the tiny alcove, but one stood up and approached the door. Then Aden's face appeared in the square spots of light created by the slats, dirt and blood caked over his skin.

"Gia! What are you doing here?"

"I saw you get arrested. I have to get you out of here."

"We were ambushed," he said. "They knew we were coming."

"I know and I'm sorry," she said. "It was all my fault, but I'm not going to leave until I free you."

"There's a guard; he has the keys. It's the only way to open the doors."

"Do you know where he is?"

"The guards took Tomas and rest of his cell up to the Armillary."

"Okay," she said trying to think quickly. She had snuck into the Armillary before, she could do it again.

"Hey!" A man shouted from the bend in the tunnel, pointing at Georgiana.

"Go!" Aden shouted at her, but he didn't need to for she had already taken off running towards the stairs.

But she didn't get far before she heard more footsteps coming down the stairs in a rushed thunder. She turned back, but there was nowhere else for her to go except the way she came, so she ducked back into the alcove and began climbing the rope again, using the knots to help her ascent.

Someone grabbed her boot and pulled down. She kicked and twisted as she clung to the rope, but then more hands joined the first and latched onto her legs. Her burning hands finally released the rope as she could not overcome the doubled force of the guards weighing her down. She collapsed onto them and continued to twist and struggle as they grabbed hold of her arms. They dragged her out of the alcove and down the hall and no matter how much she attempted to wrestle free, there was no overpowering them. And no matter how much Aden yelled and banged on the cell door, the guards could not be dissuaded from their path.

Georgiana spat curses at them and berated them the whole way up the stairs and up into the Armillary, calling them cowards and traitors to the Empyrian people. But when they reached the main chamber inside 'The Dome,' and she saw the other rebels kneeling in the center, surrounded by the Empyrian High Guard, she felt suddenly tired, as if all the air could not re-inflate her lungs. The rebels' eyes looked over at her as she was brought to them and she could see their deflated spirits as well. Tomas was among them and a quick flash of horror covered his face at seeing her, but just as quickly he looked away and replaced it with a silent, defiant mask.

Georgiana looked away too. She knew she deserved all of the blame for what was happening, but she couldn't stand the thought of Tomas thinking it too. She had betrayed them all and though it had been unintentional, she was responsible. And then another thought hit her: she was just like her father. Her beautifully naive, well-intentioned father who had managed to get himself embroiled in the Lords' snares as they fought for the upper hand. He had tried to protect her, by helping Cornelius, and in the process had betrayed the Urbanes. Then he had tried to make amends, though Lord Urbane's price was to spy for the other side, putting her father right back into the metal jaws of their power struggle. Georgiana had urged him not to; to stay out of it for his life's sake. Only now did she understand the weight of living with a betrayal like that. Only now did she realize that she had failed to learn from her father's mistakes and had followed the same path that he had tread before her. It was a bittersweet sunset. She loved her father, and despite the roots in the road that had tripped him up, she was proud of him for fighting to put things right. And she knew she would do the same. Whatever it might cost her. The footsteps from her father lay before her and she would follow them to the end.

The guards deposited her roughly on the floor next to the other rebels and the moment their hands left her she scrambled over to Tomas, prostrating herself over his chained wrists, grabbing his hands in her own.

"Please forgive me! I never meant for this to happen!" she cried, and though her words were sincere, the display had a bigger purpose. She pulled the small knife she had taken from the kitchens out from the edge of her sleeve and slipped it into Tomas' palm.

His eyes registered surprise for only a moment and then he gripped his fingers around it, effectively hiding it from the guards.

Georgiana was then pulled away from him and held firmly in place next to the group, each of her arms held by a guard. The other soldiers looked only slightly rattled by her little outburst, but it wasn't long before they all straightened and resumed their impassive expressions, spurred by the sharp clap of footsteps approaching. Several parted to make way for the newcomers.

Flanked on either side by two guards was Cornelius Saveen.

Georgiana's knees began to shake as she watched him look over the batch of prisoners with a smug gleam in his eye, but not because she was afraid; because she was pinned in place by the guards and her desire to lunge at him and put a fist through his face was going unfulfilled.

His eyes made their final stop on her and he took a few more steps closer. "I know you," he said, trying to figure her out.

"We caught her down below trying to free the other prisoners," one of the guards holding her said. "She tried to escape through one of the old passageways."

"Another one?" Cornelius raised an eyebrow and then turned to an officer. "Send a unit down there. I want to know where it goes."

A couple of them left, but Cornelius stayed and studied her once more. "You were at the tavern. With one of the soldiers that night." He smiled. "I suppose I should be thanking you. You're the reason my plan worked so beautifully."

"You'll never get away with any of this. No matter how many of us you kill," Georgiana retorted. "Your fate is already written."

Cornelius laughed. "You sound like the witch woman, Mora. Always babbling on about death and the grim future. I suppose she was talking about you and your friends here." He turned and started walking back towards his soldiers.

But Georgiana could not let him go thinking he had won. "You're right, but you don't know everything. You didn't know that she told me I would bring about the destruction of the city."

He stopped then and looked over his shoulder at her.

"My fate is tied to Empyria. If you kill us, then you'll be sealing your own tomb."

He marched back over to her, the humor in his face gone. "That witch was nothing more than a drunk. Her words were nothing more than heretical gibberish."

Georgiana let the corners of her mouth curve up. "Hmm. I wonder what she told you to make you fear her so."

Cornelius reached up and smacked the side of her face with the back of his hand. Georgiana winced and let out a sharp hiss as the stinging sensation spread across her cheek.

"I am not afraid. And tomorrow morning you will be the first to be executed. Just like your father was...Miss *Graysan*."

Georgiana glared at him, refusing to let him see the pain his words about her father conjured, but she did not have time to quip back for the sound of a distant trumpet echoed through the halls and into the grand chamber. But they weren't the uplifting scales of victory; they were the frantic blares of impending danger.

Cornelius moved away from her then and back to his soldiers, suspicion and caution vying for dominance over his face. He ordered some more men to go out and see what the alarm was about, but no sooner had they left than the sound of more warning sounds blasted from the trumpets, these ones much closer.

Georgiana exchanged a look with Tomas, but as far as she could tell he didn't know what was causing the disturbance either.

There may have been a few rebels that had escaped the roundup, but not enough to launch an assault.

A guard came running into the main chamber, stopping by Cornelius, his eyes wide with disbelief. "My lord, we're under attack!"

"I thought you said you'd gotten them all," Cornelius turned on one of his captains with a scowl.

The captain could only stutter in his defense, but the new guard continued. "Not rebels, my lord."

Cornelius turned around. "What?"

"They're from the Cities. A whole army."

"Send men to the gates," Cornelius instructed. "I want bowmen on the walls and—."

"They already breached the gates," the guard interrupted. "They're in the city."

The air in the room changed. The calm upper hand that the Empyrian soldiers had portrayed suddenly shifted and left them looking uncertainly at their leader.

Georgiana could see the fear settling in Cornelius' eyes even as he started barking orders and mobilizing the soldiers. A large number of the soldiers rushed out of the main chamber then to join the defense of the city and Cornelius ordered the remainder to split: half with him and half to take the prisoners below. She glanced over at Tomas once more and he nodded slightly. This was their moment.

Two guards came over to escort them back into the catacombs and as one reached to pull Tomas back to his feet, he sprang upwards, slashing the man's neck with the knife that Georgiana had given to him. He immediately went for the second, throwing his whole body towards the guard before he could pull his sword out.

The other rebels jumped up, and though they didn't have any weapons, they had the numbers now.

The guards holding Georgiana pushed her to the floor and rushed over to join the fight. The clash of swords on chains and the cries of men struggling for their lives rattled in her ears as she scrambled across the floor, trying to get out of the melee. She saw Cornelius' stormy face as he marched back to the fray with his sword drawn. He swung at Tomas, but she lost sight of them as a soldier's body fell in front of her. She jumped back, pressing up against one of the stone pillars supporting the room.

Then she saw Tomas fall to the floor, holding a bloody gash across his right thigh.

"Tomas!" she screamed, causing both he and Cornelius to look at her.

Tomas' face was wrenched with pain and Cornelius knew he had him beat. Cornelius let him lie and aimed his sights on Georgiana, stalking across the room towards her, no doubt set on making her pay for her previous comments.

Georgiana knew she couldn't run, but she had no way to defend herself either. Then she saw the shiny blade of the sword from the fallen soldier and lunged at it. But Cornelius realized her intention too and was faster, reaching her in an instant and pinning her wrist to the ground with his boot before she could grasp the handle.

They stared at each other a moment, anger meeting defiance.

"You won't win," Georgiana said through gritted teeth.

"You won't be alive to see if you're right," he said.

He raised his sword, but then froze, the fury on his face replaced with something else, though Georgiana couldn't quite tell what it was in the shadows. And she could hardly see beyond her own fear. But then she glimpsed something at Cornelius' neck: a long, silver blade. Slowly, Cornelius stepped back, removing his foot from Georgiana's wrist.

She stood up, noticing the other Empyrian soldiers had stopped fighting as more soldiers flooded into the room. But these soldiers did not wear the blue and brown garb of the Empyrians.

"It's over, Cornelius," the voice holding the sword to Cornelius' neck boomed and Georgiana looked to see Lord Urbane standing there, his soldiers fanning triumphantly out around him. "You're done."

Chapter Twenty-Five

Tamsin knew she was getting close. She could feel them again. Like bees returning to the hive the amon'jii were forming a swarm once more. Though she didn't know if they were regrouping on their own or if they were being drawn to this spot, by something or someone. She tightened her grip on the sword as she continued down the tunnel. She had stumbled upon it earlier amidst the still carcasses of the amon'jii. She had found his sword, but not Kellan. Burned, buried, or worse, she only allowed herself a moment to wonder, for she knew if she gave herself any longer to dwell on what his final moments had been then she would fall apart. His sword had done him proud to the very end. She hoped it would do the same for her.

A flickering glow caressed the wall ahead of her where the tunnel curved and she could hear the snarls and snapping jaws of the amon'jii. She put her back to the shadowy side and crept along until she reached the curve. She paused here and the tiny drops of water that fell lackadaisically off the tips of her hair seemed to mark the moment somehow. As if to say this was the end of the trail. The end of the adventure. If someone were to retrace her steps all the way from Jalsai, from Empyria to the marsh lands, from the mangroves to the islands, the Ravine to the anasii hada…they would stop here with a few drops of water on the rough, cold stone.

She pushed her hair behind her back and peered around the curve, to find that the tunnel lasted only a few more feet and then opened up into a magnificent cavern that rivaled even the size of the Dome of the Armillary. The inner walls were pock-marked with natural alcoves and ledges and rose up to meet the ceiling as if to resemble a wine decanter. Though the stopper was broken in various places, exposed to the night sky above, this was not enough to cause the glow she saw.

In the center of the cavern was a conical-shaped pile of sticks and reed stalks, burning brightly like a beacon, its smoke meandering up through the holes in the ceiling. Perhaps to draw the amon'jii here, because she could feel them nearby.

But it wasn't the fire that caught her attention, it was the man that stepped out from behind it.

Mr. Monstran.

His silver hair glistened like sweat in the firelight and his maroon robes seemed to absorb the shadows, creating the illusion of a floating specter. A smile crept over his lips as his eyes met Tamsin's. "I wondered if I would see you here," he said.

Tamsin walked out from the tunnel. There was no need to hide anymore. She took a few steps into the large cavern, aware of the pulsing amon'jii hearts in the shadows surrounding her, but she did not take her eyes off of Monstran.

He paced around the fire, seemingly unafraid of closing the distance between them, but then several more men stepped out from behind him, clothed in shades of black and carmine and armed with curved swords.

Tamsin paused at this, for the men moved more like beasts then soldiers, tilting their heads to look at her as they awkwardly stepped out from either side of the fire, knees bent and backs hunched as if they were getting ready to crawl across the floor. They resembled the amon'jii, stealthy and deadly, and horrifically paralyzing if caught up by the sight of them. Tamsin wondered if these men too had been tortured and manipulated by Monstran, to be his personal bodyguards against the very creatures they mirrored.

"I see you're realizing the futility of your situation," Monstran said, noticing her reaction.

Vengeance had a bitter, metallic taste, Tamsin thought as she stared at Monstran. Here she was face to face with the man who had stolen the man she loved and all she could think about was sticking her sword right through that superior smile of his. Though vengeance was unique that way, in that it took grief and loss and sharpened it into a tool so focused that there were only two possible outcomes: victory or death. Tamsin felt the familiar headache starting to build as her rage at the man before her grew, though she now knew it to be her power. It demanded to be released, to see Monstran's white hair set a flaming orange.

But there was one power greater than hers. Greater even than vengeance.

Haven wasn't gone yet. And neither was her desire to get him back.

Slowly, the headache began to ease as she regained control. She couldn't kill him yet, not until she knew where Haven was. "No," she replied through ground teeth. "I'm realizing the futility of yours."

Monstran stopped pacing, then turned to face her with a smile. But the corner of his mouth twitched slightly. "You cannot stop what is coming," he said. "It is already in motion."

"On the contrary, I've already stopped you. Your dam is broken. The amon'jii will never cross now."

"If you only would be alive to see if that were true," he said. "But this is your last night on this earth I'm afraid, Miss Urbane." Then he raised his hand and snapped his fingers.

His bodyguards lunged at her like a cluster of spiders attacking a fly. She had only time for a quick intake of breath before she had to block the first sword that swung her way. She parried the first man easily and swung around behind him, slashing the backs of his unprotected legs. The ones that followed were not so easy, having seen their comrade fall to the deadly girl with the blade, and she quickly found that she was matched in speed and strength. She had to dodge and sidestep the quick blows and though her size offered them a smaller target, they followed her relentlessly.

As she swung low, forcing one of the men to jump back, she realized she had done this all before. Her body remembered the movements, the same pattern the Red Sight had conjured for her in the battle. The earth trembled with the weight of their footsteps and the ring of steel shuddered down her arms with each collision, just as she had felt in her vision. Only now it was not northerners she fought, but these beastly men. And she was alone. Every choice she had made had been to prevent what she had seen in the Red Sight, to protect the people she cared about. But it seemed her vision was manifesting anyway, in its own surreal way.

Another man charged at her, taking advantage of her momentary lapse. He slashed at her like a man attacking a nightmare, forcing her to back up as she struggled to block the continuous blows until she was almost swallowed by the shadow of one of the alcoves.

Its breath alerted her to its presence only a second before an amon'jii sprang out of the shadow behind her. She had no choice but to dart forward, away from its snapping jaws and towards the frenzied attack of the man. The amon'jii's teeth missed her head by less than a thread, but she was unable to completely avoid the man's sword, and it sliced across her collarbone like a whip. She shoved his sword away with her own, putting a step between them, ready for his next attack.

But it never came. The man suddenly retreated back to Monstran's side, cowering like a dog that had betrayed its owner. The remaining bodyguards did the same, slinking back until Tamsin was standing alone again, though she looked around, making sure there were no other amon'jii approaching.

Monstran seemed unsurprised by their actions. He moved his head as if he were listening to something for a moment, then began pacing again. "Let me tell you about my Master, the Creator, the Enslaver. You know him as one of the Q'atorii."

Tamsin squeezed her eyes shut for just a second, feeling the burn of the cut across her collar, then refocused on Monstran, aiming her sword in his direction. She would not be fooled by his manipulations. However she felt about the story of the Q'atorii and the Ma'diin's creation would not blind her to the kind of man Monstran was. He was a man who thrived on the fear of others. Gods didn't exist; evil men did.

"You can't make a god disappear by not believing in it," Monstran continued. "He'll still be there."

Tamsin stared at him, feeling the fire build behind her eyes. "I know the story. Even if he was real, Ib'n was defeated. All of this is a hoax. Created by you!"

"My dear," Mr. Monstran said with a sickly-sweet smile. "Your education has been sorely misinformed I'm afraid." He turned his head slightly to the right. "Haven, why don't you come out here?"

Tamsin's stomach dropped. A shadowy figure stepped out from the shadows and drifted over to Monstran's side as the beastly men cowered even further. His face was hidden by a hood, but she had learned to recognize him without it a long time ago.

"Haven?" she breathed.

Haven remained still however, and though every ounce of her body wanted her to rush over to him, Tamsin held her ground too. Her one instinct that something was off was enough to hold her back. This wasn't the beaten, broken man she had last seen in the catacombs of the Armillary, begging her to stay. He stood tall, clothed in black and crimson robes, his presence towering like a mountain whose shadow darkened the entire valley beneath it. The man before her made the hairs on the back of her neck stand up like a cat's.

"What have you done to him?" she hissed at Monstran.

"I told him the truth," Monstran said. "Would you like to hear it? Or rather, would you like him to tell you…?"

"Tamsin."

Her name fell from Haven's lips like a drip of honey, slowly stretching out across the space between them, and she trembled at the sound of his voice, having longed to hear it for so long. It poured over her instincts, threatening to embalm them until they suffocated and froze, never to be heeded again.

"Come to me, Tamsin. It's alright," he continued in a soothing tone. "Everything is better now. I've seen the truth of Monstran's words and Ib'n's vision for the world. Together we can make the others see too."

She wanted to melt into the sound of him, drink him like a bittersweet wine that left her with a craving so strong she couldn't deny, but his words struck a chord of horror. "What?"

His lips turned up into a smile. "I finally understand, Tamsin. You don't have to fight anymore. Join us."

Her head quivered back and forth, unable to believe what he was saying. Join with Monstran? Join with the amon'jii? "Do you even know what you're saying? What did they do to you?"

He crossed over to her, far more quickly than Tamsin could react to, and put his finger underneath her chin, lifting her gaze up to meet his. That sweet smell, smoke and lilac intertwining like vines into an ethereal pillar of mist, blurred her senses and for a moment all she could think of was surrendering to the fog. Then her eyes lifted and collided with his, but the brilliant blue she had come to know, filled with a depth and clarity that rivaled the sea, was gone. Haven's eyes, as sharp and icy as they were, had always held a warmth whenever he looked at her. But here before her was a gaze that could've froze the sun.

She took a quick step back and his hand drifted away from her chin. She whipped her sword out in front of her, the point just barely pressing into his chest.

"Finally," a cold, reverberating voice poured out from between his lips. "The great she-hunter shows herself."

She clenched her fists around the hilt, her nails digging deep into the leather. When she thought Haven had died in Empyria, it seemed like a lifetime ago now, she had been out of her mind with grief, with disbelief, with anger. She had abandoned her life, had let time just march on without her aware of it.

Now it was different. Now those emotions were all refined, focused. They were sharpened to a point, like an arrow, aimed right at Haven. Only it was not Haven. Everything she had heard, everything Oman and Enrik and even Mr. Graysan had warned her about, was standing before her. She didn't want to say his name, as if speaking it aloud would make it real, but she knew they were already well past that. She breathed hard, like a caged animal with too much energy.

His eyes continued to stare at her. He seemed relaxed, unruffled by her display.

"You know, when you used his firestone for the very first time, you were the one that connected us. You opened up a gateway into his soul for me. I have you to thank for choosing Haven to be my host."

"You're not a god, you're a monster!" The air grew hot around her as her power begged to be unleashed.

A laugh surfaced, sending chills across her skin and Haven took a few calculated steps back, holding his hands up on either side of him. The amon'jii that had previously lurked in the shadows now stepped forward. One, two, three…more and more of them emerged until Tamsin could no longer keep count and they unfolded around him like writhing black wings. It was one against hundreds. She was strong enough to control their fire, but to repel them all physically would be…impossible.

"It may be only minutes," Monstran said, "but if you want to live…"

A drop of blood slid off her lip from her nose and when it hit the floor it sounded like an anvil had been struck.

Ib'n's voice cut through Haven's lips, tainted with triumph. "Then run, little she-hunter. Run."

"Get him out of my sight," Lord Urbane said and two of his soldiers moved in, wrestled Cornelius' sword out of his hand and began to drag him away.

Georgiana could barely believe that she was still alive and that the Cities had come to their aid. But one by one the other Empyrians dropped their weapons and where the rebels had once knelt on the floor, now they did so. The rebels stood around them, out of breath from the recent struggle, but smiling. All except Tomas, who was still laying on the floor, clutching his bleeding leg with a grimace. Georgiana rushed over to him.

"I'll be okay," he said with some effort as she knelt down next to him.

Lord Urbane, who had been ordering his men to clear the Armillary, limped over to them and then upon seeing the state Tomas was in called for a healer. "You're Graysan's daughter, aren't you?" he then asked.

Georgiana nodded, still too dizzy from their unexpected salvation to say anything.

"I was sorry to hear about his death," he said. "Though your letter convinced the Council to send an army here. So thank you."

Georgiana nodded again, though she wanted to thank him for coming to their aid as well as berating him for getting her father involved in all of this. But she said nothing. Her world had been upended and now at last there was some hope for calm, but she felt numb. How quickly things could change and as unprepared as she had felt joining the rebels, she felt just as unprepared to navigate the future without them. Lord Urbane had returned with his army to save them and to expunge the hold Cornelius had over the city. But with Cornelius' power gone, there was no need for the rebels anymore.

Where would that power go? Back to the lords? Back to men like Cornelius who could decapitate the city with a snap of their fingers?

"How did you get past the soldiers?" Tomas asked, breaking Georgiana out of her daze.

"The man you sent found us as we emerged from the mountains," Lord Urbane said. "He showed us the way through the Hollow Cliffs into the city. We waited until nightfall then a group of us infiltrated the compound and were able to get to the main gates to let the rest of the army in."

"Your timing was a little tight," Tomas commented.

Lord Urbane chuckled. "I apologize for that. I—." Then he stopped and looked around with a curious expression.

Everyone else did the same as a low rumble shivered through the Armillary, making the floor underneath them tremble. Confused whispers were exchanged by the soldiers as the rumble slowly dissipated. But then another rumble erupted, even more forceful than the last, making some men stumble.

It wasn't the Empyrians. It wasn't the Cities' soldiers. It was bigger. Lord Urbane shouted at some of the men to see what was going on, but as they disappeared down the hall, the giant, colored-glass dome above them exploded, sending thousands of fragments raining down upon them. Everyone crouched down and covered their heads as the glass shattered around them, but there was no time to escape the jagged downfall entirely.

Georgiana tried to cover Tomas as best she could, but no one emerged unscathed by the time the last pieces fell. She looked up at the great, sharp-edged hole in the ceiling and as everyone began to stand up again, shouts and screams from the outside filtered in. But then even closer shouting could be heard as men and soldiers emerged from the tunnel that led down to the catacombs. Georgiana noticed that all their clothes were soaking wet as they fled. She looked at Tomas and his eyes told her he was thinking the same thing.

"Get the keys!" he told her, pointing at one of the fallen Empyrian soldiers.

She scrambled over to the still soldier as everyone else mobilized around her as Lord Urbane began shouting orders again. She unhooked the key ring from the man's belt and took off for the tunnel. She could hear the screaming from down below, the frantic calls for help, as she descended the stairs back to the catacombs. She rounded the last corner and was knocked down by a man fleeing. She fell down the last step and landed shin-deep in water.

She stood up quickly, instantly shivering from the cold, and let out a horrified quiver of air as she heard the prisoners shouting, begging for someone to let them out of the flooding tunnel. Whatever was happening outside was forceful enough to undermine the integrity of the new cells. Within minutes this place would be an underwater tomb as the Elglas took back what was hers.

She gripped the keys tightly and waded over to the first door. She shoved them into the lock and twisted. "Push!" she shouted to the men and women inside, for the force of the water rushing from the other end of the tunnel was too strong to allow her to open on her own. Once there was enough space for the people to get through she went on to the next one.

"Gia!" she heard Aden's relieved voice when she made it to his cell.

"Hurry!" she said as she unlocked the door and the men shoved it open. They rushed out, but Aden stayed with her, grabbing the door and holding it open.

"Go to the next one!" he shouted above the sound of the rushing water.

She did and they went on like that until the water was up to their waists. Finally, they opened the last cell and urged the people to hurry towards the stairs. Georgiana went the other way though, further into the tunnel. She had to make sure everyone was out. She couldn't leave anyone behind.

She heard Aden calling her name, but then another rumble interrupted him and the entire tunnel groaned and heaved around them. Georgiana lost her footing as the swirling water doubled its force and she fell into the water. She couldn't gain traction as the current continued to push her down the tunnel and her hands grappled for something, anything beneath the water to anchor her. Then she felt a hand grip her and haul her above the surface. Aden's face emerged as she coughed and spluttered and he gave her a moment to catch her breath before they made their way to the stairs.

They took a few steps up, but rounded the corner only to see a wall of boulders sealing the way up. The last rumble had caused a cave-in. They were trapped.

Aden pounded his fists against them. "No!" he cried.

But Georgiana wasn't defeated yet. "Aden! C'mon!" she shouted, pulling his arm and going back into the water which now splashed up against their chests. They made their way along the walls, gripping the cell doors they had just opened to keep from getting swept under again. They pushed through the water as quickly as they could, but it was rising fast now. Finally, they reached the alcove. Georgiana's rope still hung from the ceiling and Aden boosted her up as she began to climb. She hurried, though her wet clothes and slippery hands seemed determined to pull her back down. She forced herself to keep going up, gritting her teeth against her own weight until she finally emerged into the small room. She hooked her fingers into the nearby grate and dragged herself the rest of the way out. The torch she had brought with her earlier was barely the size of a candle flame now, illuminating only the beads of water on her skin. Panting, she looked back into the hole. She could hear the rushing water below, but saw only darkness.

"Aden? Aden!" she shouted.

Then Aden's hands emerged on the rope and she let out a relieved exhale as she helped pull him up the rest of the way. They both laid on their backs for a few moments, breathing heavily as their bodies took in the short respite.

"By the gods," Aden said, chuckling. "Let's never do that again."

Before Georgiana could agree, another rumble shook the room, sending little puffs of dust falling from the ceiling. It was nothing like the shattering of the Armillary, but Georgiana didn't want to stick around any longer.

"What's happening?" Aden asked her as they both got to their feet.

"I don't know," she replied and they headed out down the long tunnel. She explained to him what had happened in the Armillary and Lord Urbane's army showing up, but she couldn't explain what was causing these quakes. They hurried through the tunnel and back up the stairs to the Urbane compound without further hindrance other than their own exhaustion.

Finally they made it to the top and stepped into Tamsin's old room. Something caught Georgiana's eye immediately and she went over to the balcony, but stopped short as her breath caught in her throat.

The night sky was on fire. And so was the city. She felt Aden step up beside her, the same horrified expression on his face. They watched as huge pyres rose up into the sky and new ones exploded at random throughout the city. But it wasn't at random. The fires illuminated a shape, circling above the city like a vulture, only it wasn't a bird, it was much bigger. Snarls could be heard between the roaring flames as if the sun had sent its very own warrior to destroy them. Every time it dove towards the city, a bright ball of fire would spew from its mouth and another building would be set ablaze.

Suddenly the stones above them broke and burst around them as a set of giant claws dug into the roof of the compound. Georgiana and Aden jumped back, pressing their backs to the wall inside the room. Another one of the creatures scratched at the stone as it searched for a foothold until finally one of its claws wrapped around the doorway where they had just been standing. A long, waving tail appeared over the other doorway, moving back and forth like a flag in the breeze. They could hear the creature breathing: a low thrumming deep in its throat accompanied by a slow scraping sound as it moved across the ceiling.

Georgiana didn't dare to move, but her eyes were drawn upward to the new hole in the ceiling. She saw skin like a lizard with wings like a bat covering the creature for just a moment and then she felt hot air brush across her face. She focused her eyes ahead once more, forcing her trembling hands to be still. But then she saw the edge of a black snout move into the doorway of the balcony, glistening with rows of sharp teeth. Its nostrils flared wide, trying to smell for them she knew. She didn't know if the water would cover their scent, but she did know she couldn't move. It wouldn't matter if the creature didn't smell them then; it would see them.

An other-worldly shriek filled the sky then and the creature pulled back, responding to the call from the other one still wreaking havoc over the city. With a great whoosh of air, it launched itself from the compound and flew back into the darkness to join the other.

It took Georgiana a moment and a squeeze on her arm from Aden's hand to break the icy fear still holding her in place. But then she peered around the doorway again where the creature had just vacated, feeling like a cat on its ninth life.

Aden pointed across the city towards the black desert and told her to look. There, where the glittering night sky and the shifting sands of the Sindune collided, the air seemed to spark and ignite, as if the stars on the horizon were exploding. But they weren't stars. With each illuminating burst, the outline of wings appeared.

More were coming.

As Georgiana watched, Mora's words came back to her. A long time ago, the witch woman had prophesied that she would bring about the destruction of the city and be buried beneath it. One part of that, it seemed, was about to come true.

"Then run, little she-hunter. Run."

Those were the last words she heard before the fear took over and she ran. She could still hear them behind her as she turned down another passageway. They seemed to echo in the rocky halls after her, chasing her like a shadow, snatching at her heels until she finally stumbled and crashed into the floor. But what was truly chasing her was more than shadows.

'Get up!' her mind shrieked and her hands raked across the ground in answer, grasping at anything that would help her along. But her arms felt numb and her legs were like wooden logs as she heaved herself back to her feet. The shock of what she had seen was setting in, slowing her down as it fought against her instincts to flee.

At first, she had fled blindly through the tunnels, the sound of the amon'jii's claws scraping against the stone driving her forward. But as her endurance waned, she knew she would have to run smarter, not faster. So she began choosing the narrower passages, forcing the large creatures to pursue her in an ever-thinning line. But they were relentless, voracious, and…hungry. They clawed over each other and at the walls, snapping and snarling at each other just long enough to give her an extra moment here and a precious second there to gain an inch. They could not burn her, for despite the reckless speed at which she ran she kept control of the fire raging in their hearts. But their voices lashed out after her, taunting her, cursing her. They promised a ruthless death. She wanted to cover her ears and scream.

She gripped the tunnel wall for support and her hands flexed around an edge. She quickly felt along it and though she could barely see a foot in front of her she deemed it wide enough and slipped around it. There was just enough room for her to squeeze into the crevice and she forced herself to keep moving through it, even as the walls scraped her back, her arms, and her knees. She kept going, even when she felt like the walls choked all the air from the passage, even as they pushed what was left from her lungs. The tearing and snarling and shrieking from the main passageway grew louder and she grew more desperate to escape them until she was tearing at the wall herself, pulling her body through by her fingernails.

At last she felt an edge, and gripped it tight, thrusting herself out of the narrow crevice and onto a jagged ledge overlooking the eastern landscape. She gasped as she was released and the bitter bite of the night air seized her. She stumbled forward and collapsed onto her hands and knees. She hugged herself around her knees, hoping the pressure would still her heaving chest and quiet her breathing. Surely they would hear her? She forced her lips shut, even though her lungs begged for more air, but she only allowed it through her nose. In and out. In and out as her chin quivered and the fear inside threatened to rip her open. She closed her eyes as it whispered insidious things to her, telling her to give up, that there was no way she was getting out of here alive. That everything that had happened had been for nothing. It fed off the heartbreak of her past and the horror that she had just witnessed.

No fear...

She opened her eyes as his voice floated over the breeze and stared at the sand underneath her hands. Her brows furrowed together as she slowly dug her fingers into the fine grains. She looked up, squinting against the harsh rays of the sun, and saw that the ledge had disappeared. All around her was the desert, simmering in the bright midday light.

It all seemed so real, but she couldn't understand why her mind was conjuring this now. The light, the heat, even the dryness in her throat scratched open the memory of being here before, lost in the desert.

A shadow fell across her, perhaps a cloud to bring shade to the damning heat—. Then she realized she had that same thought before, when…

The shadow transformed into a man and she blinked hard, but she already knew who it was.

"Haven," she whispered, her lips trembling.

But he was all tenderness here, gentle. He offered her some water, telling her to drink slow, and she relished the feeling of the cool liquid as it slipped down her throat just as she relished reliving this moment. The moment when she had first met Haven.

He knelt down beside her, wrapping his cloak around her and then put his arms underneath her legs and shoulders. *"Don't give up on me,"* he whispered, as if commanding her to live. Then he lifted her off the ground.

Tamsin gasped and found herself standing on the ledge once more, surrounded only by the dark night and the abyss only inches from her feet. She stumbled back against the rock face, breathing heavily as the memory disappeared as quickly as it had come.

But his last words echoed in her mind. *Don't give up on me.* They felt new, but familiar, as if her mind had been so delirious during that time that she had locked them away. But now she heard them so clearly, spoken in his smooth Ma'diinese, infusing her with the strength to keep going despite the desert's best efforts to break her. He had been the strong one then. He had carried her across the sands and protected her from the sandstorm even though it had taken everything he had to do so.

But now, they took on a new meaning, as if they were coming from Haven at this point in time, begging *her* not to give up on *him*. He was the one that needed her help now, her strength.

Hers will be the fury…

Have faith in your Watcher… he needs it right now… Numha's words whispered to her.

Hers will be the judgment…

Even the dead are with you… Ko'ran's voice drifted over the wind.

Hers will be the choice…

You are not alone… the Blue Lady promised.

Hers will be the tide that changes the forces of earth and moves Gods and queens.

Tamsin clenched her fists, feeling the words surround her like a shield. Her power seethed through her veins, preparing to be freed. She was ready. She was not afraid anymore.

She squeezed back through the crevasse, back to the tunnels that she had just fled and emerged into the hollow darkness. She could feel the amon'jii nearby, feel their heartbeats quicken as they picked up her scent once again. She heard their claws against the stone, racing towards her. She could sense the fire inside them, ready to be released.

As they neared, she didn't subdue the flames she felt building inside them. Instead, she fueled them even more, swelling the flames until the amon'jii couldn't control them and the fire consumed them from within. Earth-shattering shrieks filled the tunnels as the amon'jii lurched to a stop, twisting and contorting, clawing at their insides that were burning from within. The sounds of the dying creatures lasted only moments as they were unable to stave off Tamsin's attack and soon the tunnel was lined with motionless bodies.

Tamsin made her way back, lighting up any amon'jii that threatened her, but the further she went, the more fear she saw reflected in the beasts' eyes as they witnessed their kin drop to the ground, glowing and steaming. And then they began to retreat, fleeing back through the tunnels, screeching out warnings to the others. Tamsin followed them, knowing they would run back to their Master. Her power was sizzling by the time she made it back to the chamber, though she felt neither tired nor pained from using it. Rather it was like she had tapped into a tree with an endless supply of syrup, filling her veins with the necessary fuel to burn the entire forest.

Monstran and Haven were still there, engrossed in a dramatic conversation while the amon'jii flooded in around them, hissing and snapping and cursing her name. They both looked up as she re-entered the chamber. Haven held his hand up and the amon'jii quieted, shrinking back behind their leader.

"What has she done to them, Master? Why are they so upset?"

Haven held up his other hand, silencing Monstran as well, then he turned his hooded gaze towards Tamsin.

"Well, well. You are braver than I thought," Ib'n's cold voice resounded over the stone.

"You don't scare me."

Haven's body circled closer to her. He held out his hand and one of the bodyguards timidly placed one of the curved swords in his hand. He flexed his fingers around it, testing the grip and feel. Then he turned his attention back to Tamsin. "I'll let you in on a secret, little she-hunter: Queens are not immortal. Kings are not immortal. Kazserii, Lords, Chiefs, Warlords... even Gods. I've destroyed more of them than you could count in your lifetime. The Q'atorii fell at my hands. The Seven Deities of your ancestors, the Ottarkins, fell after them. Those who hold the most power fall the hardest. They bleed and they wail and they beg for mercy. And then they die. You call yourself Kazsera. Let me tell you: your fate will be the same as the gods and queens that fell before you."

"My fate will be my choice," Tamsin said, her determination solidifying through every muscle in her body. "And my people call me many things, but only one matters." She paused. "Haven calls me 'jha'ii.' And that's how I know you will lose. Because love is a power greater than any title or person. And *love is immortal*." Here she couldn't help but let a grin slide across her lips. "And by your own admission—you are not." She gripped her sword tightly, ready for the hate she saw in his eyes to unleash itself, but she wasn't afraid of it anymore, for when she had spoken the word 'jha'ii' something had flickered in Haven's eyes. Just for a second, there had been doubt in his resolve, and that was the first crack in Ib'n's armor. If it took ten thousand cracks like that to get through to Haven then Tamsin wouldn't waver. And she wouldn't relent.

This would be her hardest duel yet. She would either win or she would die. And this fight wouldn't be won by the sword; she would have to rely on her instincts and trust her training with the blade to keep her alive long enough to find the right words to say that would undo months of torture and manipulation. And all while her heart pumped raw, agonizing emotion as much as it pumped blood.

Chapter Twenty-Six

Blood ran freely down her arm, mixing with the dust of the earth to give her an almost black hue, though there was no time to bind it. Tamsin stared at it and a steady calm settled on her, slowing her breathing to match the beating of her heart. She knew Haven was coming for her again; she could see his dark shape getting closer out of her peripherals, but she was not afraid. She snapped out of her trance and ducked out of the way just as his sword came crashing down on the rocks where she had stood. She kicked at his wrists before he could strike again and he lost hold of his sword, the impact sending it screeching across the floor. She slashed wide and he jumped back out of the way, giving her the space she needed to cross over to his fallen sword.

She reached for it and his boot slammed down onto her forearm. He grabbed her other wrist before she could bring her sword around then her throat with his other hand until she was painfully and effectively pinned to the ground. Her mouth opened, uselessly gasping for air as she tried to free herself from under his weight.

His eyes drifted away from her face and down to her hand that was desperately trying to move her sword. Something flickered in his eyes, some recognition tapping against the icy cold, like a bird pecking against a glass window. His hand loosened around Tamsin's throat and a wild gust of air rushed into her lungs. He reached up and his fingertips brushed the bracelet that Ko'ran had given her. Lu'sa's bracelet.

He staggered back like she had struck him in the chest, his hands clenching into claws in front of him. A strangled cry tore its way out of his throat and his knees bent sharply, forcing him to the ground. He trembled like a man on fire.

Tamsin rolled away as quickly as she could and raised her sword, uncertain as to what was happening. A trick to get her to lower her guard perhaps. But it didn't make sense. He had just had her.

He raised his head and locks of dark hair fell over his eyes. But his eyes burned with pain and uncertainty.

"Jha'ii."

The word sent shivers up her spine, as if a frosty wind had blown over her skin. It was not said with the contemptuous tone that had previously slipped over his lips. The velvet had been stripped away, but the gentleness had not. That one word was racked with pain, guilt, and…memory.

He was still in there, fighting for control.

"Haven," she said his name aloud and those blue eyes bored into her like icy daggers, begging her to understand.

He hunched over, panting heavily, then his head snapped in Monstran's direction. "You lied to me," he growled. Then his face screwed together like he was in pain. "I thought you said he was ready," that cold voice returned.

It was the first time Tamsin had seen Monstran look surprised, almost to the point of horror. He had made a mistake. A big one. Haven hadn't given up.

Monstran shook his head back and forth quickly. "He was ready, Master. He was—." He was cut off as Haven, or rather Ib'n, suddenly lunged at him and seized his throat.

"You miscalculated," Ib'n snarled through Haven. "He is resisting me."

Monstran gasped for air, though he dared not raise a hand against his master. His eyes found Tamsin's and narrowed. "It's her—her fault," he rasped. "Seeing—her—has given him—hope. You need—to—kill her."

Haven's head twitched to the side, then he tossed Monstran to the ground. He turned to face Tamsin, his expression dark. He started walking towards her.

Tamsin gripped her sword tighter as her fear spiked, ready for another attack. But Haven was still in there. She could still reach him.

"Haven. It's me. You're stronger than him. You have to keep fighting," she urged.

Haven paused, his muscles clenching and contracting under his skin. "Tamsin..." His voice was strained.

Monstran had gotten back to his feet. "Haven, you know it's wrong to resist." His voice had slipped back into its seductive hiss. "It's an unpardonable sin to resist your god. Just let go."

Tamsin panicked, realizing what Monstran was doing. "Don't listen to him Haven! Don't give up. You can beat him!"

Haven's chest heaved with each breath. "I can't," he said, his eyes flickering strangely. "I can't let him out into the world. I've seen what he's going to do." He lurched over to his fallen sword, picking it up. He shifted the handle around until the blade was pointed at him instead of Tamsin. "I have to end this."

Tamsin's breath hitched, realizing what he was going to do. "No, no," she said, the words barely above a whisper as that familiar black pit began to bloom in her stomach. The one she had fallen into when she thought Haven had died in Empyria. That endless emptiness that crippled every good feeling and scattered the pieces of her life to the desert sand...

Haven's lips twitched and then he plunged the dagger towards him—

"NO!" Tamsin screamed.

Haven dropped the dagger as the hand that held it exploded into flames.

Tamsin gasped, surprised herself by what she had done and immediately destroyed the flames.

Haven hissed as he hunched over, cradling his burnt hand in the other. Then he slowly looked up at her. "You have to let me go, Tamsin. Light. Me. Up."

Tamsin stared at the smoke drifting up from his hand, relieved that he had not stabbed himself, but disturbed and horrified that he was asking her to do what she had just done. Only this time it wouldn't leave behind a bloody hand, but a corpse of ashes. "I can't do that, Haven," she said, shaking her head furiously. "Never." He was asking her to do the impossible. Her hands trembled. She couldn't kill him. She wouldn't kill him. There had to be another way. There had to be. She shook her head.

"It's the only way to destroy him, Tamsin."

"I'm going to save you," Tamsin said, her voice shaking despite her determination.

His eyes pleaded with her as he breathed heavily, desperately, then his expression melted, disappearing behind a blank mask once more. His breathing slowed and he straightened.

A laugh bubbled through Monstran's lips as he walked slowly to one side. "You can't save him, Miss Urbane, because he already has been saved. His great and terrible purpose is beyond your reach now."

Tamsin screamed and lunged at Monstran, her sword inches away from slicing him in two, but Haven countered with his own. A sharp ring sung in the air as the two blades connected and then he shoved her away, sending her sprawling to the ground.

"I am not leaving here without you, Haven!"

Tamsin rolled to the side just as Haven's sword connected with the boulder that was behind her, sending shards of rock skittering to the floor. The cavern was large, but offered only minimal places to shield herself. Her greatest strength was adaptability Oman had said, but she did not know how long she would be able to physically last against Ib'n's onslaught. Haven continued to fight him from within, giving her precious moments to breathe, but the angrier Ib'n got, the stronger he seemed to become. And despite his plea, Tamsin would not kill him. She could only hope that Haven would fight him long enough for her to think of a different plan. They were both running out of time.

He came after her again and this time his swing caught its target. She was a hair too slow and the tip of his blade sliced across her shoulder. She managed to block his next blow, but the impact knocked her backwards, nearly to the ground. She prepared herself as he advanced, but suddenly the rage in his eyes faltered and he jolted to a stop. It was Haven, wrestling for control. She usually took these moments to retreat, but the distance between them was too close. His body jerked again and she swung wide, hoping to put more space between them.

But her blade also found its target and he took a step back, examining the blood that now flowed from his side. His gaze was cold as he looked at Tamsin.

"Do it, Tamsin," he said.

She backed up. She couldn't do this. "I'm sorry Haven."

He advanced and she couldn't tell if the anger she saw on his face was Ib'n's or Haven's. She was so tired and heartsick that her instincts to flee as he approached fell on deaf ears. He didn't even raise his sword, but reached out his hand, grabbed her around the neck and flung her against the cavern wall.

She crumpled against the rocks, too exhausted to even cry out. But she couldn't stop. She had made a promise.

Don't give up on me...

She staggered back to her feet, every pain and ache getting harder to ignore, but Haven's words were the loudest and she would not surrender.

Haven and Monstran slowly turned in her direction. Monstran, dirty and disheveled, took a step back, but Haven, or Ib'n, stood still, eying her with annoyed contempt as he held his bleeding side. He looked over his shoulder for a moment and the snarls from the surrounding amon'jii increased tenfold. He turned back to Tamsin and then gave the slightest of nods.

The snarls exploded, but Tamsin was ready, and swung her sword in a quick arc as the first amon'jii advanced. She spun and slashed as more drew near, hoping to catch her with a claw or between their razor-like teeth. She held their fire-breath at bay easily, as if she were dancing with them, focusing on the ones that got close, letting the others free until they took their shot at her. They scrambled after her, often snapping at each other like an alpha-less pack of wolves after a rabbit. She was quick and small and they were large and competitive, each vying for a piece of her.

She dove directly at one as it came at her, slipping underneath its long belly and stabbing upward into the soft flesh. She rolled out of the way as the creature screamed and fell to the side, its legs retracting and spasming violently for a moment. Then a great shudder ran through it as a sigh escaped and then it lay still, as if it were another one of the boulders strewn throughout the cavern.

The creature's death gave her the pause she needed to summon her power once more and she let out a scream as she released her hold over their hearts, fueling a chain reaction of shrieks from the beasts as they collapsed to the ground, consumed by their own fire.

"Enough!" Ib'n's voice bellowed and the remaining amon'jii shrank back with lowered heads and bared teeth until they were only shadows skulking in the alcoves once again.

Tamsin kept her sword up as she watched them retreat and then her eyes found Haven.

"Would you like to see what a true god is capable of?" Ib'n taunted her. He curled his fingers and a flame shot out of the fire in the middle of the cavern towards Tamsin.

Tamsin dropped to the ground, shielding herself with her sword, but her power did not let her down and turned the flame to smoke just as it reached her. She looked up, surprised for a moment that she was not on fire. She got back to her feet, a new vein of confidence flowing through her.

Haven's face fought back his annoyance as he stared at her with venom in his eyes. His hand twisted again, but this time Tamsin was prepared for it and incinerated the flame before it was even halfway to her.

Tamsin couldn't help the smile that caught her lips and pulled them up and without missing a breath she extinguished the entire fire, transforming the cavern into a black pit, illuminated only by the few holes that scarred the ceiling.

But this only seemed to enrage him more as Haven's own lips peeled back to reveal a snarl. He didn't try to resurrect the flames, but instead knelt down and touched his hand to the ground. After a moment, the ground began to tremble and his snarl turned back into a smile.

Tamsin stumbled a little as the ground quivered beneath her, but she held her footing and raised her wits as she waited for whatever new trick Ib'n was about to unleash.

Monstran, though, did not seem to like where this duel was headed and quickly motioned for his remaining bodyguards to follow him as he tried to make for one of the tunnels. His escape was cut short as one of the stalactites plummeted to the ground in front of him, sending jagged shards exploding in all directions. He fell to the ground as the amon'jii began to flee around him, fearing what their master was concocting.

But Haven continued to smile, despite the exodus of the amon'jii and the fragile shell of rock beginning to crumble around them. A large crack burst through the rock in front of him, splitting the stone with a jarring lurch that sent Tamsin to her knees. The crack separated them and was wide enough for her to fall through if she stumbled, but it wasn't falling into it that worried her. It was what was coming up.

She felt the heat first, and then an orange glow ignited the darkness, turning the shadows to burnt amber.

Haven then rose as he summoned the blood of the earth, calling upon its molten magma to rise. To rise and cover the land in an inescapable shadow of fire.

Despite the heat pouring up from the rock, Tamsin's teeth shivered together inside her skull, rivaling the sound as more rocks crashed down around her. She didn't know how to fight this. But she couldn't let him win.

We can't let him win... the Blue Lady's words echoed in her ears, pushing away her desperation.

There was only one thing that Tamsin could think of. One thing that could either save them or kill them.

She called upon her own power, called upon that elusive strand of unbridled energy that had the force to split the sky and earth apart.

Their eyes met, and the earth rumbled and the sky howled as the chaos of nature collided in a flash of deafening white as the very air exploded around them.

"Are you alright?"

Tamsin blinked slowly against the bright light. She touched her head where she had hit the wall, but realized it didn't hurt. In fact, nothing seemed to hurt. There was a light breeze brushing her face and the air didn't smell like sulfur. She could feel the sun on her face, but when she opened her eyes the whole sky was bright as if the sun had stretched itself over the whole sky. She sat up gingerly, expecting her aches and pains to make themselves known, but she felt nothing. She felt strangely light instead. She looked up again, wondering how she had survived.

But she wasn't in the cavern anymore. Surrounding her was a field of white-plumed foxtails, waving gently in the wind just below her line of sight. The cavern was gone and with it, Haven and Monstran. She was on a shallow hill that sloped down and met the sea a little distance away. How had she gotten here? Then she remembered it had been a voice that woke her up. She turned around and saw a small girl standing a few feet away.

The girl smiled timidly at her. She couldn't have been older than five, but there was no one else around.

"Where am I?" Tamsin asked.

"In the after place," the girl replied in Ma'diinese. "You're her, aren't you?"

Tamsin's forehead knotted, trying to remember if she knew this girl. She didn't look familiar, but she was obviously Ma'diin, though she didn't know anywhere in the marsh lands that looked like this place.

"Haven said you were pretty. He was right."

"Haven is here?" Tamsin's heart leapt. She looked around again, but she still did not see anyone. She needed to find him, to get back to the cavern to help him.

"He's not here," the girl said, her smile turning into a frown. "He's fighting the bad one right now."

The bad one—? "Ib'n you mean? He's still in the cave?"

The girl shuddered at the mention of his name. "Yes. He's there. I'm scared for him. He's been fighting a long time."

Tamsin studied the girl more closely. "Who are you?"

"I'm Lu'sa."

Tamsin's breath caught in her throat. She knew that name. The girl that had died. Ko'ran's daughter. The one Haven had tried to save. The one who's death had sent him on a killing spree, giving him his reputation among the Ma'diin. But that would mean...

"He comes here once in a while, when things get too hard I think," the girl, Lu'sa, continued, unaware of Tamsin's distress. "But he hasn't been here in a while."

"So he's not...I'm not..." Tamsin couldn't bring herself to say the word. She remembered being thrown against the cavern wall from the blast of lightning and lava colliding. She remembered a sharp pain and then the next thing she knew she was here.

Lu'sa shook her head. "Most people show up here and stay, but Haven...." She shrugged her tiny shoulders. "Last time he told me you talked to him, in his head. He said he wouldn't be back for a while. Because you were coming to get him."

The firestone. "I—I tried. But, if I'm here, I think I failed."

"You can stay here with me if you want," Lu'sa said, pointing across the hill.

There was a skeleton of a muudhiif down the slope, near the edge of the grassy meadow overlooking the sea.

"He started building that last time," Lu'sa said. The girl shook her head. "He's silly. I told him he doesn't have to actually build it, but he's stubborn." She giggled and Tamsin turned her head back towards her.

The girl was now holding a kind of wooden cage in the shape of a ball. Inside was a small black bird preening underneath its wings.

"See?" the girl said, grinning. "You can create anything you want." She held it out.

Tamsin took the cage, half expecting it to disappear in her hands, but it was completely real. The bird looked up for a moment, its tiny black eyes studying this new handler, before going back to preening its feathers.

Then she noticed the dark blood still staining her hands and forearms. She gave the birdcage back to Lu'sa and then let out a shaky breath.

Lu'sa looked up at her, her eyes sympathetic. "You can still save him. Back where you really are."

Back where she really was... "What?"

Lu'sa hung her head and her lower lip quivered. "It's been really good seeing him again. I missed him. But you can't let him come back here."

Tamsin's heart beat fast. "I can go back? How do you know?"

Lu'sa scuffed at a tuft of grass with her toe uncertainly.

"Because I brought you here," a voice behind her said.

Tamsin spun around and stopped short, unable to believe what she was seeing. "You," was all she managed to say.

The Blue Lady stood just a few feet away, looking just as real as the first time Tamsin saw her when she was a girl. The air seemed to shimmer like diamond dust around her here, though she was no specter or apparition. The grass parted underneath her feet and her hair moved with the wind. She walked over to where a small table had appeared. On it was a stack of white cloths, a vase and a small bowl. She took the vase and poured some water in the bowl, then took a cloth and dipped it in the water. She came over to Tamsin and delicately began dabbing Tamsin's forehead.

Tamsin still couldn't believe she was here. "I thought I would never see you again."

The Blue Lady smiled warmly. "Not in your world. So I brought you here, to mine." She paused in her dabbing. She sunk the now red cloth back into the bowl, wetting it again. "An epic tale is filled with extraordinary people who don't know they're in one."

"I remember you told me that. On my ninth birthday."

The Blue Lady wrung out the cloth and began wiping Tamsin's hands. "But I wasn't the first to say it."

Tamsin thought for a moment. "Who are you, to me?"

"Your mother."

Tamsin had guessed it for a while now, but hearing it somehow made it all sink in. She let the Blue Lady wipe away the blood from her hands in silence for a few moments, though it seemed more of a comfort to her than to Tamsin. Because she knew she had to go back.

"Whenever you're ready," the Blue Lady said as if reading her thoughts.

But there was one thing she still needed to figure out. "Is there any way to save him?"

The Blue Lady smiled, but it was Lu'sa that put her tiny hand on her arm and Tamsin was reminded of her words.

You can create anything you want...

Then she saw the wooden birdcage again, its branches woven just tight enough to keep the bird inside. Tamsin closed her eyes and imagined...

When she opened them the twelve figures she had seen in the Red Sight were standing in a circle around her. Waiting to take her back.

"No fear," she whispered into the wind.

The one stepped forward and placed a hand on her shoulder and the meadow disappeared.

Her eyelids were heavy as she peeled them open and the blurry shapes solidified into remaining fragments of the cavern. Her fingers tightened numbly around her sword handle as she began to gain traction in the waking world once more. She could feel the amon'jii's hearts pounding faintly through the air. She could smell the sweat and blood soaked into her clothes and scattered across the rocks. A ringing lingered in her ears as she staggered to her feet.

The cavern had been shattered. Broken rocks were strewn everywhere, some piled up together over the still bodies of the amon'jii. Shards of glossy black stones, pointed like daggers, spiraled outward over the uneven ground in a circular pattern, all having originated from the scorched crack where lightning and lava collided. Even the ceiling had split open, like a cracked egg, revealing the night sky above.

But nothing else was moving. She spotted Monstran's maroon-colored robes lying across the other side of the cavern, crumpled and ripped underneath a layer of black dust. She made her way over to him, using the pommel of her sword to help her climb over the heaps of rocks and jagged ledges protruding from the ground. She flipped it around in her hand as she drew near, then realized there was no need.

Half of Monstran's cloak lay still over the ground and the other half was buried under a mountain of stone. Only an arm and a thin strand of silver hair had escaped the avalanche. She knelt down next to the still heap. She had done this, with her power. She had rid the world of this man's evil manipulations and yet a small part of her wished she had been there to witness his demise.

Then she noticed something in Monstran's hand. She pried his fingers away to reveal a small pouch and before she even opened it, she knew what was inside. Haven's firestone.

It reminded her of the After place and what she still needed to do, but before she could she leaned down close to the rocks and whispered, "You will *never* hurt him again," willing the words into the dead man's ears. Then she got up and tied the pouch to her belt.

She walked through the rubble and a sound caught her attention: a raking of claws against stone and a slight wheezing for breath. She made her way closer to the sound and saw an amon'jii, shifting against the ground in its final moments before death claimed it. She moved closer to the large body, careful to avoid its sharp teeth if it decided to make one final attempt at her, but it barely seemed to notice her. She walked around its head and then shoved her sword up into the back of its jaw. The beast shivered once and then was completely still. Then Tamsin stepped around its legs to its belly and sliced her sword down its torso. She reached her hand into the creature's body, trying to ignore the sensation of its blood running down her arm, and felt for the organ that was the cause of so much pain and yet…was the key to everything. Her fingers closed around it and she knew this was what she needed. She gave a mighty pull and ripped it out of the amon'jii's body. The dark, glistening mass felt hot in her palm and for a split moment her resolve slipped, thinking of what was going to happen, but she didn't know how long she had so she put the thought out of her mind and put the wet heart into the pouch alongside Haven's. Now, she had to find him.

A swell of thunder rumbled above as she climbed up a tall, angled ledge and looked around. For a moment all she saw was broken boulders and the fallout from the peak of their battle, then she spotted movement in one of the alcoves that was still partially intact. It was not much, but it was alive. She slid down the ledge and over to the alcove, careful with her steps, but keeping her eyes forward. She didn't know what, or rather who, she would find once she reached him, but she knew it was Haven's body. He was kneeling on the ground, one arm hanging silently at his side while the other cradled his bleeding side as his chest moved up and down in great, deep breaths. His black and crimson hood hung around his shoulders and his shirt fell in strips of ripped cloth across his chest and waist.

Tamsin lowered her sword and dropped to one knee so she was eye level with him. Beads of sweat dotted his forehead and mingled with the blood already running down from his eyebrow and the veins in his neck bulged out from the internal war he was fighting.

"Who am I speaking with?" she asked as evenly as she could muster.

His eyes flashed pain for a moment and then turned to steel. "You won't kill me because you won't kill him," the voice that was not Haven's said.

"No, but you will never completely control him. He rejects you even now," she said, choosing her words carefully, like a hunter selecting her bait.

Those blue eyes sizzled with anger and he sprang forward like an animal attacking its prey. But Tamsin was ready for it and rolled out of the way, swinging upwards with her sword as she did. He let out a harsh hiss as it cut into him. Tamsin swiftly rolled up to her feet and pointed the tip at his chest, holding him at bay.

But he surprised her and grabbed her blade with both hands. She tried to pull away, but he only held on tighter. Blood began to seep through his fingers.

His blue eyes stared at her pleadingly. "Please Jha'ii. End. It."

She shook her head and tears flung off her eyelashes. "I can't." Her lower lip trembled for a moment until she clamped her teeth shut. She knew what she had to do, but she could hardly bear it. "I love you," she whispered. But there was only one way to save him. "Ib'n, I need to talk to you."

Betrayal blazed across his face, but she did not let it ruin her resolve. She stared at him, nostrils flaring in determination. Her throat tightened as the pain left his face and that horrifyingly calm mask replaced it. His fingers slowly unlaced themselves from her blade without so much as a wince and he stood up.

"If you want to beg for his life, don't waste your breath. He's gone, she-hunter."

Tamsin still held her sword between them. "I'm not begging for his life. I'm giving you an alternative."

His head cocked just slightly. "What alternative?"

"I'm offering myself, in exchange for Haven."

"You think I would give up this Lumierii in exchange for you?" He laughed then and the sound sent thorns into her skin. "The Lumierii are stronger than any man. They possess power that no man possesses. Why would I trade him in for you when you won't live to see the sunrise anyway?"

"Because I am like no man or Lumierii. You felt me, you felt my mind, all that time ago through Haven's firestone. You've seen what I am capable of. You know I possess more power than Haven or any other person on this earth. I have what you want."

"And the moment I possess you, you will try to kill yourself, thus killing me."

"You have my word, if you let Haven go, I will not kill myself, nor you."

He paced around slowly, never taking his eyes off her as he considered her proposition. "I know you will not give yourself freely," he said. "However, I cannot deny the idea is tempting." He was in front of her in a moment, too fast for Tamsin to defend herself. He grabbed her wrist so tightly till her bones threatened to break and she was forced to drop her sword. His other hand flew to her throat, shoving her back until she was pushed up against a huge boulder. She could feel his blood oozing from his hand down her throat, though she was not strong enough to pry apart the slick fingers.

He continued to watch her as she struggled, showing no sign of weakness, but it was getting harder to breathe and she didn't know how much longer she could stay conscious…

Then it hit her. He was testing her. Fighting against her instinct, she let her hand drop to her side and relaxed her body.

Suddenly, his hand released and she choked on the onrush of air flooding her windpipe. She forced herself to calm down, to take slow breaths. The trap was set…the bait was laid…

He leaned in close and whispered in her ear, "I accept."

Blood mixed with blood. Fire mixed with fire. A red haze surrounded her as Ib'n gripped her head between his hands, whispering words, ancient words, that she couldn't understand. Thousands of years of anger and rage ripped through her, but it was the unbreakable confidence, the inevitable certainty that made her tremble in dread. She could feel Ib'n's arrogance; he believed he had already won. A terrible scream filled her mind like boiling water, melting her sanity and any defenses that defined the realm of her consciousness. It drowned out the sound of her own screams until endurance became a foreign concept. The only path forward was surrender. Then he let go.

It felt like flying, or rather like falling, Tamsin decided. For she wasn't moving, but her stomach lurched unpleasantly as her sense of reality returned. She was only vaguely aware of kneeling on the cavern floor, her hands pressed to the side of her head. She could still feel herself here, but there was another, very strong presence, who was shredding her to pieces. Ib'n was trying to take control. To rid this body of every memory and feeling that made her whole. She grasped at the pieces, but it was getting harder and harder to untangle herself from him.

This was what Haven must have felt like. How did he manage to break through?

Haven. The name resounded through her skull like a horn, sheathing her in golden armor. Yes, this is what she had come back for. Not to let herself slip away. Not to give up. To fight.

Haven was laying, face down, on the ground a few feet away. She crawled her way over to him, unable to give the strength it required to walk. She grabbed his upper arm and shook him, then again, harder, until his head snapped up, glowing eyes blazing. He looked exhausted. His blue eyes were streaked with red, his face was covered with grime and sweat, and he had a tremble that shook the hair in front of his eyes.

"I need you Haven," she gasped, struggling to maintain control. "You have to get up!"

The urgency in her voice shook him even more, but it was enough to force him to his hands and knees. He seemed to see her then, in their present state, and he reached to touch her, concern striking through the exhaustion.

But Tamsin took his outstretched hand and slowly directed it to the pouch at her hip. His eyes widened and he withdrew the heart that she had cut out of the amon'jii.

His eyes showed confusion at first, then horror as he realized what she intended. "I not do this," he said.

"You must," Tamsin urged. "It's the only way." Her fists clenched at her sides and she rolled onto her back. She could feel her grip slipping. Ib'n was pushing her out with all of his strength.

Haven stared at the heart in his hand, frozen by the weight of the task she asked of him.

"Haven!" Tamsin gasped, the muscles in her neck tightening with each breath. "There's no time. He's—he's too strong. I'm going to let go." Tears leaked out the corners of her eyes. "When I do, you have to cut out my heart. Turn me into a Watcher. Haven, look at me!"

Haven tore his eyes away from the heart, and they glistened with guilt.

She took his face in her hands. "No fear."

His nostrils flared and his bottom lip quivered, but he nodded just so slightly. "No fear, Jha'ii."

Tamsin nodded in return and shoved her knife handle into his other hand, knowing he would not let her down.

Tamsin took in his face one last time, before she was gone, and closed her eyes. With each breath she dove deeper and deeper to the place where Ib'n was, though it was like choking on water with each inhale. It was not hard to find him, for she went where the onslaught was thickest. He wanted her to run, to flee back to that meadow where she could exist in peace and comfort. That would be easier than this. It was as if the very seven hells of old had invaded her soul.

It went against every instinct, every thread of character she still had left, but she had to give up. She had to surrender.

"Now!" she screamed.

And she let go.

Suddenly there was nothing. Just an empty awareness of Ib'n's victory. She felt neither pain nor joy, only an echo of Ib'n's triumphant celebration. She was only a spectator, not even a she anymore, just a shadow with no substance, no will, no emotion. She did not feel the knife as it plunged into her chest, only aware of Ib'n's screams, of his shock as his new heart was torn away and with it the black tendrils of evil that he had unleashed in Tamsin's body.

Only when the new heart was shoved into her that Tamsin began to feel again. An aching coldness at first, and then a burst of fiery pain that ripped a scream from her throat. Her back arched in protest to the foreign object. Her vision was a blur of dark shapes and red blood and her ears were flooded with foreign words…but that voice. She knew that voice.

Then the coldness returned, sapping the rest of her strength and she thought she could make out, just beyond the dark shadows, grass waving in a meadow.

Chapter Twenty-Seven

"Numha. Numha, wake up."

Numha took a deep, wakening breath as her body responded to the sound of her name being called before her mind could completely extract itself from the dream world. She opened one eye first, then blinked a few times until Benuuk's blurry form became clearer. Something was shoved into her hands and she felt her fingers tighten around a water skin. She sat up, her body's aches starting to emerge through the lingering fog of sleep. She took a shallow sip from the water skin first, then a deeper drink once her tongue didn't feel like it had been scraped against dry desert sand. "How long have I been out?" she said hoarsely.

"A few hours," Benuuk said.

Numha groaned. She could mentally muscle her way through most things, but the fatigue of the battle with the amon'jii and the fallout afterward had caught up with her. She had only received some minor scrapes and bruises from the fight so she had helped with the wounded immediately after, going from one buurda to the next until she couldn't see straight and someone had grabbed her shoulders and laid her down on a rug.

"I'm sorry it wasn't more," the former Kor'diin continued, "but we need you."

"What's happened?" Numha asked, the last veils of sleep quickly falling away.

"Come with me," he said, helping her up off the ground. He handed her a cloak and they stepped out from underneath the cover of the buurda where she had slept.

Rain was coming down in a steady drizzle as they made their way through the camp, quickly slogging over the wet stone and tufts of grass that buttressed the anasii hada. It was strange seeing all the

Empyrians mixed in with their own people. Small clusters of the northerners had formed, but she was pleased to see her people mingling, offering water and what aid they could. Most of them were huddled underneath large buurdas or the sharply-shaped tents the northerners had erected to avoid the rain. But despite the rain there were still many that moved from buurda to buurda, carrying food and supplies. The truce was unspoken for now, between the Ma'diin and the northerners, while they tended to the wounded so soon after joining together against their common enemy.

Numha heard shouting voices ahead and rounded a tent to find R'en and a few sha'diin glaring at each other around the smoking remains of a fire.

Numha looked at R'en and noticed the blood staining her garments. R'en, always fierce, had been a force of nature all to her own in the battle, and had taken a few injuries to show for it, but the blood on her clothes was fresh.

"What's going on?" Numha asked.

"I'm going to stick a dagger in each of them, that's what's going on," R'en said fiercely.

"What did they do?" She was relieved it wasn't northerners R'en was talking with, but it left her confused.

"Not them," R'en huffed. "Their Kazserii. They're convening right now. Tamsin's not been back an hour and they're already—."

"Wait. Tamsin's back?"

R'en nodded. "The Watchers are with her."

Numha was afraid to ask any more from the seriousness of R'en's tone. There was no elation, no joy, but also no devastation. Only grim reality and the shiny blood on R'en's clothes.

"Take me to her," she said.

R'en nodded, but not before giving one last condemning look to the sha'diin. Then a scream cut through the constant pelting of raindrops against the rock and canvased buurdas. R'en glanced at Numha and the two of them hurried away. Numha dared not imagine what the scream meant, only that her Kazsera was alive. She was surprised though when they stopped in front of one of the northerner's tents. The triangular structure was closed off from curious eyes, though those that were close by looked like they had been whipped from the sounds coming from it.

Someone bumped into Numha's arm as he walked past, though she didn't say anything as she watched him enter the tent, shrouded in the dark cloak of a Watcher. R'en had said that they were with Tamsin, she realized. She decided to follow him in anyway, despite what it possibly meant. She lifted the cream-colored flap and stepped inside with R'en close behind her.

There were no candles, no fire, but the pallid gray of the day permeated the tent's thin fabric enough for Numha to make out the bodies of several Watchers huddled over a figure on the ground.

Tamsin lay there, writhing, covered in blood and grime and sweat. Even after the battle they had just won, Numha had not seen any injured to this extent. Whatever Tamsin had endured had been much worse than what they had faced.

Oman looked up, his bright eyes shining with intensity. "You should not be here," he said.

"She is our Kazsera. We're not—," Numha started, but then she paused to take in the whole scene. There were no sha'diin. No healers. Only Watchers. "What happened?"

"She's transitioning," Oman said, pressing his hands to Tamsin's chest.

R'en caught her eye again, this time with a look of pained affirmation. Their Kazsera, their friend, was turning into a Watcher.

"How…?"

Then Tamsin lurched forward, panting as if the very air was steeped in fire. Her dark hair clung in wavy strands to her face. "Something's…not…right…" she managed to get out through gasps of air. Her hands pulled at her clothes over her chest as her eyes widened with fear.

Even in the dull light it was not hard to see the dark-hued blood that covered every inch of Tamsin's torso.

Numha's hand shook slightly as she covered her mouth.

"Calm now, Tamsin," Oman said soothingly as he grabbed her wrists to keep her from clawing at the wound. "Calm now. The more you fight the harder it will be for your body to accept it."

Tamsin screwed her eyes shut. "I…can't. Something's wrong." Her breath continued to be labored, though she was not strong enough to break out of Oman's grip and he slowly eased her back down to the ground.

"Root of haava. Now," Oman said, looking over his shoulder to one of the Watchers. Then he turned back to Tamsin, whose face mimicked the dull light and lips had a purple tinge to them. "Breathe, Tamsin. Focus on that." He motioned for another Watcher to come over and hold her arms as Kep'chlan brought over the bowl. Oman took the bowl, mixed some water in from his water skin and swiftly began pounding the contents together with the handle of his knife.

"We'll go get a healer," Numha said, feeling helpless and frozen.

"No," Oman said without looking up. "They're busy with the others."

"But she is the Kaz'ma'sha—."

"Who is becoming a Watcher," he replied. "They wouldn't know what to do. Trust me. If you want to help, go check on Haven. I would—but we all must pick our battles," he said, grinding the sleeping concoction even harder.

"Haven," Tamsin gasped. "Where…?"

"He's alright, Tamsin. He's alright," he said, in that calm tone again, catching and holding her teary gaze. "He's alright."

Her breath hitched a few times, but the trust she had for Oman and his words seemed to spare her a few moments from the agony of what was happening to her. Her body trembled, but she was steady enough to drink when Oman offered her the bowl.

"Kep'chlan, more *drafii*, for the wound," Oman said.

Numha had observed satchels full of supplies near the side of the tent, but even she didn't know what *drafii* was. Perhaps he was right and that she and the other healers were out of their element here. But as horrible as it was she could not bear to tear her eyes away.

"Leave. *Now*," Oman growled at them.

"Come on, Numha," R'en said, gently pulling her away.

They headed back out into the rain, pausing just outside the tent, both hoping this would not be the last time they saw their Kazsera alive. The transition into a Watcher was something everyone knew of, but forced it from their thoughts, for even imagining it was too unpleasant. Seeing even a small glimpse of it was enough to make Numha's stomach turn.

"I just need a second," Numha said in response to the concerned look on R'en's face.

"I know," R'en said. "It's what we get for caring too much." She scrunched her nose back and forth as if to rid herself of even the smell of some unwanted emotion.

Numha knew it was just as hard for R'en to see Tamsin like this, despite her stoic front. "It's even worse than after the Duels." Then her gaze went to R'en's shirt and the trails of blood running down her neck with the rain. "You should go get cleaned up."

R'en shook her head. "Later. The Kazserii still need to answer to the edge of my knife."

"R'en—."

Another agonized scream split the air and Numha had to shut her eyes until it was over. She took a deep breath. "Her mother survived. So can she."

"What will this mean?" R'en asked. "She already has powers that no one else has, not even the Watchers. What—."

Numha held up her hand to silence her. "We won't know until—." She glanced back at the tent, but was unable to finish. There was no guarantee that the Watchers could save her. It was well known that women rarely survived the transition. Numha couldn't focus on anything beyond that right now, but she needed to. "Come on. Take me to the Kazserii," she said and they continued through the camp.

R'en led her quickly back, weaving between the tents and people with haste. They stopped just in front of a makeshift muudhiif, looking as if it had been erected with the discarded canvases of a dozen buurdas. It had no sides or doors, but was held up by a grove of spears and wide enough to keep the Kazserii assembled there out of the rain.

There were a dozen or so kazsiin standing guard around, but they parted as Numha and R'en approached.

"If she dies," Isillah's voice rang out over the drum of the rain on the canvas, "the Watcher will have to be put to death."

"What's going on here?" Numha asked sternly, joining the circle of Kazserii.

Calos looked relieved to see her, as did some of the others, but Isillah's glare was like ice.

"You have no place here, Numha," Isillah said dismissively. "As I was saying—."

"I have *the* place here," Numha replied. "I am kazsiin to the Kaz'ma'sha, who is still very much alive. If you don't want her to find out that you're offering her Watcher up to be executed, then I would choose your next words with care."

"Have you even seen him yet? The Watcher?" Isillah asked.

Numha narrowed her eyes, but caught R'en shaking her head, silently telling her she would explain later.

"We have to plan for the future," Isillah continued.

"And yours will be the same as the dam if Tamsin finds out what you're planning. Rise above your petty plays for power, Isillah," Numha warned. "Remember what happened to your former ally, Hazees. Learn from her mistakes."

Isillah glared at her until she finally scoffed. Turning, she marched out of the tent, several of her kazsiin following her.

R'en grinned, but Numha remained firm in the presence she had made in the tent, a slight scowl marring her face.

"Isillah is right, up to a point," K'al spoke up. "We have to plan for the future."

"No plans will be made here without the Kaz'ma'sha," Numha said.

K'al held up her hands respectfully. "I am only suggesting we think about what's going to happen in the next few days. Our casualties, for instance, were few, but we have to put them to rest."

Numha let go of some of her irritation and nodded. K'al was an honorable Kazsera and Numha knew she would stay loyal to Tamsin and do what was best for the Ma'diin.

"See to your wounded. Honor your dead," R'en said.

"And what about the northerners?" another Kazsera spoke up. "Two days ago they were our enemy."

"But they fought with us against the amon'jii," Calos spoke up.

"Which are now gone," the Kazsera said. "How do we know they won't come for us next?"

"The dam is broken. The amon'jii are gone. Peace was achieved." Numha said. "Ysallah, one of your own, fought for this well before any of you. Do not let her death be marred by your lingering distrust."

"Have the Watchers confirmed that the amon'jii are gone?" another Kazsera asked.

"They're a little busy right now," Numha said.

"So it's true," Calos said, concern etched across her young face. "Tamsin is becoming a Watcher."

Numha exchanged a glance with R'en, but neither had to say anything.

"Then that is what we'll do," K'al said.

"What?" Numha asked.

"Pray," she said. "To whatever gods that are left who will hear us."

The other Kazserii nodded in agreement and one by one they left with their kazsiin, leaving only Numha and R'en and the sound of the drizzling rain.

"You were born for this, you know," R'en said.

Numha was grateful for the compliment, but she didn't relish it. "There's still a lot of work to do."

"Tell me and it'll be done."

As much as the Kazserii's council had irked her, she knew there were many tasks yet ahead of them. Some could wait, but others were more pressing. "Find Kellan. We need to make sure the amon'jii are gone for good and it will be better if at least one Watcher will go with the sha'diin to scout the area."

R'en turned to her, her eyes pained. "You didn't hear?"

"Hear what?"

"Kellan didn't come back," she said quietly.

Numha took a deep breath. The last she had seen him he had been riding off towards the anasii hada to go find Tamsin. Everyone knew that his single-minded intent to protect her was not born of duty, but of the heart. And she knew, without having to ask, that he had helped save them all. Whatever he had done, had helped Tamsin. Had helped them all.

"I'll gather some sha'diin," R'en said. "We'll make sure the amon'jii are gone."

Numha nodded in thanks. She was glad for the help. With R'en after the amon'jii, the Kazserii tending their people, and the Watchers caring for Tamsin, it only left one more thing that was clear to Numha that needed doing.

"Have you seen Haven yet?" Numha asked.

R'en nodded. "When they first got back. He would not leave her side."

"I was surprised not to see him there with her."

"You won't be," R'en said darkly.

Numha was about to ask why when R'en nodded ahead. "Benuuk can take you. I'll gather the scouts. We'll be back at sundown."

Numha didn't say anything, but nodded her approval and the two women parted. She found Benuuk again and asked him to take her to the Watcher.

Numha looked to see a lone tent come into view through the drizzling sheets of rain. There was nothing odd about it, except for the dozen sha'diin that surrounded it, their spears pointed to the structure with statuesque stillness. Just underneath the canopy, kneeling on the ground with his hands tied to a pole behind him, was the Watcher.

"What is this?" Numha asked, approaching with a sense of caution. "Who ordered this?"

"Oman," Benuuk said.

Numha noticed then that the sha'diin surrounding him weren't just ordinary tribesmen. They were the Exiles.

"He won't say a word," Benuuk continued, "until he's figured out what happened."

"Oman isn't one to take chances," Numha said. If Oman thought Haven was even slightly a threat, he wouldn't allow the Watcher to stay with their Kazsera. But even this, treating one of his oath brothers like a prisoner of war, was enough to send shivers down her arms. She would have to get answers herself.

Numha was about to wade through the Exiles when a hand shot out in front of them. It wasn't one of the Exiles, but Poma, the woman from Ysallah's old tribe. Numha did not know her well, but she knew Tamsin trusted her.

"What are you doing?" Numha asked.

"I'll ask the same of you," Poma said in return, blocking their way to the tent.

"Oman sent us to check on him," Numha said. "Your turn."

"I'm making sure nobody harm's him." Her delicately angled face was sharp with focus. "Oman may question him, but he is the single most important thing to Tamsin. And I will protect him with my life." Her narrow eyes glanced at the Exiles that surrounded the tent.

"Why does Oman question him?" Numha asked.

One of the Exiles came over to them, his shaggy hair dripping with water. Hronar, Numha thought she remembered his name. "Oman told us about the Alamorgrian woman. Something the witch woman said to him when he took her to the edge of the marshes to set her free. That Haven would be a danger to us all if he left the Ravine alive."

Numha bristled at the mention of Mora, having had enough of that woman's meddling, but then she remembered what Tamsin had told them. How the northern boy, Enrik, had said there was an evil power at work that was using Haven as a vessel. That Ib'n was trying to come back into the world. What if Tamsin's predicament had not been an accident? What if Haven had turned her intentionally? "But you don't believe it," she said to Poma.

"He brought Tamsin back to us," Poma said.

"He doesn't look dangerous. He looks distraught," Benuuk said, not unsympathetically.

"Because he can hear her screaming," Poma said bitterly. "If your loved one was suffering and you were tied up like a wild animal, how would you react?"

"Like a wild animal," Numha said. "Has anyone spoken to him yet?"

Hronar shook his head. "We've been waiting for Oman."

Oman knew about this possible threat, Numha realized. The morning Tamsin had gone to the anasii hada, he had summoned the Exiles for a secret meeting. He had prepared for this.

Numha watched Haven for a moment. His cloak and hood had been removed and she could see his glowing blue eyes staring at a point on the ground through his tangled hair. His focus never wavered, but she could see the muscles of his neck and jaw were taught. He was distraught, yes, but he also looked exhausted. His clothing was torn in several places, over his chest and legs, and the deep burgundy stains that lay underneath seemed to saturate every thread beyond the tears. He was already a Watcher, but if Tamsin's condition was any indication of what they had gone through, then he would need a healer as well.

"Hronar, will you let Poma take him somewhere more private? Somewhere we can talk to him where he won't feel threatened. He brought our Kazsera back alive. We owe him our help."

Hronar rubbed the back of his neck, looking unsure.

Numha pressed him. "I don't know what Oman told you, but if Tamsin finds out that you were involved in whatever alternate plan he had, then—."

Hronar held up his hands. "Alright, alright."

Numha nodded. "Good. Benuuk, see if one of the Watchers can help with his wounds."

"I would like to help with that," a gruff voice said from behind.

They turned and saw one of the Exiles, Ardak, standing there. Numha hadn't noticed before, but he had been absent from the group guarding Haven.

"Watcher's blood is too dangerous for sha'diin," Benuuk said.

"The Watchers are busy saving our Kazsera," Ardak replied, without resentment. "And I owe Haven far more than any of you."

They looked at each other for a moment, then Numha nodded. She didn't have time to argue. It would be their heads if Tamsin lived and Haven died, but she trusted Poma's loyalty and ability. And though she had only known Ardak a short time, Numha believed his intentions were honorable as well.

"Thank you," he said, the barest of tremors visible on his lower lip before he pressed them together.

"I'll leave you to it then," Numha said, walking away from the others, confident that they could handle their parts.

She wandered back through the rain, through the maze of tents and people. Everyone had their jobs to do; faces she did not know were tending fires or bringing food to one another, erecting buurdas, scrubbing blood from clothes. Even the northerners were handing out supplies from large carts they had brought down from their stronghold. She waded through it all until she found herself back at the empty tent the Kazserii had been in. She stood underneath the dark canvas, letting water drip off her nose in a slow, rhythmic way as the activity continued around her. The battle was over, but she couldn't help feeling like she was still fighting.

She let her knees sink down to the ground, not knowing what else to do under the weight of what had just happened and the uncertainty of the path ahead. She took a few, shaky breaths. She knew the aftermath could have been much, much worse and she knew she would need to muster her strength for the days coming. But she just wanted a moment. A single moment to be vulnerable, to let the guilt of coming through unscathed wash over her, to give up the fight to her weaker emotions. Just a moment, and then she would be able to gather herself again.

Someone put their hand on her shoulder and she looked up. She recognized the northern man who had offered himself up in the sh'pav'danya. The one who had helped warn them of the amon'jii. She stood up and he removed his hand, holding it up apologetically.

He said something in his own tongue and held out a blanket with the other hand.

She nodded gratefully and held out her hand, but instead of giving it to her he opened it up and wrapped it around her shoulders.

"Thank you," she said, pushing down the lump in her throat at his act of kindness.

He said something in return and she didn't need to understand the words to understand what he meant. That it was okay to need to be taken care of once in a while.

She nodded and they stood in silence for a minute until he asked her a question. She shook her head, not comprehending, and he thought for a moment then said one word, "Tamsin?"

She took a steadying breath, then squeezed his upper arm. "She's alive," she said, hoping she conveyed enough hope through her tone and her eyes. Then she realized what she had to do. It wouldn't be easy, but someone would have to talk to the northerners. Ardak could speak a little of their language, but while he was busy with Haven someone would have to keep the alliance that Tamsin had forged. And until Tamsin was well enough to do it herself, Numha would be that someone.

She lifted her palm up in sync with her breath and then tapped on the man's chest in sync with his heartbeat. "Cuvaan," she said.

The corners of his eyes tightened a moment as he repeated the word slowly, "Cuvaan." Then he answered her with his own, "Alive," he said. He nodded, a slight smile picking up his lips.

"Alive," Numha said, smiling back.

Chapter Twenty-Eight

He could hear their hushed voices through the steady rainfall, though he did not look up from where he watched the rain hitting the ground in front of him as it fell from the tent's edge. Every once in a while he heard a scream shiver between the raindrops and it nearly broke his concentration. His whole body would tremble and his arms would tighten against the restraints that held him. But then he would focus on the tiny puddle of water in front of him again and it would keep everything else at bay. He knew it was a tenuous, fragile curtain that held the dark memories away.

A reflection appeared in his puddle: two boots approached him slowly, with only a small hint of caution, then a fair-faced woman crouched down opposite him. The ripples distorted the image, but even then, the reflection of her features was delicate, but sharp around the edges. He didn't recognize her, though that didn't cause him any concern. None of the faces he encountered here had been familiar. The canvas buurdas, their dress, their speech—it all seemed plucked from a dream he had once had, but the people were strangers to him. Except for Tamsin.

"Have you had anything to drink, Watcher Haven?" the woman asked.

The sympathy in her voice told him she already knew the answer to that. He had not eaten or drank or even slept since coming here. He had not even tried to, despite his obvious need of it. He had no wish to enter the realm of dreams and nightmares, giving up his mind's control when he had only recently been returned to it.

"Have they mistreated you?" she asked, tilting her head towards the armed men surrounding them. At his silence, she drew a small knife from her belt.

Haven watched through the reflection, but didn't move or say anything. The woman moved slowly, deliberately, and leaned forward and sawed through the ropes that tied his hands. She returned the knife and then pulled out a water skin. She extended it out to him, covering his view of the puddle.

He brought his hands forward, slowly taking the skin. He held onto it a few moments, his mind trying to reconnect a feeling that had been severed. This woman was being…kind. He didn't know how to respond. Then, slowly, he brought the skin to his lips and took a small drink.

"You need rest," the woman said, almost like she was talking to herself. "You both do."

His nostrils flared at the word 'both' and he lowered the water skin. Of course Tamsin needed rest. She was alive, but what she was living through was not pleasant or easy.

Time had slowed. Every breath of air into his lungs, every fall of his eyelashes, and every drop of blood off the edge of his sword hung suspended, such as the last note played by a string kanun if it had refused to give up its song. He recognized it: the tense space between life and death, where one is only a rise and fall of breath away either living or dying. But it was much different looking at it from the outside. Haven felt as if he were watching the desert sun as he stared at Tamsin's still form in this frozen moment, a sun that would either rise or set. If the latter became true, he knew he would remain here, in this exact time and place and never lower his gaze from her radiant face. But if the former were true and she survived—

Tamsin suddenly gasped, the sound of it shattering the crystallized cocoon of time around them. Her back arched slightly, then slumped to the ground again, but her chest began moving in a rhythmic pattern once more.

"I know you must be worried about her, but she will be alright," the woman continued. "There are others with her, helping her."

He looked up from his pool then. He alone was responsible for what she was becoming. He would protect her. His eyes conveyed what his silence did not, but he wanted the fair-featured girl across from him to understand. For he knew why she had come. He knew what they whispered. The men with spears standing guard betrayed their distrust. But he did want her to understand that they could not keep him from Tamsin indefinitely.

"I'll let you see her, but only if you come with me first."

There was no malice behind her tone, though he would not be caught off guard if she proved false. He finally nodded. He watched as she stood up and walked away, then as she turned around and realized he hadn't moved.

"My name is Poma, by the way" she said. "You can trust me."

One of the men with spears inched closer. "Watcher Oman told us to keep him here. He can't trust him."

The girl kept her face neutral without so much as a twitch, but she did take a long pause, studying Haven with an unwavering direct gaze. She wasn't afraid of him as others were. "There are rumors that Ib'n himself led the amon'jii army. That he had been resurrected. That Tamsin defeated him. Others say that the very same Watcher she fought so hard for actually led Ib'n's army, but turned at the last moment and saved our Kazsera. Who actually killed Ib'n? The Watcher or the Kazsera?"

Haven matched her steady gaze, even as the memories of that night roared through his head like an uncontrolled wildfire.

Blood ran out of her chest and down his arms until there was no beginning or ending to either of them. He said the words over and over. He knew them without thinking and yet every thought, every ounce of energy and power he had went into those words. One hand on her new heart, the other on the old. Consolidating power in a fiery dance of convergence and severance. Forever binding one to the other, yet ensuring their survival through separation. And Haven, a conduit for the ancient ritual, could not break the connection until either life or death took root.

Her new heart was beating.

And the other...

He looked down at the newly created firestone in his hand.

"You're asking the wrong question," he said at last.

The look on her face changed then, showing the barest hints of confusion. Oman's order to have Haven guarded had thrown Haven's loyalty into question and there was enough unknown about what had happened to him to cast doubt. Haven knew where his loyalty was, but he could not blame the others for their mistrust. The

Ma'diin were covered in a shadow and only Haven knew what made it. And he would not put Tamsin at more risk until he knew for sure the answer to the question they should all be asking.

Finally, Poma said, "I am loyal to Tamsin. And to her Watcher."

Haven slowly got up then and limped over to her. The sha'diin cleared them a path but did not lower their spears. They walked over to where two men were waiting for them. The younger one, who showed only the faintest traces of facial hair, pulled a cloak out of a thick satchel and handed it to him. The other, whose beard was thick and sodden with rain, looked as if the mere sight of Haven pained him deeply. A memory twitched at the corner of his mind, telling him that not all Ma'diin liked what he was.

"This is Benuuk and Ardak," Poma said, indicating each. "They've offered to help."

He put the cloak on, knowing the rain nor the overcast sky would hurt him, but feeling like it was expected. Several of the spear-wielding sha'diin followed him as he followed the three away from the rest of the camp. He lumbered down an uneven incline until they arrived at a hollowed-out cavern in the wall of the anasii hada. A small waterfall covered half the opening, pouring down from somewhere not too far above. The inside was filled with water, though there was a wide ledge of flattened boulders surrounding it, keeping the water from spilling out.

Benuuk put down his satchel on one of the ledges and began pulling things out. "There's food, water, herbs, clean bandages," he said. "And we'll get you a proper cloak when we can."

A proper cloak. That's right. The n'qab was missing from this one, he realized as he sat down on one of the ledges underneath the overhang. "What are we doing here?" he asked.

Benuuk furrowed his brow at him and then glanced to Poma for a moment. "These," he indicated the items from the satchel, "are for you."

"I would prefer to see her," Haven said.

Poma grabbed some of the bandages and stepped over. "I told you I would take you to her. But you need some help yourself first."

"I'm fine."

Poma sighed. "I have three children, Watcher. Ask them how far their stubbornness gets them." She took another step closer.

Haven held up his hand. "I can manage," he said, taking the bandages from Poma.

"Alright," Poma said, reluctantly. "We'll stay in case you need anything."

"If you wish," he said, indifferent to their proximity, though he watched them convene over by the other end of the ledges for a moment. Poma and Benuuk talked quietly together, though the other one, Ardak, still said nothing. Haven wondered why he was even here. The sound from the waterfall echoing through the cavern masked what they were speaking about, though they glanced his way often.

He took one of the cloth bandages and soaked it in the water, then rung out the excess. He held it in his hand, the water dripping from it already pink in color from the blood that coated his hands. He could manage. He had cleaned and healed his own wounds before, though the memories had been scratched out and replaced with others. The white-haired man's servants had tended to him before, washing him, stitching his wounds.

He was free of that place, so why could his mind not leave it?

He tried to shake it away, but as the water dripped from his hand back into the pool he caught his reflection. Through the ripples, his expression was a frozen, inhuman wall.

The darkness that slithered along the walls like serpents. The voices, their whispers like knives. The pressure of his own breath, marking the passage of time with the weight of a drumbeat. Pain was constant and yet nothing. Fear was constant and yet irrelevant.

'What did I say about your old life?' the voice would ask him.

'You have to accept the truth.'
'They have left you behind.'
'You belong to Him now...'

He blinked and saw Poma's concerned face kneeling before him.

She nodded supportively, encouragingly, and gently took the cloth back from him. "It's alright. Let me help you." She started to wipe the blood from his hands, but he stopped her.

There was a reason Watchers mended themselves. There was a reason...

"It's alright," she repeated. "There was a time I was fearful of Watcher blood, but not anymore. We have to take care of each other. Tamsin taught me that." She started wiping away the blood again. "Most of this is hers, isn't it?"

He nodded.

As she cleaned his hands he could see the concern and questions dart through her eyes as her gaze lingered on the marks encircling his wrists. Old scars from the restraints they had used. Back when he had resisted.

"You can ask me," he said.

She paused for a moment. Then asked, "How did you survive?"

The world had turned upside down. Fire struck its flames into the ground and water ascended into the sky. The familiar had become foreign and the foreign had become the fog-ridden shadow in which he dwelt.

"I'm not sure that I did."

She looked into his eyes, but he wasn't seeing her. Poma took a deep breath and after a moment realized that the wall did not reflect what was happening behind the Watcher's eyes.

"Will you take me to her now?" he asked.

"Haven," she said, her tone softening as if she were speaking to one of her children, "you need to rest—." Then her eyes fell to the ground next to him, where a small, red pool had begun to form in a divot in the rock. She followed the trail up to his waist and slowly peeled back the edge of his shirt. A deep, venomous-looking line cut through his side, separating his ribs from his hip. She quickly grabbed several dry bandages and pressed them to the wound.

Haven didn't flinch or wince or make any indication that he felt anything. He stared ahead, one moment seeing Poma yelling at Ardak, then Benuuk, who took off running back to camp, then the next moment he saw Tamsin, dripping with sweat and blood as she swung her sword as hard as she could at him, then pulling back at the last second before the blow became fatal. If she had just dug in a little more she would not be suffering right now. She could have ended it, but she fought for him.

He pushed Poma's hands away and started to get back up.

"Haven, stop. Benuuk's gone to get another healer. Just wait," she said.

He ignored her and half slid, half stepped off the ledge. She tried to stop him, putting a hand on his arm, but he immediately turned and grabbed her throat. The surprise had barely registered on her face before he released her. He took a step away from her, knowing he had acted instinctively, but his instincts were tainted by shadows. He raised his apologetic eyes to meet hers, but then saw the sha'diin that had followed them advance, their spears raised. He turned again and grabbed the spear before its owner could react. He pushed back and threw the sha'diin to the ground, whipping it out of his hands and then pointing it to the other sha'diin. "I'm done waiting," he growled, but then he saw the fear in the sha'diin's eyes and he wavered.

He shook his head, as if to rid some dirt out of his eyes, and then a hand appeared on his spear. It was Ardak and he looked just as guilty and confused as Haven felt, but there was a steadying presence to his manner, something that undermined the reactionary chaos of living in the dark. Some memory tried to surface in that desert in his mind, but he couldn't quite recognize it.

"All I can see is scorched land," he said. "Everything familiar has been blown away like sand. Except for the one spot that she's standing on. She's the only thing that is clear to me."

Ardak swallowed thickly. "I have returned home after being gone, exiled, for almost twenty years. But it somehow feels lonelier than before. Maybe we can help each other get back to what we lost."

Haven lowered the spear and then let it fall out of his hands to the ground. "I won't hurt her."

"I know," Ardak said curtly, as if more for his sake as a gruffness started to creep into his tone. "Come on. Let's get you to Tamsin." He then sidled over and put Haven's arm over his shoulder so he could lean on him.

"Ardak," Poma warned.

"If Oman has a problem with it, then I'll take the blame," Ardak said.

"He shouldn't be moved," Poma insisted.

"He'll see Tamsin and then he'll let the healer take a look, right?"

Haven nodded.

"Alright, let's go."

"Ardak!"

"You say you're loyal to Tamsin and to her Watcher," he retorted. "Keeping these two apart any longer will kill them faster than any cut. Believe me."

Poma looked like she wanted to say more, but something in Ardak's tone or expression seemed to change her mind and after a moment she nodded.

Haven then leaned on Ardak as they walked back into camp. His body felt heavy and he knew the pain should have bothered him, but it didn't. He knew he had been though worse. The feeling of being disconnected should have triggered some kind of urgency, some kind of alarm, but knowing he would see Tamsin, the one person that made sense, grounded him to the breath still in his lungs.

Until the footprints he left in the mud began to turn red and the ground that suddenly heaved up to meet him turned everything black.

Chapter Twenty-Nine

She heard sounds: quiet chatter, the rhythmic clop of hooves against stone, the wind brushing against the walls of a fabric tent. Normal noises that eased her passage into wakefulness. Then she heard her breath, rattling out of her lungs, and the tread of boot-clad feet getting closer.

"Where am I?" Tamsin asked.

"In my tent," a familiar voice answered.

"Mr. Brennan?"

"Apparently you set the other tent on fire," he said. "This one isn't exactly fireproof, but it'll keep you out of the sun, which is what I think they were trying to tell me."

"The sun?" And then she remembered. Everything. All of it. She gasped and tried to sit up, but a weight in her chest pulled the rest of the air from her lungs and she lay back, breathing heavily.

"Easy, easy," he said, crossing over to her. "The horsehair will keep you together better than that herb mash they had on you, but I don't want to stitch you up a second time."

She reached up to her chest and felt the crisscross of stitching underneath her tunic. She pulled her hand away again before she could fully succumb to what was inside of her, pumping blood through her veins. To what she was now.

Mr. Brennan's face was sympathetic, though he couldn't hide the speculative crease at the corners of his eyes. "The others, the ones in cloaks...you're like them now, aren't you?"

She nodded, looking away from him and up at the ceiling, using all of her energy to keep the tears in her eyes. She took slow, measured breaths. "How...how long...?"

"About three days," he said, dipping a ladle into a bucket and then offering her a sip. "I think you should wait for the others until you try anything though." He made a face then at her questioning look. "I don't think I'm going to explain things too well." He scratched the back of his head. "You missed quite a bit during your little nap."

"Oman, or Numha. They could help."

"If I knew who they were, I'm sure they could."

"The Ma'diin? The Empyrians? Did anyone…?" She wasn't sure what to ask. She had a vague memory of Oman and some others in a tent with her. But it wasn't this one. As Mr. Brennan had said, this was his tent, an Empyrian tent. If she was in the Empyrian camp, she didn't know what that meant for the Ma'diin or what had happened between them and the amon'jii. And where that left… "Haven. Where is he?"

"Haven? I'm guessing he's the one everyone's been arguing about. For being the only other person that can understand both parties other than yourself, he's not very chatty, is he?"

"He's alive?"

"Yeah, though he didn't make it easy. Whatever was on the other side of that dam did quite the number on both of you."

"But he's alive?"

Mr. Brennan chuckled a little. "See for yourself, my lady." He helped her sit up then, and when she had caught her breath, he pointed over to the other end of the tent.

She looked behind her, grimacing at the pull the motion caused to her chest, but all of that disappeared when she saw him lying on another cot just a few yards away. Haven was motionless, save for the steady rise and fall of his chest as he lay sleeping.

"Help me," she breathed, and Mr. Brennan grabbed her elbow quickly as she moved to get up.

"Okay," he said, steadying her as she wobbled a bit on her feet, "but take it easy. I think those guys out there have a spear with my name on it if anything happens to you. I gather you're pretty important to them."

But Tamsin wasn't listening anymore. She barely felt the ground under her feet as she took a step and then another and didn't notice that everything had a slightly off-color hue. Everything except Haven. Mr. Brennan let go of her when they reached Haven's cot and she slid down to her knees.

His face, even in sleep, had a pensive tightness to it. The edges of his lips were pulled slightly into a thinner line and his dark brow had a hint of a furrow to it, as if he were working out some mystery as he slept. But the anguished battle between Ib'n's malice and Haven's desperation was gone. He was himself again. From the wavy strands of hair that fell around his eyes to the curve of his jaw to the silver tendrils of his Lumierii marks that cascaded down his collarbone to his chest. His tunic was undone, revealing not only the Lumierii marks, but a path of wide cloths wrapped around his side. Tamsin reached up and laid her fingertips on it, remembering the moment her sword had cut into him. Then she watched his chest rise up and fall, over and over, as a mother would her newborn child, amazed and relieved by the sheer miracle of it and terrified that it would stop if she looked away. She traced the lines of his scars, familiar ones and new. Then she closed her eyes and let her forehead rest on his chest, breathing in that smoky, lilac scent that she had yearned for. She had dreamed of this moment for so long that it nearly ached to finally be here. To be together. To be safe. To finally have a moment where love was more than just the memory of him, more than just his name whispered in the darkness of night.

She turned as she felt something touch the back of her head and saw Haven's bright blue eyes staring at her. "Jha'ii," he said, his voice rough, but soft with velvet. Her breath hitched and she collapsed over him, burying her tears into his neck.

He stroked her hair and murmured, "Jha'ii, Jha'ii," over and over, trying to comfort her, but his own voice was heavy with emotion.

They weren't alone anymore. Every battle, every inch they had fought for, had been for each other. To get back to each other. Every broken night, every dark day, every sacrifice in tears and blood, every weary step. It had all been to end the reign of shadows that had clung to them since leaving Empyria. They had finally found each other in the wasteland that had lain between them. They were safe now. The ghosts of the monsters that hunted them might still be there, but if they didn't look back, then they had a real chance to be free.

Tamsin took the bowl of soup from Mr. Brennan with a gracious nod. She was sitting on a cot next to his desk inside his tent. Haven was asleep though night had only just begun. She never wanted to take her eyes off of him ever again, but a gentle reminder from Mr. Brennan that she needed to eat and drink prompted her to finally leave his side and let him rest.

"You should get some rest too," she told Mr. Brennan.

Mr. Brennan started to reply, but the tent flap opened then and Numha stepped quietly inside. Her face melted into a relieved smile when she saw Tamsin and Tamsin felt her own doing the same.

"I think I'll do just that," Mr. Brennan said and he slipped outside to give the two some privacy.

Numha put down the blanket she had been carrying onto Mr. Brennan's empty chair and swiped her fingers across her hand in respect.

"We're beyond that," Tamsin said, still smiling. "And it's good to see you."

"I'll never be beyond that, not after what you have done for our people," Numha replied. "And it's good to see you too. How are you feeling?"

Tamsin hadn't begun to unravel the complexity of that question, so she decided to answer as simply as she could. "Alive," she said, but she knew even that was far from simple. Physically, she felt stronger than she believed she had the right to, though she was afraid to ask why. Was it the adrenaline or something else pumping through her veins? Emotionally, she was living in the aftermath of the biggest battle of her life. Haven was alive and with her, but she had paid for it. And now with Numha's visit, she would find out what that had cost everyone else.

"Will you catch me up to speed?" Tamsin asked her, knowing she couldn't delay this conversation any further.

Numha nodded and she proceeded to tell her everything that had happened since she had left for the anasii hada: the negotiations with the northerners, Mr. Farrows late arrival and warning, the amon'jii and the breaking of the dam, Haven's return with her, and Numha's dealings with the Kazserii and the northerners since. The casualties had been few on both sides, though there were still many recovering from injuries. There was a steady truce since their union against the amon'jii, though communications had been difficult, since the only two who could speak both languages were in this tent together.

"What about Ardak? Doesn't he remember the language?"

Numha shook her head. "He seems hesitant to talk to the northerners. He's been very protective of Haven though. And you."

This did not surprise her, but she wondered why Ardak had not offered his knowledge to them. He was the one that had taught Haven the northern language after all.

"What about the other Exiles?" she asked. There had not been much time to reunite them with their families after they returned, but it was still a promise she intended to keep.

"They are just as protective as Ardak, annoyingly so," she added with an amused smile. "Though Enok has taken an interest in the northerners in quite a…remarkable way."

"Oh?"

"He's learning their language; their *written* language. I told him it's not our custom and that he should ask you when you're feeling better."

"No, it's okay," Tamsin said, thinking of Enok's intellectual character. "Let him." She remembered when she had first started teaching Haven to read, how the Empyrians and even her own mother had thought it a precarious idea. But if there was peace between the northerners and the Ma'diin now, then perhaps it could benefit them both. She knew the Ma'diin followed the oral tradition when it came to preserving the stories of their culture and she wanted to respect that, but she also thought their culture was extraordinary and deserved to be preserved beyond the memories of the storytellers.

"Thank you for handling all of this, Numha," she said. "Have plans been made to return home?"

"Scouts have been sent out to follow the amon'jii's retreat and to see the water damage done to some of the outlying tribes. We should be able to begin moving people back soon. R'en said there hasn't been a trace or trail of the amon'jii and the extra water should keep any stragglers at bay."

"R'en led the scouts to follow the amon'jii?"

Numha's expression turned then. "The Watchers were on the eastern front when the amon'jii attacked. They took the brunt of it before the dam fell."

"But I remember. Oman, Kep'chlan, there were others, they were there with me in the tent."

"Many were wounded. Oman and Kep'chlan were the only two left that could help them. And when you came back, Oman did everything he could to save you."

"Where is he now, Numha?"

"He wanted to make sure you would live before he left."

"Where is he, Numha?" she repeated.

Numha sighed. "He's on his way to the shaman stones."

"Why would he go there?" Tamsin shook her head.

"Because he didn't want anyone to see. During the battle, one of the amon'jii must have ripped his cloak. No one knew. And he's been helping people, night and—."

"Day," Tamsin finished. She put the bowl of soup down and put her face in her hands. The cost reared its ugly head. Oman was going there to die. "But he didn't say goodbye."

Numha sighed and looked away for a moment. "Sometimes we don't get to say goodbye the way we want to."

"No. There has to be a way. When did he leave?" Tamsin asked. She was feeling strong enough. She could catch up to him, tell him that he didn't have to die alone.

"Just after sunset. Tamsin—he wanted you to have this." She reached over and grabbed the blanket she had set on the chair earlier.

Tamsin realized it wasn't a blanket. It was Oman's cloak. And this was his goodbye. Tamsin took the cloak, feeling the weight of the strong fabric between her fingers. The Watchers were ruled by ancient rules, the same ones that she was now bound to. Once broken, those rules could not be undone. Though now with his end certain, she wondered if that weight had been lifted along with his cloak. She hoped beyond hope that as he walked away into the night, he felt lighter and that he knew the depth of her gratitude for him. Numha was right: sometimes one didn't get to say goodbye the way they wanted to. But that's where hope stepped in.

Numha finished relaying the last bits of information to her before finally leaving to let her rest, promising to update the others on her well-being to avoid the swarm of visitors that had initially surrounded the muudhiif before she was moved to the northern camp.

But rest eluded her. She sat in the silence for a while, her mind going back and forth between Haven and what Numha had all said to her. She was glad the road behind them was over, but she knew the way ahead would be hard as well. She thought she had evaded the Red Sight and its deadly angles, but she knew now that even though she had avoided most of the bloodshed she had witnessed in her vision, it still had taken what it thought it was owed.

Oman had met fate's sharp talons, and perhaps his end had been foretold by the Red Sight, but Kellan had also been lost. She felt cheated somehow, as if fate had punished her for challenging it.

Challenging fate was not for the timid of heart, for fate had a dark side, and she fought back to claim what was hers.

She got up from the cot, still gingerly, but she went over to the table with the washbasin. She cupped her hands in the water and splashed her face, as if she could wash away the loss from her mind. But as the water dripped off her nose and eyelashes, and the water began to settle back in the bowl, she caught her reflection. It was the first time she had seen herself since…

Haven had told her a long time ago what the world looked like as a Watcher. Colors were different. Light and shadows seemed to be reversed. The darkness that once held dominion over the night was like a tame bird, guiding one through with ease what had previously been off limits. And occasionally, a color broke through like the shattering of a prism.

This was what Tamsin stared at now. She knew she was different, she could *feel* it, but seeing it startled her more than what she wanted to admit. They were her eyes, but now they glowed like golden amber saturated with honey.

Chapter Thirty

Tamsin's cloak billowed around her as she watched the northerners prepare to leave. After several weeks of healing, packing, and helping clean up after the flooding, the northerners were finally ready to go home. The entire army gathered at the base of the outpost, cinching saddles, tying down the last remaining supplies in the wagons, and finishing the final head count as the squadrons organized.

"It's been years for some of us," Commander Ruskla said, who was standing next to her and watching the preparations with his icy eagle eyes.

"Thank you for delaying your journey a little longer and staying to help restore the outer marshes," she said, her n'qab pushing against her nose in the wind. There was still a lot of work to do, but seeing the Ma'diin and the northerners working together made the load lighter to bear.

"Perhaps there's hope for our peoples to coexist after all," he said. He tipped his head to her and then joined the rest of them.

His countenance towards her the last few weeks had been respectful, but distant, and she realized it would take some longer than others to get over her charade when she had first met them. And he had been busy since then, but she was grateful to part as peaceful neighbors. The alternative could have been much worse.

She saw Lt. Farrows waiting patiently near the edge of the group then, watching her under the brim of his hat and as the Commander walked away she went over to him.

"I want to thank you, Lieutenant, for everything you did. I didn't deserve your trust and you gave it anyway."

"Are you sure you don't want to come with us?" Farrows asked.

"Quite sure," Tamsin replied. Even if she had wanted to, the Empyrians wouldn't know what to do with her, now that she was changed. And a part of her ached to see her father and mother again, but the ache of missing Haven if she left would be something she couldn't live with. And she was a grown woman, a leader in her own right. Her people were here now. Her place was here.

"Well I hope I get to see you again someday," he said a little sadly, because they both knew that would probably never happen. He looked like he wanted to say more, but he gave her a nod and then joined the rest of his squadron.

She watched him go for a moment and then saw Mr. Brennan coming towards her with a horse in equal step next to him. She recognized the black coat of the horse she had ridden weeks ago and his ears pointed in her direction as they approached. She unhooked her n'qab and though she knew her eyes were different now, she hoped they wouldn't frighten the creature. The horse's nostrils flared for a moment and then his head bobbed up and down, clearly not needing to see her face to recognize her.

She smiled. "I still don't know his name."

"Apollyon," Mr. Brennan replied. "After the god who liked to throw people into the darkest pits of the seven hells."

Tamsin raised her eyebrow. "Hopefully that's a reflection of his color and not his temperament."

Mr. Brennan chuckled. "You'll have to find out for yourself." Then at Tamsin's puzzled look he handed her the lead rope. "He's yours."

Tamsin's mouth fell open. "What?"

"He'll take good care of you if you take care of him. And taking care of horses isn't too different than taking care of people," he said, echoing the words he had told her when they first met, only now they held a tone of advice. She was responsible for an entire race and if she would care for them the same way she would care for a horse, with kindness and mutual trust, then she'd be alright.

"Thank you, Mr. Brennan," she said, taking the rope and letting Apollyon nuzzle the palm of her hand.

He patted the horse on the neck and then took his leave and she knew he was leaving her with more than just a parting gift. Apollyon would be her access to freedom during her reign and a reminder of the world she left behind, but that still very much existed.

"Don't worry, we'll think of a better name," she whispered conspiratorially to Apollyon, then she and her new black steed watched as the northerners finally departed. She spotted Enrik atop a horse and waved, but she had already said her goodbyes to him earlier. The only thing left to do was go back home before the sight of the retreating northerners growing smaller left a pang of nostalgia.

Apollyon was already saddled and ready so she climbed up, with just enough difficulty to make him toss his head in her direction. He was at least fifteen hands high, but she knew with practice that they would manage. She re-hooked her n'qab and then gripped the reins in her gloved hands. Not far away, another group of sha'diin were waiting for her to escort her back, but she wanted to taste this new freedom. She tapped her heels against his flanks and they walked away, but she tapped them again, slowly gaining speed until they fell into a comfortable rhythm with each other. She rode past the waiting Ma'diin, unable to keep the smile from her face as the thrill of speeding across the warm landscape sent her arms and legs tingling. Apollyon seemed to feel it too and she could sense his eagerness, so she slackened her hold on the reins and let him take control of their pace. His head darted forward, quicker and quicker with each pound of his hooves until it seemed they weren't really running anymore, but flying. Tamsin laughed out loud, but she couldn't hear it over the wind in her ears.

Finally, the rocky terrain ended and they barreled into the first line of water that once again encompassed the marsh lands. Apollyon slowed against the resistance and they waded through to the nearest mud flat where much of the Ma'diin army still remained, both breathing heavily from the joyful exertion. Tamsin slid off his back once they were on dry land again and walked him over to several Ma'diin that were eying Apollyon with wary glances. She saw Poma there and was relieved to see her children with her again as well. Those that had been sent to the islands beyond the mangroves had started to return and she was glad that they had been given the chance to have happy reunions, instead of tragic ones.

Mikisle was brave enough to come up to her first, though his eyes were wide as he looked up at Apollyon. "What is it?" he asked.

"He's a horse and his name is Apollyon," she said, taking his hand and showing him how to let the giant animal smell him.

"Lyon," Poma's youngest, Cairn, murmured and pointed, unable to articulate the full name yet.

"Lyon it is," Tamsin said, but before she could greet them all properly she saw Ko'ran walking over, looking a bit out of breath. "What is it?" she asked, instantly wary of why he was here.

"Haven left. I've been searching for hours, but I can't find him anywhere."

"He left—what does that mean?"

"I found him by Lu'sa's grave marker today. I tried talking to him, but he—he wouldn't say a word. Then he disappeared."

"It's okay, Ko'ran. We'll find him," she reassured him, but she felt the sudden prick of urgency as surely as she felt the pull of gravity against her feet. Her duties as Kaz'ma'sha had kept her busier than she would've liked these last few weeks and when she couldn't be with Haven she had a small number of people that stayed with him, including Ko'ran and Ardak. Ardak had been extra diligent with him, and Tamsin knew it was his way of making up for lost time, but he still had not told Haven who he was. Tamsin understood why he wanted to wait, but she also knew it weighed on him more and more with each day that passed. Haven's wounds were healing, but he had days when he seemed stuck in some kind of dark void where the world around him was shrouded by an invisible veil and he barely uttered a word. Until he was back to his normal self, she feared him being alone. She was supposed to meet with some of the Kazserii after the northerners had departed, but they would have to wait. She handed the reins over to Mikisle and asked him to look after her horse until she got back. She gave Poma an appreciative nod and then followed Ko'ran away.

They walked through the Ma'diin camp until they reached her muudhiif. It was not nearly as large as her previous ones, but the sha'diin had done well in the amount of time they had with providing her a private dwelling until they returned to the inner marshes. She wanted to grab a few things in case they were going to be gone awhile, which she anxiously hoped they wouldn't be.

They stopped when they got inside, for Haven was right there. He was kneeling on the ground on the other side of the muudhiif, his side turned to them. His shoulders moved up and down with the force of each breath, as if his body were trying to contain a storm within.

"Wait outside, Ko'ran," Tamsin whispered, her tone indicating the order was not to be questioned. Then she crossed over to Haven, pausing to grab the washbowl as she noticed red stains on his hands. She knelt down in front of him, setting the washbowl down and gently taking his hands in her own. Bloody patches crisscrossed the tops of his knuckles. His eyes slowly met hers and she was taken aback by the grief she saw there. "Haven?"

"They've taken everything from me. I went to her grave today and I just..." he looked down at his hands. "She died in that water. She died and I can't remember her name. She was important, like you. How many others have died and I can't remember them? Ib'n—he's taken everything." His hands clenched into fists, forcing the anger to stay within his control.

He was swimming in a river of shadows, trying to get home, but drowning in the current.

"For every glimpse of something, there's endless layers of..." His nostrils flared and his lips twitched, unable to express the depth of the darkness that existed in his mind.

But maybe he didn't have to. Something Ardak had said, that it was like Haven was stuck in a nightmare...it gave her an idea. She had had nightmares before, when she had Haven's firestone. The sh'lomiin believed she had been seeing Haven and she believed it too.

"There were bones on the ground. And blood. Dripping from here," she said, touching the corner of her mouth.

Every muscle in his body froze. Everything except his eyes, which watched her with cautious precision. The edges tightened around the icy blues, trying to decide whether he was predator or prey.

She knew she had his attention. "The white fire burned everything and yet it left no ashes in its wake. You wanted to scream, but you couldn't. Because the white fire was the only light in that place. The darkness was like smoke, suffocating you with lies, hiding the voices that tormented you."

"Jha'ii," he whispered, not quite a warning, but not quite a plea.

She took the small rag, folded neatly over the edge of the washbowl, dipped it in the water and then began dabbing his knuckles. "I saw you in that place," she said. "Every night when I went to sleep, I saw you in my dreams. I would wake up, screaming and sick. But you haven't woken up yet, have you?"

He looked like he wanted to speak, like he was desperate to, but she knew the stranglehold he was still under.

"Even with the dreams, I know what I saw was just a scratch compared to what you lived through. And you did live through it, Haven. You lived. You're here, with me, right now. I need you to wake up and be here."

His mouth opened slightly to ask a question, but nothing came out.

She knew he didn't know how. Neither did she, but she knew where to start. "I was going to run away with you once before. If you want to, I will leave tonight with you. We can go anywhere. Just us. We can go far away, leave everything behind us." She reached down then, unhooked the pouch that held his firestone and offered it to him. "Or we stay," she said, "and we help each other live with the darkness."

His fingers closed around hers over the pouch, squeezing tightly, and he bent down until his forehead was touching hers. "Jha'ii. Salah'ii. Ena'ii," he whispered. *My heart. My refuge. My everything.*

"Beh'ii. Avan'ii. Ena'ii," she replied. *My breath. My fortress. My everything.*

He lifted his head, his eyes full of ice and fire and...determination.

Tamsin slipped the bracelet off her wrist then, the one that Ko'ran had given her and placed it in his palm.

He touched it gently, as if he were holding a dried flower petal. "Lu'sa," he breathed.

Chapter Thirty-One

"What in the seven hells happened here?" Mr. Brennan asked as they approached the gates of Empyria. Or rather what was left of them. Boulders and rocks littered the path and they had to weave their horses around them to get inside. More of the same was in the courtyard and there were a few people moving about with wheelbarrows clearing debris. There were black scorch marks on the walls that were still standing.

"Looks like one of the seven hells," Farrows replied. He nudged his horse forward and they continued through the courtyard and into the city, followed by their small group of soldiers.

They saw more of the same the farther they went. People cleaning debris from the streets, mending broken carts and doors and burning what couldn't be saved in large heaps, sending lengthy streams of smoke into the air. But the biggest stream of smoke came from one of the compounds, rising into the air like a ghostly tower and spreading its permeating stench onto every surface it could cling to. It looked like the city had suffered a siege against an army of fiery catapults. They rode down to the docks to see if the Commander had arrived yet with the boat crew and though they didn't see them the docks were just as busy as the streets had been. People were loading supplies onto boats and crossing over to the eastern bank and others were helping offload people covered in bandages. Across the water, the bridge to the Armillary had been severed, leaving a jagged gap in the stonework.

Farrows dismounted and took in the scene, at a loss as where to even begin processing what he was seeing. Fortunately, one of the women who was helping load supplies noticed them and walked over.

"What happened here?" Farrows asked.

The young woman was tall and lean, with a mane of blonde hair pulled back into a loose braid over her shoulders. "Where did you come from that you don't know?" she asked, eyeing his clothes and then the others atop their horses next to him with a bit of scrutiny.

"We've just arrived from the Empyrian outpost at the dam. We sent riders ahead, but did not hear a reply."

"We've been a bit occupied," the woman said. "Civil unrest followed by an attack from flying demons has kept everyone pretty busy."

Farrows and Mr. Brennan exchanged a look. "Flying demons?" Mr. Brennan asked.

But before the woman could answer, one of the soldiers behind him called out. "Gia?"

Farrows glanced back and saw Lieutenant Riggs' boy dismount from his horse and weave through the others.

The woman's eyes widened. "Enrik?!" She rushed over to him and the two embraced each other tightly, the relief visible on both their faces. After a quick moment they pulled away, but the woman, Gia, kept a grip on his arms. "I didn't know where you went. You've been at the dam this whole time?"

"Not the whole time," Enrik shook his head. "But that's a long story."

"About as long as mine," she replied.

"What happened here?" Enrik asked.

Gia took a deep breath and then looked around at the others a moment more. "Come with me," she said, then she called over to one of the men loading a boat, "Aden, I'll be back soon."

Farrows ordered the rest of the men to stay and help at the docks, with Gia's grateful nod of approval, then he, Mr. Brennan, and Enrik followed Gia back through the busy streets. She filled them in on what had happened, giving a brief account from when Cornelius shut down the city to the day the army from the Cities had arrived. They walked until they reached the small courtyard where the Archive building was…or had been.

The Archive building lay in ruins before them. The steps that had once led up to the impressive structure now led up to a crumbled heap of boulders, broken walls, glass, and wood. Parchment was strewn about everywhere. Scrolls and books lay in shredded heaps as people sorted through the rubble.

"I mentioned flying demons before," Gia said, waving her hand out for them to see.

Next to the shattered remains of the building was another conglomerate of boulders that appeared to have crumbled from the building next to it, but when Farrows stepped closer he saw that there was a shape to the conglomerate, a continuity to the rocks that flowed from one to the next.

Enrik was the first to see it for what it was. "Oh lords," he said under his breath. "They came here."

"What are you talking about?" Farrows asked. But as he circled the structure, it became more and more familiar. "It looks like one of them." It had been dark when the creatures attacked them at the edge of the marshes, but even in the black of night it was impossible to forget the hideous monsters. "It looks like…"

"The statues that guarded the front gates," Gia said. "Except they weren't statues at all. Whatever they were, they woke up."

"There were more," Enrik said. "On their way from the south."

"There were," Gia said, "But they all turned to stone like this one and dropped into the desert just beyond the southeast wall."

"Turned to stone…how?" Farrows asked.

Gia shrugged her shoulders. "We don't know, but if those other ones had made it here, you probably would've come back to a graveyard instead of a city. Why have you come back?"

"We fought our own demons," Farrows said, "versions of this one." He pointed to the stone creature. "And the dam broke during the fight so there was really no reason for us to stay anymore."

"It broke? How?"

"Well," Farrows scratched his head, thinking of all the strange things that had happened in just the last few weeks, "there's a rumor…"

"It was Tamsin," Enrik piped in excitedly.

Gia's eyes flashed in surprise. "Tamsin? But she's—."

"In the marsh lands," Enrik said. "She rescued me from the tunnels where Mr. Monstran was and—."

Gia raised her hand to stop him. "Hold up." Then she smiled and a chuckle burst through her lips. "There's someone else who needs to hear this story too."

"Who?"

She shook her head as if she couldn't believe herself the words she was about to say. "The person who led the army from the Cities here."

"Still no change?" Lord Urbane asked, lifting the spyglass to his eye and moving it until he found what he was looking for. The stone creatures looked like the humps of a great serpent as it meandered through the sand, but in reality they had not moved from where they had fallen out of the sky only weeks before. The only change was that they appeared to sink a little more each day as the Sindune sought to reclaim them, the desert wind slowly burying them, grain by grain, as it whipped sand over them. But Lord Urbane would not take any chances and kept lookouts posted day and night until it could be decided if anything could be done with them. The creatures they had assumed to be statues at the front gates and lain dormant for centuries. They had no clue what had awoken them or what had turned them back to stone, and without that knowledge it was impossible to know how long they would remain asleep this time.

"No change, my lord," the lookout guard replied.

"My lord!" another guard called up to him and ran up the stairs to the top of the wall. "I've just received word: soldiers have returned from the dam."

Lord Urbane handed the spyglass back to the lookout guard. "Where are they now?"

"Some are on their way here, sir. Miss Graysan is bringing them. She said they have information you need."

"Very well," he said, and followed the guard slowly down the stairs, pausing on each one to support his bad leg. He would forever be grateful to the young Ma'diin boy, Samih, who had sheltered him in the desert after the attempted murder by the corrupted Empyrians at the dam site, but the weeks of traveling between Empyria and the Cities had only aggravated the wound he had received. Samih had wanted him to rest further, but Lord Urbane had insisted on returning to Empyria. And every decision since then had only worsened it. The healer he had consulted had said he was lucky to be walking on it at all, but if he did not take time to rest, he was going to end up bedridden.

But there was so much yet to be done in the aftermath of the attack and there was a stubbornness in him that refused to sit idly by while others did the work. The caravan to take Cornelius back to the Cities was still being arranged. His top-ranking officers had sworn a new oath of loyalty to Lord Urbane and the well-being of Empyria's citizens, but Cornelius himself would be taken back, in chains, to be tried and held accountable by the Lords Council. Letters were streaming in by the hundreds from the Cities, as communication had been restored, and Lord Urbane had a dozen a day it seemed to respond to, updates on the city's repairs, detailed accounts of the civil unrest that preceded it, a list of crimes committed under Cornelius's regime, inventory, supplies and aid that they required, and the restoration of power to the rightful lords of Empyria. That last continued to sit on his desk, opened, but yet to be signed, for the last week. The words had struck him, curiously more significant now than before all this. As a ruling lord, he should have signed it and been done with it, once again sealing his own authority over the city. But the ruling powers of Empyria had been corrupted even before Cornelius. And it wasn't the other lords that had rebelled against Cornelius's reign, but the people. Ordinary citizens had risen up and banded together to fight against the injustice that was bombarding them. They had organized the information, written the letters that had persuaded the Council to send troops. They had provided refuge for those seeking shelter and escaping persecution. They had defended their city and the people within its walls and were now rebuilding it. It was these people that deserved a voice in their own city. It was a radical notion, especially for one of title, but Lord Urbane couldn't redirect his moral compass. Empyria, he predicted, was on its way to becoming an independent entity once more, no longer a province of the Cities, but an ally. No longer a territorial division under the Council's rule, but a trade partner in its own right. Talks had already begun between himself and some of the rebel leaders and even had Lord Urbane wanted to keep Empyria within the fold, he knew it could cause conflict even worse than what they had already endured. Navigating the fallout already felt like a joint task. Lord Urbane still had command of the army he came with and much of the Empyrian force, but the leaders of the rebellion had very much solidified their authority in the people's eyes.

Coming down from the wall, he saw the soldiers the guard had informed him of approaching with Miss Graysan. Georgiana had not only provided key evidence to Cornelius's atrocities with her letter, but had proved herself to be a fortress of selfless strength to the Empyrians. She had a careful manner, especially when he was around, which Lord Urbane suspected had something to do with his hand in forcing her father to act as a spy. This dangerous involvement between the rebels and Cornelius had ultimately led to Mr. Graysan's death, and Lord Urbane felt the sting of this every time Georgiana was around, though he knew his guilt was nothing next to the pain she must feel. And perhaps it was this reason why that decree lay unsigned on his desk. Not one, but two lords had been involved in her father's death, and though she would never say that to him directly, Lord Urbane could not disagree with her.

But he saw no trace of this in her eyes this time as they approached. On the contrary, her eyes sparkled over her beaming smile. "Lord Urbane," she greeted him. "May I present Lieutenant Farrows, Mr. Brennan, and Enrik Riggs, who have just returned from the dam."

The disbelief on the men's faces was hardly disguised. Lord Urbane had grown somewhat accustomed to the shocked looks he received when people, who had previously thought him dead, saw him for the first time. Many of the rebels knew of his continued existence before his return, including Georgiana, but those that had been stationed at the dam did not. He had received a message, brought by one of the returning soldiers days ago, of their impending arrival, but without further knowledge of the ones in charge and the reason for their return he left it unanswered, preferring to keep them in the dark until he had a chance to speak with them. He knew Cornelius had ultimately been behind his attempted murder at the dam, but he still didn't know everyone involved in the attack. He wasn't afraid of a repeat attack, but he wanted to flush out the depth of their loyalty to Cornelius and sever it if need be.

Though the grin of genuine happiness on Georgiana's face, the first one he had seen on the girl, made him wonder what he was missing. "Lieutenant," he addressed the first man, "Are you the ranking officer here?"

Lt. Farrows blinked a few times and shook his head slightly, having to physically shake off the shock of seeing him. "Yes, my lord. Um, of the ground contingent at least. Commander Ruskla is making his way upriver with the boats. And apologies, my lord. We had no idea—."

"It's alright," he said, lifting up a hand. He knew Ruskla and knew him to be a fair man. "How many are returning?"

"Everyone," Farrows replied.

"Everyone? For what reason?"

"The dam's been destroyed."

Lord Urbane's eyebrows went from being furrowed to rising up to nearly his hairline. He looked over his shoulder at the guard who had fetched him and then to Georgiana. "You were right: that is some important news." Before he could ask how, he realized something. Even as important as that was, it didn't explain Georgiana's elated expression.

"That's not even the tip of it," Farrows said.

"How was it destroyed?" he asked, his brows once again furrowing.

"Not how, but who."

Lord Urbane tilted his head.

"Tamsin."

Now it was Lord Urbane's turn to look shocked. He had suspected Tamsin had gone to the marsh lands, but to hear her name from men who had actually been there… "You saw her? She was there? Is she—did she come back with you?"

"We saw her," Farrows said, "but she did not come back with us. She chose to stay."

"She chose? Which means she's alive?"

Farrows nodded, but Mr. Brennan stepped forward. "We each have our own stories of Lady Tamsin," he said. "She's alive, and well," he added, "but there's something you should know."

"Tell me."

Emilia looked through the windowpanes to watch Lavinia in the gardens. The mid-morning sun was twinkling over the shrubs and flowers lightly and Lavinia was gently swaying the tiny infant in her arms side to side as she danced to the left and then the right. Both seemed content and just the sight of them made Emilia sigh. Though it also made her wistful, seeing them together. Enlightened now to her past and true heritage, she knew that she had never had that with her own mother. There had always been a distance between them and Emilia had thought it was because of her mother's disapproval of her rebellious inclinations, but perhaps it went further than that. They had never known each other for the first few years of Emilia's childhood and maybe by the time they reunited it was already too late to create a connecting bond. Lavinia, though, seemed at home caring for this baby. Another baby that was not her own, and yet she stepped into the role like it was made for her.

Lady Allard stepped up next to her and watched Lavinia and the baby as well for a moment. "I didn't think you would still be here," she said.

"I decided to take the day off," Emilia replied, a little amused by her own remark. But it was true; she had been working at the Council building for weeks now, ever since her debut, and she often didn't get home until well after dark. Some nights she would have a tray sent to her room and other nights she was too tired to eat. But it was a good tired. Her business wasn't just about filling up her social calendar, but actually using her time for something useful. The last several weeks had been filled with meetings and getting acquainted with the other lords and how things were run within the Council. She was learning about her own duties and what was required of her on top of sorting out the crisis with Empyria. Even after they had voted to send an army there with Lord Urbane at its helm, there was still a lot to uncover about the amount of corruption lurking in the Delmarian ranks. Commander Garz had been tried and sentenced, along with several of his officers, and every letter detailing the events in Empyria had to be documented to ascertain the names of those involved within the desert city. Emilia was pleased to be used a resource in these proceedings, having lived there most of her life.

"Has there been any news about Madame Corinthia's family?" she asked.

Lady Allard shook her head. "Nothing yet. Though I don't think Lavinia is in a rush to get rid of him."

"And what about you? Have you finalized your plans to leave?"

"Nearly." Lady Allard had made plans to go back to her seaside home of Alstair, where she said she still had relatives, but Emilia knew she was still anxious about news of her husband still in Empyria. She didn't want to impose on Lavinia anymore, but she was hesitant to leave until they had word from Lord Urbane.

Emilia had made no such plans yet. She had the option to stay, being the reigning member of the Urbane house, but the truth was she had just been too busy to look for a place of her own.

"We're a house of orphans and outlanders," Emilia said as she reflected on this, though it didn't seem like such a bad thing now. Nothing like when she had first arrived.

Sherene came rushing into the room then with Mr. Brandstone right on her heels. "Miss Emilia! Lady Allard! It's here!"

Emilia and Lady Allard both turned around to see the two elbowing each other slightly.

"I'm perfectly capable of delivering it on my own," Mr. Brandstone said, casting an annoyed eye at the day maid.

"Yes, but I wanted to be the first to tell them," Sherene countered.

"Tell us what?" Lady Allard asked.

"Lord Urbane has sent a letter!" Sherene cried happily.

Mr. Brandstone frowned at her and pulled an envelope from his coat pocket. He handed it to Emilia. "It just arrived."

Emilia unfolded it and began reading the contents, trying to ignore all the impatient eyes upon her. After a minute, she said, "He did it," and looked up with a smile. It had worked. All of their efforts at the Council had paid off and Lord Urbane had been successful in taking control of the city. She continued reading and tried to summarize to the others what he said. There had been an attack on the city and they had nearly failed totally. They had prevailed, but parts of the city had been destroyed. Efforts to rebuild were already underway. Concerning Lord Saveen's coup, arrests had been made and trials were underway. When they were finished they would return with the prisoners.

"Does he say anything about my husband?" Lady Allard asked.

Emilia could see the tension in her eyes. Cerena was such a calm, steadying presence in the house, that Emilia forgot sometimes how hard it must have been for her to leave without her husband.

"He's alive," Emilia told her. "He'll be returning to the Cities. And he'll be coming with—." She stopped, trying to make sense of what she was reading.

"With whom?" Lady Allard asked.

Emilia swallowed thickly. "My mother. But she—she's been arrested and tried."

"What?" the other three said simultaneously. But Lord Urbane's letter didn't go into further details about it.

Emilia finished reading and then handed it off to Lady Allard. She turned back to the window as she contemplated this new information. It would be weeks before anyone returned from Empyria. Weeks before she would know what her mother had done and if she would end up paying for them.

Lady Allard gasped quietly, her eyes darting over the letter. "He also says the dam has been destroyed," she said. "There was some altercation to the south, but they are on good terms with the Ma'diin now. And—." She gasped again, her eyes growing wide.

"What!? What does it say?" Sherene asked.

Lady Allard gave her the letter with a smile. Sherene scanned its contents quickly while Mr. Brandstone couldn't help but look over her shoulder. Her hand then covered her mouth and her eyes glistened as she held up the letter like it was a victory banner.

"I have to show this to my Lady," she said and she rushed out of the room.

The rest of them joined Emilia at the window as they watched Sherene shuffle quickly outside and over to Lavinia. She talked animatedly and then held up the letter for Lavinia to see.

Emilia knew what she was telling her: not only was Lord Urbane safe, but their daughter, Tamsin, was safe as well. He had heard from several reliable sources that she was alive and in the marsh lands. Emilia hoped Tamsin had succeeded as well in what she had set out to do. And though their meeting had triggered an avalanche of strange and sometimes painful events, in the end they had both gotten something that they needed. For Emilia, it was a purpose and a chance to make an impact with her own voice.

Epilogue

It had been a month since the northerners departure. A month since the Ma'diin had left the anasii hada and returned to the marsh lands. A month since Haven had let her into the darkness with him and had begun to heal the scars that plagued him. A month since the light had finally broken through the cracks and begun to claim dominion over the shadows.

Tamsin listened to the birds outside the muudhiif walls as they began to wake up with the first rays of morning, welcoming the light with their bright calls. She loved to experience the first minutes of the day through the feathered creatures, when the rest of the world was still quiet and their crystal-clear songs skipped back and forth over the water. Before she was the Kaz'ma'sha and the duties and responsibilities of rebuilding an empire took hold. Before she was a Watcher and was governed by rules outside of her will. When she was just Tamsin. When she could look over and see Haven fixing the handle of one of his knives or doing whatever task he was set upon.

This particular morning he was wrapping the head of a spear with thin strips of reeds, dipping them first in a bowl of water and then when they were pliable, twisting them together to secure the sharp stone to the stick. He looked up when he noticed Tamsin watching him then nodded next to him where a pile of fish lay lifeless on a small reed mat.

"You went fishing last night?" she asked him.

"No one else fishes in the dark," he said. "It's almost too easy."

Tamsin smiled. She was learning firsthand how alive the night was now that she could see in the dark as Haven and the other Watchers could. She wasn't completely nocturnal as she had originally learned the Watchers to be because of this gift, since she was still Kaz'ma'sha to the rest of the Ma'diin who still lived in the daylight, but she had been exploring the marshes with Haven while everyone else slept. And beyond that she was pleased whenever she witnessed him doing something that seemed so normal. His memory had slowly been returning, but every little detail helped, even if it was as small as remembering how to catch fish.

He paused his work for a moment and as if hearing her thoughts, said, "I remembered something last night. I brought you fish before."

She smiled again. "That dinner party in Empyria. You put them right on the table."

"Your mother did not like me."

"I think I was the one she did not like at that moment," Tamsin chuckled, remembering how stunned everyone had been. "What else do you remember from that night?"

He thought for a moment. "I let you see my face. And you…" He reached over and took her hand, intertwining his fingers into hers as the memory played out. "You took my hand and you told me you weren't afraid of me."

"No fear. You used to tell me that."

He furrowed his brow a little. "And now, after everything that I…what I became…you're still not afraid?"

Tamsin shook her head. "Are you afraid of me? After what I've become?"

"Terrified," he said, unable to keep the corner of his mouth from twitching up into a smile.

Her smile widened and she sidled in closer. He put the spear down and wrapped his arm around her as she sunk into the moment and his embrace. They were finding their way through the shadows together. Every day brought with it new revelations that weren't exactly new, but brought up a soup of questions, memories, and feelings. Wading through it all was slow going, but it was bringing their paths closer together. They were connected by the darkness as much as the light and realizing that was as much of a breakthrough as anything else.

Her hand went idly up to her chest, running her fingers unconsciously up and down the scar that was there even as her mind wandered to happier things. She realized she was doing it only when she felt Haven's hand encircle hers. She lay her head on his shoulder, feeling the slight rise and fall with each of his breaths, and then a gentle pressure on her hair as he kissed the top of her head. Yes, it was mornings like this that she cherished the most.

"Kaz'ma'sha?" a soft, feminine voice floated in from outside.

Tamsin sighed, suspecting that the sha'diin had a sixth sense about when she was awake. "I'll be with you in just a few minutes, Mishana," she said, trying to soak in the last few moments with Haven before her responsibilities took hold. Mishana was a new member of her kazsiin. Within the last few weeks, many of the Kazserii had solidified their allegiance by offering their own kazsiin to Tamsin. She had wanted to refuse, but Numha said it would be an insult not to except. So Tamsin's circle had gone from two to twelve, a number Numha assured her was fit for the Kaz'ma'sha. And she and R'en had meticulously vetted each candidate based on skills and personality. It was an honor to be kazsiin to the Kaz'ma'sha, and R'en wanted to make sure any future candidates knew what was required. Mishana was young, but eager to prove herself and had volunteered to be the early morning guard of Tamsin's muudhiif.

"Kazsiin R'en is here," Mishana continued. "She needs to speak with you."

Tamsin wondered if it was about the ceremony for the new kazsiin. It was to take place tomorrow and was to be a celebration of the women who had earned their place among Tamsin's inner circle.

"Alright," Tamsin said begrudgingly, looking up at Haven with a frown, not wanting to leave his side even for a moment. "Tell her—."

But she didn't get a chance to finish as the flap was whipped open and R'en entered with an irritated look on her face. It wasn't often that she didn't have some version of irritation etched into her expression, but something else was there as well, an edge of urgency in her body language. "Tamsin, you need to come with me," R'en said, forgoing the sign of respect and her title.

Tamsin didn't mind this from some, including R'en, and she would sometimes tease her for it, but she sensed now was not the time. Haven stood up first, already his demeanor changing into the protector. Tamsin stood up more slowly. "What's wrong?" she asked.

"They're back. A group of the northerners showed up on our borders this morning."

"What? How many?"

"Only seven. They're camped near the *baiina* crossing. I've sent more scouts farther north to see if there are more."

"Has anything happened?" Tamsin asked, trying to keep a rational head while her heart beat faster.

R'en shook her head. "No. Numha's with them now, but they keep asking for you."

"Take me there. No more than a dozen sha'diin as escort R'en," Tamsin warned, knowing if it were up to R'en she would send an entire village. "I don't want to spook them if they're here on friendly terms."

R'en nodded with tight lips and went to gather the men and canoes.

Tamsin turned to Haven, who was already adding knives to his belt. If the sha'diin didn't spook them, Haven surely would. "It would be pointless to ask you to stay here, wouldn't it?"

He sent her a look that confirmed it and she would not argue it.

"Alright, let's go," she said, but Haven stepped in front of the doorway, blocking her.

She knew immediately what she had forgotten. It had been over a month and remembering that she needed a cloak to go outside had been the one thing her mind still let slip. Haven had introduced her to the many layers a Watcher wore that went beyond tunics and jerkins. Any seam between clothing was covered in a wrap. Thin leather guards were worn over the wrists and hands, frayed like palm leaves at the ends with a loop around each finger so as not to restrict any movement. There was even a special half-cloak that could be worn that still provided the hooded n'qab, but was less formal, Haven had said. Even at night, though, it was dangerous, to be without any form of cloak. The daylight tended to sneak up on one when one was hunting amon'jii. The cloak needed to be a second skin. And she knew forgetting it did not lighten Haven's instincts to protect her.

She went back to her annex and lifted the lid on her reed basket next to her sleeping mat. Kneeling down, she saw her cloak folded nicely inside. Sitting next to it, cradled in a little nest she had made with the one shawl she had brought with her, was her firestone, for she had not gotten accustomed to carrying it with her everywhere yet like Haven did. She reached out for her cloak, but paused, her fingers hovering just above the fabric. Her lips formed a tiny circle as she forced air into her lungs and back out again. Her hands started to tremble so she gripped the edge of the basket tightly, closing her eyes against the feeling of dread the rose through her like a moving tide. She knew it would pass, but some days the near misses crept up on her and felt more like she was on borrowed time. Like an executioner had an ax to her neck, but whispered 'not yet.'

Her breath hitched as she suddenly felt arms around her.

"Breathe, Jha'ii," Haven whispered into her ear, his chest pressing into her back as he wrapped himself around her.

She let go of the basket and gripped his arms tightly, not caring that she hadn't heard him come in, or that she was falling apart in front of him. She tried to do as he asked, and focused on breathing and the feeling of his strong body next to hers. And he didn't let go, not until her breathing had returned to normal and she felt the panic ease away like a cold shadow. She never wanted to be weak in front of him, but instead of letting that rip her ego apart, she knew he probably felt the same, and letting him be the strong one sometimes was helping him get back to who he was.

He eventually released his arms and he helped her stand back up, turning her around to face him. She nodded silently, letting him know she was alright.

She bent down and gently picked up her cloak and began putting it on, though making a show of doing all the fastenings so Haven could see. She hooked her n'qab in place last, and though it didn't really hinder her new eyesight, it was always the one that affected her the most. It was the one that reminded her, truly, of what she was now and what everyone saw first when they looked at her. Numha had recently confessed to her that she was working with the weavers to come up with something a little lighter and less masculine for her that would still protect her. Haven grunted in approval when she had finished and they walked outside together. R'en and the sha'diin were waiting for them so they got into the canoes and headed out, scattering the birds that had opted for a lackadaisical morning bath.

There were a few canoes lingering in the water as they reached the northerners camp, silently keeping guard until the Kaz'ma'sha arrived. And though Tamsin had ordered only a dozen sha'diin to accompany them, she knew R'en had more hiding in the surrounding reeds, just as she had done when Tamsin first arrived to the Kor'diin's tribe. Only this time Tamsin was not on the receiving end. The northerners had made camp on an uncluttered mud flat, spacious enough to house several small tents around a campfire. And it was relatively open compared to some of the other neighboring flats. They had wanted to be found.

Numha was already with them and came over to meet Tamsin as they pulled the canoes up. Tamsin stepped out and walked over to where the Empyrians were gathered around their cooking fire, with Haven less than a step behind. Some of the men were already standing and the ones who weren't quickly stood up as they approached.

One stepped forward and Tamsin smiled at the unexpected face. "Lieutenant Farrows. It's good to see you, but I'm surprised to see you back here."

"It is indeed good to see you again Lady Tamsin," Farrows replied. "You look very well. I hope we have not caused your people any alarm by our presence." He glanced behind her at the dozen sha'diin waiting on the bank and then at Haven looming next to Tamsin.

"That depends on your answer," she said, though she said it kindly. "Why are you here?"

"Your father sent us," he replied with a smile.

"My father? Did he return to Empyria?"

"He did and when he found out you were here he wanted us to come back immediately to find you."

She hadn't thought about her father in a while and it was with a twinge of guilt that she realized the last time she had seen him was fooling him into thinking she was returning to the Cities with him. "I'm sorry that you've wasted your journey," she said, "but I still haven't changed my mind. I'm staying here."

"That's not why he sent us," Farrows said. "We told him everything that had happened here, and to you, and he has a letter for you, but before that I think we need to fill you in on what's happened in Empyria." He motioned to one of the tents.

"Lead the way," Tamsin said, but she exchanged a quick look with Haven from behind their n'qabs, sharing a silent look of cautious curiosity. They followed him to the tent and Farrows held the flap open for them, but as soon as they entered Haven put his arm in front of Tamsin, effectively stopping her. "Haven? What is it?"

There wasn't much inside the tent; the Empyrians had traveled light this time, only bringing the necessities, but there was one other man already in the tent who was organizing a stack of parchments. The man looked up as they entered and then dropped his eyes away, bowing slightly, as if he were apologizing for not being prepared.

Farrows stepped in after them. "Ah, Lady Tamsin, Mr. Haven, this is our scribe, Mr. Harvus. He's offered to help you write any letters you may want to send back."

Haven took a few steps closer to Mr. Harvus, not threatening, but intimidating enough to make Mr. Harvus back away.

"Haven," Tamsin said, trying not to sound too harsh. He walked a fine line within the shadowy realm where his memories lurked and sometimes he seemed to disappear there when one revealed itself and he was working to figure it out. But Tamsin didn't recognize Mr. Harvus and she didn't know what about him had triggered Haven's response.

Haven took a step back at the sound of her voice, allowing Mr. Harvus to slink along the side of the tent past him.

"I think I'll wait outside until you're done," Mr. Harvus said nervously, clutching the parchments to his chest and then slipping outside.

Tamsin turned her head after him, her brow furrowing. His face wasn't the slightest bit familiar, but something had tugged at the far recesses of her mind when he had spoken.

"Do you two know Mr. Harvus?" Farrows asked, glancing between them.

Tamsin looked at Haven, whose own hood remained rooted to the doorway, and shook her head. "I'm sorry, Lieutenant, no. But

I appreciate the help. I admit it has been some time since I've written...well anything."

Farrows smiled. "It is no problem at all. But first—."

"But first," Tamsin echoed. "Empyria. Tell me what's happened."

And he did. He detailed everything that had been told to him after their return to the desert city. Cornelius' reign, the rebellion, Lord Urbane leading the army from the Cities, and the attack from the flying creatures. And everything else, he told them, would be in her father's letter.

Tamsin was silent for a minute as she processed everything. She was glad that her friends and the people she cared about had made it through and that Cornelius was being brought to some form of justice. But she felt strangely removed from it all, like Farrows was telling this to the wrong person. She felt she had given up the right to this knowledge when she had chosen to leave Empyria. Or maybe she hadn't given up the right, instead, for a long time, she had just given up the expectation that she would ever leave the marsh lands alive.

Farrows handed her a folded piece of parchment then and stepped outside without a word, giving her some privacy.

Tamsin looked down at the letter, recognizing her father's wax seal stamped across the edge. She broke it open, feeling a wave of nostalgia as she saw her father's handwriting.

My dearest Tamsin,

First and foremost, I want to say how proud I am of you. I have gathered accounts from the Empyrian soldiers that returned from the dam of the events that have transpired there and there is no doubt in my mind that many lives were saved because of your actions. And your sacrifice. You have done something that no man or woman was able to achieve before you. As much as I wish for your return it has been made clear that this is not your intention. I want you to know that I respect your choice and I will not try to persuade you of where your place is. Though if I had been able to make the journey and been able to see you in person, I may have tried. Or I may have been awestruck by your strength and tenacity, a popular sentiment by those who see you, I am told. It is hard for me to imagine you outside of my memories of you climbing trees in the garden or hiding under my desk as a little girl. I find myself wondering if the life I had built for you was never destined for you at all. I can only hope that where I failed to prepare you for this life, you have succeeded. And despite my shortcomings and secrets, you can forgive me. I love you very much, my dearest child.

Haven moved in closer. "What does it say?" he asked, a note of caution creeping into his voice, as if he did not trust the letter's contents.

Tamsin realized he must be thinking her father was writing her to persuade her to come back to Empyria. She gave Haven a reassuring smile. "He writes that he loves me and that he's proud of me," she said, feeling her throat tighten as she thought of her father writing this. She could almost hear the tenor of his voice as she continued reading further down the letter. "He echoes what Farrows told us, about the attack on Empyria."

"The afain'jii," Haven said.

Tamsin nodded. "He says the city is safe for now, but there was a lot of damage. The Archive building was completely destroyed."

"I remember it," Haven said. "You were teaching me about the symbols."

"Yes, I was teaching you how to read them. It's when—." She paused as her eye caught something her father had written.

"What is it?" Haven asked.

Tamsin's eyes darted back and forth over the page, trying to keep up with the information her father had written. "He says they found something in the ruins, something he had forgotten about. He and my mother—Irin—had been working on. They—." She gasped, her hand making the parchment shake slightly. She reached up and unhooked her n'qab, rereading the words that made her breath quicken, just to be sure the thin veil had not distorted the truth.

Haven moved in front of her, unhooking his own n'qab. His bright, concerned eyes connected with hers and she felt evermore the weight of the letter in her hand.

"They may have found a cure," she breathed.

"A cure?" Haven's eyebrows furrowed. "For what?"

The light of hope was like the sweet touch of wine on her tongue, but with it came the bitter sting of foreboding: that her 'epic tale' was not over. That the peace they had forged was about to get thrown back into the fire. That her odyssey would lead them right back to Empyria.

"The sun curse."

Here Ends Book Three of An Empyrian Odyssey

Preview
Book Four of An Empyrian Odyssey

"Here," Tamsin said, holding out the spyglass. "For the one I lost."

Enrik smiled, but shook his head. "You keep it."

Tamsin nodded and placed it in her lap. She couldn't help but wonder what would've happened if she had never forgotten the spyglass in the first place all those months ago when Enrik and Georgiana had showed her their secret perch above the Empyrian wall. Would she still have slipped and fallen in the river? Would they all be sitting here now?

"Can you believe that we're all still here?" Georgiana asked aloud, dangling her legs over the edge freely.

"After everything that's happened," Enrik added.

"We're right back where we started," Tamsin said.

They all exchanged a long look and the rest didn't need to be spoken. They might be back at the beginning, but none of them had been unchanged by the time that had passed. Or the fact that none of their families had remained intact. Their journey's had been separate, the challenges they faced very different than each other's, but it didn't change the solace they took in each other's company. They sat in silence a little longer, listening to the sound of the river rush beneath them, reminding them that no matter what happened, time kept going.

Finally, Enrik sighed. "Well, should we go?"

Gia nodded and they stood up. "Tamsin, are you coming?"

"Not just yet."

Enrik made a face. "Tamsin…" he warned.

"I promise nothing will happen this time," she said, laughing. "Go, I'll see you tomorrow."

Gia squeezed her shoulder lightly. "See you tomorrow." Then she and Enrik climbed back down and out of sight.

Tamsin took a deep breath in and let it go slowly, savoring the sound of it as it faded into the deep, constant tones of the water below. It was a peaceful moment of which she had learned to surrender to, for there had been so few of them this last year. It was nice to be alone up here, but she did not feel alone. Her friends and loved ones were here and knowing they were safe felt like wrapping a familiar shawl around her shoulders. Though there was one person she was eager to get back to.

Her eyebrows knitted together as the feeling shifted. She wasn't alone, not just metaphorically, but actually. No one else was around her, but the sense of being watched by someone rippled across her skin like a breeze.

She stood up, staring across the river to where its banks met the mighty walls of the Hollow Cliffs. It wasn't the solstice yet, but what if...

She lifted the spyglass up to her face. Peering through the small end she lifted the instrument until she found the break in the darkness where the Cliff's edge met the star-speckled sky. She moved it slowly to the left, following the ridge line until it dropped away into the desert. She lowered the spyglass away from her eye, thinking it had been a silly thought, but the feeling of being watched persisted. She raised the spyglass back up and this time moved it slowly across the ridge line to the right.

Her new heart beat heavily in her chest, and she didn't know why until she saw them.

Her hunch had been right. Standing atop the Cliffs were the silhouettes of two figures.

All those months ago, she had seen Haven for the first time standing atop those very cliffs with the others of the Ma'diin party that had come to Empyria. And until now she had assumed it had been them, or other Ma'diin, every time Gia and Enrik had seen them. But something was different this time and there was only one way she was going to find out.

She tucked the spyglass in her bag and made her way down the ledge. Her sha'diin were still waiting for her by the bottom of the steps and followed her wordlessly as she made her way back through the streets. She still had to fight the urge to look behind her as their footsteps shadowed her own, as it was still taking some getting used to be followed constantly. As a girl, Sherene had never been very far, and even in public Tamsin had always had a chaperon. But this was more than just a safety measure or social rule; this was a show of loyalty and strength and honor. She was Kaz'ma'sha to them all and as much as she wished it would never come to it, she knew each of them would lay down their life for hers. But even so, there was one person they still kept a healthy distance to.

She made inquiries when she got back to the Urbane compound and was directed up to the main level. She stopped at the top of the stairs and saw Haven's dark form near the veranda. She turned to her shadows. "You may leave now. Haven is here."

The sha'diin nodded and flicked their fingers off their hands in respect and went to rejoin the rest of the Ma'diin where they camped inside the wall of the compound. Tamsin didn't know who she was going to find out on the cliffs and she preferred to go with the one person the sha'diin steered clear of. But as she walked across the room she saw that he was actually sitting with his back against a pillar near the veranda.

She went over to him and was about to speak, but stopped. He was sound asleep. His breathing was slow and heavy and his head tilted slightly over one shoulder.

She smiled, remembering a moment like this many months ago. It had been raining then and they had shared biscuits together while she badgered him with questions. He had fallen asleep then too.

She knew he wouldn't have fallen asleep now unless he was truly exhausted, so she walked quietly away, leaving him to rest.

She would go to the Cliffs alone. She didn't want the figures on the Cliffs getting spooked by more than one or two people.

She went back down, through the servants' deserted halls, and to the stables. There were a few horses stabled there and their ears perked up as she walked in. Apollyon poked his head over the door and nickered quietly. She grabbed his tack and he only pawed his hoof once in impatience as she saddled him. She was a decent enough rider; her height gave her a disadvantage when it came to lifting heavy saddles onto the creatures. She walked him out of his stall and then climbed up, whispering into his ear that she would give him a good brushing as soon as they got back. She patted his neck and gave him a little nudge with her heel.

There was no way to avoid the Ma'diin who were still up and seated around the fires, but at least no one would follow her this way. The sha'diin were nearly as wary around horses as they were around Haven.

"Kazsera, where are you going?" One of the sha'diin jumped up. "Kazsera!"

But Tamsin didn't stop and cantered past them and out of the courtyard. No one tried to stop her either as she made her way through the city gates and out into the open. The moon was breaking over the city's walls as Apollyon galloped over the sand, sending puffs of chilly dust across the landscape. The chill of the night did nothing to dispel the sense of freedom she had not felt in weeks. And her ability to see in the dark now almost blinded her to the fact that her horse could not, though he seemed to be just as excited to be running freely beyond the confines of the walls. She eventually slowed his gait as they neared the cliffs and led him down to the bank for a quick drink from the river. Then she found an outcropping to tie his reins around and walked the rest of the way herself.

She let her instincts take over when she reached them, choosing the path that she had taken so many times with Haven. It felt like no time had passed at all as each step and each rock under her hands felt familiar. Her body remembered where to go, even as her mind thought ahead to who she was going to find once she reached the top. She came to the landing where she and Haven used to practice her powers and paused, taking a moment to re-imagine their nights together. She had learned the Ma'diin's language here, had first created fire here, and as silly as it seemed now, it was where she had first truly been alone with a man that wasn't her father or a tutor. It was where the course of her future had changed and she had started to become the person she was now, learning things she would never have known if she had stayed in the Cities.

She looked over to the spot where Haven's buurda had always been setup and noticed something. The buurda was gone, but she had never seen the large crevasse in the rockface behind it before. Either the buurda had hidden it well or her sight had just not been as good as it was now in the dark to spot it. She had to stoop only a little, but it was easily wide enough for her to fit in. Haven had never mentioned it, but as she ducked her head in to get a closer look she saw that it actually opened up even wider about a meter in. She took a couple steps in and was greeted by a steep staircase of crude rocks.

She had come to find the individuals on top of the cliffs so she didn't hesitate and began to climb. There wasn't any fear or worry. There wasn't any doubt. It wasn't even confidence, but rather just a feeling that she was going exactly where she was supposed to. She took a deep breath when she finally made it to the last step and her head broke aboveground, filling her lungs with the cold night air. She did a little turn, taking in the expanse of the dark desert below her, stretching out like a beautiful and deadly ocean, broken only by the glimmering lights of Empyria…and the two figures overlooking it all.

They were turned away from her, only a few yards from the edge of the cliff, though their cloaks were perfectly still.

Tamsin took a few steps closer and opened her mouth, but then shut it, unsure of what to say as she didn't even know who they were. Her own cloak billowed around her in the heightened wind, gripping around her legs as if the wind itself was insistent she keep her feet put. Suddenly the idea of leaving Haven and the sha'diin behind seemed incredibly foolish.

"Tamsin Urbane, Irinbaat, Kazszura'asha, Baagh'dovuurii, Kaz'ma'sha of the Ma'diin, the Fury and the Flood," a man's voice floated over the wind from beneath one of the hoods. His voice cut through the howling air with the precise edge and clarity of a prism. Both of the figures turned around to face her and Tamsin's mouth fell open slightly. The two men, or at least they resembled men, had eyes whiter than winter clouds and their chiseled faces shimmered like ice around the edges. They did not appear to be old and yet their unnervingly vacant expressions seemed to mask an ancientness underneath.

"We've been waiting for you."

Pronunciation Guide

Afain'jii (ah-fane-<u>jee</u>)
Alahkiin Zakar (ah-lah-<u>keen</u> zah-<u>kar</u>)
Aluuva (ah-<u>loo</u>-vah)
Amon'jii (ah-mahn-<u>jee</u>)
Anasii hada (ah-nah-<u>see</u> <u>hah</u>-dah)
Baagh (bahg)
Baagh'dovuurii (bahg doh-<u>voo</u>-ree)
Baat (baht)
Buurda (<u>boor</u>-dah)
Cavahst (kah-<u>vahst</u>)
Empyria (em-<u>peer</u>-ree-ah)
Fairmoore (<u>fair</u>-moor)
Fluazan (<u>flaw</u>-zahn)
Fuh'diin (<u>foo</u>-deen)
Haava (<u>hah</u>-vah)
Hafakii (hah-fah-kee)
Halcyona (hall-see-oh-nah)
Haniis (hah-nees)
Havakkii (hah-vah-<u>kee</u>)
Hiita (<u>hee</u>-tah)
Ib'n (<u>ee</u>-bin)
Ireczburg (<u>ear</u>-ex-berg)
Jalsai (jahl-sa-<u>ee</u>)
Jiin mughaif (jeen moo-<u>gah</u>-eef)
Kapu'era (kah-poo-<u>air</u>-ah)
Kaz'ma'sha (kahz-mah-<u>shah</u>)
Kazsera (kah-<u>zay</u>-rah)
Kazserii (kah-<u>zay</u>-ree)
Kazsiin (kah-<u>zeen</u>)
Kazszura'asha (kah-<u>zoo</u>-rah-<u>ah</u>-shah)
Kor'diin (kor-<u>deen</u>)
Lumierii (loo-mee-<u>air</u>-ee)
Lumii veritaas (<u>loo</u>-mee vay-ree-<u>tahs</u>)
Ma'diin (mah-<u>deen</u>)
Muudhiif (moo-<u>deef</u>)
N'qab (nee-<u>kob</u>)
Pa'shiia (pah-<u>shee</u>-ah)
Pak'kriin (pahk-ee-<u>kreen</u>)
Pentiyan (pehn-tee-<u>yahn</u>)
Q'atorii (kah-<u>toh</u>-ree)
Sh'lomiin (<u>shee</u>-lo-meen)
Sh'pav'danya (shih-<u>pahv</u>-dahn-yah)
Sha'diin (shah-<u>deen</u>)
Shafaii (shah-<u>fah</u>-ee)
Shriiski (<u>shree</u>-skeh)
Skiishiv (<u>skee</u>-shehv)
Tiika (<u>tee</u>-kah)
Vas'akru (vahs-ah-<u>kroo</u>)

0

The completion of this book took patience, perseverance and the support of my family and friends. This book endured through a pandemic, preschool, and, funnily enough, a laptop starting on fire. But I think it was worth the wait and in the end the story unfolded as it was meant to. So I send all my thanks and gratitude to my family, my faith, my friends, my reviewers, editors, babysitters, and everyone who read *The Dark Solstice* and *The Hour of Embers* and still choose to follow Tamsin and Haven on their journey. These characters have been with me for years, sometimes challenging me and other times blessing me. They've helped me to grow, to become a better writer and human being. I hope your patience was rewarded and whatever your connection to the story may be, I hope it has added value to your life.

2

ABOUT THE AUTHOR

N. L. Willcome lives in northeastern Wisconsin with her husband, Bill, and her son, Kypling. She received a B.A. in English Literature from the University of Wisconsin – Madison in 2011 and is a work-from-home mom, author, and yoga asana instructor. *The Crown of the Desert* is her third novel in An Empyrian Odyssey series. Her other works include *The Dark Solstice, The Hour of Embers,* and *The Magic Carnival and The Adventures of Landon Knight,* a children's chapter book.

Nlwillcomeauthor.wordpress.com

Facebook.com/NikkiWillcome

Goodreads.com/nlwillcome

Made in the USA
Columbia, SC
26 May 2023